VANISHED

THEO BAXTER

INKUBATOR
BOOKS

Published by Inkubator Books
www.inkubatorbooks.com

Copyright © 2023 by Theo Baxter

Theo Baxter has asserted his right to be identified as the author of this work.

ISBN (eBook): 978-1-83756-183-4
ISBN (Paperback): 978-1-83756-184-1
ISBN (Hardback): 978-1-83756-185-8

VANISHED is a work of fiction. People, places, events, and situations are the product of the author's imagination. Any resemblance to actual persons, living or dead is entirely coincidental.

No part of this book may be reproduced, stored in any retrieval system, or transmitted by any means without the prior written permission of the publisher.

1

There was a rare moment of quiet in the Conner household. All you could hear was the occasional clink of cutlery against porcelain dishes. The nicest we had, as per my father's breakfast request. He was sitting at the head of the table, shoveling eggs into his mouth. My mother sat next to him, her face illuminated by her phone. She occasionally took a small bite of her eggs, but her eyes never left the small screen in her hands.

I sat on the other side of my father, separating him from my daughter, Isabel. She politely ate, making as little noise as possible, everything I put on her plate. Thankfully, my father was distracted, his eyes cast down at his plate, focused on the never-ending mountain of scrambled eggs I prepared.

"Mommy?" Isabel asked. "Why aren't you eating?"

I opened my mouth to answer her, but before I could my father dropped his fork, causing everyone at the table—except my mother—to flinch.

"She doesn't need to eat. She's fat enough as it is," he said, his eyes boring into my daughter's skull.

Isabel gulped and turned back to her plate. Thankfully, she chose not to engage, and for once my father was too busy to challenge my eight-year-old. He went back to his plate, jostling the table as my mother went for hers. She hardly noticed that her fork hit the wooden table, and brought it back up to her mouth empty.

My mother, Helena, chewed for a moment before calmly removing a large piece of wood that must have come off the old wooden spatula I'd used from her mouth and setting it down on her napkin as if it were a fish bone. Did she even know she was eating eggs and not a filet? I wanted to ask her, but there was no way to get her attention. Her eyes were glued to whatever was happening on the little screen, the bubble she occupied whenever she was forced to eat meals with us.

It's a defense mechanism, I reminded myself. *You'd do the same if you could.*

Isabel nudged my leg under the table, bringing me back to reality. I took a bite of my eggs—they were pretty good. I was starting to get better at cooking. It was always just the basics, but they were quite tasty.

It probably sounded bizarre, but other than the fact that my father had stayed at the table for this long, which was indeed strange, this was a fairly typical morning for us. I think that was what made me so tense that morning. Usually he ate a bite or two, complained about my cooking, kissed my mom on the forehead, and then disappeared into his office. My mom would either sit at the table silently scrolling through her phone, or disappear into the house shortly after my father left. Either way, it felt like she wasn't at the table at all.

That left Isabel and me to eat our breakfast at our own

pace and have a few moments of sweet solitude away from the specter of my parents and the tension they brought into every room. Isabel could chatter away, talking about all her plans for the day while I tried as hard as I could to get her to take a couple of bites between her excited ramblings; and I didn't have to worry about my parents getting annoyed with my child.

Today my father decided he liked my eggs, so he sat at the breakfast table for longer than usual. Isabel was starting to squirm in her chair. She wasn't finished with her plate, but I could tell she was done with breakfast. It's hard to keep an eight-year-old still for any amount of time, but this eight-year-old was used to being able to get up and run around, ask questions, and giggle with her mom after sitting still for five minutes in the morning. My dad hated it when Isabel was fidgety, and I worried about—

Well. I worried about what he would do, or say, to her.

"Isabel, do you want to go to your room?" I asked gently, when I first saw her shuffle in her chair.

"That brat isn't going to eat in her room," my father answered, before Isabel could even look up from her plate. "She can sit still and have a nice breakfast with her family, can't she? Or are you raising a feral cat under my roof?"

I felt my shoulders tense, ready to throw myself between my father and his granddaughter.

"I'm okay here, Mommy," she whispered, careful not to make too much noise—my father hated noise.

He snorted and went back to his plate. His pile of eggs didn't seem to be getting any smaller, though he continually lifted his fork to his mouth as though he was eating them. His eyes were bright and ready to rage at any moment. The earlier comment about my weight could either be the beginning of an eruption or just a jab as it was.

My hands shook as I brought my fork to my plate and scooped up the yellow, jiggling yolks, bringing them to my mouth.

"What, are you afraid of the eggs you made? They won't poison you. For once, they're actually pretty good," I heard my father say through his chews.

I bit down on the fork and forced myself to chew longer than I needed to. The eggs rolled around in my mouth, coating my tongue in a slimy film. I had let them go cold. They were too hard and too soft all at the same time. The salt made me thirsty, but the texture made me want to spit them out in my dad's face. My stomach was already turning with anxiety. I worried about what he would do if he knew what I was thinking.

Isabel could tell I was upset, and she shuffled closer to me in her chair. "Mommy, when you finish eating maybe we can play with my dolls. Or we could practice our drawing. I got further in that portrait book you gave me, and I think I'm gonna be able to draw your nose right this time."

My father rolled his eyes before jamming another forkful of eggs into his mouth. My mom glanced at us over her phone, and then turned away from me and my dad in her chair. I could sense that he was getting annoyed with Isabel. His morning peace was interrupted and there was no way for him to get it back.

I tried to get the situation back under control. "Sure, honey, we can practice your drawing. For now, can you sit and finish your eggs?" I asked.

"I don't want to finish my eggs. I don't like them anymore. I want to go draw. Can I go draw?" Isabel asked, her voice rising out of the quiet whisper I taught her to use when she was at the table.

From my left I could hear a grunt—my dad was losing his patience.

"You can go draw if you'd like. Say thank you and excuse yourself."

"I don't want to go alone, Mommy. I want you to come with me."

At that I could see my father's knuckles go white around his fork. He was annoyed. My father hated Isabel. To him, she was the living embodiment of his disappointment in me.

"Mommy? Can you come with me? Are you done?" Isabel asked, tugging my sleeve.

She tugged so hard I dropped the fork onto the wooden floor. It fell with a thud and my father's fork clattered to his plate. I sat up and was met with his seething expression.

"Does that kid understand that *some* of us aren't finished eating yet?" he growled through gritted teeth.

"Yes, of course she does. She's just a little impatient, that's all," I said, shaking Isabel's hand off me and trying to settle her back in her chair.

She refused, squirming from my hand like a fish. "*I'm done eating, and it looks like Grandma's done eating too. She hasn't touched her eggs in a while,*" Isabel said, pointing across the table at my mother.

I grabbed her hand and pulled it back to her plate. "Isabel, I've told you countless times it's rude to point."

"It's rude to make assumptions as well; have you told her that?" my father asked. He turned to my mother. "Are you done with your food?"

My mother didn't say a word. She kept staring at her phone, silently stabbing a fold of fluffy scrambled eggs with her fork, and slowly bringing it up to her mouth, as if my father wasn't breathing over her as she did.

"Looks to me like Helena is still eating. You know what they say, when you assume you—"

"They say you shouldn't make assumptions," I interrupted, holding Isabel back in her chair, cutting my father off before he could start cussing, which I knew would make Isabel cry out that he put a dollar in the cussing jar. My father called her a 'narc' every time she did, and he was already on edge. No need to make the situation worse.

"Isabel, why don't you go upstairs and get your art supplies set up. I'll come join you when we're all done here," I told her, trying to ignore my parents. My mother could at the very least answer my father. It wouldn't calm him down, but it would keep him from exploding.

"No, I want to go with you!" Isabel cried out.

I froze in my chair, not turning to see the reactions behind me. It got quiet. The only sound was the clink of my mother stabbing her eggs with a fork. I couldn't hear my father breathing—that was a bad sign.

"Isabel, please—"

"Mommy, just come with me! You finished your food, and I've finished my food. We should go play! I want to go play!"

"Will you shut her up?" my father roared.

Across the table I saw my mother shrink away, as if she was trying to jump into her phone. I closed my eyes and moved Isabel back in her chair, putting my body between her and my father. "She's just a little impatient, like any eight-year-old would be."

"It's impolite to rush people when they're in the middle of a meal. She should know better by now."

"I'm sorry, kids are—"

"I don't care about how kids are *supposed* to act. This is *my* house, and when you're under *my* roof you'll keep your damn kid under control and not let her bother us. I don't want to be pissed off, Maggie. I don't *enjoy* being angry, despite what you probably say to people behind my back. If you're going to raise this girl, you need to be raising her right, not letting her run around this house like some kind of wild animal."

Isabel's eyes lit up with rage. "I'm not an animal! And we only play wild animals in my room, we don't play it around the house."

I wanted to smile, to celebrate my little girl sticking up for me. I couldn't, not right now. Not when my dad's chair was scraping back from the table and he was unfolding his massive body to tower over us.

"You need to shut this kid up and teach her some manners, Maggie, before she ruins somebody else's breakfast. And if you don't manage to keep her under control..." my father trailed off, staring at me.

He didn't need to explain. The bruises up and down my mother's arms were explanation enough. When he felt I was sufficiently threatened, he turned on his heels and walked away, leaving his half-finished breakfast on the plate. His booming footsteps faded as he wandered off into the maze of the house.

Isabel was quiet as he walked away, her little hand holding onto my sleeve. I stood up and started to clear the table.

"Mom, are you finished with your plate?" I timidly asked.

My mom said nothing, didn't move her eyes from her phone. She waved the plate away, and then left the table.

Soon, her footsteps faded away as well, in the direction of the main sitting room.

I looked at Isabel and smiled. "The sooner we clean up, the sooner we can draw. Do you remember the song I taught you?"

"Obviously, Mommy; we sing it every day."

As we cleared the table and washed the dishes, I thought about the insane living situation I was subjecting my daughter to. It's not that I didn't want to leave. I knew this wasn't the right environment for a kid. No one should be living in a place where they had to tiptoe around an abusive parent or grandparent. The problem was my father—he thought he had the town convinced that we were the perfect family. A loving wife and dutiful daughter in a beautiful, historical family home. He pretended we were living the American Dream. He was an influential man in our town; after all, he owned half of it. Joseph Conner got into real estate early and managed to amass a fortune in property, land, and cash. This meant he could pay off just about anyone in town and cut off anyone he didn't like.

If I ran out and hid in a neighbor's basement, my father would find me and drag me back home. If I tried to give Isabel away, he'd bring her back. According to him, the day I decided to keep her was the day I sealed my fate, and I had to live with the consequences of my stupidity. I didn't mind—Isabel was the only light in my life. I wished I could do better for her, and I thought if I could just finish remodeling my parents' house, they'd let me go. Once they didn't need me anymore, I would be free. Until then, I would do everything in my power to protect Isabel from my father.

I knew it was selfish, believe me. It was the kind of situation where normal logic went out the window and all I wanted to do was survive. For a long time, it wasn't that bad —my parents were reluctantly charmed by Isabel's curious nature.

There was a change when she turned eight, as I started to remodel my parents' home. I couldn't explain it, and I couldn't explain why I didn't just leave.

2

My home had never felt so large as when I was tasked to remodel it.

My father wanted the house redone. As far as he was concerned, the house was old and unfashionable and if I was going to live there well into my twenties, I was going to have to earn my keep. He also didn't want any strangers coming in to do the work.

"They won't appreciate the treasure they have here. Those young contractors don't know a solid house when they see one. They'll try to turn this place into one of those modern glass-paneled monstrosities and ruin the character we have here," he grumbled at me when pitching the project. "You appreciate this house. You should be the one to fix it."

He had a point. A lot of the new remodels were casting aside the beautiful Victorian features of the houses in town and replacing them with floor-to-ceiling windows—not a great idea in a town with as many storms as we had—or turning them into post-modern steel-coloured boxes. I was more into the elaborate wood carvings and fixtures of the old Victorian buildings, the bright colors, towers, and gables, even the widow's peak and accompanying widow's walks that dotted some of the houses closer to the seaside. It was a shame to see the character of these houses torn down for the modernist blocks with no personality.

I couldn't remember when I started, but it was just as well because there was no way to tell when I would be finished. Despite the fact that they didn't go anywhere or really do anything, my parents were on a tight schedule to get the remodel finished. At first, I thought this might mean they were planning on selling the house and moving to another town—if that were the case, maybe I could sneak away with Isabel and start our lives over again. I had completed at least a quarter of the house before I realized it was all a pipe dream. My parents were tied to this old house, and they'd die in it if they could.

Every day I got to work early, preparing breakfast for everyone and creating a plan for the day. I often presented these plans to Isabel as some kind of game, to make sure she would be helping me and staying out of the way of my parents. It was summer, school was out, and there weren't very many children in the neighborhood, so it was better for Isabel to stay with me than play alone and hurt herself. She helped me to sort through boxes and closets, helped sand and re-stain old furniture. I even taught her how to embroider so she could help me repair the cushions on some old chairs. Some of the furniture had been in the Conner family for generations and was desperately in need of a tender hand. Neither of my parents was handy, and we had enough money that when a family heirloom broke, they'd just buy something new to replace it. But of course, my father didn't want to get rid of the broken item, so it would get shoved into a room that we rarely used. Sometimes it felt like most of the house was occupied by broken things and we tried to live our lives around them.

Isabel didn't always want to play my 'fix the furniture' game. I mean, she was an eight-year-old. No matter how precocious, there comes a time when all they want to do is play with their dolls or color in a coloring book. As the summer trudged along, it got harder and harder to keep track of her. Remodeling the house wasn't a novelty anymore, and she had clued in that 'fix the furniture' wasn't so much a game as a chore.

"Please, Issie, just stay close to me, okay?" I asked her.

"Why? You're so boring. You never want to play. I just want to play witches. Can't we go up to the tower and brew something in a cauldron?" she whined, kicking the molding of the hallway we were in.

I had finally finished clearing out the rooms on this floor and was starting to work on the floors in the hallway. Isabel wasn't allowed to run around the hallway with the sander, and she was having a temper tantrum about it.

"I always want to play with you, my love, but I have to get some work done first. If you just have a little patience—"

"Patience for what?" came a sweet quiet voice from behind me.

I jumped, startled at the noise. It was like the wind coming through a creaky door and for a split second I thought it was a ghost. I turned to see the bony frame of my mother peeking out at us from one of the doorways, her hands waving away the dust that was perpetually floating in the air. How long had she been standing there?

"Mommy says I have to have patience because she has to work, but I want to play witches and she won't play with me because she said she has to sand the hallway," Isabel sang.

My mother barely moved her head to acknowledge my daughter. Instead she smiled her tight, angry smile at me and said, "Maggie, I hope you know this has to be finished. I won't have you dilly-dallying on the house; we have to live in it, after all."

"I know, Mom," I replied. "I was just telling Isabel that we can play witches once I'm done with the hallway for today. It needs sanding and re-staining, but after that it will need some time to dry before I can get started on the wallpaper in the halls. It's so dark. Don't you think it might be nicer to have something a little bit brighter?" I said, trying to cheer her up.

My mother said nothing, just turned and walked off down the hall.

Isabel bent down and whispered in my ear, "I can make sure she doesn't come back. That way we can play for a while before you have to finish the job." She immediately took off down the hall after my mother, turning a corner and disappearing into the gloom of the stuffy old house.

"Isabel!" I cried after her. My parents could be irresponsible with my child, and the house was in such a state that I hated it when Isabel ran off and I didn't know where she was going.

She moved faster than any eight-year-old should, particularly when she wanted something. Other parents had to know what I meant—blink and all of a sudden, your kid was knee-deep in a mess you tried in vain to warn them against.

I stood up, moving my materials to the side so they weren't in danger of being knocked over, and I chased her down the hall. The fumes from the wood stain were hitting me, and as soon as I turned into the hall I saw no sign of my mother or Isabel. The hallway appeared to be longer than it ever could have been, like it had been stretched though a black hole. At the end must have been my daughter because I could hear her footsteps—they weren't far off. I started down the hallway—slowly because I was afraid of tripping over my feet.

The first door I came across was a little closet—the house was full of these. In another lifetime they were probably used by housekeepers and butlers to store linens and porcelain. There was even a dumbwaiter in the house, that I hoped to repair to its former glory. I closed the closet and kept going down the hall, hoping to avoid my mother and coax Isabel back to the hallway I was working on.

I tried another door—this time to a little anteroom that I knew was once the 'smoking room'—it was now my father's storage area where he kept boxes and boxes of old paperwork: rental contracts, lease agreements, and bills of sale from his sprawling real estate business. Not that my mother would have gone in there, but it was likely that Isabel forgot what she was chasing her for and started a new game, as boisterous and cooped-up eight-year-olds might do.

"Isabel? Are you in here?" I whispered. "Isabel, come back here. You're not in trouble, but I need you to stick by me, okay?"

I didn't want to step into the office. I knew if I did, I'd hear about it later. My father had an eerie sixth sense about his things, his papers, his mysterious documents that my mother and I knew nothing about. A whole world of business that he refused to explain—probably because it wasn't exactly morally righteous to be bribing half the town's authorities.

"Issie!" I hissed. "This isn't funny at all."

"I would have to agree; this isn't very funny at all," a voice boomed behind me. "Not only are you snooping around where you aren't supposed to, you've left your work all over the floor in order to do it."

I gulped and turned around to face my father. His arm reached around me to slam the door, causing me to flinch.

"I made sure to set it to the side. Isabel ran off and I was just—"

"She lives here, Maggie. Your daughter knows her way around the house. What are you afraid of? You have work to do. You don't have time to be playing hide and seek with your bored kid."

"I wanted to make sure she didn't go anywhere she isn't supposed to."

"I won't," piped up a little voice behind my father. Isabel was innocently standing in the hall, as if she hadn't run away from me at all. "I was just in the bathroom, but I didn't tell Mommy. I'm done now. I can help with the hallway."

My father looked back and forth between me and my daughter, clearly trying to determine if this was a joke or not.

I just shrugged my shoulders and shook my head—the universal parental sign for, *Kids, right? They're all nuts.*

My father took me by the arm and led me back around the corner to the hallway I was working on. "You need to finish your work before you go off to play. The last time I checked there was only one eight-year-old in this house. As a grown woman, I expect you to be able to finish what you started without some kind of recess period." He let go of my arm and stalked off down the hallway. Just as my mother did, he turned a corner and disappeared.

I whipped around to face Isabel. "What have I told you? Don't go off alone. You could get hurt!" I yelled, exasperated.

"I'm sorry. I thought I could chase Grandma Helena and make sure she was too scared to come back, but she went into her library and locked the door. Then I had to pee, and I didn't think you'd be upset because I wasn't gone too long. I went as fast as I could and I came back, but then I saw Grandpa Joseph and he looked mad, and you always told me to hide from him when he looked mad," Isabel sputtered and started to cry.

I wrapped my daughter in my arms and kissed the top of her forehead. "Sweetie, it's okay. I just worry about you," I whispered into her hair.

"You worry about me too much. None of the other kids have helicopter moms like you," she replied.

"Where did you learn that phrase?" I asked.

Isabel just shrugged and went over to my repair gear. She found a pair of safety goggles and put them on, sitting herself down on the little stool I had brought for her. She wasn't going to reply. It was the secret of kids saying oddly mature things—they just learned them and never explained how.

I pulled on my own safely goggles, picked up the electric sander beside her and got back to work.

THE SANDER WAS POWERFUL, and loud. It meant that I could hardly hear anything when I was working with it, and the vibrations from the machine traveled up my arm and down my body, drowning out the footsteps and creaks of the floor. It took me a while to realize Isabel had run off again. I ought to have expected it; whenever I paused to take a break or switch arms, she pestered me with questions about games we could play, what we were going to eat for dinner, and why the sky was blue.

Where did that little kid run off to now? I asked myself. It's possible she just went to the bathroom again. The noise from the sander was deafening; I wouldn't blame the kid for trying to get a little break from it. I stood up and dusted myself off, ready to go look for her, and met my mother's gaze at the end of the hall.

"Where are you going?" she asked. "You can't be finished yet, are you?"

"Of course not. I just want to look for Isabel."

My mother rolled her eyes. "You are far too overprotective of that girl. Just keep working. Let her be. She's eight. Do you really think she wants to be sitting next to a sander all day?"

She stood at the end of the hall until I picked up a broom and started sweeping the debris from the work I had already completed, waiting at the end of the hall but staring at her phone. Once my mother was satisfied, she wandered off, probably in the direction of her library where she could bury herself in a book or her phone and forget everything that was going on around her.

I thought about what I could do to brighten this place up —some yellow floral wallpaper, maybe? Or a leafy green with gold accents. I had seen it at the hardware store, in the premium wallpapers section. It was a little decadent, but it matched the vintage grandeur of the house. Would my mother even notice if I replaced the faded pink wallpaper with something more modern?

I tried to focus on cleaning up. My mom had a point;

Isabel lived here too. I shouldn't hover over her, especially while she was on holiday from school. I swept the dust and sanded wood into a little pail I'd brought with me.

Still, I couldn't help but worry. My father was easily annoyed by Isabel, and I didn't want her to cross his path. During the school year it was fairly easy; she was gone most of the day and kept to herself in the evening with homework and quiet craft time. This period of 'rest' wasn't as restful for me as a parent. It meant I had to find ways to entertain my daughter all day long, while I was working, and with limited funds.

One of these days, we'll get out of here, Issie. I'll figure out a way.

I SANDED the rest of the hall, working faster than I had before. Isabel still wasn't back, which meant she was tucked away somewhere, either playing a game or reading by herself. She was probably up in the attic, playing witches by herself. It made me feel sad, and sorry that I couldn't give her a sibling to play with. I was also an only child, so I knew what it was like to have to entertain yourself. I surveyed my work and decided I could probably sneak away. If my parents asked, I'd just tell them the sander was starting to overheat and it needed a rest.

I swept up the debris and tucked my materials to the side again, lining them up against the wall so they wouldn't block anyone's path. I figured Isabel wouldn't go following my mother, knowing it could get her in trouble, so I headed off in the opposite direction.

I checked the attic first, sneezing and waving away the

floating dust bunnies that greeted me as I went up the stairs. Isabel was nowhere to be found, which I thought was strange. *She probably realized that witches isn't a fun game when you're playing alone,* I thought as I moved over to the window. It was a nice day out, not a single cloud in the sky. Isabel knew it was okay for her to play in a small part of the backyard, but it wasn't safe where I hadn't got the chance to clear it. My parents never took care of their property the way they should have. It was only now that I was older and a little more skilled that the house was becoming livable again.

Isabel wasn't outside, so I went back through the house to try and find her. She wasn't in her room, wasn't in the main sitting room, and wasn't in the kitchen waiting patiently for me to make her a snack. Those were her usual haunting grounds, so where could she have gone? The library was my mother's domain, and Isabel said it smelled like old people, so there was no way she had wandered in there.

Was she hiding in one of the closets, playing a game of hide and seek and waiting for me to find her? The thought made me panic. How long had my baby been waiting for me, expecting me to realize she was gone and come looking for her? Was she feeling scared or hurt or hungry? I picked up the pace as I ran back upstairs to the hallway I had been working on.

My materials were untouched—a good sign. It meant my father hadn't come through here, and Isabel was still in hiding, wherever she was. I went back down the hall toward my father's office storage. Isabel might have gone in the direction of my mother knowing she was too busy in her own little world to pay any attention to her. I crept down the hall, opening door after door very slowly so I didn't spook my daughter. I avoided my mother's library and went into the spare bedroom next to it.

I was about to leave when I heard a muffled sneeze coming from inside the closet. My heart started to race. Unsure of what I might find, I moved across the room as quietly as possible and creaked the door open to find Isabel tucked into a corner of the closet, wiping her nose with the back of her hand.

"The book is really dusty, Mommy," she said, looking up at me with her big innocent eyes.

"Where did you find it?" I asked her, bending down to give her a hug.

"On the table by the bed. It doesn't have anything on it, see? So I wanted to see what's in it. It's really dusty. It keeps making me sneeze."

I took the book out of her hands and tossed it into the closet. "You should have just left it, baby. You don't know whose it is."

"I was gonna put it back," Isabel whined, rolling her doe-like eyes.

"Were you? And I bet you were just coming right back, even though I told you not to run off, huh? I was so worried about you. I went up to the attic and thought you might have been hurt. I looked all over the house for you, and the more I couldn't find you the more worried I got."

"You didn't look everywhere for me," Isabel said, point-blank. "That would have taken way too long."

"You're right, this house is huge. But I looked everywhere I could think. I went to the kitchen and almost made you a snack to lure you out of your hiding place."

"You didn't look everywhere. You didn't look for me in the crying room," she said.

"The what?" I asked, feeling the blood draining from my face. I had made sure never to mention that place. I made sure never to talk about that—

"The crying room. You said you looked everywhere for me, but you didn't look in there, did you? So that means you couldn't have looked *everywhere*. You just looked in the places where you thought I would be," Isabel rambled on, but I wasn't paying attention.

She was right. I hadn't looked in the crying room.

3

My dad didn't hate me when I was a kid. I had plenty of memories of him taking me to the beach that was only an hour away. He'd swim with me, and we had this game where I'd jump to avoid the surf and he'd hoist me in the air so it felt like I was flying over the small waves. Sometimes my mother would come. Oftentimes she'd stay home, but I never understood why. I had heard my parents fighting and had been afraid that one day they'd get a divorce and I'd have to move and leave the only home I'd ever known.

As I got older, my father seemed to be more frustrated by my presence. I went to my mom more often with questions, trying to wake her up out of her perpetual depression. That, for some reason, would make my father angry. In those moments he'd play hide and seek with me, and he'd lock me in the crying room.

He didn't call it that, of course—I did. I quickly realized that he used those moments as revenge for me paying more attention to my mother than to him. The problem with living with a narcissist was that you could never live up to their expectations, nor understand how much they needed you to focus solely on them.

The first time he locked me in that room, he only left me in the tiny space for about fifteen minutes. Just enough for me to "learn my lesson," or so he'd said at the time.

"Serves you right," he'd said as he'd unlocked the room. "You ought to show some respect to the person who *actually* parents you. Not that brain-dead zombie who can barely cook or take care of you."

He's right, I remembered thinking. *My mom barely notices whether or not I'm in the room. He must have been sad, thinking that I was playing favorites.*

Of course, I understand now that no kid should have to choose between their parents like that. No other kid had to weigh out the consequences of favoring one parent over the other. Kids weren't taught what this kind of abuse looked like, only what physical or sexual abuse looked like. For the first ten years of my life my father never hit or hurt my mother in front of me. I didn't know why she was so reserved or cold. I only knew what my father said—that she was a lazy mother, and he was the only person I could rely on.

Maybe that was why I was still living at home now. Somewhere deep down I still believed that my father was the only person I could trust. I hadn't trusted my teachers because even though they had to know what went on at my home, they had only been speculating. And I never trusted the neighbors because they were all nosy gossips who my father claimed just wanted to besmirch our family name around town. I hadn't even trusted my friends because they weren't family, and family were the only people who could understand family. That circular logic swirled in my brain until I had become a rebellious teenager who found the perfect time to sneak out of her house. I'd learned how to lie to my parents so that they thought I was at a friend's house when really, I was at a house party. Still, whenever I had been caught out, or got too close to a stranger, my father would bring me back to the crying room and lock me in there.

"You need some time to think about where your loyalties lie," he'd said at the time. "My father did this to me, taught me some harsh lessons, and I became a successful family man and businessman; a pillar in the community. You need to learn some discipline," he'd add firmly.

That became his new mantra. Respect turned into discipline, and my teenage years were spent in and out of the crying room.

I remembered the last time I went in there. I had told my father I was going camping with some friends. One of their parents had a cabin on a small island, one of those rustic remote buildings with no cellphone service and a 'if it's yellow let it mellow' sign above the toilet. I had begged him to go, claimed that all my friends were going and I'd be left out if I didn't go.

"It's a popularity thing. If I don't go, then Ashley will think it's because I think I'm better than her and then it'll turn into a whole thing. Please, *please,* can I go?" I had begged. I had known peppering in my worry about losing status would get him to agree. My father was always a very proud man. Eventually he'd caved and I had been allowed to go. I had told him it was a three-day trip to that remote island with my friends.

Of course, that hadn't been where we were really going. Ashley had booked us on a train to New York City, where we had planned to spend the weekend with her much older boyfriend, and his friend Nate Moore.

"Nate really likes you. He thinks you're very cute and mature for your age," Ashley had said, enticing me to break every rule my father had put in place and go with her.

We had known our parents wouldn't let us spend the weekend with our older, secret boyfriends. I had known my father would flip if he had known I had a boyfriend, one he hadn't hand-picked from our town's elite. It had been a risk, but I had been dying to see the big city lights and live my adolescent fantasy of getting as far away from my family as I could.

We never even made it to the city. Ashley's father had found out where we were really going—her little brother couldn't quite keep that secret. Her father had called my dad, and the two of them had driven down to the city to meet the train. I had no idea how many red lights they drove through or how many speeding tickets they got, but they were on the platform when we got out at Grand Central Station. My father had been livid. He had grabbed my arm so hard I almost lost feeling in it.

When we had returned home, he'd thrown me in the crying room. "Well, I hadn't planned on you being home for the next three days, so you can go ahead and camp in here," he'd said as he'd slammed and locked the door.

He hadn't opened the door until Monday at dinnertime, the time I had said I'd be home from Ashley's cabin.

After that weekend, I had run away and ended up living with Nate, who got me pregnant and blamed me for it. Nate, who hated me when I started caring more about my daughter than him. Nate, who was the reason I was shipped back home to my parents, no longer their innocent daughter.

Since I came back, I had barely heard anything about the crying room. My father never even threatened to throw me back in there anymore. I was glad. It made me think he had changed. That maybe we could have a fresh start as a family.

"Mommy?" Isabel asked, interrupting my dark reverie. "What's the crying room?"

It was on the other side of the house, the part I hadn't started working on just yet. I avoided the room as much as I could, and I never brought it up with Isabel—nor my parents.

"It's ancient history, darling. Where did you hear about it?" I asked, biting back tears as the memory of the crying room surged and faded away.

"I saw it in a dream. I thought it was a wall, but then the wall was a door, and we were in it together. How can the wall be a door? Is that real?" she asked.

"No, honey, it's not real. In a dream anything can be anything." It was going to be just fine; plenty of kids had strange dreams. Who knew? Maybe my father had threatened to put her in there—I'd have to find a way to stop that from happening.

Isabel nodded solemnly. "You shouldn't go to the crying room. It's a bad idea to reopen that wound."

My kid was weird. I didn't understand why she was suddenly talking like the Oracle in some Ancient Greek myth. Maybe I should try to find her some kind of day camp or daycare, so she could socialize with other kids and not say such weird stuff. Her precociousness was charming, but that was bordering on being creepy.

"Of course, my darling. I won't go into the crying room," I told her, smiling through my sadness. I knew that I would have to go back there eventually, to that tiny hidden closet in the parlor. I had to go back and tear away the scabs that grew over those memories as I cleaned the space. Once I did, I was determined to seal that door and never set foot in the room again.

But that wouldn't be for a long time. I had more to do in this house. There were floors to finish and wallpaper to put up, and hundreds of pieces of old furniture to fix. Not to mention the roof that leaked anytime there was a storm.

"Can we go play witches now?" Isabel asked, tugging at my sleeve.

I shook my head and looked down at my daughter, the brightest light in my otherwise dim life.

4

I cracked open the first can of wood stain. The fumes stung my eyes, and I got up to go find a fan or a window—anything that would keep me from fainting or getting sick from the smell—benzene, formaldehyde, and arsenic—what a combo. I had to admit, I kind of liked it, the same way people loved the smell of gasoline. Carpentry made me feel free from my parents and their dysfunctional household. I loved the feeling of building things, making something from nothing, and getting lost in the intricacies of a project.

This hallway was not one of those passion projects. I had finally finished sanding the full length of the hallway. It took me hours. It seemed that any time I made some progress, the length of the hallway doubled. After making dinner and putting Isabel to sleep, I went back, ready to spend most of my night staining the floor, lost in my own world.

The stain was thicker than I was used to. As I stirred the liquid, it felt more like molasses than the usual oil- or water-based stains I used. I asked my father to buy some, but he refused, so I had to dig through the garage to get it. *It's probably just old; needs a stir before I can use it.*

I got up, taking the can with me, to find some thinner or mineral spirits to revive the old wood stain. Coming down the hall, I could hear my parents in the middle of an argument. Their voices were muffled, but I didn't need to hear them to know what was going on. Likely my mother was deep in her book and my father was getting bored. Either that or he wanted control of the TV and my mother wouldn't give it up. I paid it no mind as I passed the hallway and went down to the basement. I had set up a little workshop down there, with all the essentials for basic carpentry work. I wanted to set it up in the garage, but my father refused.

"What would the neighbors think?" he bellowed. "They'd think we're too poor to afford a professional to come work on the house. I don't wanna hear their questions or their judgement when I go into town. If you need a workshop, you can have one in the basement."

That was the end of that conversation. I set up in the basement and hid my tools and my work down there—just in case anyone cared enough to check on me.

Our neighborhood used to be pretty lively. There were families up and down the street, people who had lived in this town for generations. Their ancestors built a small house, and they built additions and remodeled the structure until the whole street was dotted with manor-like buildings that had Victorian exteriors and modern interiors. In the past few years, people had started moving away and the street was now mostly vacant. It gave the part of town we lived in an eerie quality. You half expected to see tumbleweeds rolling down the street or hear the screams of banshees from every roof. I didn't really know what happened. I guessed that people got tired of the constant upkeep that came with having an old house. Or maybe their kids grew up and moved away toward better opportunities and bigger dreams. I was never sure. All my old friends had gone, so there really wasn't anyone I could turn to when my parents' screams cracked the foundations of our home.

I stirred some mineral spirits into the wood stain, losing myself in the swirl of two liquids coming together. It was romantic, I thought, to see something truly become one like that. I didn't even hear the thumps coming from above me until I had started making my way back up the stairs. There was only one thing it could mean—the argument had escalated. My mother wasn't humoring my dad's anger. Instead she had probably retreated further, causing him to get even meaner.

Judging from the noise, they were probably in the sitting room. The sound of my father yelling got louder as I went up the stairs, but still I couldn't quite make out what he was saying. He must have been drunk because his words sounded like they were slurring together. I didn't hear my mother at all—either she was talking quietly, or she was staying silent.

After a moment of hesitation, I moved toward the sitting room. The door was slightly open, and I could see my parents through the crack. My father was still unintelligible, but it was clear how he was feeling. He kept yelling at my mother and then pushing her around or boxing her ears. It was like watching a prize fighter hitting a punching bag. My mom just took his hits and popped right back up. Throughout the ordeal she was silent, and her eyes were vacant. My mom disassociated when my father got physical with her, but this was something else. Watching them was cruel. My mother looked like a corpse. Her skin was paler than usual and her eyes had no life behind them.

My father, on the other hand, was larger than life. He was at least two heads taller than my mother on a good day, but now it looked like he could carry her in one hand. He overpowered her in every sense of the word. I wondered if maybe I was subconsciously blocking out what he was saying in order to protect myself. He kept going at her, and every time he did he got bigger, meaner, angrier. She wouldn't react—she couldn't, at this point. Her face had a completely neutral expression. It was clear that my father thought she was mocking him.

I couldn't take my eyes off them for a moment. I didn't know what to do. I couldn't call anyone—the police wouldn't come by without checking with my father first. All I could do was watch, keeping my breathing as quiet as possible and trying to keep my shaking hands from dropping the can of wood stain and tearing my father's attention away from my mother and onto me.

It was selfish. I wanted to scream at my father, fight him with whatever I could, but doing so meant I'd probably wake Isabel, who was sleeping upstairs. I didn't want her to see this. I was trying as much as I could to protect her from my father's anger, and if she tried to get in between us...

I didn't want to think about that.

Instead I watched as my father kept screaming and my mother just stood there. She was as rigid as a corpse and seemed to hardly notice as my father got louder and angrier. She wasn't bleeding or bruised. If you had told me my father was striking a ghost I would have believed you. Maybe this was the reason no one lived around here anymore. There weren't any banshees screaming from the roofs of the old houses; there was only the sound of my mother as she navigated my father's anger.

I couldn't watch for very much longer. My father's behavior was making me sick to my stomach, and I still had a lot of work to do. If I wanted to avoid a rerun of this episode, I had to finish staining the floor before the morning.

I FELT guilty leaving my mother like that. She didn't often *feel* like a mother, but it was still selfish to prioritize the work I had to do over her wellbeing. I knew she'd be fine; he wasn't about to kill her. My mother had long since lost that motherly feeling. She could have abandoned me and I wouldn't have noticed. The only times her presence was felt was when my father was occupied with her or if she was nagging me to get some project or another finished. She was mostly checked out of our lives, barely lifting her gaze from the phone or the book in her hand. Even when she didn't have a physical distraction she was off in her own world, so occupied by her thoughts that she barely registered the presence of me or my daughter. She wasn't warm. She didn't ask questions.

When I was growing up, I often blamed her for the way my father acted—if she would just pay some attention to him, maybe then he'd be satisfied, he'd stop blowing up in our faces, wouldn't be so angry all of the time. Maybe if she had been paying attention, she would have done her best to send me to a child psychologist. That person could have made me understand what was happening, maybe even helped me avoid the rebellious years of my adolescence.

I trudged up the stairs, first to check on Isabel and then to go back to my work. I opened the door to her room as quietly as I could and crept in to find my daughter fast asleep in her bed. The soft moonlight was shining on her face and she looked like a porcelain doll.

I had absolutely no idea how to help her. It was getting harder and harder to hide my father's behavior from my daughter's curious eyes. She saw the way he recoiled whenever she spoke up, saw his face go red with anger when something was out of order. She knew what kind of man he was, and was starting to adopt the same kind of emotional behavior. I saw her get moodier as the days went by—today was the perfect example. When she didn't get her way, Isabel ran off to take matters into her own hands, with no thought as to why I might be worried. I did the same thing as a kid. It led to my rebellious streak as a teenager and everything that came after it.

What if Isabel inherited my father's anger? Or my teenage rebellion? Or even my mother's indifference? She was a smart, curious kid and I wanted the best for her. I wanted to make sure she didn't end up in the same cycle as I did, but what could I do for her? I had no family to send her to, and if I left her with someone in town, I ran the risk of my father finding out about it.

Isabel stirred in her sleep just as my father's voice roared up the stairs. I closed the door as quietly as I could, before going back to my work in the hall. Hopefully, it didn't disrupt her peace. I hoped his voice didn't give her nightmares.

My father fell asleep soon after. At least I thought he did; his voice was no longer traveling up the stairs and I didn't hear any more thuds coming from the sitting room.

I shook my head to stay awake and got back to working on staining the hallway floor. The wood stain had thickened again, I wasn't sure how. It was old, I guessed. Or maybe my father *had* bought new wood stain, and he bought some kind of gel-base that I was unfamiliar with. I decided to pour it onto a palette just in case. The stain poured out of the can thick and dark, darker than I expected. I hoped this was what my parents wanted, or that they wouldn't notice. There was a reddish tint to it, which could match the fading strawberry-tinted wallpaper up here.

I dipped a rag into the stain and got to work massaging it into the freshly sanded floor. It was redder than I'd thought, brighter, like blood. I didn't think much of it at first, just kept staining the floor—I was so tired, there wasn't any way this was really blood. It was just my eyes playing tricks on me, or the full moon making me go mad. I pushed the thick red stain around on the fresh wood and was hit with the bitter scent of iron—I was wrong. It was blood.

I shook my head thinking it was all a dream. Maybe I had sniffed a little too much stain—formaldehyde and arsenic were a powerful combination—but when I dipped my rag back into the palette, there was no mistaking what soaked through the white cloth.

It was blood. I was pushing blood all over the floor, simultaneously trying to clean and tint the floor. *It's a finish, Maggie. You're imagining things,* I told myself. *There isn't any blood.*

Just in case, I ran to the bathroom to wring out the rag I

was using. Blood poured down the sink. The rag wouldn't come clean.

I looked into the mirror and blinked. "You're awake. You're staining the floor with wood finish, not blood. Wake up, Maggie Conner. Wake up!" I screamed, flinching immediately. I pinched my cheeks to stay awake—I was awake, wasn't I? If I was awake, then what I was seeing was real, and it was just really dark wood stain with a red tint. That was all it was.

I opened the window and stuck my head out—it could have been the fumes playing tricks on me. I took a few gulps of fresh air before going back inside. The rag in my hand was wet and dark, but when I smelled it, it had that familiar chemical smell of formaldehyde and arsenic. It had all been a dream. I was tired, that was all it was.

I took a couple more gulps of fresh air and headed back to work. The fresh wood was stained unevenly with a dark color—I was right, it had all been just a strange dream. Now I would have to make sure to do at least two coats, to cover up the untidy strokes I had done. I dipped my rag into the stain, paying closer attention to the color this time. It was back to its loose consistency, and when I dragged the rag over the floor it turned the old wood into an expected dark oak color. My hands were shaking and I felt nauseated.

It's the chemicals, Maggie. The formaldehyde and the arsenic, they're poisonous—why do you think people sniff paint? To get high and forget reality. It's just a break from reality.

Still, my hands were shaking. Each time I dipped my rag back into the wood stain I could feel my muscles tense up and I worried that I was working blood into the floors of my parents' house. I brought my nose to the floor to check—it didn't have the metallic smell of blood. It just smelled like chemicals—chemical acidity and the musk of old wood.

See? You're just tired, Maggie.

Living in this house was taking its toll, and even if I couldn't leave, I had to make sure it wouldn't drive me insane.

5

My head and back were aching, but I was finally done. I had lost track of time hours ago, and it would take a day for the floor to dry, but I could add it to my growing list of achievements when it came to this old crumbling house. It was only a little past midnight, which meant that a lot of the drying time could be done before I had to start playing hallway security guard to make sure no one stepped on it.

Slowly, I made my way up the stairs to my room—on the third floor, right across from Isabel's. Up here it could sometimes feel like we were living alone, as if we had a small two-bedroom flat in an old house. It could be a fairy tale. All that was missing was a fairy godmother and a happy ending.

But I couldn't sleep. It wasn't too late—I had expected to be up all night but the adrenaline pumping though my veins post-weird-blood-hallucination had made me work faster. I could still get a decent amount of sleep before Isabel inevitably woke me at the crack of dawn, but my mind was racing and my eyes didn't want to stay closed. I was thinking about the blood and all the work I still had to do on this house.

Thinking about how much stain I had left and whether I could use that on some of the furniture.

Thinking about my daughter and worrying that she would never have a normal childhood, or that her childhood would cause damage to her mental health.

Thinking about my *own* mental health and if I'd ever be able to recover from my parents' abuse.

Thinking and daydreaming, tossing and turning, watching the hands turn on the retro alarm clock by my bed.

After an hour of trying—and failing—to bore myself to sleep, I decided to just take a sleeping pill and knock myself out that way. I stumbled into my bathroom and opened the medicine cabinet. I hated taking drugs. It reminded me of Isabel's father and all the lives he ruined dealing illegal uppers and downers. Nate singlehandedly caused the opioid crisis in my town and left people strung out when he died. The pills in my cabinet were all prescribed to me, a cocktail of painkillers, sleeping pills, and psych drugs that doctors recommended to keep me "sane." I didn't really believe them; I knew they were all under my father's thumb and were probably trying to keep me in a state where I was unable to defend myself.

I only took them when it was really necessary. Times like these when I knew I wouldn't be able to sleep without some mind-altering help.

I took a small bottle of sleeping pills—tranquilizers, really—and counted out how many were left, comparing it to the tally I kept in a hidden notepad. Ten pills were left, ten pills in the count. I popped one in my mouth, adjusted the numbers for sleeping pills, and rolled the little notepad back into its hiding place—an old bottle of children's cough syrup.

There was a part of me that truly believed my father would start stealing these drugs from me, given the chance. He barely ever left the house. It was no wonder he was always so bored, and boredom bred stupidity. There was no telling when he would get sick of using alcohol to mend his wounds and turn to drugs instead.

So what if he did? What if one day he mixed some sleeping pills into his beer? He'd fall asleep and wouldn't wake up again. Imagine that, I thought, smiling to myself.

Guilt crept in at the edges of my thoughts. The idea that any daughter would want her father dead was evil, but I didn't think my father was a typical dad. For the first half of my life he had me convinced that my mother was a clumsy woman who bruised easily and was too shy to really connect with her daughter. It was no wonder that now, as an adult, I was staring at a medicine cabinet full of anti-depressants and medications for the treatment of psychosis.

My eyes were finally starting to feel heavy. I stumbled back to bed and waited for the heavy quilt of sleep to cover me. If my father were dead, I could fix up the house at my own pace. I wouldn't have to worry about his anger toward my daughter and the failure she represented to him. Maybe my mother would come alive again, and we could finally have the warm loving home I wanted for Isabel, just the three of us. If my father were dead, I probably wouldn't have to take all these prescription medications and I wouldn't have to worry about Isabel's mental health.

Maybe I didn't need a fairy godmother after all. Maybe all I needed was for my father to finally die.

6

I woke up late the next morning. My daughter was uncharacteristically quiet. Usually she woke me by bursting into the room the moment the sun came up, jumping on my bed and singing about her plans for the day. Having never been much of a morning person, this was only tolerable because of how much I loved my daughter, and I prayed every day to be woken up by something normal, like an alarm clock.

Today I finally got my wish, and it caused me more anxiety than trying to quiet Isabel and stop her from knocking her head on the ceiling.

My daughter was curled up in a ball at the foot of my bed, sound asleep.

"Isabel?" I asked, gently shaking her awake. It was 8 o'clock in the morning. We needed to hurry to get breakfast done and on the table. "Issie, can you wake up for me, please?"

Her eyes immediately burst open and a grin spread across her face.

"I *knew* you were awake this whole time! I came in and I tried to wake you up, but you wouldn't wake up, you were just staying asleep, so I was like, 'Mommy?' and you just sorta muttered in your sleep and that's how I knew you were playing a *prank* on me. But I wanted to prank you back by pretending that *I* was asleep and that you woke up *super-duper* late. So I crawled to the end of your bed, and then I pretended to be asleep and I waited, and I wanted to change your alarm clock but I didn't know how so I didn't, and I waited because I *knew* you were awake and I was right. You were awake and I pranked you back, right?"

Where do kids get their energy in the morning and how can I get some?

"Um, yes, baby, yeah, you pranked me right back. You got me," I said, as I stretched my arms overhead and let out a big yawn. The worst thing about taking a pill to sleep was the grogginess I felt the next morning. I needed some of whatever my eight-year-old had to shake myself into reality.

"Are we gonna make pancakes today?" she asked, staring up at me.

"Sure. Go back to your room and change and meet me in the hallway. We can make pancakes today," I replied, gently pushing Isabel out of my room so I could have a moment of peace before my day began. There was no special occasion, but I was pretty sure we had everything we needed for pancakes. I wanted to give Isabel as many of these cozy memories as possible in the hopes that they would suffocate the bad ones in her mind.

I DIDN'T SEE my parents until we were cleaning up. I had made a few extra pancakes and was writing instructions for heating them up on a sticky note when my mom walked into the kitchen. She sat down at the table behind me without saying a word.

When I saw her, my heart leaped into my throat. "Mom! You scared me," I exclaimed.

She didn't respond. She merely crossed her arms on the table and I almost jumped again.

Both of my mother's hands were wrapped in bandages. I tried to say something, but when I opened my mouth nothing came out. She didn't seem upset at all, her face had a calm look, but she had to be in pain. When had this happened? Was this what was going on last night when I left her and my father alone?

"Stop panicking, Maggie. I'm fine," she said in a measured and cold tone. "However, I do need your help with some things as I am unable to use my hands at the moment."

"Wh-what happened?" I stammered.

"That's not important. Come with me." My mother got up and started walking out of the kitchen.

I hurriedly wrapped up my note and trotted after her. "Are they burnt, or is it a cut of some kind? Mom, we should take you to the hospital so they can check you out." I reached out to stop her, but my mother flinched away from my touch.

"Maggie, I already told you that what happened with my hands isn't important and doesn't concern you. The only thing that matters is that I have some work to do and I obviously cannot do it myself, so you will have to help me. I'm sure you can put away your silly little crafts for a day to help your mother with some paperwork."

This behavior wasn't completely unusual for my mother,

but I was still stunned at her answer. For as long as I could remember she had always been cold and distant but this was on another level entirely. She was acting as if it were completely normal to be walking around with both her hands in bandages. It was obvious that she was hurt, and it had to have happened sometime last night. Was that why my parents were so quiet after I saw them fighting? I just couldn't understand why she wouldn't say; we both knew what my father could be like. If she would just tell me what happened, then maybe I could help her.

She's just protecting you, Maggie. That's what all this boils down to, doesn't it? You would do the same with Isabel. You would try to protect her from the truth as much as you can.

Growing up, I craved my mother's attention more than any other person. She never wanted to engage or play with me, and as I got older she pulled away more and more. Nowadays we barely spoke to each other. She was always lost in her phone or in a book. Occasionally I caught her staring at the wall and quietly crying, but any time I acknowledged it, her mood would change rapidly. She got angry and spewed judgmental comments about my life.

My mother stopped abruptly, tearing me out of my reverie. She cleared her throat and gestured to her pocket. "The key is in there."

I reached into her pocket and pulled out an old skeleton key, using it to open the door of an office I had never noticed before. Renovating this house was slowly opening my eyes to everything I had ignored when I was hell-bent on running away. This office must have been my mother's only sanctuary in our home. She led me in and sat down at a desk, waiting for me to sit across from her. There were papers everywhere, piled on the desk and on a chair next to it. It looked like every bill that had piled up in the twenty-four years of my life, plus realty contracts and other mysterious legal documents. I had no idea what to make of any of it.

"Do you need me to organize this stuff?" I asked.

My mother just shook her head. She swept some papers aside and revealed a file full of legal papers. "I need your help with this. I can't sign anything with my hands right now. Can you pull up a chair, and I can start explaining it to you?"

I took a long look around the room hoping to find a chair that was unoccupied. This place was like a black hole of our family's legal and financial history. I couldn't believe I hadn't come across it before. I carefully moved a stack of what looked like old gas bills to the floor and pulled up a chair next to my mother.

She handed me a pen and started flipping pages.

"Am I signing this with your name? Should I be practicing your signature?" I asked, confused about my role. Were we about to commit some kind of fraud? "Does Dad even know what's going on?"

"This doesn't concern your father. I have a little inheritance coming in. Sign with your own name; you'll be my proxy. I'll send a document explaining it when I can actually type," she explained.

I could tell I probably wouldn't be getting much more out of Helena Conner today so I just went along with it.

She must know what's going on. She wouldn't have asked you if she didn't. Your mother is selfish, not stupid.

The papers were never-ending. Each had to be signed, initialed, and dated, and my mom flipped the pages before I could read what I was signing. My dad was a smart businessman and he drilled into me from a young age that I was never, *ever,* supposed to sign anything without reading it first. Hopefully, my mother read these and knew what she was doing. I did the best I could to read names or legal terms that jumped out at me. I didn't know if it was the formaldehyde fumes from the night before or if I was still tired from the sleeping pill, but the words on those pages were jumbled and I couldn't focus my eyes on any of the details.

"Mom, slow down. I can't even see what I'm signing."

"Don't worry about it, Maggie. It's a family inheritance; what more do you need to know? The money comes to me, eventually it will come to you, and when it does you can read the documents in detail."

"Who are you inheriting from?"

"Some relative who died. I've already gone over the paperwork with a lawyer. Who do you think sent these?"

"I didn't realize you were getting mail delivered."

"*You* signed for it a week ago, remember? The piece of registered mail that was delivered to the house. Honestly, Maggie, you live in such a dull haze sometimes."

Slowly it came back to me—an express delivery person coming to the house and requiring a signature for an envelope. Isabel was hiding behind me, playing with the little red ribbon around her neck. The delivery man didn't even notice her. He made some comment about me living in the house alone. I snapped at him that I wasn't alone, I obviously had my daughter with me, and he rolled his eyes. I slammed the door in his face after that, and dropped the envelope on the front table.

"Right, I remember that guy. He seemed quite rude," I said, as my mother tapped her foot on the side of the desk, waiting for me to sign another page written in the most confusing language of all—legalese. I was so distracted I didn't even hear my father's footsteps as they came down the hall. He barged in just as I was about to put pen to paper and I instinctively knocked a pile over in order to cover up what my mother and I were doing.

"What are you two doing in here?" he growled.

"Mom needed my help sorting out some bills," I answered, my hand still on the page I needed to sign, buried under old bills and assorted paperwork. I couldn't put my finger on why, but I didn't want my father to know what we were doing. My mother was silent.

"Sorting out bills?" my father snorted. "With what money?"

"They're all old bills. We were organizing them since this room's a mess, right, Mom?" I said, nudging my mom in the side. She was practically catatonic.

My father rolled his eyes and strode into the room. He grabbed my mother by the arm and pulled her out the door. "Well, that doesn't sound like a two-person job. C'mon, Helena. I need a second."

"A second for what?" I asked, calling after him.

"A game! I'm bored, not a single one of you has even asked how my day is, and your *kid* is making a racket upstairs. I'm annoyed and I want to play cards, so your mother is going to play with me while you organize whatever mess she's made. I swear if a single dime is out of place..." he trailed off down the hall, dragging my mother by the arm like an insolent child.

She didn't make a sound.

IT WAS GOING to take me ages to get through that paperwork. I tried going back and reading from the beginning, but I just couldn't focus. The words on the page kept sliding out of focus and I kept having to look away. The inheritance contract was making me nauseous. I kept having to take breaks, go to the kitchen to pour myself water or coffee just so I could parse through the legalese on the page. Someone had, thankfully, flagged all the places where a signature was needed, so that was easy, but deciphering what it all meant was impossible.

Upstairs I heard a crash, like someone threw a glass to the floor. It was probably my father, angry that my mother beat him at whatever silly little game he decided they'd play. It renewed my resolve to figure out what this paperwork meant. There was more in this file that needed to be filled out—financial information, tax information, insurance information, basically a whole profile for the life of the beneficiary. Within these documents I found requests for my information as well, but I didn't know why. There was no information on the benefactor or how he was related to my family. Could I trust some random papers I found in my mother's secret office? What if this was a scam, or a ploy by my father to launder our family finances through him, ensuring my mother and I stayed trapped in this house forever?

I hoped she wouldn't ask for the key to this room back. Not only was this the only door that locked in this ancient house that I didn't have the key to, but the mess of paperwork could hold the key to my and Isabel's escape. If I spent some time in here organizing everything, I could put together a plan to stop my father, or even escape this town, and all that would start with this strange inheritance.

I threw my head back and tried to stretch in my mother's uncomfortable office chair. It was one of those leather-and-metal rolling chairs from the sixties that sold for hundreds of dollars to people who didn't know how uncomfortable they were. Sitting in it hunched over the desk was giving me a backache. I closed my eyes and rolled my neck, taking long deep breaths to curb the motion sickness these papers were giving me.

When I opened my eyes, Isabel was sitting across from me.

"Tell me about him," she said.

"Tell you about who?"

"My father."

7

I stared at Isabel. She wasn't smiling, and was sitting very still, her hands crossed in her lap waiting for my answer.

"Why do you want to know about him?" I asked.

Isabel shrugged her shoulders and waited for me to get on with it. Her expression was strangely solemn. This wasn't the boisterous eight-year-old I knew.

"What made you think about him today? Was it something you read in one of your books?"

Isabel didn't respond. She just waited.

"When I was young, just before you were born, I was really angry at everything. I was angry at my mom, I was angry with my dad—your granny and grandfather—and I just wanted to get as far away from them as I could. Sometimes I did this by going out with my friends and lying to your granny and grandfather. One time I did it and your grandfather got really, really angry with me—"

"Where did you go?" Isabel interrupted.

"I went to go meet a boy. My friend Ashley had a

boyfriend, and he had a friend named Nate, and we went to meet the two of them in the city, but I told your grandparents I was going camping, and—" My breath caught in my throat as I thought about the crying room. I didn't want to go there with Isabel. It was enough that she knew of its existence.

"What happened, Mommy?" she asked. She wasn't whining for me to go on the way she usually did. Instead, Isabel nudged me forward the way a psychologist might, with a detached curiosity that encouraged self-reflection.

"Well, I was sad because your grandparents were upset. But at the same time I was sixteen, and I was selfish, and I didn't want to do what they told me to do. Nate became my secret boyfriend and one day I ran away from home so I didn't have to hide from my mommy and daddy anymore. I didn't want to live at home. I wanted to live with Nate. What I didn't know was that Nate was involved in some very dangerous business. Soon after I ran away to be with Nate, he died, and when the police found me they sent me back to your granny and grandfather. When I came home, I told my mommy and daddy that I was pregnant with you. I was very sad because Nate was gone, but it's okay because it brought me you."

"Do you regret it?" Isabel asked.

I had to think about that for a moment. I wanted to say no, that I would never regret running away from home, but that wasn't entirely true.

"Whatever happened, it brought me you, and I could never regret you," I said. That was the simplest way of explaining the truth of the matter. The circumstances surrounding my daughter's birth were regrettable, and it caused the relationship I had with my parents to fracture in a way that was impossible to put back together. That being said, Isabel was perfect. She was my twin in almost every way. Through some magic of the universe, she hadn't inherited any of Nate's aggressive qualities. I wouldn't give her up for the world.

Isabel examined me from across the desk. After a while, she nodded and got down from the chair. "I'm going back to my room. I love you, Mommy," she said, before slipping out the door.

That kid is getting weird. I need to find a way to socialize her.

I COULDN'T STOP THINKING about Isabel. She'd been so serious when she asked me about her father, it felt like I was talking with a therapist, not my eight-year-old. Did she read about someone's absent father in a book? Or was this something she thought about frequently? I hoped I could give her everything she needed as a mother, but maybe she felt there was something missing. Something a story could explain.

What I told her wasn't untrue, but it was a very sanitized version of what actually happened.

After that incident with Ashley that landed me in the crying room, I was temporarily determined to be the perfect daughter. I thought that doing so would make my family perfect, that I was the real reason my parents fought and if I could just put my head down and do exactly what was asked of me everything would turn out fine, my father would suddenly become a reasonable man, and my mother would re-engage in both our lives.

That turned out to be a very misguided wish.

My father got angrier and more aggressive. Like he was trying to control me by turning his fist from iron to steel. I couldn't handle the pressure, and soon went back to my rebellious ways. I remember I didn't talk to Ashley for a month after the cabin incident, and when I finally confronted her she refused to speak to me. I started crying on the spot, feeling as though the only ally I had in town had turned her back to me.

That was the day I met and fell "in love" with Nate Moore. He came up to me after Ashley's rebuff and comforted me.

"I've had my eye on you for a while," he said.

I looked at him like he was crazy, and he just laughed.

"I didn't mean that in a creepy way. Only that I've seen you hanging with Ash and I thought you were cute."

I remembered blushing. Nate was tall, with dark curly hair and bright brown eyes. His smile could light up a room and melt everyone in it. From that day on we were basically inseparable. Nate told me he was eighteen, had dropped out of high school early and was working on getting his GED instead.

"Institutional learning is not really my bag," he had said. "I want to contribute to society and do school on my own time, you know? I don't need to learn calculus and who the presidents were in the nineteenth century to be able to work for a living."

I was dazzled by his intelligence and rejection of what was supposed to be a "normal" way to do things.

Oh, how wrong I was.

I didn't find out until later that Nate was just a smart-ass drug dealer. He didn't go to school because he was twenty-three, and didn't graduate high school because he was a burnout. By the time I realized all that, I was pregnant with Isabel and there was no easy way of turning back.

I remembered the day I ran away from home. Nate was waiting for me in his beat-up car around the corner from my house. He wanted to wait out front but I knew his car would be a giveaway. No one in our neighborhood had a dirty car like that—my father made sure of it. The second Nate pulled up to the curb, everyone would be at their window to see what was the deal with the dirty car. I had stuffed as much as I could into a backpack the night before, and I left it under the back porch behind a garbage can, where I knew my father would never find it. That night I waited until my parents were asleep, knowing my father would be too drunk to wake up, snuck out the window and grabbed my bag. I hopped the back fence, snuck through my neighbor's yard, and made my way to Nate's waiting car. We screamed and squealed the whole drive to his place.

It might have been the happiest night of my life. Having no idea what would happen, that night was the most hopeful I'd ever been. Even if it didn't work out with Nate, I had my whole life ahead of me to make mistakes and fix them. I imagined leaving and going to the city, finding a little place for myself, and getting a job as a secretary. I knew deep down that Nate wasn't going to be my soulmate, but he got me out of my father's house, and for that, I was sure, I'd be grateful forever. It didn't take long before those hopes and dreams and fantasies were completely dashed.

Nate styled himself as an entrepreneur—a self-made man on the path to a fortune. Little did I know that meant he had graduated from selling dime bags of marijuana to grams of cocaine and heroin. The people who came over to his house made my father look like a peaceful man. Still, Nate loved me and took care of me. He made sure to hide the worst of his crimes so I could plead ignorance if he ever got arrested—I naively believed this would make a difference. He was a drug dealer but he was still helping me get my GED, and when my father came banging on his door Nate hid me from view and kicked my dad to the curb. Nate was not what I expected, but he was still the man who comforted me when Ashley made me cry. I also still believed he was eighteen at this point. Showed how sheltered I was, I suppose. As far as I knew, we were the same. Two teenage runaways escaping abusive homes and indifferent parents, who were just doing whatever they could to survive. I wanted to get a job but I knew I couldn't work in our town without my father knowing, so I relied on Nate's income and hospitality to get by. I thought our mutual trauma would bond us and that we'd build a life together, for the time being at least.

Once again, everything changed abruptly. My period was late. I couldn't go to a doctor nearby, so Nate drove me to a clinic one county over. They confirmed what we both suspected—I was pregnant. Another tick on my teenage runaway bingo card. He immediately drove me home and I remember he didn't say a word the whole drive. I was in shock. I kept staring down at my belly like I would suddenly develop X-ray vision and see what was going on inside me. I could feel the anger pouring out of Nate, but I was too afraid to say anything.

"I could get rid of it," I whispered while we waited at a light.

Nate slammed my head into the passenger side window.

"Don't be stupid," he said, before dropping back into a sullen silence.

I didn't even cry after he did it, but sometimes it felt like my ears were still ringing from the bash on the windshield.

That was when things went downhill. Until the drive back from the clinic, I had still believed in my dream of getting away from my parents and leaving them in the dust. After that day I wasn't so sure. Nate's temper became worse, his patience shorter, and he stopped protecting me the way he used to. Every day he hit me in one way or another. There were days when he'd beat me up, and there were days when he would just slap me at some time, to "keep me in my place."

I only fought back once. I hardly even remember it. Nate was getting ready for some of his suppliers to come over, and he was stressing out about cash, counting it over and over and over again. I tried to move past him but my growing belly knocked some bills down on the table, so he grabbed me by the neck and started choking me. I kicked him in the knees and ran to our room, where I promptly passed out from stress.

I was woken up by a police officer shaking me awake. Nate's body had been found in our front room, covered in blood. He'd died from a stab wound, probably inflicted by one of the suppliers Nate had been waiting for. He was always short of money, and they got angrier and angrier every visit. I always tried to warn him one of these days they wouldn't be so patient with him—I was just glad I wasn't awake when my prediction finally came true.

The police saw the bruises on my arms and neck, and figured out what was happening with Nate pretty quickly.

"You have any family around, dear? Anyone we can call?" I remembered one of them asking.

I had just shaken my head, still too shocked to answer. *At least he doesn't know who I am,* I had thought. I remembered lying about my age after the police revealed to me that Nate was twenty-four, five years older than the age I thought he was. I hoped they would just leave me alone and I could continue living by myself. I could find a job somewhere, maybe be a cashier at a supermarket. It would be a hard life, but it was better than going back to my father's house.

Sadly, I didn't have that kind of luck. One police officer took pity on me—an abandoned pregnant woman—and in doing so found out I was lying about my age. He thought he was doing me a favor, that he was putting me back on the right track and helping me avoid the kind of trouble that had killed my boyfriend. There was no way he could have known why I ran away from home in the first place. I tried to fight it, tried to come up with options, I even tried looking up orphanages or one of those nunneries that took in pregnant teenage girls—but the fact was, as a minor, all these decisions had to be signed off by my parents. I didn't have any control over my life, and to an outside eye there was no reason why I wouldn't want to go back to my father's house. He was wealthy, he owned a giant home, and he was family.

When he had greeted me at the door he'd made a show of how worried he had been and how relieved he was to see that I was coming home in one piece. I guessed the police told him about my "condition," because he was holding up a onesie with "grandaddy's little girl" on it.

He should have been an actor or something. The performance he gave to the kind state patrol officer who didn't know what kind of man my father *really* was, was Oscar-worthy. Of course, he ruined the act a moment later by saying something very nasty before pulling me through the door.

When the door closed I saw that a dark cloud had rolled over his expression, and being so close, I could smell the alcohol on him. He didn't say a word, just dropped the onesie on an entryway table and walked away.

His silent treatment lasted until Isabel was born, then months of being ignored by my father turned into years of tiptoeing around him, careful not to disturb his "peace" while dealing with a crying, screaming baby. I had been as careful as I could be and kept Isabel as far away from her grandfather as I could. His patience wore thin, but I'd managed to always get between my father and Isabel.

Somehow, eight years later, Isabel was still with me. Whatever sway my father had in this town had finally worked in my favor. I didn't know how long it could last. I didn't know how much longer I could go shielding Isabel from what was really going on—she had already found the crying room. It was only a matter of time before…

Don't think about that now, Maggie. You can't think about that right now.

Right. I had work to do. I had to finish reading and signing these papers. I had to finish working on the house. My to-do list was endless. I didn't have time to drown in my sorrows.

8

"Maggie, we're out of food. You have to go get some groceries," my mother called through the bedroom door, waking me from another strange nightmare. I'd been having them more often lately, ever since Isabel mentioned the crying room. In it, I was running down a hall but the maze of my house turned into a wallpapered labyrinth. There was only one path, and it led to the crying room. No matter which way I turned, that was always where I ended up. I slowly moved toward it, but before I could open the hidden door, I woke up.

I sat up in bed, my whole body sweating. The dream felt so real I had to pinch myself to make sure I was awake.

"I'm up. I'll go," I called back, but didn't get an answer.

My mom had probably walked off already. I had spent the whole previous day going through the papers she had given me. They didn't seem to make any sense. Whenever I tried to focus on the page the words would get all jumbled up and turn into gibberish. I wondered if there were law school reading primers in "legalese."

After Isabel's interruption I never got my focus back. I kept thinking about Nate and what my life could have been had I just woken up and left the house before the police came. Would Isabel's life have been any better if I was a single mother without my parents? I eventually gave up, figuring I would have a day or two before I had to send off the pages. I locked the door behind me and kept the key in my pocket, just in case my father got curious about my mother's office. She didn't seem to care that I hadn't given back her key. Maybe she was passing her sanctuary on to me, like a little chain of inheritance.

I dragged myself out of bed and over to Isabel's room to wake her up.

"Rise and shine, my petal! It's a gorgeous day out, and we need to go to the store. Are you ready?" I asked, grinning from ear to ear and pulling back the curtains to let in the day. There wasn't a single cloud in the sky and the sun's rays were so strong they almost lifted the gloom from the house.

"Mommy, I don't want to. I don't feel good," Isabel mumbled from under her covers.

I could see her squirming in bed, so different from the still figure haunting my office the day before. She was back to her usual chaotic self.

"What's wrong, baby? What doesn't feel good?" I asked her.

"I don't know, my head hurts and I feel all sweaty," she replied.

"Did you have nightmares?"

"No, I didn't have any dreams. But I feel all sweaty and clammy. Like I have the flu, but I don't have a cough or anything."

I felt Isabel's forehead. She didn't seem to have a fever,

but I didn't have a thermometer around to check. She wasn't lying about the clamminess. My hand was sticky with sweat when I pulled away from her.

"Maybe you should stay in bed, honey," I said. "You can take a nap and I'll bring you some soup. How does that sound?"

Isabel didn't say anything. Just nodded and pulled the covers back over her head.

I patted her hair and tucked her in, tickling her and causing her to giggle as I did.

"When you come back I want to hear another story. A good one this time, not about Dick and Jane or my dad or anything. I want an original story," my little princess commanded from her bed.

I saluted her and turned off her light.

She'll be fine up here. There's no reason for anyone to come into her room. Besides, when have they ever shown any interest in Isabel? I had to reassure myself as I got ready. Being at home meant I could make sure my daughter was okay. Being away from her, even for a little while, made me feel anxious. I couldn't control what she was doing or where she was going. I wouldn't be there to protect her if she got in the way of my parents.

She'll be okay, Maggie. Your mother is always surprised to see Isabel, like she has forgotten about her own granddaughter. Your father is more occupied with your mother than your daughter. Isabel is asleep. Everything is going to be okay.

I pulled myself together and left, trying to shake my fear of leaving the house. The sun practically blinded me the moment I stepped outside, sending shivers down my spine. I wanted to run away, and I wanted to crawl under the house at the same time. I fought my anxiety every step I took down the path. I still had trouble breathing when I started walking down the sidewalk. I felt shaky and sweaty. *It's probably the sun. It's so dark and cool in the house this is just a shock to your system.*

The car hadn't been working, and it wasn't exactly practical. My father, when purchasing it, didn't bring his family into consideration and bought a very flashy foreign car. All looks, no substance, and nearly impossible to repair. The few times I brought it in to a mechanic they told me the repair would cost twice as much and take twice as long because they needed to source parts from one place or another. I gave up trying to repair it, and if my dad ever asked I told him the carburetor was on backorder, which seemed to calm him down. I did my groceries by hand, taking a cute little wagon with me when I felt there was too much to carry. If it wasn't for the sun beating down on me, I might actually enjoy the walk.

I didn't have very much to do—just some groceries to pick up and some hardware essentials for the renovation. Our town was small enough that it wouldn't take me very long. Soon I could be back with Isabel. I kept reassuring myself that I knew exactly what I needed. There was no reason for me to worry. Isabel wasn't well. She'd just be asleep. Besides, it was early, and my dad usually didn't really get grumpy until the evening. The sun was blazing and I didn't want to stay out for very long; my shoulders would burn. The sooner I finished the sooner I could get back indoors. *Don't dawdle. If you see someone you know just smile and wave. Don't get into small talk or you'll be sucked in for hours.*

Like in any other small town, everyone loved to gossip. Living in a sleepy town could be boring. Gossiping about the local wealthy, abusive, powerful drunk was a great way to pass the time. Despite the fact that everyone knew what went on in my house, no one stopped it and no one ever asked or confronted me about it. They treated me with kid gloves anytime I ran into them, like I was a porcelain doll about to break. It would be nice to have someone I could talk to, someone who didn't know my life and didn't look at me or my family like we were goldfish swimming in a bowl.

"Maggie!"

I jumped hearing my name being called. What had I forgotten? I turned around and saw a woman with a mess of bright red hair jogging in my direction. It was Lana Cabot. Lana and her husband Bill had moved in across the street at the start of the summer. The pair were childless, semi-retired yuppies who jumped at the chance to leave their high-powered city life behind—or so I'd heard. Like I said, gossip was a pastime for a lot of people around here.

"Hi! Lana, right?" I said as she approached me, her smile beaming brighter than the sun.

"Yes! I have been wanting to say hello to you! I thought of coming by your door but um..." Lana trailed off.

I knew the answer without her explaining.

"That's all right, it always happens eventually. Are you settling in okay?" I smiled and started walking, hoping she'd get the hint.

Lana was more determined than that. "We are. I think Bill is having a harder time adjusting than I am. He isn't used to how quiet it can get, but I think he'll find a groove. We have our business, which is much easier to run from a big house than a two-bed in the Upper West side. You should come by. I can give you some samples." Lana reached out to pat my arm but I twisted out of her way. We each flinched away from each other like there was an electric force field separating us.

"Maybe. We'll see. My hands are pretty full lately, with it being summer, and I don't have childcare for my daughter so..."

"Oh, you can bring her by. You know most people think CBD is just like cannabis but it's actually not. It's a cannab*idiol* which means it comes from the same plant but doesn't have the same psychoactive effect on the body—"

"I know the difference. My high school boyfriend smoked weed." *That wasn't entirely a lie.*

"Oh, wonderful. Yes, you young people are more well-researched on the subject. I find myself having to explain what we do a lot more often here..." Lana trailed off again.

I had to get out of this conversation before it took over my day.

"I get it. Town gossip is run by those nosy old ladies who think every newcomer is up to no good. I have to go, though. I have a lot to do, and I need to get back. My daughter is napping but I don't want to leave her for long."

"Well, we're across the street if you ever need anything." Lana smiled. She had really kind dark blue eyes. It was like staring into two sapphires. She really did mean well, and it seemed like maybe she wanted to be friends.

Why would a middle-aged woman want to be friends with you, Maggie? She has a whole life already set up. She just wants to know what's going on in the house, just like everyone else. My father's voice was an undercurrent of all my thoughts. As much as I wanted to reach out, it felt too dangerous to bring someone into my life. I could lose Isabel, and I didn't think I could survive that.

I shoved the thought to the back of my mind and smiled back at her, trying to form a response that was kind but not inviting. "Thanks, I'll keep that in mind."

"Even if you just want to talk. Being a mom can be lonely."

"Sure, I'll keep that in mind." *It is too hot. I want to get back home.*

"Really, anything you need. I don't have kids at home anymore, but I take care of my nieces and nephews often."

Please, Lana, just let me be.

"I believe it. You have very kind eyes. I have to get to the store now. Bye, Lana." I turned and scurried away from her. I was probably much ruder than I needed to be, but I was starting to feel panicky. I wanted to get home. I needed to finish my chores. There was bile rolling around in my stomach, ready to release itself on the sidewalk, and the longer I talked to Lana the more likely I was going to throw up. I was racing against my body now to finish what I needed and get out of the sun.

The rest of my walk was uneventful. I found a pair of headphones in my pocket and put them in my ears, not to blare music; just to discourage anyone from talking to me. I was on a mission and I wanted to get it over with.

When I made it to the grocery store I spent a solid minute cooling down in the frozen foods aisle before quickly gathering what I needed. I could feel eyes on me as I moved about the store, accompanied by concerned glances and whispers from the other shoppers. My skin was crawling by the time I was ready to check out.

"It's nice to see you out and about." The cashier held my hand with my change in it for a little too long.

I felt fidgety and uncomfortable. I'd known this woman for years. There was a time she wouldn't even look at me because she thought I was damaged goods. Now, all of a sudden, she was being nice to me? Nothing had changed, or did everyone's guilty conscience come out to play for the summer?

"Thanks," I said, awkwardly untangling myself from her grip. "It's a hot one out there. You're lucky you guys have air conditioning in here." I smiled and packed my things, feeling her staring at the back of my head. *Have I grown an extra limb? Why is everyone suddenly acting like my life matters?*

It was difficult to explain this contrast. Growing up, following my mom around, I heard people whisper about her. She often went out wearing dark sunglasses, drawing comments about her snobbishness from the other women in town. Maybe they believed she was that pretentious, but I was sure their husbands knew what those sunglasses were hiding. Who knew, though, maybe the women knew too? As I got older and my father's erratic behavior got worse, people stopped paying attention to us. There was no pity in their eyes, only a collective desire to turn their heads from what was going on under their noses.

The sudden sympathetic attention was jarring and made me more suspicious than if they had continued ignoring me and my family. What's more was that no one ever asked about Isabel, proving to me that they didn't really care about my family; they only cared about hearing the latest gossip about us.

I left the grocery store ready to run the whole way home. I still had errands to run, but I didn't care. This trip had already taken too long with Lana's interruption, and having all eyes on me at the grocery store made me feel sick. I could get wood glue and caulk another time—hell, I could probably order them online or something, and avoid going into town altogether. All I could think about was getting home to Isabel. She was probably awake now. She might even have left her room to go looking for me—

"Ow!" I yelped. My silly little wagon hit a rock and went tumbling into my leg, spilling my groceries everywhere. Served me right for losing myself in my worries. I bent over to pick them up but another set of hands beat me to it. It was Charlie Barrows, another newcomer.

"Oh, you don't have to do that—"

"Let me help you—"

We both started talking at the same time, both stopped and laughed at the same time.

"Sorry if I cut you off," I said. "This little wagon is useful but so annoying."

"I know what you mean," he said, gesturing at his own little cart, full of kibble bags.

"Your dogs must be hungry," I said, picking my cart up again.

"It's not for mine, it's for my grooming business. I figure if I give them the good stuff, they won't hate coming to me so much and it'll be easier to trim their hair and nails." Charlie blushed and stood in front of his cart, trying to hide the evidence of his plan. He was cute, tall, with bright ginger hair and soft eyes. If we had met in high school I wouldn't have given Charlie a second glance, but years later that gawky earnestness was what was so attractive about him.

"Is that why you bought up all the pine two by fours? I needed some for a renovation project and Tony's Hardware was cleared out. Tony mentioned you had been in there, buying out his stock."

Charlie blushed even harder. "That was me. I was trying to build a doggie mega-mansion. I'm thinking of expanding into a kennel. With all the city transplants coming in, I figure they might want something like that. Also, it's kinda fun for the dogs to get their zoomies out on a playground."

"Tire them out so that they're pooped when you need them to behave? I do the same thing with my daughter," I said, laughing.

As soon as I said "daughter" Charlie froze. Typical of any man. You can flirt with them or have a relaxed conversation with them—until you mention that you're a mom. No man wants to be a stepdad.

"You know, I've never seen your daughter. Does… um… does she like dogs?" he sputtered.

"To be honest, she's in more of a cat phase at the moment," I answered. "Cat people really, really hate dogs for some reason."

"That's because they think dogs are dumb in comparison. I get it; I was that way too. You should show her videos of a whippet or a Manchester terrier. Basenjis are also pretty cat-like. Obviously, I'm biased, but hey, it might be nice for her to get a little puppy love in." Charlie's passion for dogs came out in his smile, his eyes, even his hands got more animated as he talked about them. It was hard not to get pulled in by his obvious and wholesome love for the animal.

"Thanks. I'll look them up. I have to get back. I left her at home with my parents and… um—"

"I'm sure she's super bored. I get it." Charlie blinked awkwardly, waving as he backed into (and tripped over) his cart. It was a nice distraction but I had to get back.

Before I could take a step away, Mary Albertson grabbed me by the arm.

"I saw you fall, honey. Are you all right?" she asked, her nose merely inches away from my face.

I turned but Charlie was already crossing the street—the only hope I had to save me from possibly the nosiest person in town. She held my arm in a death grip as we walked down the street.

"I'm fine, Mary. I didn't fall. My dumb little wagon tipped over and spilled my groceries."

"Ah, I just wanted to make sure you were okay. Do you need help getting home?" She talked to me in that high-pitched, fake-soothing voice that people usually reserved for adorable toddlers and the invalid. It was unbelievably condescending. The only reason I let her do it was because Mary had probably been slowly losing her mind since the day I was born. She was always dressed in bright, mismatched prints, and it seemed she never brushed her wildly curly hair. It gave her the effect of an artsy banshee looming over your fence, trying to gather your family secrets—or maybe a colorful version of the grandmother from *The Addams Family*.

"Mary, I'm fine. I have to get home." Without Charlie, my anxious antennae perked back up. I was hyper-aware of the time, the heat, and of having to make awkward conversation again. Charlie had soothed my rolling tummy, and Mary pumped bile into my throat. I had to get away from her, but she was stronger than I realized.

"Why do you have to get home? It's a gorgeous day out. Don't you want to bask in the sun a little bit?" she asked.

"Well, for starters, I have a bunch of frozen meat in my

wagon. If I bask out in the sun for too long, it'll go bad—" I started to answer.

But Mary cut me off. "Why did you buy so much food?"

"I'm not going to shop for groceries solo when I have other mouths to feed."

"What other mouths? Honey, you know your mom's not there, right?" Her sympathy was syrupy, coated in a fake gloss of sweetness.

"Yeah, but she still has to eat." At that point I didn't really care if I knocked Mary to the ground. She may be old but she was clearly strong enough to stand on her own. I swung my arm around.

She jumped back, cowering behind a car for a moment, before following me back down the street. "I was only trying to—"

"You were hurting my arm, Mary. Sorry for being so aggressive, but your nails were digging into me."

"I apologize, dear. I'm only trying to help."

I didn't have time for this. I was on the verge of abandoning my groceries and sprinting away from her. Wasn't it enough that no one dared walk down my street anymore? Or that I was followed throughout the grocery store?

"Mary—" I cut myself off before saying anything too mean. *She's nosy but harmless. She means well and goes about it awkwardly. She's an old lady and feels guilty for letting your family life go down the drain.* "Mary, I really don't need your help. I'm sorry if I hurt you, or if you think I meant to. I just need to get home. I left Isabel sleeping and she's unwell. I'd like to get her something to bring down her fever."

"Isabel?"

"My daughter, Mary. My daughter Isabel is at home and

she needs me. I don't have time to argue with you about my grocery habits."

"Sweetheart, you don't have a daughter. Now, why are you buying so much food that's just going to go to waste? I've seen your trash bins; they are absolutely overflowing with wasted food, and that's only going to attract raccoons or foxes, which is dangerous. I know you are a new homeowner so you probably don't understand what kind of pests animals and rodents can be. Did you know they can get into your pipes..."

Mary continued talking but I barely heard her. The sun was too much for me and my anxiety of being away from home. I could feel a wave of nausea and panic coming over me, and it felt like I was about to faint. How could she say that? She had surely seen me take my daughter to school, or heard Isabel playing in our yard. If Mary was paying attention to my *dumpster bins,* she must also be paying attention to who was living in my house, yet here she was acting as if I was living alone. I understood that everyone in town was collectively ignoring my father's behavior, but acting as if my family didn't exist was going too far.

I could hear a faraway voice arguing with Mary, but I was too panicked to listen. I sat down on the hood of a nearby car, trying to quell the panic attack I could feel coming on.

Breathe, Maggie, breathe in through your nose and out through your mouth. One nostril at a time. Count to four.

My head was spinning, my palms were sweating, and I had to swallow the vomit at the back of my throat. The car I leaned against was too hot, but so was the pavement and the sun and the air around me.

"Maggie? Are you feeling okay?" a delicate voice pierced

my anxious thoughts. It was Lana. She was the one arguing with Mary.

"I just feel a little hot."

"Yeah, the sun's really beating down on us today, huh?" she asked.

I shook my head and looked around me. I was closer to home than I'd realized. Just about a block away. I must have been walking faster than I'd thought. Lana kept herself an arm's length away. She was holding my wagon and smiling.

"Mary Albertson is a crazy neighbor, huh?" I said, smiling weakly.

"She sure is. Last week she knocked on our door to tell us the light was out in the third floor guest bedroom. I don't even know how she figured out the layout of my house."

"She knows everything, trust me. She's been inside every one of these houses and has it mapped out down to the square foot." We both laughed. I was glad to know that, finally, I wasn't the only one who thought Mary was a menace.

"Do you want some water? I was out for a walk and I saw you. I used to get panic attacks all the time. It was part of the reason Bill and I moved out here. Some cold water always helps." She offered her bottle, keeping her distance.

From the outside, to someone like Mary it would have seemed rude. As if Lana was implying that I was crazy. Yet I appreciated the gesture; I needed the breathing room. Needed someone to acknowledge that I wanted to be left alone.

"Thanks. I have to get home. I—"

"I know, to your daughter. Please, keep the bottle. I'm headed by the grocery store anyway. I can just pick up another. I'll see you around, Maggie." With that, Lana waved and walked away.

I took a moment to finish the bottle, letting the panic settle back into my stomach. Being a block away from the house made me feel calm. From here I could see the lights were still out in Isabel's room and the curtains were drawn. *She's still sleeping, which means she's safe.*

I hurried back to the house, desperate to get out of the sun and get away from all the socializing I was forced to do. I knew I had a lot of work but all I wanted to do was sleep. Sleep off my day, sleep off the people I saw, sleep until finally my stomach was settled.

"What took you so long?" My father was waiting for me in the entryway, his arms crossed, standing like a guard to my own home.

"I ran into Mary Albertson. She's as nosy as ever, kept talking to me about foxes getting into the garbage bins," I said.

My father didn't answer, he just turned and disappeared into the darkness.

I breathed a sigh of relief, happy to be back in the cool darkness of the house. I dragged the wobbly wagon into the kitchen and started unloading my hoard, the hoard Mary called a "waste."

I still didn't understand why she said what she did. That I was alone, or that I didn't have a daughter. It was truly strange.

She's getting older, Maggie. She just doesn't remember. The comment was so flippant, Mary probably didn't even know what she was saying. Besides, I was already halfway to a panic attack. I probably just misunderstood her.

Somewhere behind me I heard a gentle creak coming down the stairs.

"Mommy?" asked a tiny voice at the door. "I still don't feel very well." Isabel appeared in the doorway, wearing a nightgown and her red ribbon, holding one of my old stuffed animals. Isabel looked young and ancient at the same time, patiently waiting for me to take her back upstairs. She was such a serious kid, an odd product of this house.

I decided it didn't really matter what Mary did or didn't remember. My daughter was real, was made of flesh and blood, and she needed me to take care of her.

9

I was getting exhausted more easily than I used to. The combination of Isabel's energy and drastic mood swings, renovating the old house, and my parents' escalating anger toward each other must have been taking its toll. I wished I could just relax for a day, have a long bath and maybe a glass of red wine or something, anything that could shut the world out so I could take a moment to myself.

That's selfish, Maggie. Your family needs you. Especially Isabel. What is she supposed to do without you?

Was it really so selfish to want to spend some time alone and forget my worries for a minute? Maybe even go to the dog park and chat with Charlie for a little bit, have a glimpse of what a normal life could be. I was sure my parents could handle themselves for a while. They were grown adults. They could cook for themselves for a night. I'd have to find a babysitter for Isabel, or even take her with me. If I took Isabel with me to the dog park it would come off as so casual Charlie would never think that I had intentionally come around hoping to talk with him.

I started daydreaming about what my life could be like. Long after this house was finished, I could maybe build a little guest cottage in the sprawling backyard for Isabel and me. My parents could keep the giant house. I didn't really care about it. Isabel would miss playing witches or princesses in the tower attic, but she was eight. Soon she'd forget and come up with new characters to play, and soon after that she'd be a sullen, rebellious teenager who didn't need an attic tower at all. I could visit Charlie at the dog grooming business he had, maybe even help him out a bit. Isabel could have a job that would teach her a little responsibility, and being around dogs would be good for her mental health. There was some study I remembered reading about saying how "dog therapy" was becoming more popular among children who came from traumatic households.

Not that Isabel was traumatized. She couldn't have been, not yet. I protected her from all that.

"Are you done with those yet?" my mother asked.

I looked down at the papers in my hand. It was her mysterious inheritance, all the pages finally signed and completed, ready to be sent away. "Yes, I'm finally done. I still don't know what it's for—"

"I told you, I have some money coming in," my mother said, cutting off my sentence as she entered the room. "You'll need to go to the post office to send these back to the lawyer. There should be an envelope in the file they were in."

Sure enough, buried under the pages was a pre-addressed envelope to a lawyer in the city. I made a mental note of the name so I could look it up later, while my mother was rushing to get the pages in there.

"Mom, slow down, the pages aren't in order," I said, wrestling the documents from her hands.

"What does that matter? Some intern is going to reorganize these anyway," she said, continuing to shove the pages into the envelope.

My hands were shaking as I tried, in vain, to stop her. I knew my mother was trying to do this quickly, before my father could come barging into the room, but this was irresponsible. What if we messed up, or missed a page, and she ended up losing whatever inheritance she came into?

"Mom—Mother, let me do this, okay? If we shove paper in here it's only going to make the pages ball up and they won't fit in the envelope. Just let me do it, and I'll take it to the post office." I held her hand and looked into her eyes.

My mother's vacant gaze looked through me, to the wall behind. "Okay," she said. She untangled herself from my grip, turned, and walked out of the room without another word.

I was left staring at the door, mouth agape. My mother was weird—it's no wonder people like Mary thought I was crazy and that Isabel had oddly serious mood swings. *I guess it runs in the family.*

I sorted the pages, pressing out those that had been crumpled in my mother's hasty actions, before neatly sliding them into the envelope. The postage wasn't paid, and the document was far too big to be sent by regular mail. I would have to go to the post office and send it out as a parcel.

Isabel was upstairs reading quietly. She had found an old book by Henry James, some collection of ghost stories I didn't even know we had, and it was keeping her fully occupied. I ran upstairs to check on Isabel, to make sure she'd stay in her room for the next hour or so.

"Of course, Mother. It's not as if I can go anywhere else," was all she said in reply.

I had never realized a child could be gripped by existential angst before her teenage years, but I supposed that was what happened when you lived in a gloomy Victorian house and hardly ever went outside.

The post office wasn't far, but I still felt panicky when I left my house. Luckily, my neighbors were nowhere to be found, so I was at least able to deal with my anxiety in peace. It wasn't as hot as yesterday, but the sun was still unrelenting. I was trying to keep my cool so I didn't panic if I saw anyone and give them any more reasons to think I was crazy. I thought about the papers I was carrying, and how much my mother needed me to complete a task that, for one reason or another, she couldn't do on her own.

I understood why. People in town often stared at my mother as she walked down the streets. She was pretty, in a frail sort of way. We looked a lot alike, with wispy brown hair and green eyes. My mom had such a small face and stature that her eyes kind of looked like they were bulging out of her head. That meant that the bruises around them were always more prominent than they would have been on anyone else. I could hardly remember what my mother looked like without a pair of sunglasses on. They lent her a sophisticated air, like she was some unapproachable French intellectual—except that she always flinched if anyone tried to touch her.

Her frailty used to drive me insane, before I experienced firsthand what kind of man my father was. He wasn't always so angry, but when his temper boiled over it was impossible to cool him down. She endured countless hospital trips, always covering for my father, just like everyone else. I remember being a kid with a broken arm, a direct result of my father pushing me down the stairs, and when my mom looked the doctor in the eyes and told them it was because I was being careless, the doctor just nodded. A grim mutual understanding that they couldn't talk about what really happened.

That's in the past, Maggie. Try not to think about it now. But my heart started pounding again as I thought about how much control my father had over this town. My legs felt weak as I took myself farther and farther away from the comfort of my own home, where I could hide from the prying eyes of my neighbors. How could I just leave these thoughts behind when they made me who I was today? If it weren't for my father's anger, he never would have attacked me or my mother. If he hadn't attacked me, I would never have run away from home. If I hadn't run away from home, I wouldn't have taken up with Nate. If I hadn't taken up with Nate, I wouldn't have Isabel. Who would I be if it weren't for the sadness in my past? Was there a point where everything might have been different?

I was starting to get tired. I wasn't far from the post office, but I needed to take a moment to sit down. Once again, the summer heat was getting to me and I was starting to feel nauseous and dizzy. I sat on a bench and fanned myself with my mother's legal documents, thinking about the night my father sent me to the ER.

My dad had started drinking early that day; I couldn't remember why. He often came home from work early and started drinking. By the time dinner was ready he was barely conscious. He moved through life in a semi-conscious stupor, either drunk or hung over all the time. I still didn't know what he was trying to forget. That night, I had been late coming home from school. I had secretly met up with Nate, and we'd lost track of time. I didn't have time to take out the steak my father had requested for his dinner, and tried to make up for it by making a Bolognese. My dad loved Bolognese and I made an absolutely amazing one. I figured making his favorite meal might distract him from not getting *exactly* what he wanted.

I was wrong.

My father started by throwing his plate at the wall, before questioning my priorities and my devotion to our family. I couldn't think of anything to say to defend myself. He just kept screaming, "Say something!" and I broke down in tears.

I remembered that I collapsed to the floor and a pair of rough hands pulled me back up by the neck. My father had me by the throat and had been screaming in my face but I couldn't make a sound. I could barely breathe. I could feel blood rushing to my head and yet I felt lightheaded. I remembered thinking that finally, he was going to kill me. But he didn't.

He dropped me off at the ER. Opened the car door and pushed me out. I stumbled into the hospital where a nurse immediately rushed me to a bed. I'd had multiple doctors look at me and mutter under their breaths—something about a bad boyfriend. The truth was glaring them in the face, yet no one had the courage to speak up. The nurse, clearly new to the area, called the police, who took their time before showing up.

"Who did this to you?" a young officer asked, without even pulling out his notebook.

"Aren't you going to take notes? Isn't that what happens when the police take a witnesses statement?" I had asked.

"Well, I'd like to have a conversation with you first. Don't worry, I'll remember what you tell me. Now, I know it may seem embarrassing but a lot of young people think that getting into um... kinky *activities* is a fun time, but clearly—"

"*Kinky activities?*" I sputtered. "Are you really trying to tell me you think—"

"Calm down, dear, your voice is far too hoarse. I can hardly understand what you're saying." He tried to reassure me, tried to get me to play along, but I just couldn't take it anymore. This cop was going to put down, on paper, that a sixteen-year-old had come to hospital with bruising along her throat because she was having kinky sex with her boyfriend?

"You saw who dropped me off," I croaked, taking deep breaths with each word. "You know who did this to me."

"Yes, your father mentioned there was a boy hanging around you. From Mr. Conner's description he's just the sort of bad influence who would persuade you to do something as stupid as this," the officer said, clearing his throat and trying to get me back on track.

I glared at him and could see his face starting to go red. "How much did he pay you?" I asked, trying to keep my breathing under control.

"What?" the cop asked. "I can hardly understand you." He smiled and looked around. He was starting to get nervous about who was listening.

Good, I thought, *he should feel ashamed.*

"How much... did my father pay... you... to cover... for his... mistakes?" I spoke slowly and as clearly as I could with a half-crushed windpipe.

The cop's face went dark and red. He was angry and ashamed. I thought for a moment he was going to slap me.

"How... much?" I hissed.

The cop stood up and walked out of the room without saying another word.

That night I decided I had to leave. I was in the hospital for a few more days. I knew I couldn't call Nate, so I called Ashley instead and told her to get a message to him. Our friendship had already started to disintegrate by then, so it took some convincing, but I thought my raspy voice helped persuade her to help me. The rest of my tragic teenage story played out like the plot of a bad after-school special—my boyfriend got me pregnant, got himself killed, and got me sent back to live with my father. Years later here I was, still living under that same roof.

Why hadn't I left yet? For the logical reasons—I wouldn't get very far, I had to think about my daughter, I would feel guilty leaving my mother, and I had no money or job or skills to lean on. I would have to leave this town or else my father would be able to follow me and control me from afar.

Leaving was so easy when I was sixteen. I had my whole life ahead of me and it felt full of possibility. I was still hopeful that in a few years I could turn my life around. Eight years of tragedy had drained my ambition from me. Instead, I could barely muster the energy to walk a couple of blocks to the post office, and I was consumed with anxiety the whole way.

I knew deep down that something had to change. I had to stand up to my father and change my life. Some days the answer felt clear—maybe I could dump some rat poison in my father's beer and get rid of him that way, passing it off as a suicide. Maybe I would just let my father take some of my medication, turn the other cheek and let him overdose.

But most days I felt like it was impossible to do or think of anything except my most basic tasks; re-staining the floor, for example, or getting groceries. On days like that I felt suffocated by my father's gaze and my mother's indifference, so much so that the thought of leaving didn't even cross my mind. It was too much work to plan for, and I was unsure it would even pay off.

But, Maggie, something has to change. You can't go on forever like this.

Of course, that was true, but I still didn't know what to do.

10

The post office took ages. The line itself was at least a half-hour-long wait, despite there being only five people ahead of me. On the way back home I, of course, ran into Mary again, which drained another fifteen minutes out of my day and life.

I was exhausted by the time I got back and was met with the quietest evening I had ever experienced in my home. Isabel was enraptured by her book of ghost stories, and my parents were nowhere to be found. I hardly knew what to do with myself. Should I finally have that glass of red wine and a bath?

I decided against it. There was no way I wouldn't be interrupted while in the middle of my relaxation routine. I ought to follow Isabel's lead and just read until trouble found me. I started making dinner, distracted myself by cleaning out the fridge, and then went to get a book. I strolled into the little library my mother had built, full of books stacked haphazardly in their shelves. I scanned the titles for something that interested me, but it was mostly self-help books about becoming your own woman that were probably outdated when my mother bought them. Still, I was undisturbed by my family. It was a weird feeling and it made the house feel larger than it was.

I finally decided to go down to my workshop and get started refinishing an old dining room set I'd found. I could keep the door open and still hear if anyone needed me, and the work would help me relax more than a glass of wine ever could.

I worked for a few hours in complete silence. I was suspicious of the quiet, even though I appreciated the break from my family. It was unusual to work undisturbed, but I told myself my parents must have gone to bed early. That was the only logical reason why I didn't hear their arguments tonight.

This could be your chance, Maggie, a quiet voice nagged at the back of my thoughts, *your chance to finally leave.* It was impossible. I couldn't go without Isabel, and I'd have to pass my parents' room to get her. Isabel could start crying, and that would wake them up, ruining my chances at a clean break. I couldn't leave, not this time. I had to appreciate what this was—a rare night of peace. I decided to finish sanding the chairs and table, and then go up to bed.

SUDDENLY, I heard a squish through the darkness. I was still in my workshop but I could hear it coming from upstairs—a loud squishing sound, echoing through the halls. I had to investigate, but every fiber of my being wanted to avoid the noise and stay hidden in the basement. The squishing got louder and more frequent. It was accompanied by the sound of someone moaning. A bit of time passed, I heard a scuffle, and there it came again—a squish and a moan. The sound was familiar, but I couldn't place it. It was loud, reverberating in my ears from all directions. Where was it coming from?

I slowly crept up the stairs into the hall, where the moaning got louder. I heard a voice pleading, "I'm sorry, I'm sorry." It sounded like someone was whispering in my ear, but at the same time the sounds were echoing throughout the house. I couldn't place it. The sound wasn't coming from one direction but all of them at once. What was that noise? It was on the tip of my tongue if I could just figure it out...

Was someone in need of my help?

"Hello?" I called out but didn't get an answer. I was starting to get scared; no one was answering me.

Instead I heard the sound again, louder this time. A squish like someone was being stabbed with a knife—was that what was happening? I stopped to listen to the sound. Yes! I was right; it was the sound of someone being stabbed. My heart started racing as I thought of Isabel—was she okay, or was the moaning I heard coming from my daughter?

I picked up the pace and started running through my house, taking the stairs two at a time. Still, I couldn't figure out where the sound was coming from. I was sure of it now; it was the sound of someone being stabbed and then moaning in the aftermath. They had to have been dead by now... unless it was a recording? Was this some kind of a sick joke?

I could feel myself getting dizzy so I pressed myself against the wall trying to regain my balance. When I stopped, the sounds got louder. Suddenly it felt like the knife was right beside me and I could feel the heat from the blood on my skin. I almost threw up. I had to swallow the vomit teasing the back of my throat.

The sound didn't stop, the knife plunging into someone's body, the squish as the metal pierced skin, blood, muscle, and bone.

I couldn't think straight. I felt myself running in circles down the hallways of my house. I finally made it to the stairs, the sound still echoing through my ears. I had to get upstairs. I had to make sure that Isabel was okay. She could be hurt. This could be the sound of my little girl dying.

I fell to my knees and crawled up the stairs, flinching at the sound. I made it to my daughter's room and tried to open the door, but it was locked. I wriggled the doorknob and pushed on the door, hoping it was just stuck and needed a little push. No matter what I did, the door wouldn't open, but I could hear the sound even louder now. It was coming from my room, across the hall.

I banged on Isabel's door. "Isabel! Are you okay? Isabel, please, answer me!" I screamed, tears streaming down my face.

I heard the sound again, louder this time. I couldn't hold back the bile in my throat and finally vomited all over the carpet. Before I could agonize over how to get it out, the sound came again. The wet squishing sound, the moan as someone's last breath left their body. A man trying desperately to cling to life as, again, a knife was pushed into his body. It was happening in my bedroom, there was no doubt about it. It was happening in my room and I was powerless to stop it. My hands reached the doorknob and I braced myself for what was behind it—

"Mommy?" came a small, delicate voice.

I sat up in bed, sweating and crying. Isabel was standing

at the foot of the bed, staring at me. Her face had never looked so serious.

"It was a dream. It was all a dream," I muttered to myself.

Isabel was still staring at me. She hadn't moved a muscle.

I tried hard to get my breathing under control so I didn't worry her. "Hi, honey," I whispered. "Why are you out of bed?"

Isabel didn't say anything, she just shrugged her shoulders.

I gulped some more air. My heart rate was finally starting to slow down. "Did you have a bad dream?" I asked, trying to forget the nightmare I had just woken up from.

"No, I don't dream anymore," she explained, sitting down on the edge of my bed, "but you were dreaming. I could tell."

Isabel was being really creepy. There was no other way to describe it. I mean, kids were weird a lot of the time. Any parent could tell you, sometimes their child would do or say things that were just plain... strange. They just didn't have the kind of social conditioning we did as adults, and that led to weird stuff, like your kid waking you up in the middle of the night because they were staring at you.

This was one of those moments.

"Well," I said, unsure of how to comfort my daughter, "do you want to try sleeping in Mommy's bed tonight? Will that help you dream?"

"No, it's okay. I just don't dream anymore," she said, all matter of fact and none of that childish charm. It was like talking to a very small adult.

"Are you afraid of your dreams?" I asked.

"No," she replied. "When I close my eyes it goes dark. I go back to the place where I was before I was born, and I wait until I wake up."

"That doesn't seem very restful."

"It is. It gives me time to recenter myself and feel calm. You should try it, Mommy."

I didn't know what to say. My body was still weak and shaky from my nightmare. Part of me thought maybe this was part of it, and I was bracing myself against the sound of a knife slicing through flesh again.

"Don't worry, Mommy, you had a nightmare. I used to have those a lot too, but I feel better now," Isabel said, hopping off the bed. She padded to my side and gave me a kiss. "It's time to go back now."

I watched Isabel tiptoe out of my room, closing the door behind her.

My head hit the pillow and I spent the rest of the night staring at the ceiling, unable to get back to sleep. Between my nightmare and the nightmarish vision of my daughter standing over me, I couldn't close my eyes and rest. I kept thinking about Isabel and what she said, that when she was asleep she went back to the place where she was born. Was Isabel trying to tell me she died each night when she went to bed? If she was, that couldn't be healthy. She must have been waking up during the night. Why else would she be staring at me, waiting for me to wake up? I wasn't crying out, so she couldn't have heard me.

I didn't know what to do anymore. I just wanted to cry. What was I supposed to do for my daughter? Was it worse to stay here where at least we had shelter and food, or run away where we had each other but I couldn't guarantee my daughter would have the basic necessities of life?

I couldn't bear the thought of being separated from her. Without Isabel, I honestly didn't think I'd be able to survive, and leaving my daughter orphaned at such a young age was unacceptable.

I started sweating again, this time from the overwhelming anxiety of what I could possibly do for my daughter while not getting her taken away from me.

11

I woke up the next morning to my worst fears coming true. It was like Isabel had entered my mind in the night and acted on the most frightening parts of my anxiety.

I walked into my daughter's bedroom to find all of her pillows on the floor, and her bedlinens covering the furniture.

"I'm in mourning, Mommy," she said, as if that explained the mess.

"Mourning? Do you know what that means?" I asked, trying to replace my anger with a teaching moment.

"Of course I know what it means! Don't you? It means you have to practice what it's like when I'm gone. I'm trying to help you practice what it's like when I'm dead, don't you get it?" Isabel screamed at the top of her lungs and started trying to pull her mattress off her bed.

I ran over and picked up her little screaming body, her legs kicking at mine. I held her until she calmed down.

When finally her body went limp, I set her back down on the bed.

Isabel slumped over like a rag doll and closed her eyes.

My whole body froze—what had I done? Was she okay? Did she faint?

"Isabel?" I asked, my voice shaking. "Isabel, are you okay?" I shook her shoulder gently, trying to wake her up.

She opened one eye and looked at me, sending shivers down my spine. "I'm okay, Mommy. I just wish you would understand that." She sat up and wrapped her arms around me.

I knew kids went through weird little phases like this, but Isabel was becoming too obsessed with death.

"Has Grandpa been talking to you about dying?" I whispered, terrified that my father might be threatening her behind my back.

"No, Mommy, Grandpa never talks to me. You made sure of that," she whispered back.

She was right; I did everything I could to separate my father from Isabel, and for the most part it was easy. He didn't want anything to do with the 'thing' that had caused him so much shame. Isabel was probably the reason my father never went into town anymore, and why everyone, particularly Mary, seemed to think this house was cursed and full of crazies.

"Isabel, I understand what you're doing and I appreciate all your help, but for now we need to keep your room tidy and clean, so can you help me put all this back?"

Isabel nodded, and silently helped me to re-make her bed.

When we were done, she looked around the room and

sighed. "It just doesn't look right," she said, before turning and walking out of the room.

THAT NIGHT, after a long day of refinishing the dining set in my workshop, we trudged up the stairs to bed together, Isabel feeling heavier than ever in my arms. She was lightly snoring as I carried her up the stairs, and was fast asleep when I tucked her into bed.

As soon as her head hit the pillow, Isabel screamed. She tore the pillow from behind her head and launched it across the room. "I hate this! I hate it! I can't sleep! I won't do it. I'm *not* going to sleep with these!" she howled while throwing her pillows and toys all over the room.

"Isabel! Calm down!"

"No! I won't sleep with them. I don't like them. I hate them! I can't do it. I won't do it! No more. I won't do it anymore!" she shrieked.

I tried to collect her pillows and toys. I had no idea where this behavior was coming from, nor where she got the energy to suddenly throw a tantrum when a second before she was fast asleep.

"Isabel, enough!" I roared. In the silence, I strained my ears to make sure the house was silent.

Isabel sniffled quietly on her stripped bed.

"If you don't want to sleep with pillows, that is fine, but it is unacceptable to throw them around the room like that. You can *calmly* put your pillows to the side if you like, but you still have to sleep with a sheet, because I don't want you getting sick."

Isabel nodded and curled herself up in bed. "I don't like the pillows. They make me feel like it's hard to breathe."

"Okay, but you can't react that way. Do you understand why?"

"No. It doesn't matter what I do."

I was far too tired to deal with this. My muscles were aching from using the electric sander for hours.

"Sure, Isabel, it doesn't matter at all," I muttered, before turning out the light and going to my own bedroom.

THIS BEHAVIOR CONTINUED FOR A WEEK. Isabel refused to sleep with a single pillow on her bed, and when she helped me make her bed in the morning she refused to touch a pillow even if it had been on the floor the whole night.

"They're scary, Mommy," was the only explanation she offered for this sudden phobia.

I tried to pry the real reason out of her—was she having nightmares about her pillows, or was the pillow cover too rough? Our bedrooms were on the third floor. They were probably the maid's quarters in some former life of this house. Maybe the cold or dust was settling on her pillow and irritating her in her sleep? Any time I asked a question she would get very serious and repeatedly say the same thing.

"I just don't like these pillows, that's all."

After a few days of this I decided it was less trouble to just buy her some new linens rather than continue to have the same fight every night and every morning. I went out and bought brand-new, hypoallergenic pillows, and pink pillow cases for them. Her old linen set had ballerinas so I chose a solid color, in case the dancers were giving her nightmares or something.

"Who are those for?" a wheedling voice came up behind me and asked as I was making my decision.

I turned and saw Mary fingering the children's linens and smiling at me.

"Just needed some new sheets. Need to refresh," I said, grinning as wide as I could while also looking for whoever was supposed to be minding the old woman, because surely she had a caregiver. My interactions with her lately had been so odd I didn't feel comfortable being alone with her.

"I lost a child once. She had orange sheets—I was obsessed with orange. I think I bought orange sheets for five years afterward, just to keep her close to me," she added, staring down at the sheets and blinking back tears.

She must have been going through some kind of episode. I'd heard that in the early stages of dementia some patients didn't even realize the reality they were experiencing was just a memory. I patted her hand and left Mary with her memories, hoping that one of the store associates would find her and help her home. I didn't have time, and frankly it scared me that she couldn't remember my daughter. *Though I guess, if she also lost a child, it could be triggering for her to hear about Isabel. Every time I talk about my child she hasn't seen in a while, she is reminded of the baby she lost, and it sends her into a spiral.* I thought Mary was nosy and mean, but even she didn't deserve to have lost a child. I couldn't imagine how I would act if Isabel was taken from me like that.

The thought brought tears to my eyes. I had to sit for a moment on a bench outside the store to collect myself. Watching families come in and out of the shop made me feel like throwing up. I had so few friends in town, no one to help me with Isabel. No one I could go to for advice on what to do when your child suddenly rejected the pillows on her bed. Mary was a lonely old lady. She probably felt some kind of kinship with me because of that. *I ought to be a little kinder to her. She can't control what's going on in her brain.*

I CAME BACK and Isabel was at the door, waiting for me.

"I've been quiet, just like you asked," she said, but her voice sounded hoarse.

"Are you okay? Have you been coughing?" I was starting to think this was all due to some kind of dust allergy—pretty common and it would explain the sudden aversion to pillows.

Isabel just shook her head and took the bags from me. "I'll help you with the bags. I wanna see them."

Isabel sounded cheerful, like her normal curious and happy self, but I noticed when she was climbing the stairs her breathing was labored and raspy.

"Isabel, are you okay carrying these?" I asked.

"Yeah, I'm fine," she replied, but she still had to take breaks at every landing to catch her breath.

The hypoallergenic stuff I bought should help. It's probably dust from living in an attic all this time and barely going outside, I thought.

Isabel seemed excited about all her new linens—maybe that was the issue all along. She was just annoyed, having an only-child tantrum and not knowing how to express her feelings. I was sure this would solve everything.

That night, Isabel got into bed and fell asleep almost immediately, her head resting on a new pillow.

A FEW DAYS LATER, it all came to a head. Isabel had spent the morning helping me in my workshop. I was almost done with the dining set; it would be ready to be sold after a coat of varnish and some drying time. I let her go after the morning to play in the backyard, hoping the fresh air would help her strange breathing problems that looked like asthma attacks.

She was a little old to develop asthma, I thought. Most children showed signs of the condition when they were younger. But maybe there was more dust in the air, or the summer cooped up indoors had triggered something that was dormant for the early years of her childhood. I wasn't sure. I couldn't be sure because of what happened later that day.

I was fixing up a snack when Isabel came running into the kitchen holding her neck. She was frantically gulping for air and then collapsed on the ground muttering to herself. I dropped the fruit I was cutting and ran over to her tiny body. She was wheezing and rolling around on the ground—at first I thought she must be having a seizure.

"Isabel, honey, can you hear me? What's wrong?"

"I... can't... Mommy... breathe..." she said through strained breath.

I could feel her heart pounding in her chest as I lifted her little body into a seated position. That didn't seem to help at all. Isabel pawed at her neck, pulling on the ribbon she insisted on wearing every single day. She started crying as she gasped for air, muttering about not being able to breathe and trying to wriggle away from me.

"Isabel, I'm here. Let me help you, let me take this off—" I said as I tried to loosen the ribbon, but in her panic Isabel pushed me and started to crawl away. She started coughing uncontrollably and couldn't stand on her own. I had seen this before. Isabel was having an asthma attack. I had to get her to a hospital; they'd have the right equipment to get her breathing again.

"Isabel, I'm sorry, we have to go." I grabbed her by the waist and my daughter shrieked. She flailed her legs and arms, trying to worm her way out of my grasp. All I wanted to do was help her. Couldn't she see that? *When you're panicking like that, you can't see anything at all,* I reminded myself. It was true. How many times had I descended into a blind panic in my own life?

"Issie, please, try to calm down. It'll help you breathe," I wailed. I had to get a grip before I started crying and wheezing myself. "Try to name five things you can see, okay? That'll help you stop panicking. Tell me five things you see and what colors they are, okay?" I said into her ear.

Isabel nodded but she was still crying. "I can see the table, it looks dark. There's something white on it, I think. It-it looks kind of blurry," she sputtered in fits and starts, dragging oxygen into her lungs.

I carried her down the hallway to the door, determined to get her medical attention as soon as I could. The ambulance would take too long. I could probably get Lana to drive me to the hospital if I needed—

"What do you think you're doing?" my father's voice came out of nowhere. Suddenly he was in front of me, blocking the front entryway.

"Isabel is having an asthma attack. I have to get her to a hospital now. Get out of my way!" I demanded, trying to shove my father from my path.

"She can't leave, Maggie. You know that." My father stood at the door with his arms crossed over his chest.

I was shaking with panic and anger—how could he say that? "Daddy, I have to go. I know you hate that I had her but—"

"Maggie, I don't think you understand. That child *cannot* leave this house," he repeated. "I've put my foot down," he said.

Isabel was still wheezing in my ear but her body had finally relaxed in my arms.

"I have an inhaler," my mother said from somewhere behind me. "She can use this. One puff will be fine for a girl her size."

I turned around and saw my mother holding out an inhaler.

"Take it, Maggie."

I looked between my parents in shock. I didn't know what to do. My mother was helping, for once, and my father wasn't budging from his place by the door. Isabel was still coughing through her strained breath. I put her down and took my mother's inhaler, holding the mouthpiece in front of Isabel. My parents' gaze bore holes in my back as I administered the stimulant to Isabel's lungs.

She was okay. Her breathing got better after one puff, just as my mom said.

"You could probably use it too," she added, "anytime you need." With that, my mother turned and walked away down the hall.

My father kept his guard in front of the door. "She can't leave, Maggie," he said.

"Why not? She's going to have to leave sometime to go to school or when she makes friends or—"

My father put his hand up to silence me. "I don't care. She can't leave. She can stay here, you can stay with her, but if you go out that door you're going alone. I'll make sure of that," he said, and walked away down the hall. He teetered a little bit, clearly already drunk in the middle of the afternoon.

Isabel looked up at me and held the puffer out.

I took it from her and puffed some air to clear my lungs. My heart was beating in my ears—in all the confusion I barely noticed my own panic attack and breathing difficulty. I had to sit down next to Isabel, who was already feeling better, swinging her legs back and forth and singing some nursery rhyme to herself.

"Mommy, I was worried about you. You seemed really scared, like you were getting all dizzy and shaky."

She was right; I was scared. My mouth was dry and my chest still felt tight. The thought of going back to my workshop was giving me a headache; there wasn't nearly enough fresh air down there. The real reason for my panic was what my father had just said. That I could leave, but Isabel couldn't. He was holding her hostage—as long as she lived here, my father would control Isabel's comings and goings. If I wanted to leave with her it would have to be in the middle of the night—the same way I had escaped when I was sixteen, except this time there wouldn't be a car waiting for me. He knew I would never leave without her. That was how he could keep me here, trapped in my own house forever.

"I think I'm gonna go upstairs, Mommy. I want to go play witches. Are you going to come too?" Isabel asked.

I was still feeling lightheaded, and knew I couldn't go back to my restoration work. Isabel bounded up the stairs and I slowly followed behind. My breathing was taking longer to bounce back than hers. I was too drained to dissect what my father had said, or how he'd known I was trying to leave.

12

Isabel and I played witches for the rest of the afternoon. The game was pretty simple, so simple I often forgot who came up with it—me, or my daughter. We sat in the tower attic and pretended to be witches brewing a potion in a large cauldron. The cauldron was an old cast-iron urn I'd found that I emptied out. We pretended to pour in frogs' legs and eye of newt, and every day we worked toward creating the perfect potion for one ailment or another. It was methodical—we would try a recipe, and one of us would taste-test it and critique its "magical powers." The game usually entertained Isabel for hours and hours on end. The fact that we kept trying and "improving" these potions seemed to satisfy her very curious mind. Today, she got tired of the game early.

"Mommy, I just don't see the logic in it anymore. I think I'm growing too old for witches. These magic potions don't change anything anyway. I think I'm going down to my room to nap," she said, before stalking out the door and stomping downstairs.

It's fine, you knew it was going to happen one day. Every little girl outgrows her mother's silly childhood games eventually, I thought as I trudged back downstairs. I figured I could get to work organizing my mother's secret office, now that I knew it existed. The room looked like it hadn't been touched in years. It desperately needed a solid coat of paint and the baseboards needed to be replaced. I also hoped that doing so would make my mother more engaged in my life and create an ally against my father.

I was just thinking about the office and what I could do to improve it when I heard a knock at the front door. I froze, waiting for my father to answer it. I had no idea who it could be. I wasn't expecting any visitors—not that I knew anyone who would visit—and as far as I knew neither of my parents ever had friends over. For a moment I wondered if maybe it was a member of the police force, coming to collect a bribe from my father. If it were, maybe I could sneak out and corner him, explain how desperate I was and that he had to help us. They couldn't turn a blind eye anymore, not when a child was involved.

The knocking got louder and louder. Clearly my father wasn't going to answer, so I made my way to the front door. I saw Mary's nose smushed up against the glass as she was trying to see inside.

She didn't respond to my wave, just kept knocking on the glass pane. We had a door knocker; did she not see we had it? Maybe she was having another memory attack and didn't realize it was there.

Taking pity on the woman, I went over and answered the door. "Hello, Mary. How are you doing?" I asked, as gently as I could.

"I'm well, dear. I came to check up on you and see if you maybe needed my help with some things," she said, smiling at me. Her smile was disturbing. It was too sincere.

So sincere I could tell there was absolutely no feeling behind it. She probably just wanted in to see what was going on for herself, so she could go off and gossip about the Conners to anyone who would listen. Then again, if she was having an episode of dementia or another mental illness, she might just be off on her own planet while trying to communicate with me back down on Earth.

"Why don't you come inside, Mary? We can have some tea," I said, smiling. Tea would be nice. She could calm down, and once this little episode was over, Mary would go back home safely. I opened the door and gestured for her to come inside, looking out on the street to see if anyone was with her, making sure she was okay.

"This house is so much bigger on the inside... It's like a giant maze or something," she said, smiling as she took it all in. "Have you been fixing it up?"

"Yes. It's big and old and needs a lot of work. The house takes up a lot of my time."

"I bet. Why don't you get someone to come work on it for you? You could dedicate your time to other things, and I'm sure it wouldn't be very expensive."

"I'd prefer to do it myself. I have an idea of how I want things to look."

That was only half true. I did have an idea of how I wanted things to look, especially since my parents were rarely interested in *what* I did, only that I continued working. I didn't want to do it myself, but the deal I made with my parents was that I would work on the house, alone, in trade for room and board for me and Isabel. If I didn't work on the house myself, I'd be out on the street with my daughter. *Which might not be that bad, with the way things are going.*

"Are you sure you have the expertise to do it? It's a big undertaking," Mary said, stroking the wallpaper in the halls.

"For the most part it's just aesthetic. The house has good bones, and there's been no flooding or pest-related damage. The floors need refinishing and the rooms need to be cleared out, all stuff that is easy to learn on your own. If I have any questions I just ask the guys at the hardware store in town. They're usually happy to teach me."

"That's so resourceful, dear. I'm happy to hear it," she said, cocking her head and stroking my arm.

Mary was acting like I was a teenager who'd just started her first job or something. It honestly wasn't *that* hard to learn how to do some casual carpentry or home repair. But Mary was part of a different generation—the same as my mom's, women whose husbands did all the work and whose job was to cook, clean, and raise children. They didn't talk back to their husbands or get their hands dirty. It wasn't in the homemaker's job description.

"How about that tea? Why don't we take it in the kitchen? I haven't really finished with the sitting room just yet," I said, leading Mary by the elbow. I could hear footsteps upstairs, and I couldn't tell whose they were. I was determined to keep Mary feeling safe so that hopefully she could leave sooner rather than later. I led her to the little dining table in the kitchen and put the kettle on.

"Is chamomile okay? I don't like to have caffeine this late in the day," I said, rummaging through my cupboards.

Mary's eyes were roving around the kitchen, like she was

trying to memorize it for later. "Mm-hmm, that sounds fine. Your kitchen looks pretty well stocked," she said. "If I were to place a bet, I'd say you have enough food for a family of four in here."

"What makes you say that?" I asked.

"Well, I can see your pantry from here. There's plenty of staples. And I saw you at the grocery store the other day. You were laden down with bags. I was just wondering what you do to keep it all fresh. I don't see a freezer or anything in here."

"We have a freezer; it's in the garage. And I cook the food; that's how I keep it fresh."

"You must have to throw out a lot."

"I have to get rid of some. You've had kids, Mary, you must know what that's like. They go through phases where all they'll eat is macaroni with hot dogs and you have to trick them into eating something else." Isabel had been going through such a phase recently. I had been using the witches game to sneak vegetable smoothies into her diet, or else she'd end up getting scurvy or something.

"Honey, I don't know what you mean. We don't have kids, at least not young ones," she said.

That must be her dementia talking. How could she forget her own kids? I remembered them. Her one daughter, Amelia Albertson, had been the class clown. She was taller than her mother, and built like an Amazon. The last I heard she had dropped out of college and was working at some tech company in San Francisco. Maybe Mary was talking about another kid, the baby she had lost and kept a secret.

"Of course, Mary. You were telling me about your loss the other day. I didn't know about it. I'm sorry to hear that—"

That was the prime moment that my eight-year-old decided to race through the kitchen from the backyard into the front hallway in the brand-new pair of dress shoes I'd picked up for her. I'd bought them when I got her new linens, thinking she was getting to the age where she'd need something like that anyway, and she ought to have a little treat if she was so terrified to sleep. I flinched as she stormed through the room, stopped to stare at Mary for a second, before shrugging and continuing on.

Mary didn't seem to notice. She was focused on my own expression. "Maggie? Margaret, are you okay? You look like you just ate a lemon," she said, her voice sweeter than it needed to be.

"I just—I'm sorry about that," I said, gesturing to the path Isabel had taken.

Mary looked past me but didn't seem to understand what I meant.

Rather than try to explain and risk triggering the old woman, I brushed it off and continued, "Never mind, I just mean... You were talking the other day about your own loss. I'm sorry if I reminded you of it."

Mary shrugged it off like it was nothing. "Things like that happen. What we need to do is grieve and move on so we don't get stuck in the low points of our lives—do you know what I mean?"

At that moment Isabel started trying to tap-dance in her new dress shoes out in the hall.

Mary ignored her and continued talking. "While I do think about that child sometimes, what her life could have been had I not lost her, I worked through my emotions at the time so that I could move on. I had another daughter—you remember Amelia, don't you?" she asked, and waited for my answer.

I was so distracted I barely heard her question. "I'm sorry, just give me a—" I went out into the hall and hissed at Isabel to stop dancing.

"Why, Mommy? She doesn't even notice me," she said.

"That's no reason to disturb us. Mary wanted a quiet conversation with Mommy and you're being very rude. Now come in here and apologize to Mary. You didn't even acknowledge her when she came in."

"Maggie?" Mary asked. "Who are you talking to?"

"It's just Isabel. She's very sorry for disturbing you, *aren't you, Isabel?*" I said, giving her the sternest look I had.

Isabel bit her lip and called out to Mary, "Sorry, Mrs. Albertson. I didn't mean to disturb you two," she said, before running off up the stairs.

Mary came over to the doorway and looked around in the hallway.

"She ran off," I explained.

"Who did? I didn't see anyone." Mary's eyes softened again.

I didn't understand—Isabel had run past us a minute ago and Mary didn't even notice her. Was every woman in this town prone to ignoring kids under the age of ten? Mary Albertson was almost as detached as my own mother.

It could be that Isabel is a trigger for her. Maybe her lost daughter would have been Isabel's age now, and it's playing tricks on her perception.

"That's fine. The water's boiled. Why don't you sit down?" I told her.

I didn't know how to deal with this. Mary had never been

my favourite person in town. The fact that she was nosy enough to know everyone's business yet never helped me or my mother when I was young and vulnerable always rubbed me the wrong way. I knew memory problems ran in the family, because Amelia would talk about the weird stuff her grandmother did in the early days of her dementia. Stuff like thinking Amelia's stuffed animals were real and leaving pet food out for them, and imagining that dead relatives had come back to life. Despite that, I couldn't bring myself to feel sorry for the woman in front of me. Because of her history in town and how invasive she was being with me lately, it made me think that this could all be an act so she could learn the secrets of what was going on inside my house.

As if in response to that thought, I heard my father scream my mother's name somewhere upstairs. I jumped, but Mary didn't hear a thing. She fiddled with the string on her teabag and stared at me.

"You know, dear, I have a few books on grief that really helped me through. Would you like me to loan them to you?" she asked.

"What do you mean?"

My father was getting louder. I could hear his heavy footsteps upstairs. Based on how loud he was, I thought he was in my mother's office. Did he finally break in there? I hadn't gotten the chance to add another lock to the door.

"Oh, some self-help books people gave me to cope with loss. Loss of a child, loss of a family member, loss of a spouse —they repackage it, but it all boils down to the same advice. Self-help books can be a little 'lame,' I know, but they are a good first step in the process of moving on."

"Helena, get back here. I'm not finished with you," my

father's voice rang out as clear as if he'd been in the room with us.

I flinched and looked up.

Mary followed my gaze. "You should probably take a look at those pipes. I know you said the house has good bones, but these old houses always need their plumbing looked at."

So she isn't totally crazy. She definitely heard my father yelling and is playing it off as the house's plumbing acting up. Maybe I was right that Mary's "dementia" was an act to get her nosy self into the house and start spreading secrets and lies about my family.

What would she have to lie about? Everyone knows Joseph Conner abuses his wife and kid, and runs the town with an iron fist. He's the type who prefers to be feared, not loved. The town gossip doesn't need to lie her way in here to find that out.

"You're probably right," I said. "Who knows what's been growing in the pipes."

"Exactly! The house has been practically abandoned for years now. You might be flushing out a rat's nest without even realizing it." Mary chuckled and sipped her tea.

There it was again, that suggestion that she was floating in and out of her own little world. I could see right through it now.

"Well, I had them checked. There certainly aren't any animals, but rust can build up anywhere..." I laughed, hoping to drown out the sound of my mother shrieking upstairs. This was turning into a game of chicken; who could react first to the circus surrounding us?

"It's impressive that you've moved back here after the funeral. I would have assumed you'd sell this place as-is and leave town. That's probably what Amelia would do if I died," she said, chuckling. "I think it's wonderful that you've decided to stay and fix up the house. Are you planning on living here for a while, then?"

Funeral? What on earth was this woman talking about? Did someone in her family die? Why would she think that would affect me?

"I'm sure Amelia would stick around. She isn't heartless," I stammered, unsure of how to continue this game.

The thudding got louder upstairs. The walls started quivering each time my father landed a blow.

"No, she has a whole life on the West Coast that I am *not* welcome in," she said.

It was not a surprise. Mary was the sort who believed in telling the "harsh truth," no matter how much it made her daughter cry.

"By the way, what did you think of the funeral?"

"What funeral?" I asked her, as a picture frame was knocked off the wall.

"Your mother's funeral, my dear. It's been a few weeks. Surely you can talk about it now; the process of grief has to start some time."

My mother screamed at my dad. Her words were muffled, but it was clear that she was up there.

"Mary, this isn't funny," I said, trying to hide how angry I was. "I don't know what kind of *information* you are trying to get out of me, but this is the wrong way to do it." My voice was quivering and I was getting louder.

My mom kept yelling at my dad in stops and starts, likely between him striking her.

"Sweetheart, I'm not trying to make a joke or get anything out of you. You've been shut in this house, and while the whole town wants to keep acting as if nothing is going on—"

"Sometimes it is none of your business what's going on in a home, *especially* when you can't even keep straight who's alive or dead in there!" I stood up, knocking my chair against the ground.

Mary recoiled, spilling some hot tea on herself.

"My mother is upstairs. We both know my dad is up there using her as a punching bag. You really have the gall to call it a plumbing problem? You act like you care, yet you haven't changed a bit! None of you have. I couldn't count on a *single person* in this town when I was growing up, and even now that I have a child we're still nothing but a sick joke in your eyes. Get out of here, Mary. Get out of my house, now. I don't care if you have a caretaker, if this is your dementia talking or what. I want you out of my house, now," I demanded, pointing to the door.

Mary looked at me in complete shock.

The house was silent. We were all waiting to see what she would do.

"You're right, dear. We should have said something long ago. Your father, he's... he has a hold over all of us." Mary smiled weakly and tiptoed past me.

I stood, shaking, in the kitchen until I heard the front door close.

A moment later my mother walked past me into the kitchen. Her lip was bleeding and she had clearly been crying. I put my hand on her shoulder, but she brushed it away. My mother turned on the sink and rinsed out her mouth. Without saying another word, I pulled a bag of frozen peas out of the freezer and went over to her. I wrapped the peas in a towel and held them up to her swollen lip. Her skin was warm; she flinched against the cold.

I stared into my mother's eyes, willing her to say something. She didn't say a word, just closed her eyes and leaned into my hand. A drop of my mother's blood fell onto my hand as she took the frozen peas from me and walked away.

13

My hands were shaking as I locked the door and went upstairs. Mary had me in a rage, my mind racing with angry thoughts. How dare she come into my home and act as if my mother was dead and my child didn't exist? Mary was manipulative, using her apparent confusion to gain access to my home. What did she want with us anyway? What could possibly be so interesting to her? What was she going to gossip about that people didn't already know? I felt like a pariah whenever I walked in town. I could see everyone staring at me as I walked the streets. What did Mary gain from sneaking in here?

She must have some other agenda. All that talk about grief... Maybe she was trying to find a way to get through to you, to help you, that tiny voice of reason called out at the back of my mind. She was being drowned out by my anxious and bitter thoughts.

I looked down at my hand, at the drop of my mother's blood staining it. She was real. My family was alive. There was no funeral. There was only Mary's manipulative provocation.

I began pacing the upstairs hallway, trying to come up with ways to get her back.

I could come to her with "news" that Amelia was hurt.

I could create some town rumor about Mary, destroy her own reputation.

Fighting fire with fire was what I knew—that's what growing up with an aggressive parent got you. Either you checked out or you adopted their method of dealing with the world.

Stop, Maggie. Take a deep breath, take one of your fast-acting anxiety pills. You're on the verge of a panic attack. Do some breathing exercises. I repeated this mantra to myself as I climbed the stairs to my room. I didn't even count out my medication the way I usually did, just threw a pill into my mouth and swallowed. I splashed cold water on my face and washed my hands.

The spot of blood got bigger. It must have spread and I didn't notice. I kept scrubbing it off my hand but it didn't go away. The water started running red, darker and darker. The spot still didn't go away—had I cut myself when I was helping my mom? My sink was running red with blood and the tiny spot grew until it was covering my hands with thick, dark blood. I switched to hot water to get the stain off my hands but it wasn't a stain anymore. I was washing blood from my hands, scrubbing and scrubbing, but it just kept bleeding and bleeding. I brought my hands up to my face. They were covered in blood but I didn't see a cut anywhere. If I was losing this much blood I had to sit down; I was going to pass out soon—but I had to get the blood off me. I had to get this off, but I didn't know how. My hands were shaking even more; I couldn't control it. I checked the bottle to make sure I had taken the correct dosage—nothing was different.

I kept washing my hands. I was going to wash them until they were raw, at this rate. The blood was starting to drain down the sink. I made the water hotter, so hot I could barely stand it, but that seemed to do the trick. Finally the thick blood coating my hands was starting to run down the drain. The water went from deep burgundy to a washed-out pink color. Finally it was all off my hands, including the spot of blood from my mother's lip.

So much for avoiding a panic attack.

I was still shaking, and now my hands felt raw from the hot water. I went over and locked my bedroom door so that I wouldn't be disturbed, and I wrapped myself in my bed. I vaguely recalled a burrito technique that could relax anyone who was freaking out. I needed a minute, maybe an hour, to myself to recover from this day.

"Mommy! Mom! Mommy!"

I woke up to Isabel jumping on my bed. "Issie, how did you get in here?"

"The door, obviously, how else?" she replied, plopping herself down at the end of my bed.

I could have sworn I'd locked it, but who knew? This house was old, and this part of the house was run down. She probably jiggled the door and popped the lock easily.

"It was hard to get in," she said, as if reading my thoughts, "but I managed. I really had to show you what I've been working on."

My heart wasn't racing anymore, but my mouth was dry

and my head was pounding. I wanted to go back to sleep and forget about my day. I wanted to escape into the world of dreamless sleep where I didn't have to manage my family.

"You can't go back to sleep. It's too early. You have to come with me," Isabel whined, crossing her arms in front of her chest, mimicking her grandfather when he was barring the door. "You're not allowed to sleep. You're not allowed to be in bed. You have work to do, and some of that work is being my mom."

"Okay, grumpy puss, I'll get up," I said, smiling weakly at my daughter. I didn't feel as anxious as I did before, and hiding in bed wasn't going to get me anywhere. I might as well get out of bed for something small, like playing with my kid.

"Finally," she said, jumping off the bed and running out the door. Isabel beelined for her room and I slowly followed her, longingly looking back at my bed. Isabel had been drawing. Balled-up paper was strewn all over her room.

"You're going to clean this up, right, Michelangelo?"

She rolled her eyes and dragged me by the arm to her desk. "Yeah, yeah, but first you need to see my masterpiece," she said.

On her desk was a sprawling drawing. A roll of kraft paper covered the little table. In crayon, Isabel had drawn a scene that would rival a master's war-time painting. It was incredible, for an eight-year-old. At first glance I was hit with a wave of pure emotion. She used every color in the box, creating a disturbing and impassioned triptych that I didn't understand at first.

"Do you like it?" she asked, smiling up at me.

The first image looked like a pregnant woman who was crying. She was standing in front of a table piled high with green bills with dollar signs everywhere. Behind the green bills was darkness. She used black and red and brown to create a black hole that was swallowing the money and taking up every bit of empty space on her crude canvas.

The second panel was terrifying. The pregnant woman was surrounded by the black hole. It was holding her around the neck. There was the outline of a white hand holding her neck, which was colored with red. In her belly was the image of a baby crying, reaching up, trying to help her mother. The baby had a red ribbon around its neck in place of the umbilical cord. The pregnant woman was reaching behind her toward a large knife floating in the air.

The third panel was all drawn in red. The knife was red, the pregnant woman was red, the baby was red, even the dark shadow was colored in red. The shadow was melting into the ground and had red knives poking out of its body. The pregnant woman was crying red tears and she was flooded with red. She was holding a red knife and her mouth was open in a scream. It was clear that the pregnant woman had stabbed the shadow, killing him with her red knife. There were red droplets falling from the knife to his body. In a small corner of the square, there was a yellow bell.

"That's the ambulance," Isabel said, pointing to the bell. "They're coming and they have the sirens on, but I didn't know how to depict the sirens."

My mouth was hanging open. I was completely speechless.

Isabel looked up at me examining my reaction. "Do you think it's good?" she asked.

I could only nod. It was true; the drawing was incredible, especially for an eight-year-old. I was expecting stick figures and a little circular sun or something, but this looked like it was drawn by someone three times her age. I couldn't get over the subject matter. My mouth was dry and my heart started pounding all over again.

"Mommy, you look scared," Isabel said.

But I didn't respond. I didn't know what to say.

"I know it can be scary, but sometimes it's necessary. It wasn't your fault. Even I could see that. There are bad people in this world, people that no matter what we do, they won't get any better. Those people need to die, especially if they hurt us."

I was frozen to the spot, staring at my beautiful daughter more afraid than ever. I wondered if maybe I was hallucinating or still dreaming in the other room. The crayon was thick on the craft paper. I touched it and my hands came away red.

"Mommy, I know you don't like to think about it. I just want you to know that I don't blame you at all, and I think you've done an incredible job with your life."

I turned to look at my daughter, still unable to believe that she'd created this. Where did this scene come from? How could her little mind come up with this?

"I love you, Mommy," Isabel whispered, hugging me around my waist. "And I want you to remember that sometimes bad people need to die. They just aren't good for us or for humanity in general." She ran out of her room and disappeared.

I couldn't move. I was consumed by the drawing. Isabel in my belly, me murdering the shadow, who I assumed must be Nate. I hadn't told her the full story. Was this all from Isabel's imagination? I tried to remember what I had told her about her father. I didn't say anything, I only said he was gone—right? That must have been it. I wanted to protect

Isabel from the truth. I would never have told her that her father was a drug dealer. Not only that, but I didn't even remember what happened that night. After Nate beat me, I passed out and didn't wake up until after the police had arrived. Isabel must have made it up, but who would give her this gruesome idea? No eight-year-old imagines bloody murder for a crayon drawing.

Either my daughter was a budding serial killer, or something else was going on in this house that I didn't know about.

14

That night I collapsed in bed, emotionally and physically exhausted from my day. I couldn't remember a time where I had ever been so tired. Maybe back when Isabel was first born? But even that was a blur. I remembered a tiny baby squealing and crying, my father getting annoyed at her, and many dirty diapers, all wrapped up in a sleepless cloud.

Isabel's drawing was disturbing. It made me scared for my daughter—and scared for living with her too. Was I raising a tiny serial killer?

I couldn't tell. That was what it looked like. All this time I had been trying to keep her away from my father's rage, only to find it percolating inside her. This rage seemed to be genetic, but it skipped a generation. At least, I thought it did. There were so many periods of my life that I couldn't quite remember anymore. The night where Nate died was one of them—I remember blacking out when Nate attacked me, but what if there was more to that night? Something that my baby remembered from her time in-utero.

It can't be, Maggie. The police arrived, and you were asleep. You passed out after Nate tried to strangle you. If you had stabbed him you'd have been covered in blood. There would have been a police investigation. You might even have been sent to jail.

Isabel had lived a pretty sheltered life for an eight-year-old. This whole summer she'd barely been outside, and only ever in the backyard. Every time I went for groceries, she'd been unwell, so I always left her in her bedroom.

It was all for her own protection, but at what point did that just cycle back around to damaging my kid's psyche?

ISABEL KEPT HAVING these panic and asthma attacks that made me feel sick to my stomach. She would suddenly start coughing and wheezing, drawing her breath in slowly and shaking her hands while pointing at her throat. There was nothing I could do for her; the inhaler I had wasn't effective. Isabel would start turning blue, her lips would get cold, then all of a sudden—just as suddenly as it started—she would be breathing normally again.

When I asked her how she was feeling, she would always say the same thing: "I feel fine, Mommy." And then she'd immediately go back to whatever she was doing.

I tried keeping a diary of these attacks so I could tell a doctor, but there was nothing in particular that triggered them. I kept a record of what she was doing and what foods she was eating, but there was nothing that strung these attacks together.

She also continued asking strange questions, often about her father, but also about my life.

"What do you do when I'm at school, Mommy?"

"Mommy, why don't you ever go outside and play with the other Mommies?"

"Mommy, do you have a job? What is your job and how come you know how to fix so much?"

Then the questions started to change, to complicated philosophies about life and death.

"Mommy, do you know that some people believe that when you die, an echo of your spirit inhabits the place you died at? So if you died in a tree then your spirit would stay inside that tree forever? Do you think that if I died, but I was a tree, I could change the tree and bend the branches to my will?"

"I believe in karma, but there's this other concept called dharma which refers to powerful concepts that hold up society and it means everyone has to conform to their duty and do what's right. But I think that can change, because depending on the circumstances your duty changes. Do you believe in karma?"

"Mommy, am I reincarnated? I think I was reincarnated from a frog, because I've had a pretty short life so far."

She also started swearing. I had no idea where she learned it, but one morning when I came in to wake her up, the first words out of her mouth were: "Fucking hell, Mommy, it's way too early for that."

"Where did you learn that word?" I asked her, but Isabel just shrugged and turned away from me in her bed. I had to pinch myself to make sure I wasn't dreaming or hallucinating a little teenager in place of my daughter. I continued on with my morning thinking I must have imagined what she said—my eight-year-old didn't know how to swear, and I was overly cautious to not curse around my daughter.

She could have learned it from a book. It must have been

where she was learning these concepts of Buddhist philosophy. My parents had a pretty extensive library that I barely ever touched. It was only logical that Isabel, who was way more curious than I ever was, started poking around in there. She had nothing else to do, and it was getting to the part of the summer where it was too hot to do anything but lie around in the air conditioning. She stopped asking to play witches, calling it a "stupid and juvenile pastime," preferring to sit in her room and read instead.

A couple days into this odd, sudden change, Isabel was sitting on the steps leading to my workshop. I was mixing some paint to repair a wall on the second floor when suddenly she screamed, "Fuck!"

I jumped, thinking it was my father who came downstairs, and almost spilled the paint everywhere.

"Isabel," I yelled, "watch your language."

Isabel didn't say anything. She just gave me the finger and stormed out. I could hear her stomping as hard as she could above me.

Did my daughter just give me the middle finger? I asked myself. I certainly didn't imagine that, and I had no idea where she would have learned that. I checked the titles of the books Isabel was reading; they were all classics and wouldn't have any of that language in them.

I wasn't going to stand for this. My child wasn't going to be the one to bring her classmates down in the next school year. I dropped what I was doing and chased Isabel up the stairs. I thought she'd turn left and head to the library, but she turned right, headed toward the part of the house I tried to avoid as best as I could. She was headed in the direction of the crying room, a place she knew I wouldn't follow her to.

"Isabel! Stop right there," I cried.

Isabel stopped in her tracks and slowly turned around to face me. Her face was dark, her mouth in a tight frown. "What?" she deadpanned.

"Where are you headed?" I asked, tiptoeing nearer to her.

Isabel smiled. "You know where I'm headed, and I know for a fact you won't follow me there."

"Stop, Isabel. I don't know what has gotten into you lately, but this is getting ridiculous—"

I cut myself off because all of a sudden Isabel dropped the book in her hand and collapsed to her knees. She was wheezing again, struggling to breathe and pulling at her ribbon necklace. I resisted going to her, thinking that it was a trick. She was going to draw me in and push me away, or even push me into the crying room.

"I'm not falling for that trick," I said.

But Isabel kept wheezing and coughing, acting like she couldn't get a full breath in. "Mommy," she croaked, "I'm not lying. I can't... I can't breathe." Isabel rolled onto her back and kicked at the floor, clawing at her neck.

I saw her skin start to go pale, her lips slowly turning blue. Her eyes started rolling to the back of her head, like the was being fast-forwarded through her strangulation. My leg twitched as I resisted running to her.

This is a trick. Maggie, this is a trick. She's tricking you.

"I'm not... tricking you... Mommy," Isabel groaned. "Help... me."

I stood there as tears stained my eyes, watching my little girl slowly die. I had seen these attacks too many times now. I knew she'd snap out of it. This time, however, it was going on longer and she sounded more desperate. She stopped making sounds. Her mouth was open trying to gulp down a little more air, but she couldn't. Was I wrong? Was Isabel really dying?

As I had that thought, she turned on her belly and popped back up. She was fine. This was a trick, or maybe I'd had a seizure. There was no way for me to know.

"What the hell, Mom?" Isabel asked. "You were just going to watch me die?"

"Of course I wasn't. I could see that you would get better. And watch the way you speak to me, young lady. That's inappropriate."

"Well, I think it's inappropriate that you stood there and *watched me die*. What kind of a mother are you, anyhow?"

"Where is this coming from?" I asked, my voice shaking. "What happened to my curious and sweet little girl?"

Isabel didn't answer. She just shrugged like a sullen teenager. I thought I had a few years, at least, before it got to that.

"Seriously, Isabel, what is going on? What's with the potty language out of nowhere? Who is teaching you this?"

"Grandpa," Isabel said, as if it were obvious.

From somewhere downstairs I heard my father roar with laughter. He must be getting a kick out of this, turning my child into a little monster. I wondered if maybe he was the one putting murderous thoughts into her head. I knew he'd always hated Nate. Maybe he was the one telling Isabel that someone murdered him, and she got confused and drew me instead. Now that I knew it was my father, Isabel's sudden shift seemed obvious. To him this was a joke—the sweet girl who becomes an angry bitch overnight. It was his revenge for my rebellion.

"When did Grandpa teach you this?" I asked. "I told you not to bother him, didn't I?"

"Yeah, but I wasn't bothering him. I dunno. Sometimes when you're downstairs for a long time I see him. Or when you go out. He asked me how I was doing once, when I was having trouble breathing, and then he said I could come to him if I needed anything. One day I saw him in the library and he told me which books I should read," she said, shrugging again. "I don't know, Mom, sometimes I run into my grandfather. The house is big but it isn't so enormous that I just wouldn't run into the other people who live here."

It was so matter of fact when she said it, I don't know why I hadn't thought of it sooner. Whenever I was out of the house, whenever Isabel wasn't in my sight, all those times my father knew Isabel was alone he was probably putting ideas into her head and turning her against me.

"Isabel, why don't you go up to your room and relax, okay? You must be tired after one of your breathing attacks. I know it's your grandfather's fault for this, but I don't want you talking like that, okay? It's unrefined. I'd rather you express yourself with some of the fancy language you've learned in the books you've been reading."

Isabel didn't say anything, just nodded and dodged me when I tried to pat her shoulder.

As a mother, it hurt me that she was already rejecting me. But as Maggie Conner, I knew who was behind it.

Joseph Conner, my father, the man who needed to be loved above and before all else, who would stop at nothing to control everyone in his world.

15

What disturbed me the most about what Isabel said was that my father just "happened" to be around to teach her in his image. Whenever my eyes weren't on Isabel, his were. To me it seemed like he ignored my daughter, didn't care much for her and wanted to pretend she didn't exist. Clearly, I was wrong. To me he acted one way, but behind my back was a different story.

For the next few days I watched my father like a hawk. I made sure to always be working near him, making excuses to be in the same room and follow him around the house if I needed to.

"Why are you following me, Maggie?" he grumbled, stumbling drunk throughout the house.

"I'm not following you, Dad, I'm working on this part of the house today. Right now I'm making sure you don't fall over," I replied.

My father looked at me through squinted eyes, suspicious of everything I said. He had the power to know what you were thinking by reading your face, so I kept my expression as neutral as I could. When my father was satisfied, he pushed me into the wall and kept walking down the hallway, laughing to himself.

"You think you're some kind of hero, don't you," he roared, "saving your kid from me. As if I was ever the problem. You and your mother are the problem." My father kept muttering as he stumbled down the stairs.

I moved to follow him, but from downstairs I heard him yell.

"Don't even try to follow me. You have work to do."

I DO REMEMBER a time before my dad became a complete, drunken asshole. He was a regular dad. I don't know what changed. He was a loving man who would get angry sometimes but not more often than anyone else. Looking back, I now realized that all that time I thought I had the coolest dad, he was abusing my mom without me knowing. I wasn't entirely sure when that changed, but it did and it changed on a dime.

One day, my mom served us dinner and my dad took a bite that was too hot, so he dumped a bowl of hot soup on my mom, right in front of me, and then started laughing.

"It's funny, right? I look like a clown and now so do you." His laughter was infectious and soon I was giggling too.

My mother didn't cry. She looked between my father and me before calmly cleaning herself up. She had to apply aloe for days afterward, and hid from the two of us. I didn't understand that the soup that I thought was too hot, that caused my father to burn his tongue, had also burned my mother's skin.

It all devolved from there, until finally I became my father's target. He started slow—just a few slaps here and there—but eventually I was also a victim of his rage. By then my mother was so tightly wound that I doubted she *could* say anything. She was totally detached from what was happening in our house, and I followed suit.

I couldn't let that happen to Isabel. I had worked so hard to keep her out of it, keep her away from my father. I wasn't going to give up, and I wasn't going to let him do whatever he wanted.

"Issie, can you come help me paint?" I called up to my daughter. When I didn't get an answer, I called up again. "Isabel! I don't want to have to ask you again!"

"She's not up there," my father's voice came from behind me, as if out of thin air. "She's in the library. I gave her another book to read. *Crime and Punishment*—she needs to learn a little about that, since you refuse to discipline your own daughter."

"Our definitions of discipline are different, Dad," I said, pushing past him and rushing downstairs to our library. The house was big and confusing. The library was probably the coziest room in the building. I had finished working on it. All the chairs were freshly stuffed and they were, hands down, the best work I had done so far. I could probably have sold them for an obscene price, but I wanted to keep them so I could cozy up to my daughter.

Isabel was sitting in one of the chairs, reading a complicated Russian novel that was bigger than she was.

"Isabel, can I get your help with one of the rooms upstairs? I'm painting. You love painting."

Her eyes peeked over the top of the book, and she snuggled deeper into the chair. "Grandpa says I have to read this because I don't know what punishment really means. What does punishment mean, anyhow?"

I felt shivers wash over me, crawl up my spine and down again. It was like looking into a horrible mirror. Whatever I did, I couldn't let my father do this to Isabel. Not any of it; no beatings, none of his emotional manipulation, and especially no crying room.

I felt like giving Isabel that book—which she couldn't possibly understand—was my father's first step toward abusing his granddaughter.

"You have to go out."

It was the next morning, and I was still in bed, hoping to have an extra few minutes before I had to start my day. Isabel had refused to help me paint, and my muscles were aching from working at double speed so I could keep an eye on her.

"Maggie, did you hear me? You have to go out."

My mother's voice was so quiet, sometimes it felt like I was making her up in my mind.

"I heard you. What do you need?" I asked, wrenching myself from my peaceful bed.

"Groceries," she replied, and left.

Groceries would take forever, and I was sure we had everything we need. Why was my mother telling me to go out for groceries? I hurriedly got dressed, woke up Isabel, and ran downstairs to the kitchen. The stench hit me before I got there—the smell of food gone bad. Someone had opened all the cans in my pantry and spilled their contents all over the floor. The same person left the freezer and the fridge doors open, spoiling all the food that had been inside. Whoever did this worked all night with only one goal in mind—to make sure we had no food in the house.

"What a mess!" my father said, behind me. "I don't think they left a single can unopened. They even spilled my beer!" His worry was so exaggerated I knew it was a joke. Some practical joke he concocted in the middle of the night.

"You're not sleepwalking again, are you, Mags?" he asked, smirking at me.

"No. I'm not sure who did this," I mumbled, bracing myself for what my father would do. Surely I hadn't started sleepwalking again, right? I'd remember doing this, wouldn't I?

Would you? some part of me questioned.

"It must have been some crazy bum. Saw an unlocked door, took the opportunity to mess things up, and ran off without a trace. You gonna call the police?" He chuckled and walked off upstairs.

So this was why we were in need of groceries again, all of a sudden. Cleaning the kitchen and going out for food would take me all day. I wouldn't be able to work on the second-floor rooms, nor would I be able to entertain Isabel for that long.

You could just lock her in her room. There was a little voice at the back of my mind that sometimes had really horrible ideas. Ideas that made me think maybe manipulation and abuse really were hereditary. Maybe it ran in the family and there just wasn't a way of breaking that cycle. That was the voice suggesting that maybe I needed to lock my daughter up.

It would be for her own good. If she's in her room, your father won't be able to hurt her. He won't be able to teach her curse words or taunt her with Crime and Punishment *or some other weird novel. She'd be safe. She wouldn't be happy about it, but at least she'd be safe.*

My mom walked past without saying anything to me. She waded through the sea of wet, spoiled food and opened the fridge.

"Mom, there's nothing in there," I called to her, but she ignored me.

She looked around in the fridge and closed it again. "Maggie, you need to go out," she said as she wandered past me into the hall.

I did need to go out, but I also had to stay in. I had to make sure Isabel was okay, I had to clean the kitchen, and I still had work to do upstairs. There weren't enough hours in the day to deal with this mess.

"What are you going to do?" my father asked from the stairs. "I can always watch Isabel. She is *my* granddaughter after all. I ought to be able to watch an eight-year-old for an hour or two."

"It's fine, Dad, I can watch her."

"*You* have to go out and get groceries."

"Why can't you or Mom do it? I don't understand. Why am I the one to *do* everything in this house?"

"Because, young lady, we are letting you live here rent-free. You think I haven't noticed that you didn't bother getting a *job* and contributing to society? You can live here while you fix up the house and run errands for your mother and me. We're old, and neither of us has the energy to be running around this town trying to keep this house from falling down around our ears. Is it too much for us to ask for our only daughter to *help us*?" My father started raising his voice, and his fist started quivering by his side.

I knew I had gone too far. Questioning Joseph Conner was never the right way to go.

"I'm sorry! I'm just a little, um, scared. About what happened last night, or how it happened. It's a lot to clean up."

"Well, then you better get started," he said before storming up the stairs, muttering to himself about how ungrateful I was.

It wasn't true. I was extremely grateful that my parents let me live here, let me raise my daughter in a comfortable home rather than risking poverty. I didn't have very many skills, hadn't finished high school and didn't go to college, so being my parents' errand girl and pro-bono contractor was the best job I could get. Now I had to figure out how to be everywhere at once so I could do my "job" and protect my daughter.

"And by the way," my father called to me, "I had planned to hand my business down to you, but if this is how you're going to act when faced with a little hard work—"

"It's all right, Dad, I can handle it. I swear, I'll handle it."

I could handle it.

ISABEL HELPED me with the kitchen. She found the sea of food hilarious, which meant she was eager to help for once. It became a craft project, a food fight, an art piece—honestly, it felt like I had my eight-year-old back. She was giggly for the whole day. This was all I wanted—quality time with my daughter so that I could erase my father's influence. I knew that as soon as I left, my father would be able to take over and keep teaching her curse words, or worse.

"Isabel, I need to make a call. Can you help me?"

"With a phone call? Why do you need help with a phone call?"

"I'm going to see if the grocery store can deliver our food, so I need help making a list of all the food that went bad. We're going to replace it and they're going to deliver it right to our door."

"Oooh, fun, like a Christmas list!" Isabel jumped up and down, excited to get started on her letter to the pantry Santa Claus.

That was the only solution I could think of—I'd start getting things delivered to the house. True, it meant I would lose the sweet time I had alone, away from the doom and gloom of this house. But I'd rather that than risk my daughter's sanity.

I NO LONGER LEFT THE house. When my parents needed me to go to the post office, I called and scheduled a pick-up at our door. The grocery store delivered everything we needed—it was actually even easier than going to the store every week. They saved my order and added exactly what they thought I needed based on the last time I bought it. The hardware store did the same. I was always asking them for advice and wasting time debating between products in the store. Deliveries made my life easier.

They also made my life quieter. I didn't really run into

Mary anymore, nor did I run into the cute dog groomer, Charlie. That was okay; I didn't need to. I had my daughter, and protecting her was my priority now. It didn't help my reputation as the local recluse. Lana tried to come over once, concerned for my well-being.

"I know you're a dedicated mother, and you're working so hard on this house. I made you a CBD bath bomb and some bath salts so you can relax," she said one day. A surprise visit from a kindly neighbor, nothing like Mary's strange inspection.

"Thanks, that's really sweet. I appreciate it," I replied, glancing back at her husband, Bill, on the road. He looked like he was her bodyguard, watching the road for potential paparazzi or stalkers who wanted to attack Lana. "Does Bill want some water or anything?" I asked her.

"Oh no, he's fine. He's just a little awkward. Wanted to come with, but didn't want to disturb."

Sure, I thought, *wanted to make sure the crazy lady across the street didn't attack his wife.*

"Well, let him know I said thanks. I know the business is both of yours, so I appreciate the thought." I smiled weakly.

"I'll let him know. I'd better head back. We've got errands to run. You enjoy that now," she said with a wave.

I waved back and closed the door. The longer I spent locked up inside, the more awkward my social interactions were going to get.

It was nice of Lana to come by. Nice of her to recognize that I was probably stressed out and needed to relax. Still, I didn't know how to connect with her. I spent my days watching an eight-year-old and bracing myself against my father. My mother barely factored into my life. She didn't help me with Isabel, but she also didn't provoke my father. She might as well have been a ghost.

The same could be said for you, Maggie. What do you do with your life, other than haunt your childhood home? You play with your daughter, you paint and refinish the fixtures in this house. If it weren't for the phone calls you make and deliveries you receive, someone might think this place was abandoned, filled with phantoms that couldn't move on from their bleak lives.

16

I kept working, as it was the only thing keeping me sane. While we lived in a giant home, it was getting harder to avoid my father. My mom seemed to be doing just fine, but I hardly ever saw her. Even when I did, she barely spoke. If we were all ghosts, she was the one fading the fastest.

The house felt strange, like a haunted fun house. Sometimes I found rooms that I was sure never existed. Like my mother's office, or I once found a room full of my old toys. It was completely stuffed with old bicycles, dolls, Halloween costumes—you name it, there it was. It was the room my childhood went to die in.

"What is all this stuff?" Isabel asked as we cleared everything out.

"It's trash, honey." Most of the toys were broken. Not a single doll that I could see had all her limbs, and the Barbie dream car didn't have any wheels on it. The toys were in such a state that I felt bad donating them. It was better to throw it all in the trash.

"You're not going to throw this out, are you? It's our house," Isabel said, clinging to the dollhouse.

I wanted to get rid of it. My mother had the dollhouse custom built for me. It was a replica of our house, down to the very last detail, but it was a mirrored version—everything was exactly the same, but slightly different. It had an eerie quality, like it had been dragged out of a surrealist painting. An entire floor was missing, the doors were off their hinges, and the stairs were all on an angle.

The one thing that struck me, that I didn't really notice until Isabel started playing with the dollhouse, was that all the rooms were identical—even the rooms I had already remodeled. The library was full of puffed-out reading chairs, and you could smell the fresh paint in it; but the rooms on the second floor, especially near the crying room, had peeling wallpaper and broken furniture.

"That's my room," Isabel said as she opened another door, another piece of the toy puzzle. "Look, there's my book and my bed, and there's my toy that I sleep with. Wow, Mommy, did you make this for me? I love it!"

I peered over her shoulder at the little replica of my daughter's room. There it was, replicated exactly. *Your mother must be working on it; that's why you haven't seen her in days.*

Yes, that explained it. She was hiding it as a surprise for Isabel.

"We should put it back for now. Obviously, whoever's working on it isn't quite finished. We ought to let them reveal it when they think the time is right," I said.

Isabel was disappointed but soon found another doll that turned out to have all its limbs and she forgot about the dollhouse.

I couldn't forget, though. It was too strange.

OTHER STRANGE THINGS kept happening at home, making me think the house was haunted. Could a house be haunted by a memory? Or by the trauma and emotions of its residents? If so, that would explain what was happening in my home. The dollhouse, which Isabel insisted should be on display in the library, kept changing as I continued painting, staining, and refinishing the house. I asked my mother if she was the one updating it, but she just ignored me. Even so, ever since I put it in the library, she spent a lot of her time sitting and staring at the dollhouse.

It was a good setup for me. As long as my mother was in the library, I could leave Isabel in there. She loved playing with the dollhouse, saying there was so much to explore with it. I didn't understand the appeal, since it was a copy of the house she lived in.

"Mommy, you don't understand. With the dollhouse we can explore without you being afraid. I could live in the dollhouse and I bet you'd feel more safe," was Isabel's only explanation.

The rooms I worked on took no time. It might have been a consequence of being shut in, but I lost track of time. My body wasn't governed by sunrise and sunset, since I didn't have to run errands that had to be planned around "opening hours." Because of that, I sometimes kept working until past midnight, but I rarely noticed. I would fall asleep for a few hours and when I woke up, it was morning. No matter the time, everyone else in the house adjusted their waking hours to match my own. Isabel was never into TV, and everything was on-demand nowadays anyway so it didn't matter to her when she watched them.

"I want to be close to you, Mommy. I want to protect you too, you know."

She was back to talking like an eight-year-old. Isabel claimed to have finished *Crime and Punishment*, but I knew that was impossible. It took college students months to get through that doorstopper of a novel; there was no way she was done. She probably just dropped it when something more interesting—the dollhouse, probably—came along.

Since I wasn't working on a typical schedule, I was able to get a lot more done on the second floor. My parents' bedroom was easy since they didn't want me in there anyway. All I had to do was refinish the door and reinstall the lock, which was rusted over. It took me a whole day just to refit the lock.

"You're stalling," my father said as he stood over me watching me install the new lock.

"I'm what?" I asked, my head buried in work.

"You're stalling, and you know it. This door doesn't take a whole day," he said, before going into his bedroom and lying down for a nap.

Down the hallway was the crying room. Isabel had put a silly sign up at the top of the stairs, pointing to the right. It was drawn to look like blood dripping, and she wrote: "This way to the crying room. Do not turn right."

Just being on that side of the house made my skin crawl. My father was right; I was stalling. I was looking for work on this side of the giant Victorian manor, hoping that it would delay the inevitable. I knew that having to work on that room would stir up memories that I didn't want to revisit. Years of my father's abuse, all boiled down to one thing—the dark, suffocating closet completely hidden from view.

The crying room was tiny, no bigger than a hall closet.

Being in there made me panic. There was never enough oxygen, and no matter what I did, I could never control my breathing enough to manage that panic. I couldn't breathe. It was simultaneously too hot and too cold. It was impossible to be comfortable. I couldn't really sit down, and it was too small to move around. The room was designed to torture you.

My dad locked me in the room when he was sick of the sight of me, which was often, or when I had defied his authority and needed to be reminded of my place. I wondered if he ever put my mother in there. It would explain her detachment.

I remember it always smelled like soil, which I couldn't understand. The crying room wasn't in the basement, it was up on the second floor. I came from a family of black thumbs so we didn't have plants that could have died in there or anything. I remembered once trying to follow some ivy to see if it wound up around that side of the building, but there was nothing.

It was so dark I couldn't see my hand in front of my face. Whenever my dad locked me in there, it took me a while to adjust to the light after I got out. Keeping the lights low and only using lamps helped when the crying room episodes were more frequent, which just added to the strange moodiness of our home.

I was pretty sure he was the one who built the crying room. Either that or it was an old maid's hallway that had been boarded up. That made sense to me since the door was hidden. When the door was closed, it looked like it was part of the wall. There was barely even a seam to indicate a doorway. The lock was hidden by an old light switch panel, which my father called a relic from a bygone age. Whenever people asked, he said he refused to take it out because it reminded him of how old the house was and how beautiful the craftsmanship was back then.

I wondered sometimes if people knew that I was crouched just behind the wall while he was waxing poetic about Victorian craftsmanship.

If it were up to me, I'd close the whole thing off. Fill it with cement and cover up the door to the little room, and forget that the crying room was ever there. Unfortunately, it wasn't up to me. My dad wanted the house to be restored to its former glory, and that included the crying room.

It took a long time for me to sleep that night. For once, I actually followed the rhythm of the sun and went to bed at a decent hour. My whole body was exhausted as I dragged myself up to my room from my workshop in the basement. As I came to the second-floor landing, I heard a strange crying noise. It sounded like someone was stuck.

"Isabel!" I called out, but no one answered.

The crying was coming from the direction of the crying room.

It's just an animal, Maggie. A racoon or a fox or something, I thought, trying to reassure myself that I hadn't accidentally trapped anything in there.

The crying got louder when I moved toward the room. The door was open, and I could see a tree blowing in the wind just outside the window. I wanted to go in there. I wanted so badly to go in and check on whoever was making that sound, but I felt paralyzed with fear. I couldn't take another step.

"It's just an animal, Maggie. It's an animal, and you're exhausted. Just go to sleep."

I turned and walked the other way, trudging up the stairs to my bed.

A COUPLE OF DAYS LATER, it happened again. I was dragging an old door up the stairs that I had just finished refurbishing in my workshop in the basement. Of course, my mother and father were downstairs and refused to help me. When I got to the second-floor landing, I heard it again. The muffled sounds of someone crying, louder this time than it was before. I dragged the door to where I needed to hang it, trying to ignore the sounds that were coming from the crying room.

I tried drowning out the sound by banging the heavy door onto its hinges, but it only got louder. It wasn't an animal, it was a human. *You're imagining things, Maggie. You passed your parents in the library downstairs. Isabel is up in her room, asleep. You are just inventing that noise because you're afraid of the crying room.*

I tried to ignore it. Tried to drown it out through my repairs, but no matter what I did I could hear it—the sound of someone sobbing and choking in the crying room. Was this a vague memory come back to haunt me?

I put away my tools and ran back down to the basement, popping my head into the library as I did. My mother was staring at the dollhouse, a book open in her lap. My father was asleep. *See? It couldn't have been them.*

I ran back upstairs to Isabel's bedroom to check on her. She'd been helping me in the basement before I forced her to come upstairs and sleep. When I got upstairs, her door was closed, which was unusual for her. Our rooms were the only two on this floor, so we rarely closed her door. I liked to be able to see into Isabel's room, make sure she was okay throughout the night.

"Isabel?" I gently knocked on the door, not wanting to wake her. I just needed to make sure she was in her room. "Are you awake?" I tried opening the door, but it was locked. I jiggled the little handle trying to force it open, but it didn't work. I couldn't make sure Isabel was in there because I couldn't hear her through the door. My body felt cold and hot at the same time as a wave of panic took over.

I ran back downstairs and stopped just before the crying room. The sound was louder than before, and it confirmed my worst fears. It wasn't an animal, it was the sound of a little girl crying. Her breath was wheezing and her sobs were clear from out in the hallway. There was someone in the crying room, and I couldn't find my daughter.

I ran into the room, spinning around looking for the light switch I knew was the catch. I knew I hadn't worked on this room, not since my parents asked me to refurbish the house, yet it seemed there was fresh wallpaper on the walls. Whoever did it had covered the light switch and made it so that you couldn't find the door. I ran my hand over the walls, trying to feel the subtle crease where the door was. The sound of crying got louder and started mixing with my own.

"Isabel, I'm coming for you, I promise!" I was convinced she was in there.

My father must have put her in there when I was dragging the heavy door up the stairs. He was pretending to be asleep all along, I was convinced. I scratched at the wallpaper trying to peel it down and reveal the door, but it was too thick. My head was spinning as I tried to formulate some kind of plan. I had blades downstairs; those could help peel it away. Using a steamer would take too long. I didn't have time; she'd run out of oxygen before I could coax the wallpaper down.

Finally I felt a bump. It was subtle, like someone was intentionally trying to hide the fake light switch. I worked my fingers around it, trying to find an air bubble or a gap of some kind. My nails were short and dull from all the work I was doing in the house, so I pawed at the wallpaper as tears streamed down my face.

Suddenly I was knocked backward off my feet. I felt an arm around my waist and a hand clasped my wrist.

My father bent down, bending my wrist backward, ignoring my yelps. "What the hell do you think you're doing?"

17

My eyes were blurry with tears as my father wrestled me away from the wall. I reached out, pawing at the wallpaper, but he was too strong for me.

"I'm going to ask you again, what the *hell* do you think you're doing?" he asked.

When I wouldn't answer, my father flung me against the wall. I hit my head and slid down the wall. I could still hear someone crying. Their sobs were ringing in my ears.

"Is it Isabel?" I cried. "Did you put her in there?"

My father laughed, stepping back into the room. "Do you really think I'd do that? That I would put that child in there?"

I only nodded as I glared at him. How dare he laugh, how dare he take joy out of my misery. He was an ugly, horrible man, and I wished I had the power to kill him then and there.

He threw his head back and laughed as if reading my thoughts and dismissing them. "I know you wish I was dead.

I know you probably dream about it at night—that I would just disappear and you'd get this whole house to yourself. My whole fortune in the palm of your hand for you to blow it all on some idiot boyfriend all over again. Sorry, it isn't all that easy."

"I can hear someone in there. I don't know who it is, but I can call the police—"

"And tell them what? That you're hearing crying through the wall? This town already thinks you're crazy; you'll just be inviting them in for a show." He laughed again, making a mockery of my panicked sadness.

I tried picking myself up, but I felt dizzy and disoriented. My whole body was trembling as my dad strode toward me.

"Tell me the truth, you little wimp. Do you want me dead or what?" he asked.

"Yes," I sputtered, "I do. I'm afraid of what you'll do to my kid. I'm afraid she's going to grow up just like me, and end up a zombie just like Mom. So yeah, I do wish you would die or just disappear." Tears were streaming down my face and I couldn't stop them. I couldn't get a handle on myself. All I could hear was someone sobbing and my father laughing.

"Well that's just too damn bad," he spat. "Because if you want to get rid of me, I'll take that little brat of yours. Yeah. You want to kill me? That's fine, but you'll be killing her too. I won't let you get away that easy."

My eyes widened in horror. I had no idea how he'd do it, and I didn't want to find out. "You can't. It's not possible. You can't take her away from me," I cried, tears and snot streaming down my face.

"I can do anything I want." My father punched the wall beside my face, denting the drywall and splitting the wallpaper just to prove a point.

I was shaking all over and wanted to vomit.

I heard his laughter thundering in my ears, but cutting through all of that, I heard the tiniest voice ask, "Mommy? Are you okay?"

Isabel was standing at the door, bedraggled and confused.

I quickly wiped my eyes so she wouldn't see me crying, and stumbled over to my daughter. I held her in my arms, touching her head and arms to make sure she was okay. She was alive, she was well, she was right in front of me, my own flesh and blood.

"I'm fine, honey, I'm fine. Where were you? You weren't in your room."

"The door got stuck and I couldn't open it, so I slept in your bed. I hope that's okay."

I felt like a balloon was deflating in my chest. Isabel was fine. Whatever I'd heard must have been a fox—they had a strange, human-like cry. My father hadn't touched Isabel. She still didn't know the fear and confusion of the crying room. Isabel was okay.

"That's okay, honey. You can sleep in my bed tonight, and tomorrow we'll fix the door," I said, turning Isabel around and sending her out the room.

Before I could leave, my father grabbed my arm. "Remember what I said. If I go, so does she." He chuckled as he brushed past me, ruffling Isabel's hair. My father danced down the steps, and I heard him slam the door to the library before he sent something crashing to the ground.

I COULDN'T SLEEP. My whole body was on edge. Every noise I heard woke me up, even when it was just a tree rapping at the window. Was it an animal? I could have sworn the noise I heard was human. It was so real there was no way my imagination came up with it—I was never that creative. Maybe I was right. Maybe this house was haunted. No ghost needed to come near this place, and it didn't have to be built on top of an ancient burial ground. None of that mattered. This house was haunted by my father's rage.

18

My dad's tirade didn't end there. He spent the next few days tormenting me, imitating a little girl's cries and laughing when I came rushing toward him. He roped Isabel into his little game too. She didn't understand how torturous it was. She was having a fun time with her grandfather. Once, as I was putting her to bed, she slapped me across the face and told me to snap out of it.

"Snap into reality, Maggie. This is your home, and it's the only home you've ever had," she said, before turning away from me in bed.

That was my father's influence. All this time I was so worried that he would start abusing my daughter the way he had done with me and my mom, I never thought he'd turn her against me.

Isabel needed a therapist. That would fix things. A therapist could examine why Isabel had such drastic mood swings. She could talk to a therapist without feeling like she had to be careful around me or my parents. If I found someone who was willing to work with me, maybe we could find a safe way to leave this house.

The only problem was getting her out of here. My father was adamant that Isabel wasn't allowed to leave—at all. Maybe we could arrange some kind of phone session, though then I couldn't be sure that my father wouldn't interfere in some other way. It needed to be somewhere outside his jurisdiction—somewhere where my father couldn't follow us.

"I'll be in Grandma's office, okay?" I whispered to Isabel as I helped her get ready. "I'm going to work on a surprise for her, so you can't tell anyone I'm in there, okay?"

"How come?" Isabel asked.

"Because then she won't be surprised. Just trust me, she's going to love it, but only if she's surprised. If Grandpa asks what I'm doing, you can tell him I'm in the basement working on a dresser—that's what I'll be doing this afternoon anyway."

"Okay." Isabel shrugged her shoulders. She asked, "Do you want me to come with you?" She was starting to pick up on how nervous I got when I left her alone, and had taken to telling me her daily schedule as we got ready in the morning.

I preferred it when she was outside, or in the library. Sometimes, when she squirmed and fussed, I knew my father had roped her into one of his little games.

"No, honey. I'd rather you played outside in the backyard today. That way you can get a little vitamin D—you're far too pale for a kid your age," I said, tickling her.

She giggled and swatted me away playfully. "I'd rather be pale than have sunburn. But fine, I think I need to run around a little and blow off some steam. I've been very moody lately and I think it's making me quite mean." She turned and went out of the room, whistling some nonsense nursery rhyme I had taught her.

I felt relieved. I could watch her from my mother's office as I made my phone calls, and I doubted my father would go out. He'd rather sit in front of the TV than do any form of exercise.

I went to the office and opened the phone book—the one directory I could think of. I was sure half of those names would be out of date, but for some reason the internet connection in this house was abysmal and I didn't want to deal with it today. I was teetering on the last sane nerve I had. A battle with technology was not what I needed.

I made a list of potential doctors and called one. My palms were sweaty as the phone rang.

"Hello. Dr. Jackson's office."

"Hi there. I... um... My name is Maggie—Margaret Conner, and I—"

"Oh... yes. Hi, Maggie. Yes, I do... I know who you are."

It was not entirely a surprise that she knew me. I lived in a small town. "Yes, well, I was just calling to inquire about an appointment for my daughter."

"Your daughter?"

"Yes. My daughter. I wanted to make an appointment for her, but... um... well, she can't leave the house at the moment so I wanted to know if Dr. Jackson makes house calls, or perhaps can conduct an appointment over the phone?"

There was silence on the other end of the line.

"Hello? Sorry, I didn't quite catch your name."

The receptionist cleared her throat. "Oh, it's Sandy. Sandy Jackson. My father is—"

"Oh, Sandy Jackson. I remember you. You were on the swim team, right?"

"Right. I was. Back in high school... anyway—I'm not sure if Dad— Dr. Jackson—is going to be able to make... er... house calls."

Figures. The sins from your past come back to haunt you, Maggie. I wasn't exactly nice to Sandy in school. She was a bit of a nerd and I had a blanket no-nerds, I-hate-everyone policy back then.

"Would it be possible to do a session over the phone?" I asked. "It's just that... well, she can't leave the house. It's a sensitive situation for us and... um... due to extenuating circumstances, my daughter is —"

"I'm sorry. Dr. Jackson is unavailable for that kind of appointment, but I think maybe another doctor would be. My dad's schedule is really full, so it's hard to fit in new patients. And he likes seeing his patients. Like, in person. I'm... sorry about that, Maggie—Miss Conner." She hung up.

I sat listening to the dial tone for a minute. Was this how all the phone calls were going to go? I didn't even get to speak to the doctor. His vindictive daughter got in the way. The Jacksons had lived in this town for generations, so they knew the exact reason why I couldn't leave my house, why I was talking to them like a stranger. I wondered how much money Sandy had received to keep my daughter from getting help. Just like the police in this town, my father's influence could stop any productive conversation in its tracks.

Forget it, Maggie. You don't have time to dwell on this. Your goal is to get Isabel some help, not wallow in self-pity.

I moved on to the next person.

"Dr. Bartesc speaking."

"Hello, Dr. Bartesc. My name is Maggie Conner and I was looking for a therapist for my daughter."

"Your daughter? Is this Margaret— Was your father Joseph Conner?" he asked.

I hesitated for a moment, thinking about the last phone call I had. "Yes, but please don't let that—please don't hang up."

I heard Dr. Bartesc put something down and sigh. It felt like an hour passed before he spoke. "What seems to be the issue, Maggie?"

I breathed a sigh of relief. "It's my daughter. She's showing signs of psychosis, I think. Like, I feel like she's turning into a little psychopath."

Dr. Bartesc chuckled at the description.

I was sure I wasn't the only parent to describe their child that way. "I want her to talk to someone. Someone completely unrelated to the family so she doesn't think she's going to get into trouble for saying anything, you know?"

"Yes," Dr. Bartesc spoke in a calm, soothing tone. "A lot of parents want the same thing for their child and hope to get some peace for themselves as well."

"Exactly! So I wanted to book a consultation with you but—well, there's a slight problem." Once again, I stumbled. "I can't bring her to your office, I'm afraid."

Dr. Bartesc inhaled sharply, like he was waiting for the "catch" and here it was. "Why is that?"

"You know my father, right? Well, he's become a bit of a recluse and I think he would feel uncomfortable letting Isabel—my daughter—leave. I also don't want to take her too far away from home. She's been having these horrible asthma attacks lately and she panics when she's far from home."

"Does she? What kind of symptoms does she have when she panics?"

"The usual, I think, for asthma. Breathing problems, heart palpitations, she gets sweaty and dizzy the further into these attacks she goes."

I could hear a pen scratching on the other end of the line. Was Dr. Bartesc taking notes on my daughter, or was he making notes about me? I couldn't tell, and I knew I had to put my anxieties to the side for now.

"It sounds to me like you have a solution in mind. Why don't you tell me what it is?" he asked.

"I wondered if you could do her sessions here, at our home. Or even over the phone if you're unable to come over. I just want someone for her to talk to, someone who can help with her intrusive and angry thoughts, and I'm trying to do the best I—"

"I'm going to stop you right there. I am afraid I might not be the man for the job. I am always committed to helping children find the help they need. However, I make it a point to meet with them in person, and I think many child therapists do as well. This is because children don't often have the same breadth of vocabulary as adults, and so they talk with their bodies as much as their mouths. Most child therapists will want to be in the room—or at least on video—with the young patient. Sadly, I can't pay house calls at the moment. I've suffered a bit of an accident this summer so I'm stuck at home, much the same as you."

Another dead end. At least this one was nice about it.

"So you're saying you can't take her on." I must have sounded exasperated, because I could hear Dr. Bartesc's sympathetic silence coming through the line.

"I do have a colleague that might be able to help. She

may be a little busy as well, but I can give her a call and tell her to expect to hear from you, if you like. She's a specialist in atypical behavior stemming from difficult situations."

"Yes!" I exclaimed. "Of course, I'll take your friend's number," I said, scrambling for a pen. I took it down, and put it to the side.

I had a few other people I wanted to call first. I wanted someone more experienced with kids, who lived a little closer to home. Maybe if it was nearby, I could sneak Isabel out for a session or two. If what Dr. Bartesc said was true, it would probably be best to try and work out a way to get Isabel to a therapist in person.

I spent hours on the phone, and I got nowhere. I exhausted all my leads and no one had been nearly as helpful or understanding as Dr. Bartesc. I felt traumatized after listening to people's judgmental voices over the phone. It was like they knew what was going on in my home, and looked down their noses at my choices as a mother. Didn't they understand how hard it was to escape a situation like this? Where was I supposed to go? Who was I supposed to turn to? I couldn't raise a child on love alone, but I was trying my best to do what I could in the situation I was in.

Not that anyone cared. They either hung up on me, laughed at me, or accused me of lying to them. All of them, except Dr. Bartesc. He made me understand *why* he wanted to see Isabel in person, and he knew my family but didn't get angry with me for being in a situation that was out of my control.

I looked up his referral but couldn't find her in that ancient phone book. It was possible she was new in town, or lived out of town. I supposed I wouldn't know until I called.

I passed the paper between my hands while I stared out

the window. I had written the specialist's phone number on the back of my father's old business card, ironically. I could hear him calling out to Isabel from downstairs, but she ignored him. She was playing in the garden, digging up flowers and making a bouquet.

Isabel saw me looking at her and waved. I waved back.

I finally called. "Hello. My name is Maggie Conner. I got your phone number from Dr. Andrei Bartesc. He referred me to you because you're a specialist in 'atypical behavior stemming from difficult situations'?"

"Hello, Miss Conner. Yes, I am Dr. Esmeralda Bolton. I am a specialist in trauma, if that's what you mean."

"Oh, I didn't realize— Sorry, he didn't describe it that way."

Dr. Bolton gently chuckled over the phone. I could tell she wasn't making fun of me, or trying to make me feel uncomfortable.

"That's okay. Andy Bartesc likes to use flowery language sometimes when he wants to protect a patient. Is this for you?"

"Oh, no, it's for my daughter. I understand that you probably want to see her in person, but I'm afraid we aren't able to leave the house at the moment. He said you might be willing to do a house visit?"

"Yes, I have done house visits before for previous patients, usually those who are agoraphobic or have other health concerns that means they are unable to leave the home. I'm sorry, did you say this was for your daughter? May I ask how old she is? Only you sound pretty young over the phone."

My stomach twisted itself into a knot. "She's eight. You're a child psychologist, aren't you?"

There was a pause over the phone. I could hear a mouse clicking in the background, like the doctor was reading something on her computer.

"I see. I have an email here from Dr. Bartesc advising that you were going to call…"

"I thought you were a child psychologist. I called asking for help for my daughter."

"I apologize. I actually don't work with children. I'm a psychologist specializing in trauma, mostly post-traumatic disorders, but I also see patients who are recovering from traumatic situations."

"I'm sorry," I continued, "I think this is a mistake. He must have meant to give me someone else's number. I'll leave you to your day."

I could hear Dr. Bolton start to say something on the other end of the line, but I hung up and started to cry. She was my last resort, the only hope I had to get Isabel some help in this town. No one would take her, and I didn't understand why. It couldn't have been that hard to come over to my home, but no therapist was willing to do so.

They probably want neutral territory where they wouldn't have parents or grandparents overhearing the session and making the kids clam up. I respected it, but it left me in an impossible position—how to keep my daughter sane when no one was willing to help.

19

Outside, Isabel was still picking flowers. She had created a number of bouquets, all laid out by the back porch. The garden was a mess, but I didn't mind. I'd never had much of a green thumb, so I wasn't planning on attacking the weeded-over mess that passed for a garden. All the more power to my eight-year-old to decide what was pretty enough to be picked.

After getting off the disappointing phone call with Dr. Esmeralda Bolton, I sat and watched Isabel play. She was so innocent and charming, my heart broke knowing that I didn't know how to help her. Later, I wished I had been closer to her that day.

Staring down at her from the office, I saw it starting. She always started coughing. It was small and spread out, like she got a piece of food caught in her throat and was trying to casually dislodge it without drawing attention to herself. My body tensed, ready to spring into action. They happened faster, her asthma attacks; one moment she was breathing just fine, the next she was clawing at her throat, unable to breathe.

I felt paralyzed with fear as I watched Isabel fall to her knees, coughing. I couldn't hear her but it looked as though she was coughing up a lung. Could our neighbors hear her? There was no one right next to us, but I wondered if she was loud enough for the Cabots to hear. If I wasn't here, would they have come running to save her?

I jumped up from the desk and ran downstairs. My legs weren't working as quickly as I wanted them to. I felt as though I was moving in slow motion.

My father popped his head out of the library as I ran past. "Where's the fire?" he gruffly asked.

I ignored him and blasted through the kitchen, onto the back deck. It was too late, and I didn't have an inhaler anyway. Isabel was on the ground, her mouth open in a sort of silent scream. My daughter's face and lips were greyish blue, and her eyelids were fluttering as she held onto her neck.

"Isabel! Isabel, Mommy's here!" I screamed as I ran toward her. I tried sitting her up, but Isabel's body was stiffer than a board. I couldn't get her to bend, couldn't get her muscles to relax. I searched for the inhaler, hoping it would turn up in the grass, but there was nothing.

Isabel's muscles started to twitch. For a moment I relaxed, hoping this meant her episode would be over soon —but it was the opposite. She started to convulse in the grass as she dragged tiny gasps of air into her body. The high-pitched wheeze made my ears ring, and her body was blurry as tears streamed down my face. I looked behind me and my father was standing in the doorway of the house.

"Do something!" I screamed. "Call an ambulance!" My

hands were hovering over Isabel. I tried to remember what you were supposed to do if someone was having a seizure—you had to make sure they didn't hurt themselves, wasn't that it? There weren't any rocks around her, and because she had been making bouquets there were little pillows of flowers all around her body. I tried to banish the funeral scene from my mind.

I turned back, and I saw my parents watching. "Why are you just standing there?" I screamed. I got up and ran toward my father. "Can't you see, she's going to die if we don't help her. You need to call an ambulance or something. We need to get her some help!"

"She's fine," he said. "She needs to work it out. Just leave her alone." He turned to go back into the house.

But I grabbed him by the arm. "I know you hate her, I know you hate what I did, but this is beyond that. You can't just leave an eight-year-old to die like that. She might be having an allergic reaction or a seizure. This is more than just asthma, more than a panic attack. She isn't doing this to take attention *away* from you—"

My father didn't wait for me to finish. He swung his arm around and swept me off the back deck.

I landed with a thud on the grass, the wind knocked out of me. My head was throbbing and I was dizzy getting back up.

My father was coming toward me, his face getting redder with each passing step. "Don't you dare call an ambulance for her. She doesn't matter. She is just some kid, an embarrassment. Aren't you ashamed of her? Now is your chance to get rid of her. Besides, you know you can't take her away from here. If you take her to the hospital, she'll never come back."

"I don't care," I lied. "I don't care if they take her away from me. At least she'll be safe." I was crying ugly tears now. I could feel snot pouring down my nose.

Sometime during our argument my mother calmly descended the steps to the garden and was standing over Isabel, keeping watch over her. "She doesn't seem to be getting better," she said calmly.

I couldn't take it. If they wouldn't act, I had to take matters into my own hands. I ran past my father, slamming the door behind me. There was a phone in my workshop. I just had to get there and I could call 911. Once I did that, there was nothing my father could do—they'd be coming. I threw a chair in front of the door and ran down the stairs to the basement. I picked up the phone just as I heard my father roar with anger upstairs.

"Hello, 911, what's your emergency?"

"I need help. My daughter is choking. She has asthma. I thought it was an asthma attack but it's not. She's convulsing and her lips are turning blue and—"

"Ma'am, I know it's hard but I need you to stay calm. What is your address and the nearest intersection?"

The phone call was a blur. I had no idea what she asked of me—my address, how to get into the home... I didn't know. I was crying the whole time. My voice shook so badly that I had to keep repeating myself.

"The ambulance is on its way, ma'am. They'll be there soon."

IT WAS ONLY TEN MINUTES, but it could have been ten hours and I wouldn't have known the difference. The ambulance came. I had run upstairs and was lying in the backyard with my daughter. I didn't know who opened the door for them; it must have been my mother. My father was screaming at me in the backyard, telling me I was stupid for doing this, stupid for inviting these men into our home.

She wasn't dead, not yet. They could still help her. It was just an extreme attack of some kind. I had to get her some medicine, start tracking her symptoms, and Isabel would be okay.

"Ma'am, where's the child?" I heard someone call out.

I was crying, my father's voice ringing in my ears.

"She's there! She's on the ground. She's turning blue, can't you see that?" I cried, tears streaming down my face.

The paramedics looked confused.

"Did you move her?" one of them asked.

The other one stopped his partner and came over to me. "Ma'am, what's your name?"

"Maggie Conner," I replied.

He nodded and crouched down in front of me, looking deeply into my eyes. His gaze was comforting, like he wanted to coax me to relax.

I started to breathe more slowly, mimicking his own breathing.

"Your daughter was convulsing, is that right?" he asked.

I just nodded. The tears were still streaming down my face, but I wasn't as panicked anymore.

"Can you pick her up? Children are sometimes scared when it comes to an ambulance. I don't want her convulsions to get worse."

I nodded, and he helped me up. I collected Isabel's tiny little body, her torso shuddering as she tried to breathe.

The paramedic smiled at me, gently taking her hand to

measure her pulse. "She's gonna be okay. Her pulse is still strong," he said, guiding me through the house.

His partner ran ahead of us. I saw my mom at the stairs, hiding from the paramedics but staring wide-eyed at my daughter.

When we got into the ambulance, they let me put Isabel on a stretcher, and I brushed her hair away and gave her forehead a kiss. Her eyes were still wide, and her body was still shaking. She looked at me, through me, and beyond into the ether. I sobbed, terrified that this was the last time I would see my daughter.

"You can ride with her," the calm paramedic said. "There's another bed set up, so you might have to lie down."

I nodded and followed him into the ambulance van, and lay down on the gurney, holding Isabel's hand.

Then, everything went black.

20

I felt like I was underwater.
I could hear people talking, but they were all far away and their voices were muffled. I couldn't think straight. My thoughts were coming to me slowly. I was drowning, but I didn't feel wet.

We sedated her in the van. She was hysterical.

This patient is on haloperidol and fluoxetine. Didn't you know that?

How were we supposed to know?

Well, did you ask her?

Listen, we're here to administer emergency services. Sometimes there isn't time to—

Get out of my sight!

I remembered getting into the ambulance with Isabel. She was still convulsing and struggling to breathe. The paramedics had her lying on a gurney. I was lying on a gurney beside her. There wasn't enough space to sit so they let me lie down. That's when everything went black.

They must have sedated me.

The nurse was angry with them. She kept talking about my medications—anti-depressants and the psychosis drugs I had been prescribed by doctors who couldn't understand what was going on in my house. I didn't need more tranquilizers—but of course, the paramedics didn't know that.

My body felt heavy, but I desperately wanted to get up. I wanted to know what happened to my daughter. Was she still alive? Was she being treated at this hospital, or had they transferred her to the children's hospital? Did someone call CPS? If I woke up, would I be reunited with my daughter?

Soon, the medication took over again, and I fell back asleep. Back into the quiet darkness of tranquilizers, sedatives, and an IV drip.

"Miss Conner, are you awake?" I heard the echoing voice of a nurse calling to me. She sounded very far away. I opened my eyes and saw her haloed head; she looked like an angel wearing hospital scrubs.

"I think so. I think I'm awake, but I can't tell. I'm feeling so tired," I mumbled. My mouth was dry and my head felt foggy. It was hard to cobble together a sentence.

"Can you sit up?" the nurse asked, her voice sickly sweet.

"I'm too tired," I said. My eyes were closing again. I could hardly keep them open. I had to ask about Isabel but I didn't think I'd stay awake long enough to hear the answer.

"Where's my daughter?" I rasped.

The nurse cocked her head—because the light was behind her, I couldn't quite see her face. It gave her body a nightmarish quality— yes, she was an angel, but her darkened face made her seem like the angel of death. I hoped today wasn't the day she was coming for me.

"What do you mean?" she asked, sweetly again.

"My daughter. I came in with my daughter. Where is she? Is she okay?"

I heard a rustle of papers and the angel appeared in front of me again.

"I'm afraid I don't see anything about a daughter on your chart. You were sedated when you came in here. Are you sure you weren't dreaming?"

Her face morphed as she spoke. Dark clouds swirled around what was supposed to be her face. She looked like a black hole or an eclipse, sucking me back into the darkness.

"Where's my daughter?" I muttered, as the darkness took over and I fell back into a dreamless sleep.

I WOKE up a few hours later. I was in a private room. Everything was bright and white and clean. It was the opposite of the moody darkness of my home. I was still tired and felt stiff. There was a throbbing pain in my arm where they had inserted the IV, and my whole body felt like lead.

I managed to push myself up onto my elbows so I could take a look around. I was alone. The room was empty except for a chair and some medical equipment. It was a private room; I wasn't sharing with a stranger, but I also wasn't sharing with my daughter.

She must be at the children's hospital, I thought. That was the only explanation—the children's hospital was better equipped to treat an eight-year-old.

Outside it was dark. I had slept away most of the day.

Isabel didn't have me to put her to sleep. She must be terrified. I was terrified for her, scared that I would never see my daughter again, afraid that the paramedics had told someone what was happening in my home and that my daughter was already being processed through the foster care system.

I could feel myself panicking, but the trace amounts of sedative coursing through my bloodstream were keeping me from freaking out. Something felt wrong. Everything felt too far away to be real. My head was hurting, and I felt confused. Where was everyone?

Just as I had that thought, a nurse swept into my room carrying some pillows. She smiled when she saw me. "Miss Conner, you're finally awake! Must have been a nice sleep."

"Where's my daughter?" I asked, stopping the nurse in her tracks. I was sorry to be so abrupt, but I had to know Isabel was safe.

"What do you mean?" she asked.

I could see she was confused but trying to stay positive; the smile on her face didn't break for a second. If you had told me it was a mask, I would have believed you.

"My daughter Isabel—we were brought here in the same ambulance. No one has told me anything about her condition or where she is. Why isn't she in the room with me?" My voice was trembling now. No amount of sedation could pacify a mother's worry.

The nurse ignored me and went about her business, checking my vital signs and replacing the pillow that was behind my head. "I think you must be confused. You came in alone. You claimed you took too many pills and were feeling nauseous. The doctors found you mixed your medication in an almost lethal way. It's very lucky you came in when you did. You could have been very sick for a long time."

"I don't remember taking any pills today. I remember the paramedics. They were kind. They put me in the van beside my daughter. He said my daughter would be okay, that her pulse was strong." I grabbed the nurse's arm, causing her to stifle a shriek. "Is she at the children's hospital?" My grip was harder than I intended. I could see in her eyes that she was in pain. I wanted to apologize, to tell her that a mother's worry made her strong, practically superhuman, but when I opened my mouth no sound came out.

The nurse peeled my fingers off her arm and laid me back down in bed. She was gentle but strong. Clearly she'd done this before; I couldn't get out of her grip. The room started spinning around me as the nurse called out to someone in the hall.

"Get her down!" she screamed. "She's too strong for me!"

That's not true, I thought. *I can barely move my arms. You're the one holding me down.*

The nurse and an orderly held me down in bed as another wave of sedative exhaustion took over. The last thing I remember seeing was the nurse's face eclipsed against the fluorescent light of my hospital room.

I WOKE up again an hour later. The room was still spinning, and the lights felt even brighter than before. I was beginning to think the hospital was trying to keep me sedated, because any time I tried to wake up I fell immediately back into that black hole of unconsciousness. This time as I blinked my eyes open I saw my father leaving my hospital room.

That explains everything. He was probably trying to cover up that I had come to the hospital, scrubbing himself clean of the scandal. If my father was here, that meant there was something the nurses wouldn't tell me. I needed someone other than that Angel Nurse, the one who was stronger than she looked, who always had a deranged smile on her face. I needed to find someone who could tell me where my daughter was being held and if she was okay.

Just as I was thinking it, the nurse came in.

"Where is she?" I asked, as soon as the door closed behind her. I was still lying back on my pillow. This time I was too tired to get out of bed.

"Good morning to you too. Well, good evening, I guess. Are you feeling a little better?" The angel wasn't so angelic.

I could hear the vitriol in her voice, but didn't she understand I just wanted to know about my baby? I needed to know where she was. I had to stay awake.

"A little. I feel pretty groggy."

"That is completely normal. You've been sleeping all day."

"You mean I've been drugged all day," I muttered.

The nurse turned around sharply. "What did you say?"

"Nothing," I said, smiling as best I could. "Just that I can't believe I've been here all day."

She nodded, satisfied with my answer. "Sometimes we need rest. Our bodies need that time to recharge, and when we aren't giving that to ourselves, well, it often results in our bodies breaking down. They stop listening to our demands to stay awake and ignore what's going on inside of us."

This nurse, who seemed like the brightest flower in a bouquet, had something else to her. Was she conspiring with my father? No matter what I did, I couldn't focus on her face.

The light in here was too bright, and she kept turning away from me. Was it something in the sedative?

"I know I asked before, but where's my daughter?" I asked her.

She froze again, this time fiddling with something in the IV bag. "Sweetheart, I don't know what you mean. You arrived here alone."

"Then they dropped her off at the children's hospital before I came. Who is going to pick her up? Is she alive? She was blue in the face when I called the ambulance."

The nurse swung her body toward me. There it was again, the same eclipse as before. Her head haloed by the fluorescent light behind her. When she looked directly at me my stomach churned.

This must be a dream. That's why I can't focus on her face. This has all been a crazy dream. I'm still asleep right now.

I needed to wake up and get out of this bed before they sedated me again.

"My dear, you don't have a daughter."

"Did my father tell you that? I saw him in here, talking to someone."

"Your father? Honey, no one has been in your room."

The room started to swirl around her. All of a sudden everything got brighter. I squinted my eyes against the light, trying to fight the oncoming darkness.

"Please, no. Please, don't put me to sleep again," I said. I could feel it at the edges of my consciousness. "Whatever he did, please don't let him do this again. I have to stay awake for Isabel. I don't know what my father said but please don't put me to sleep again."

"What did you say?" the nurse turned to me and asked. Her face was smiling, but it was still shrouded in darkness.

The room was spinning again. I could feel myself falling. I had to stay awake. I had to get out of here.

"Don't put me to sleep again. I just want to see my daughter, please!" I could feel tears stinging my eyes. Was the nurse sympathetic? I didn't know. I turned away from her and tried to lift myself up on my elbows, but the drugs were starting to take effect—either that or they hadn't worn off yet. I fell back into the bed, onto my left side now, using the momentum to roll myself onto my front. I could hear the nurse scrambling to come around the bed.

"Miss Conner, please, we're trying to help you. Get back into bed."

"Where is my daughter?" I yelled. "Why won't you let me see her?"

"You don't have a daughter, Miss Conner. You came in here alone. Don't you understand? We're trying to help you, but I can't help you if you won't get back into bed."

I felt nauseous. I knew I was going to throw up. It took all my strength to shove the nurse off me. She tumbled backward to the ground, her arms over her face like she was cowering from the light. I had a headache. Pain was pulsating through my temples and I could feel vomit teasing the back of my throat. Whatever the hospital had given me was still in my system. My body wanted to rest, but I couldn't let it. I had to get out of there and find Isabel.

"Miss Conner!" the nurse screamed as I swung my legs off the bed. As I did, the room spun, everything turned by ninety degrees and I was on my back again, this time climbing up the wall. The nurse tumbled down beside me onto the bed, unable to keep herself upright as the world tilted sideways. The hospital was connected to my father. I had to escape before they did something to Isabel. He could use this opportunity, while I was trapped and drugged, to get rid of the granddaughter he never wanted. I trudged to the door and pulled it open toward me. The world righted itself as I tumbled out into the hall.

The hallway was dark compared to my room. It took a moment before I could adjust my gaze. Hospital staff and other patients stared at me, and I could hear an alarm going off in the distance. Everything around me was happening in slow motion. From one end of the hall, I saw my father and two orderlies running toward me. My legs still felt heavy, and the flashing lights hurt my eyes.

Get out of here. Don't stop, just go! the little voice inside my head screamed and I started running down the hall away from my father. He must be behind all of this—the sedation, the nurse lying to me, the "accidental" combination of medications. His footsteps echoed down the hall as I struggled to escape. I knew I wouldn't be able to beat them, so as soon as I had the chance, I turned a corner and slipped into the first room I saw. Luckily for me, it was just a supply closet. I could hide in there for a while. Hopefully, they would just run past me. I just had to wait it out for a little while, wait for the drugs to pass through, and get out of this hospital. I would probably look insane, roaming the streets in a hospital gown, but the town already thought I was a recluse so what did that matter?

I locked the door and threw my weight against it. I was exhausted. I spent the last bit of my energy dragging a nearby shelf in front of the door. That would keep me safe until they ran by me. That would keep me safe until I woke up again.

I WAS WRONG.

I woke up again just as I had before, feeling like I was being held underwater. The nurse was there, her face framed by a halo of fluorescent lighting. I had the distinct feeling that the room was sideways and I was being held up against the wall. I tried to move my arms, but they were glued to my side.

"It's for your own protection," she said, grinning down at me.

I could hardly move my head, but I felt the leather strap across my forehead. The bed was too tight, the covers too constricting.

"I don't feel comfortable," I mumbled.

"It's not very comfortable, I'm afraid. But like I said, it's for your own good. Once you calm down, maybe we can undo some of the belts." The nurse patted my forehead and walked away.

I realized I couldn't follow her with my head. My arms were strapped to the bed, my forehead pressed against the pillow. I tried to kick up my legs, but they were also restricted. I looked down and could see a belt across my chest.

You're restrained in your bed. They've got you now, I thought. I prayed everything was okay with my daughter. I hoped I would wake up from this nightmare and finally be able to go home. I wondered when they would stop pumping me full of sedatives. I couldn't even sleep; my head and stomach were in too much turmoil.

"Hey!" I called out. "I don't feel well. Can you loosen these? Or stop the medication?"

No one answered.

The room spun again. I was looking down at the ground,

but the ground was the ceiling. I could hear a clock ticking somewhere. It was getting louder and louder.

"Hello! Can somebody help?" I cried, but no one answered me.

All I could do was lie there and wait for this nightmare to be over.

21

"*How are you feeling today, Maggie?*

I'm exhausted, I've barely slept, everyone refuses to tell me what happened to my daughter, and I'm being treated like I'm a crazy woman—how the hell do you think I feel?"

"I feel great!" I said, smiling at Nurse Caplan.

Angelica Caplan had been my nurse since that first night in the hospital, and she came to check up on me while I was held there. According to them, having someone consistent would help me recover. I, personally, disagreed. Having Nurse Caplan around did nothing but remind me of the day I went into the hospital and was drugged beyond my own understanding before being chased through the halls by my father. His influence knew no bounds.

THE NEXT MORNING, after my nightmarish ordeal, I woke up to an older man sitting in the chair next to my bed. I was still strapped down, but thankfully the restraints around my head were gone. He was kind, he smiled at me, he waited until I was properly awake to tell me that the hospital was keeping me for a few days, under "observation."

"Do you know what I mean by 'observation'?" he asked.

I knew that tone. I knew I had to play along, or else I would never be released from here.

"I'm guessing the hospital needs to keep me for a few days to make sure I'm not in any danger."

The old man nodded.

I wasn't sure if this was another strange dream, but finally the walls weren't spinning and I could actually see his face. I guessed it was real and I was being kept at the hospital against my will while Isabel was somewhere... else. I still didn't know where.

"The nurse said you came here alone, but that you believe you came here with your daughter?"

I know for a fact that I came here with my daughter in an ambulance. What I don't know is where the ambulance took her.

"An ambulance brought me. They sedated me and I blacked out. I woke up here but I think I was having hallucinations. I kept waking up and falling asleep. The last time I woke up I was strapped to the bed."

"Did that scare you?"

"Wouldn't you be scared if you woke up from a nightmare into another nightmare? I couldn't tell what was real and what was a dream. At one point it felt like the whole room turned on its side," I said, trying to keep the anger out of my voice. That wouldn't help me here. I had to answer their questions, I had to make sure they thought I was okay, and I had to go home.

"I understand. That was probably a side effect of all the

medications mixed up in you. Antipsychotics, antidepressants—the ambulance sedated you but they didn't realize you had these kinds of drugs in your system. That's why the effect was so powerful."

"When will I be able to go home? Or at least be able to lie in my bed without restraints all over me?" I asked.

The old man—the hospital psychiatrist, I assumed—sighed. He leaned his head back and stared at the ceiling. "We can't keep you against your will forever. Once the hospital sees that you aren't going to be a danger to yourself, we have to let you go. I would recommend a longer stay, however. You seem to be under a great deal of stress. You talked about your daughter—"

"Is she okay?"

"Yes," he reassured me. "Your daughter is fine. She's been sent home and is being taken care of."

My stomach tied itself back in knots. I must have looked worried because the doctor tilted his head as he observed me. I ought to have done nothing, or swallowed up that anxiety. Anything that showed my inner turmoil could keep me strapped to this bed longer, putting my daughter's mental health at risk.

"Are you concerned about her?" he asked. "Do you feel she is unsafe at home?"

"No, no, not at all, she should be fine. I'm just worried that... that it will take me too long to be better. For her, you know? I want to make sure I'm able to take care of her."

"Of course you are, just as any mother would be. I'll try to visit again, but it seems that you're tired right now. I was only here to observe. Why don't you rest for a little while longer and we can get back to your mental state?" He got up from his chair, patted my hand, and left the room.

The doctor seemed familiar somehow, but I had no idea where I had seen him before. Maybe he just had one of those faces, because I couldn't place him. He was right; I felt exhausted. I should take this time to sleep. As a mother, I didn't know when I'd get the chance at an uninterrupted night of sleep again. The interaction felt dreamy. I wasn't yet convinced that I was actually awake, that the doctor was real, and his assessment meant anything.

But it hammered home one thing—I had to behave, or else I'd be going nowhere.

I DIDN'T SEE the doctor again. I hoped that meant I passed his little "test." All that was left was for me to *not* piss off the nurse who was caring for me—again—and I would be able to leave the hospital in a few days.

"The combination of drugs in your body could have been lethal. You're lucky the ambulance arrived when they did," the nurse kept saying to me.

"Would probably have been luckier if they hadn't tried to sedate me on the way over," I grumbled.

The nurse pressed her lips together to keep herself from saying anything. I was right—the doctor basically told me as much—but obviously she didn't like being talked back to by her patients.

Keep a cool head, Maggie, and you'll be out of here sooner than if you scream and complain. I knew that, no matter whom my father paid, the hospital couldn't keep me for very long. The psychiatrist told me so—after a certain point, a consenting adult who was capable of making their own decisions could check themselves out of care. I was waiting for that moment to come. The doctors were still coming around to make sure my vital signs were consistent and regular. I was still getting put to sleep against my will. But that couldn't last too long.

"Is there a chance I can see the psychiatrist again?" I asked Nurse Caplan. "I think it would be nice to talk to him a little bit, for my personal well-being. It feels strange not talking to anyone." I smiled up at her as sweetly as I could. Now that I could see her face, I noticed Nurse Caplan was sporting a large bruise on her left eye, and a couple of smaller ones on her right arm—I guessed it was from the time I tried to escape but couldn't get the room to stop spinning.

"I suppose I could arrange an appointment. I'll check with your primary care doctor," she commented before scurrying out of the room.

Another doctor came, different from before. He wasn't as kind or gentle, and he wasn't as honest with me when it came to the circumstances surrounding my hospital stay. Every time I asked a question about the day I was admitted, he quieted down and asked why I needed to know that information. It was infuriating.

I decided to stop trying to "figure out" the hospital. They worked in mysterious ways, and I wasn't interested in solving that. I just wanted to go home—the sooner the better. Instead of asking for clarification and care, I asked for books and magazines to pass the time. I was polite and quiet with Nurse Caplan, and I was very gentle when she started helping me out of bed and taking walks with me around the hospital. I said please and thank you with a smile, and waited until I could be released.

It took three days, but finally I was allowed to leave. My legs were weak from lying in bed all day so I needed to be wheeled out to the waiting room where, of all people, Lana Cabot was waiting for me.

"Bill and I saw the ambulance the other day, and I made sure to ask where they were taking you," she explained.

"Wow, thank you, Lana. You really didn't have to do that. I could have made my way home. I have money for a taxi and—"

"Nonsense. You're our neighbor. That's what neighbors are for." Lana smiled and helped me out of the chair.

She had a comforting presence, the kind of person you knew had been a great mom. The kind of mom who listened to her children, helped with their homework, and made elaborate breakfasts on weekends. She was the kind of mom I aspired to be.

She helped me into the backseat and sat with me while Bill drove us home. He was a little more awkward. The dad who wasn't connected to his emotions but still supported his children no matter what they wanted to do. The type of dad who could be found on the sidelines of a basketball game or in the front row of a play, cheering enthusiastically.

"Thank you for picking me up. This is really too much. I didn't even realize you'd be here."

"Bill needs to practice his driving. Growing up in Manhattan you learn a lot of things, but being comfortable behind the wheel of a car is certainly not one of them," Lana teased.

Bill rolled his eyes. "Lana's been checking up on you," he said, looking at me through the rear-view mirror. "She's been calling the hospital every day for updates on your condition."

I couldn't believe it. I had barely ever spoken to Lana, and I was sure Mary had persuaded her that I was crazy. I never thought that she could be an ally to me in this town.

Lana smiled at me sheepishly. "I had a friend who went through a similar situation. She had agoraphobia, and once she got confused and took the wrong medication and ended up in the hospital. She was in there for days as doctors kept throwing drugs at her, hoping something would work."

"Why didn't she just tell them what her medication was? Surely they would have found something that could make her better."

Lana shook her head. "She felt so anxious and panicked from having to leave her house that she couldn't speak. She was like a mute at the hospital. It took days for me to find someone who would listen to me. No one would let me in to see her—they restricted it to family, but she had no family in the area who understood her condition. I finally managed to get through and tell them of her condition, which made things easier. A kind psychiatrist intervened and made her feel comfortable enough to communicate with the medical staff. She was in the hospital for weeks." Lana brushed tears away from her eyes.

I didn't know what to say, so I just patted her hand.

"Doctors are sometimes so busy they forget they're treating people," Bill added, before going silent again.

A man of very few words, but he chooses them very well, I thought.

"Thanks for checking on me," I said. "I hope I didn't worry you too much."

Lana waved away my concern. "We have to look after

each other in our neighborhood. The rest of the town acts as if it's going to swallow them whole if they set foot on our street." She chuckled, but I could see that underneath her laughter it really hurt her feelings.

I felt guilty; after all, my family was the reason no one in town dared step on our street. The Conners were cursed, as far as they were concerned.

"If there's ever anything I can do, please just let me know. We're right across the street, not far away at all. And I can give you my phone number so you can call whenever you need it," she added.

I stared out at the other cars on the highway and let my mind wander.

"Actually," I said after a few minutes of silence, "there might be something you can help with."

"Of course, hon, whatever you need."

"It's my daughter," I continued, hoping what I was about to say wouldn't make the Cabots turn the car around and beeline for the psych ward. "She's been acting incredibly strange lately."

"She must be going stir crazy. This summer has been hotter than usual, and she doesn't have school to keep her occupied." Lana giggled.

Bill gave her a stern look in the rear-view mirror.

"It's actually not that. I mean, she's as restless as any other eight-year-old, but her behavior can't be explained that easily. She's been a little…" I trailed off, unsure of how to continue.

Lana stroked my arm gently, encouraging me to continue.

"She's been really weird lately," I blurted out.

Lana and Bill both laughed.

"That's not what I thought you were going to say at all," Lana said. "Don't worry, she's eight. Kids go through a phase where they say the weirdest, creepiest stuff and then one day they just grow out of it."

"Our kid used to go up to the ticket collector at the subway and ask if he lived in the subway tunnels and if he could show her around his lair," Bill added. "We had to start walking four blocks to the next stop because we were so embarrassed."

I giggled along with them, relieved that I wasn't the only parent who went through this.

Then I thought about her changes in mood, the influence my father had on Isabel, and I continued. "It's not just that. Some of it I can explain away as my daughter deciding she's going through a goth phase, but some of it is more concerning. Her mood will change on a dime, and then she'll go back to being completely normal. And I mean she'll go from reading in her room to entering a destructive mode, completely tearing her own bed apart. Sometimes she tries to play pranks that are absolutely cruel, usually on her grandmother, and the minute it's over she apologizes profusely and acts like it was a completely different person playing the prank. At first I thought the apology was an act, but as time has gone on, I think she's disassociating or something in those moments."

"Kids go through behavior issues like that sometimes, especially when an adult isn't paying enough attention to them," Lana said, her voice getting softer.

Bill coughed and cleared his throat.

Lana sighed. "Bill likes to think city-living is better for kids. Keeps them from getting bored and going through destructive phases like that."

"You learn the consequences of disturbing others much faster than when you live in a vast town or suburb like this one," he muttered, still glaring at Lana, looking like he was begging her to shut up.

"It's not the destruction that scares me, it's the changes in her personality. She's an entirely different person when she goes through these episodes, and it scares me. She also keeps talking about things she could never have known, people she could never have met. It's like she's infiltrated my brain and is pulling out all the pieces of a puzzle I haven't given her yet, and I don't know what to do about it. And then there's her panic attacks."

"Isabel is having panic attacks?"

"That's just what I've been calling them. They come on suddenly and disappear just as quickly. She starts coughing and wheezing, like she's just having an asthma attack. Then, she starts choking and clawing at her throat. The attacks end with her face slowly turning blue, and after the last one— the reason I called the ambulance in the first place—she's started having these strange seizures. The attacks used to be over in seconds, but they've been getting longer and longer. She coughs and drags in dregs of a breath, holding her throat, and I don't know what to do about it. The hospital didn't tell me anything, only that she was perfectly fine. Even the paramedics didn't seem that worried about her when they picked us up."

"Have you tried to find help for her?" Lana asked. "There must be at least one child therapist or physician in this town that can help."

I shook my head. "I've called every therapist and they won't see her. Isabel can't leave the house, and none of them will make house calls. We don't have a pediatrician right now. We're on a couple of wait lists but everyone seems to be full up. I wish my old doctor hadn't retired, or else I'd call him." I stared into my hands, fighting back tears.

Lana held my hand and Bill drove in silence.

"Maggie, are you a religious person?" she finally asked.

I just shrugged my shoulders, unsure of how to answer her question.

"It might be worth it to talk to a priest," she continued. "If your daughter is suffering from panic attacks and you can't find medical help, it could be another avenue for you."

"What do you mean? Like my daughter is possessed or something?"

"She could be," Bill added. "We live in homes that have had many lives before us. There's no telling what kinds of spirits live inside their old walls. Not all of them are going to be kind ones."

I was suddenly very weirded out being in a car alone with the Cabots.

"Bill is a believer in the paranormal. I am open to believing anything if it can't be proven wrong. Who knows, maybe an exorcism could work on little Isabel, but also maybe a priest can give you advice. Advice that medical professionals can't."

I wasn't really sure what to say to that. I just nodded and stared out the window. The rest of the drive was silent.

22

The Cabots waved to me from their driveway after dropping me off.

I stood on the porch waving to them until they went inside, mostly because I was afraid to go in. I wasn't sure what would be waiting for me on the other side of that door. Would it be three starving family members who had gone without a meal for the weekend? Or my father might be screaming at my mother and daughter for who knew what reason. I had no idea what to expect.

Which made it very surprising when there was nothing going on.

"Hello?" I called out as I entered the house.

It was silent, but I could hear the sound of the TV coming from the living room.

"I'm home!" I yelled, but no one answered. I listened carefully for the sound of my parents upstairs, or Isabel's plodding footsteps. There was nothing. It was like I was walking into an empty home. I crept down the hall and poked my head into the living room. My parents were in there, watching some old sitcom.

"Hi, you two," I said. "Did you miss me?"

My mother didn't turn around. She barely even blinked.

My father stood up and put his hands on his hips. "You left the house a mess. Your mother was cleaning up after you all weekend. Also, thanks to your little 'vacation' we're behind on the remodel. You still have the rest of the second floor to do, and also the third floor. I don't care if you've made that your little apartment; I expect it to be repaired and refinished just like the rest of the house. No use skimping and having the wood rot or something."

Then he brushed past me. The smell of his beer followed him out of the room and down the hallway. I hadn't realized it, but my body was braced for the worst. When my father walked past me with barely even a shoulder bump, I finally exhaled. I turned around and ran up the stairs as quietly as I could, before my father could realize he hadn't boxed my ears on the way to his umpteenth beer of the day.

I took a walk around the second floor to review what needed to be done. The parlor, the room that contained the crying room, still needed to be finished. The walls needed to be repainted, and the floor definitely needed to be restained. Years of my father's angry footsteps had left their mark. There were scratches on the floor, and I was dreading the day when I would need to sand it and try not to remember which scratches were made by the furniture and which had been made by my own fingernails. I shuddered and left the room, closing the door behind me.

I'll add it to my to-do list and deal with it tomorrow, I thought.

Isabel was lying on her bed in her room. She had that

dusty old copy of *Crime and Punishment* in front of her, dutifully reading with her finger on the page to keep her place. I wondered why she'd started reading it again.

"*What was taking place in him was totally unfamiliar, new, sudden, never before experienced. Not that he understood it, but he sensed clearly, with all the power of sensation, that it was no longer possible for him to address these people in the police station, not only with heartfelt effusions, as he had just done, but in any way at all, and had they been his own brothers and sisters, and not police lieutenants, there would still have been no point in his addressing them, in whatever circumstances of life.*"

She was reading aloud to herself in the quiet of her room. A book that was way too mature for her age—it was even beyond the comprehension of most people twice her age. I had never read it, though I did remember my father grumbling about it. He always called the people in this town uncultured because they hadn't read as much as he did. To him, the fact that he made his fortune from nothing meant there were cultural markers he had to tick off, things like going to the opera and reading Russian literature. It enraged him to find out that people who were born into wealth didn't really *do* these things. They got by on money alone.

"Guess who?" I said, gently knocking on Isabel's door. I was expecting her to run into my arms after three days away from me.

"Oh, hi, Mommy! Mommy, what does 'effusions' mean?" she asked, keeping her index finger on the page.

"Um, it kind of means the gas that something is giving off. Like it's pouring off or something."

"Oh! So this means that the heart is like giving off a lot of passion and stuff, right?" Isabel cocked her head waiting for my answer.

I just nodded. Seeing my little girl reading was making me want to cry. I went over and sat down next to her in bed, closing the book and putting it on her nightstand.

"Make sure you put the bookmark in," she cried. "I don't want to lose my place; it's getting good."

"Is it? Are you liking *Crime and Punishment*?" I teased, kissing her little forehead.

"I dunno," she shrugged, "but it's fun to read. There's a lot of stuff in the book. It just keeps going and going and going."

Isabel snuggled into my arms and I pet her hair. We sat there like that, in silence, for a little while, and I soaked up the calm of my strange little girl.

"Is everything okay, Mommy? You seem sad."

"I'm not sad at all. I'm just so happy you're okay."

"Why wouldn't I be? You weren't home so I stayed in my room, just like you asked."

"You're feeling better after the other day? No lingering breathing problems or anything?"

"What do you mean? Like I ran out of breath or something?"

"Yes. The other day, you ran out of breath so badly you turned blue. You kept holding your neck and I got so worried I called the ambulance, don't you remember?"

Isabel shook her head.

I blinked, confused at her reaction. The moment was still so fresh in my mind, so terrifying to think about. I couldn't forget Isabel's tiny body convulsing in the backyard, and the strange moment I put her in the back of an ambulance just before I lost consciousness.

"You went to the hospital, honey," I continued. "I don't know what happened after that. Mommy had to go to the hospital too and they didn't tell me what was going on with you." A single tear rolled down my cheek, and Isabel wiped it away with one of her tiny fingers.

"It's okay, Mommy. I don't remember, so neither should you. You should just forget about what happened. It's not really that important. Besides, I'm feeling as good as new, which means my breath is perfect. Do you want to see? I can hold my breath for ten whole seconds and it's not even that hard! I've been practicing—watch."

Isabel plugged her nose and puffed out her cheeks. I wanted to laugh but all I could see were her little blue lips gasping for air. I unplugged her nose and playfully deflated her cheeks.

"I believe you, but I don't want to play that game right now. Why don't we do something else."

"Do you want to go upstairs and play witches? It's almost magic hour, which is the perfect time because then maybe our spells will do something unexpected!" Isabel said, jumping up from the bed. "Please, Mommy. We haven't played witches in so, so long."

"Of course we can, my pet. Let's go play witches and then later I'll make us some macaroni and cheese."

"Perfect!" she said, running out of the room.

I paused for a second, looking at the copy of *Crime and Punishment* that sat on my daughter's nightstand. *Crime and Punishment* was a punishment in this house. Inside my father's copy of those pages was a running tally of how many times he'd sent me to the crying room. He would write down the date whenever I went in on the page he was re-reading. Often, he'd call a quote through the wall, reminding me of why I was in there. To be punished for some crime he'd made up in his own head. It didn't matter what it was, or whether or not I *actually* did it. The point was to be punished, not to be judged fairly.

"Mo-om!" came a cry from up the attic stairs. "Hurry u-up, please!"

"Coming!" I said, putting the book down and running after my daughter.

WE PLAYED witches until the sun went down. I forgot about making dinner for my parents, so they were undoubtedly starving, but for some reason today I didn't care. They'd left me in the hospital for days and barely acknowledged me when I finally arrived home. They could wait for their dinner. Isabel and I ate by ourselves in the kitchen. I put some leftovers in a bowl for my parents and left it in the living room.

"Mommy, did you miss me?" Isabel asked as we made our way back up to our rooms.

"Yes, I missed you a lot." I tried to forget about the conversation I had with the Cabots on the ride over. An exorcism didn't make any sense. My daughter needed help with her mental health. She didn't need some priest terrorizing her about being "possessed."

"That's good," she said yawning widely. "I missed you too. It's been such a long time."

I gave her a hug and told her to go brush her teeth. Isabel plodded into the bathroom and I stood guard outside. Downstairs I heard the faint voice of my father yelling at something—it was either the TV or my mother. Likely it was both. Having this undisturbed time with Isabel was more of a vacation than lying in that hospital bed. What good did all that "observation" do me? None. I came home to the same situation I was in before. My father still abused us, my daughter was at risk of becoming his next target, I still had nowhere and no one to turn to, and I still had the rest of the house to repair. A whole weekend lost, and for what? For doctors to treat me like I was lying to them, or like I was crazy. What was the point in calling that ambulance if my own child didn't remember what happened? Did they pump her full of sedatives too?

I didn't want to think about that.

Of course you did the right thing, Maggie. Your daughter was turning blue and had convulsions. There was nothing you could do for her here.

But if I hadn't called the ambulance, I would never have been restrained at the hospital. They wouldn't have given me the wrong medication and knocked me out for three days. Most of the problems I faced, beyond those related to my own flesh and blood, happened outside, far away from my home. I was tempted to never leave here again.

"I'm done! I want to read now," Isabel said, grabbing my hand and dragging me over to her bed.

"What story do you want, my dear?" I asked.

Isabel yawned and pointed at *Crime and Punishment*.

I couldn't do it. I didn't want to ruin the placidness of this day with what I might see in there. "I don't think I can do that tonight; it's way too dense. I'll fall asleep long before you do if you make me read that book."

Isabel rolled her eyes and pulled another book from under her pillow. A murder mystery that I remembered from my own youth.

We snuggled into each other as I read to her, enjoying the rest of the evening.

Isabel fell asleep quickly, but I stayed in her bed reading the book. It was nostalgic, and Isabel had pulled out my favorite from the series. The heroine—the plucky granddaughter of a famous detective—has to solve a mystery involving a haunted house. The house had sat empty for years, and no one dared go inside, but all of a sudden there were lights turning on and off at random inside the old house. The heroine determined that the house's electrical wiring was faulty. She managed to save the day before the entire house burned down. When she got to the property, she found the old caretaker was still living in the garden house, too afraid to leave his employer. He had no idea the woman who'd owned the house had died years before. The old caretaker had a beautiful garden and the heroine rallied the town to help clean up the old house and allow the old man to expand his garden.

It was the sort of wholesome tale that only existed in chapter books for young girls.

I TOOK my time with my nighttime routine, trying to bask in what had been the best day in recent memory. I felt calm and connected to my daughter for the first time in days—not including those I spent in the hospital.

Still, the fact that she couldn't remember any of the attack that sent us both to the hospital worried me. I didn't know if maybe she was just saying that to protect me, or if she really didn't remember. The attacks had been happening more frequently and were so much more severe. If I had been able to go with her to the hospital, or if my doctors had *listened* to me, I'd probably have a rational, medical explanation by now. Instead I had speculation and supernatural reasons.

Bill seemed to take ghosts and hauntings really seriously. Could he really believe that Isabel was possessed? That was impossible. Possessions didn't happen outside of horror films and scary stories. My house had never been haunted. It wasn't built on some ancient burial ground and as far as I knew there were no disturbed spirits beneath the foundations. It was silly to even entertain the idea of a priest. I hadn't pegged Bill and Lana as religious—city people often weren't—but maybe they were the exception to the rule. Maybe that was why they'd decided to retire to some quaint town in an old Victorian mansion.

I suppose it's not a bad idea. If you can't find a child therapist willing to talk to Isabel, a priest might be the next best thing. I had been raised Catholic, thanks to my overbearing Irish Catholic paternal line. I associated the religion with itchy school uniforms and too many rules to keep track of. Somewhere in the vague repository of my Catholic memories I remembered that a priest's main job was to provide counsel to his congregants—to be a shepherd to his flock. Maybe he could help. That way, if Isabel really was possessed, he could do something about it.

Maggie, stop being ridiculous, I thought. *Isabel isn't possessed, she's just—*

What?

What was going on with my little girl? It wasn't a ghost, or maybe it was, and I had no medical help to diagnose her. What could be wrong with her that one day she was a sweet and precocious kid, and the next she was choking and shaking on the floor?

23

I kept tossing and turning, unable to sleep. Was it really a ghost inhabiting my daughter's body? My house had never been haunted by ghosts—only the cloud of my father's abuse. Maybe it took a child who was a little more sensitive, a little less concerned about her parent's mood, to connect with it. It would explain Isabel's strange behavior and the way she could just appear seemingly out of nowhere in this house. I knew the place had many secret rooms and passageways from its old life, but I had never thought to find them. Maybe Isabel was being taught the secrets of our home by a long-gone spirit.

It's nice to have a playdate for her. Maybe possession isn't such a bad thing.

I closed my eyes and tried counting backward from a hundred, but I couldn't even get to ninety before I was worrying again. I just couldn't believe it was a ghost, and that a priest would be able to magically fix my daughter. There had to be some kind of normal explanation for this, a medical condition that I could get her treatment for.

I rolled out of bed and pulled my laptop out from under it. The Wi-Fi worked better up here. Maybe I could do a quick search and find some explanation that was more logical than an old Victorian ghost living through my daughter.

I didn't quite know where to start. Do I just type in *My daughter seems like she's been possessed by a ghost—what do I do?* into the search bar and hope for the best? I wanted to move away from the idea that she was incurable outside of paranormal intervention. I made a list of her symptoms and started from there.

- mood swings
- personality-type mood swings (acting like she's twenty years older).
- breathing attacks that seem like asthma
- seizures/convulsions

I wished I could get her records from the hospital. Then I'd at least know what the hell happened after we got out of that ambulance. My parents must have picked her up, but they would never have asked any questions that would help me now. I doubted my father even got out of the car, and it was hard to tell if my mother was present. If anyone was possessed in this house, it was more likely to be her—a woman who barely spoke, just stared aimlessly into the distance, waiting for something to happen to her.

No, she wasn't a ghost. If it was possible to be possessed by a zombie then, maybe, that's what was going on.

I didn't have time to analyze my mother. All I knew was that they picked up Isabel, she wasn't hurt, and they didn't pass along any information from the hospital. Come to think of it, they didn't even ask about *my* hospital stay. If they didn't ask me what my three days were like, there was no reason for them to ask about Isabel's. My daughter didn't even remember going to the hospital, so I couldn't ask her what they did. It was likely that, just like all these other attacks, Isabel's breathing cleared up in an instant while I was unconscious in the ambulance. Had she even made it to the hospital? The more I thought about it the more I realized that the nurse never gave me an answer when I asked. The psychiatrist who visited me only said that she was "okay" and that she was being taken care of, but didn't offer any details beyond that.

She probably felt better in the ambulance ride, and they dropped her back at home. Lana and Bill hadn't said anything about the car being taken out, so it was entirely possible that my parents spent the whole weekend in front of the TV while Isabel was hiding upstairs in her room.

Poor kid. Maybe she is better off being haunted by a ghost.

I went back to my search. There were a couple of websites I found that had more clear information than my weekend speculation. Either required medical attention, which meant I had to somehow get Isabel out of the house and to a doctor.

The first was PTSD, post-traumatic stress disorder. I had read about PTSD before, but always in veterans or people who survived major disasters. It was the reason my father hated going into the city. He claimed everyone in the subway was a Vietnam vet suffering from PTSD. Little did I know there was a lot more to the disease. You could get PTSD as a child from witnessing abuse of a parent or from experiencing it yourself. I had probably exposed Isabel without even realizing it, since no matter what I did, she could probably hear her grandfather's tirades all over the house. That resulted in "disorganized and agitated behavior"—explaining Isabel's episodes of destroying her bedroom and claiming that her pillows were smothering her. Had my father attempted to smother her without me knowing about it? I wouldn't put it past him.

The diagnosis of PTSD in children is almost the same as the diagnosis of PTSD in adults: 1) after exposure to actual or threatened death or serious injury, instead of evidencing fear, helplessness or horror, they may respond with disorganized or agitated behavior; 2) symptoms of re-experiencing, repetition and re-enactments where children may have frightening dreams without specific content; 3) avoidance of stimuli associated with the trauma; 4) hyper-arousal, where it is noted that children may also exhibit physical symptoms such as stomachaches and headaches.

Isabel's constant tummy aches and sickly feeling whenever I suggested going outside suddenly were clear. Her grandfather had an extreme and violent reaction to Isabel leaving the house, so she got sick whenever I suggested it, probably fearing her grandfather's reaction. She went along with his activities and then complained of nightmares. She saw the violence inflicted on my mother, and then drew scenes of a woman retaliating. What I thought was a drawing of me, pregnant with Isabel, murdering her father was probably Isabel re-enacting my mom being pregnant with me, and her fantasies of attacking my grandfather.

PTSD was treatable, usually by a therapist. That road led to a dead end, I already knew. But there were specialists and other doctors, people who were used to dealing with traumatized children—maybe that same woman that Dr. Bartesc recommended could find someone for Isabel. I could delay the inevitable by calling him and getting a referral to someone else. It would at least buy me some time to formulate a plan to get Isabel out of the house without my father knowing.

Searching for a potential medical diagnosis online was a minefield. Every other link I clicked told me that my daughter likely had brain cancer, or some virus with an unpronounceable name. PTSD was looking like the most likely culprit, until I came across something called temporal lobe seizures from the *Mayo Clinic* website.

It said that these kind of seizures began in the temporal lobe of the brain, which was what processed emotions and was responsible for our short-term memory. It also said that déjà vu, euphoria, and feelings of fear might be related to these kinds of seizures.

Again, that explained Isabel's odd behavior—from her strange fear of pillows to the odd drawings of her father, Nate. It could have been a sense of déjà vu that made her draw those things, unaware of what really went on. In the drawings I remember she seemed alive in my belly, like she was egging me on, but that was impossible. If she was having trouble with short-term memory, that could explain why she didn't remember her ambulance ride, or even the strange breathing attack that preceded it. According to my poor research, temporal lobe seizures could occur from having a lesion on your brain, so there was no way for me to see if there was something wrong with Isabel until a doctor got her into an imaging machine.

The thought of Isabel having a lesion or bruising on her brain filled me with guilt. She probably had this because of me. If I'd had the courage to leave Nate sooner, he wouldn't have had the chance to abuse me when I was pregnant. If he hadn't abused me when I was pregnant, then maybe Isabel wouldn't have any of these strange behaviors.

It was all a chain, wasn't it? A chain that began with my shitty decisions and ended with Isabel's shitty quality of life. How long could I keep this up before CPS intervened, or Isabel ran away from home, just like I did? This was what all those liberal pundits called the "cycle of abuse." It was enough to make me scream.

Reading more about PTSD and temporal lobe seizures made me feel sick to my stomach with guilt. I thought I was protecting Isabel, but of course, she was still affected by my father's behavior. He didn't have to touch her for Isabel to understand how ashamed he was of her, or how annoyed he was that she existed. He yelled at me and treated Isabel as a plaything, something to be cast aside when he was bored of her. She watched as my mother in her near-catatonic state accepted my father's rage and did nothing to escape or fight back.

What kind of lesson was that teaching her? Throughout all of this, the alternative I had come up with was to lock my daughter in her room near the attic, for her to get lost reading complicated books and playing make-believe whenever I had time to spend with her. She was either going to experience second-hand abuse, or turn into one of those shut-ins who were discovered in a basement at the age of thirty. This was no fairy tale with a prince coming to save her at the end. It was real life, where changes in behavior were more easily explained by medical conditions than paranormal activity.

I felt like a terrible mom.

You're doing the best you can with what you have.

No, no, I couldn't convince myself otherwise, not this time. I was a shitty, selfish mom who wanted to hold onto her daughter for her own happiness, sacrificing her daughter in the process. Isabel would be better off someplace else. Maybe the Cabots would be willing to take her, at least for a little while, until I managed to save a little money and find a way out.

I DIDN'T SLEEP VERY WELL that night.

The whole point of that search was to give me some peace of mind, find something more concrete and treatable than a ghost. Instead I managed to make myself feel so guilty that I barely got a wink of sleep. I kept dreaming that Isabel would wake up as a sixteen-year-old and run out of the house with nothing but a backpack. I chased her down the stairs, all the way to the door, while I turned into my father and started screaming obscenities at her as she drove away in her father's car.

I woke up in a cold sweat to Isabel standing at the foot of the bed.

"Are you okay, Mommy?" she asked, her eyes as wide as dinner plates.

"Sure I am, sweetie. Why do you ask?"

She turned and looked at the clock above my door, glancing back at me with concern. "It's late. You usually wake me up and make me breakfast. I'm really hungry, but I'm not sure if you'd let me go downstairs and make breakfast myself. Besides, I don't think I'd be able to reach all the ingredients."

I sat up in bed. She was right; it was almost ten in the morning. I usually woke up at the crack of dawn, ready to work for the day. My body felt heavy, like I was back in the hospital under heavy sedatives. I was exhausted. The very last thing I wanted to do was be a mom that day. But I knew I had to. I had to make up for the time I'd lost, time that I'd never be able to get back and that probably messed up my child—but not permanently. The sooner I could get her help, the better her life would be. Based on all the symptoms I noted, and what I found online, it could be either temporal lobe seizures or PTSD. Knowing the environment Isabel had grown up in, it was probably PTSD. So that was the first step—being able to present an actual problem to a doctor, not a bunch of mystery symptoms that they could brush off.

The next step was getting out of this house. I couldn't give up this time. No more excuses, no more fear of my father. What else could he do to me that he hadn't done already? I'd survived the crying room before; I could survive it again. Even if I only got as far as the Cabots' house—at least they could come up with a plan.

My father was a shut-in. When I went into town no one asked about him anymore. Everyone knew he was an angry drunk who never went farther than his own porch. The few people who walked down the street and past our home ignored his porch-side tirades. He wouldn't follow me if I got far enough. Even when I was a teenager, he gave up chasing me when he realized I wouldn't do his bidding and come home. We had the car. It was ancient, but it still ran.

There was a puzzle to piece together but ultimately, I knew it was possible to leave for a little while. Leaving for enough time to get Isabel some help was the first piece of the bigger puzzle—how to be a less shitty mom.

24

I wanted to go through with this sooner rather than later, before I chickened out again, but I knew it would take a little bit of planning. The last time I tried to leave the house in a hurry, it was only with the help of an ambulance—outside authority that my father didn't dare contradict. I knew I couldn't call 911 again; they'd probably consider it a prank call if when they closed the door I told them what I really needed was to escape my father.

No, this time I had to do it on my own—no Nate Moore waiting for me a block away, or an ambulance to cover it up.

I STARTED IN THE GARAGE. I used the excuse that I wanted to mix two different wood stains to get the exact color on a wooden dresser I found in the upstairs parlor.

"If you want it to look brand new, I have to do it. They just don't make a wood stain that color anymore, at least not that the hardware store could find. I don't think a plain walnut will look nice. This wood was originally stained in an Art Nouveau style and with its age, a plain walnut stain will look dingy," I explained to my father over breakfast.

He was chewing and staring me down like a pit bull. I must have had a really good poker face because he bought it.

"I'd rather you do that than stink up the house. I hate that smell."

"I won't be long, and I'll make sure to cover the car. But I wouldn't poke your head in there; the smell gives you a headache, remember?" I felt like a little kid asking permission to play at a friend's house, yet I was only going into the garage for a couple of hours.

My father didn't answer. He just pushed his bowl away and walked out of the room. A minute later I heard the TV come on—he would be busy rotting his brain and liver for the rest of the day.

"Mommy, can I help? I love mixing colors. I find it to be wonderfully poetic," Isabel asked, pulling on my arm.

"Sorry, honey, the fumes won't be very good for you either. It's better if you go upstairs and do some arts and crafts. I've left a few things out for you. I ordered a book on origami so you could start folding paper cranes for us. How does that sound?"

Isabel slumped off to her room. I'd probably pay for that later with a very restless child, but oh well. It was necessary. I turned and looked at my mother, who stared at me through squinted eyes.

"You're planning something," she said. "I can see it in your eyes."

Now she notices?

"I'm not, Mother. I'm just trying to refurbish this house, just as you asked. It needs to return to its former glory; don't you remember saying that?" I said, but she didn't answer. She stood up, and I could hear her footsteps go up the stairs and end up in her secret office.

It was fine. As long as she didn't get in the way, I didn't care what she knew. I was doing more than she ever did. I wasn't going to let myself turn into a passive mother.

I DID MIX the wood stain and varnish in the garage—that part wasn't a lie. But I did it quickly, in less than a few minutes. I spent the rest of the time using what little knowledge I had to assess the state of our car. It wasn't bad, definitely would need a few repairs, but it could run. I doubted anyone had used it in ages. I usually walked to run errands around town and my parents never left the house, so it had just been sitting here. Once we cleared the dust out of the pipes, maybe changed the transmission oil or something, the car would run just like new. Luckily, my father's small fortune meant he always bought the best of everything, including automobiles, though this one was foreign and sometimes the parts for it took a while to get into the shop.

I opened the door leading inside and screamed. My father was waiting on the other side of the door, his arms crossed against his chest.

"You've been in there for a long time," he said. "Anything I should be concerned about?"

"Nope." I smiled. "I'm all done now. It just took a long time. I took breaks so I didn't get too sick from the fumes, so I could finish up the furniture in the parlor right away." I tried to sound chipper and positive, but braced myself for my father's irrational reaction.

He did nothing, just turned around and went back to the kitchen, swaying gently along the way. He was at the best part of his drunken stupor—if anyone could have a "best part" of their drunken stupor.

The rest of the day was spent fixing up furniture, an activity that was easy to get lost in. I tried not to think about Isabel's condition so I could stay positive about my plan. If I wallowed in my despair, I would give up, and I was trying to avoid that. My goal on the day we left would be to get her to the children's hospital. They would be able to provide some sort of treatment plan, and they were more likely to have staff at the hospital that understood both conditions. I would try to stay strong if and when any of the doctors or nurses dismissed my concerns.

I SPENT the next day studying my father's routine. I knew if I blatantly followed him around all day he'd get suspicious that something was going on, so I made another excuse. When he left the breakfast table, I listened for where he was going. As usual, he beelined to the living room and turned on the TV. That worked perfectly for me.

"This lamp needs rewiring," I said, bursting into the living room. I ignored my parents as I fiddled with an ancient floor lamp in the corner. I had already rewired it; the living room was the first room I had worked on and it didn't take very long. "I think I did a bad job last time. It keeps flickering."

"Why don't you try changing the bulb before you rip that precious antique apart?" my father asked, but I was ready for him.

"I did, but it looks like the bulb isn't the problem. It's been flickering on and off for weeks and I don't want it ruining your vision."

"I haven't noticed anything." My father harrumphed and turned the volume up on the TV.

He was in a decent mood after breakfast—not drunk, not hangry. This seemed like it would be the best chance I'd get to make my move. I wanted to be sure, so I took my time with the lamp. By the time lunch rolled around my father had already had more beer than I could count.

"How many of those have you had, Dad?" I asked.

"Is my drinking of your concern? Don't you have anything better to do? The last time I checked you were a mother. Doesn't your daughter need her diaper changed or something? What the hell are you still doing here anyway? Are you babysitting me or something?" He was raising his voice and starting to get out of his chair.

He might be in the weeds but he can still move pretty quickly.

"Sorry, I-I didn't mean—"

I didn't get to finish my sentence before my dad whacked my head against the brass lamp stand. I blinked away the stars in my eyes and saw him standing over me.

"Mind your own business, you piece of shit," he said, before lumbering out the door.

I checked to make sure I wasn't bleeding or anything before heading upstairs. The lamp was fine, but my confidence was shaken. He was a big man, my father. Strong no matter what time of day it was, with eyes that bored through me straight to my soul. He could probably see past my poker face. I was an idiot for thinking I could keep an eye on him all day without him noticing.

"Whatever you're planning, don't do it," my mother said.

She was standing at the top of the stairs, looking down at me. "You don't know what he's capable of."

"You're one to talk."

"I am. I know. You shouldn't take your father lightly. Whatever you are planning, it's probably better if you just deal with it at home. Running off into the world with no money and your father chasing you around town will probably end up with you in the crying room and Isabel—"

I ran past my mother into my room before she could finish that sentence. I had a plan. All I had to do was stick to it. I could easily pack a bag in the middle of the night and put it in the car while everyone was asleep. No one went into the garage; they wouldn't know anything was under the tarp that covered our car.

She's being paranoid. Can you blame her? She's lived her whole life under your father's thumb, that little sympathetic voice cried.

I knew that, I knew all that, but I couldn't let go of the resentment I had toward my mother. Would she have done the same for me if she saw the symptoms of PTSD? I had no idea. Probably not. She probably suffered from the same and never saw anyone about it... didn't even try.

Now that I thought about it, my mother's constant passivity was probably her disassociating from the situation she was in. The hours she spent staring at the TV or the dollhouse in the library was her version of escaping this situation. I ought to feel lucky she was around to warn me, but it had been too long to salvage our relationship now.

IN ORDER for my plan to work, I had to leave before my father got too drunk and lost control of his emotions. It sounded counterintuitive—*don't wait until he's wasted, go when he's a little bit buzzed.* I knew, from years of experience, that my father was a mean drunk. The more he drank, the meaner and more violent he was. If I waited too long in the day, he would stop at nothing to drag my daughter and me back. But if I left a little earlier, when he was still in control of his faculties, his shame at appearing drunk in public would take over and he wouldn't chase us. I was used to calculations like this. I had seen my mother do them my whole life. It was a delicate dance to tiptoe around my father in order to maintain his good mood.

An hour or so after breakfast was the perfect time. I could claim to be busy in the kitchen, which was why I wasn't working on the house—preparing a more elaborate breakfast would take care of that. While I cleaned, my dad would start his journey toward the land of blackout-drunk. Just before lunch, I could sneak into the garage and open the door. Feed my parents, and Isabel, and when they were back in their comfy chairs, rotting their brains in front of the TV, I'd leave in the car. It would be easy to sneak Isabel past them at that point. The car would be loaded—I'd do that either before breakfast or in the middle of the night to avoid being detected. My dad would be ensconced in the alcoholic haze of his lunchtime drink, and I could put the car into neutral to push it out of the garage.

With any luck, I could get it part of the way down the drive before hopping in and driving. My dad might notice, he might try and run after the car but he wouldn't get too far. He'd be too embarrassed to leave in that state, and still sober enough to care.

It wasn't a perfect plan. I still had my mother's voice in the back of my head telling me it wasn't going to work, but it was the best I had.

I PACKED MINIMALLY. I was still planning on coming home, whatever the consequences. Isabel needed someplace to go back to. I figured she might be held overnight for observation, especially if it was seizures, so I packed a change of clothes for each of us, and a few snacks too.

In the middle of the night I tiptoed down to the car and put a bag into the passenger side. I considered trying the car —would it be too loud? Would it wake up the whole house if I were to rev the engine, just to make sure it worked? I let it be, preferring to sleep rather than feel the potential disappointment of a stalled car.

In the morning, I made pancakes for breakfast.

"What're these for?" my father asked when he sat himself down at the table.

"Isabel asked for them," I answered, piling them onto his plate. *Eat more,* I thought, *maybe you'll be in a better mood.*

"You're turning that kid into a spoiled brat," my father complained, but he ate more pancakes than the rest of us combined.

Just as I predicted, my father went straight to the living room, flipping on the TV to some old football game. I took my time cleaning up in the kitchen, so I could count how many times he came back for a beer.

"Don't you have anything better to do?" he asked after his third beer. He didn't wait to hear my answer, just turned and left the kitchen.

Yes, actually, I do have something better to do, I thought. I finished up my work and went to collect Isabel.

"Honey, I need your help downstairs," I called up to her from the second floor, trying to mask how shaky my voice was. I had kept a secret from my daughter and it felt like I was kidnapping her.

Isabel bounded down the stairs, wearing her clacky dress shoes.

"I wanna wear these today. I love 'em. I love the noise they make, *clack, clack, clack!*" She tap-danced down the stairs and finished at the bottom in a flourish.

My father whipped around the corner, slamming into her as she did. "What the hell is going on around here? We don't live in a circus tent so why am I hearing some carnie?" he roared, picking Isabel up by the arm.

Isabel's whole body went stiff. She started wheezing and crying, her eyes bulging out of her head.

25

"This kid is a spoiled brat!" My father had an iron grip around my daughter's arm. "She's squirming like a little snake. Wouldn't need to do that if she was some innocent little kid—what did she have to do with you little plan, huh? Where do you think the two of you are going?"

"Ow, stop. You're hurting me!" Isabel squealed.

"Aww, shut up, you little brat!" my father screamed.

Isabel went limp in his grip. She started breathing funny and coughing while trying to worm her way out of his grasp.

I knew where this was going; I had seen it all before. Soon her lips would turn blue and her skin would go all grey and pale. "Dad, stop, please. You don't know what you're—"

"Well, if she'd just shut up, and you would just stay put, then—"

My father was interrupted by Isabel throwing up at his feet.

In his disgust he let her go, tossing her to the ground.

As soon as her little body hit the hallway floor she started to convulse. Her breathing attack was faster this time than ever before. In a flash she went from coughing and wheezing to clutching her neck while her mouth was open in a silent scream. Her voice was hoarse from screaming while no sound or air could escape.

"Issie! Isabel, it's okay, I'm here! Mommy's right here!"

I figured something like this would happen. With my luck we were bound to be intercepted sooner or later; I ought to have known there was no escaping this house. I was starting to think that maybe this house wasn't haunted—it was cursed. Cursed with my family's trauma. Generation after generation of angry drunks soaked the walls with whiskey, beer, and blood.

"Non potes adiuva me," Isabel drawled.

I couldn't understand what she was saying. I took Spanish for a single semester in high school, and it sounded like she was saying something about helping her?

"Honey, I can help. Tell me how I can help. Is that what you want?" I said, trying to keep her steady. I'd read online that when having a temporal lobe—or any other—seizure it was bad to try and steady someone's head, in case they broke something. It was better to clear the way, put something soft under them. I tore off the lightweight cardigan I was wearing and stuffed it under her head.

"Non potes adiuva me!" Isabel screamed, her voice raspy and asthmatic. Her eyes were as big as saucers and they dug their gaze into me.

I shivered at that look. Everything around me dropped away and all I could see were Isabel's giant pupils drawing me close. She wanted to tell me something, but I couldn't tell what.

"Stultus es stupri," she hissed, spitting up at me. The veins in her neck were bulging.

"What is she saying?" my mother whispered, her hand on my shoulder. "What's wrong with her?"

"I don't know," I replied. The language was familiar, but it wasn't Spanish. "I can't recognize it."

"It's probably some stupid made-up language. Kids are always doing stuff like that to mess with you, make you think you're crazy," my father growled, before chugging more of his beer.

Isabel's head whirled around to face him. "Maxime odio te. Hoc fecistis. Hoc fecistis!" she spat.

My father had never looked so pale. He was terrified of my eight-year-old girl, scared enough to take a step away from us.

"What did she say to you?" I asked, but he didn't say anything.

"It's you. It's your fault, hoc fecistis!" she screamed. It was the loudest she'd ever been during these attacks.

I felt my mother tense up behind me and I couldn't help but burst into tears.

Isabel whipped her head back to me. "Non es multo melius," she snarled.

I realized why I recognized the language. It wasn't Spanish, it was Latin—that explained why it was so similar. The last time I spoke Latin was in Catholic school. I went to a private Catholic school that, for some reason, still taught their students rudimentary Latin. Probably for no reason other than so they could charge an exorbitant amount of tuition.

Where did she learn Latin? I had never taught her. I barely remembered any of it myself, except maybe the Hail

Mary and a few other prayers and things to do with church. Did she learn from one of the dusty old books that she found in the attic or the library?

"Much better?" I tried to puzzle out what Isabel was saying. "I'm not much better?"

She didn't respond. Instead she regressed back to the stage where all she could do was claw at her neck and try to drag in a flimsy breath.

Even my daughter could see I was just as weak as my mother. I was just as passive, and at the end of the day I'd be the reason for this family's downfall.

"Ignave!" Isabel continued. "Coward! Sera est et recipere non potes, semper! You can't take it back!"

If only she knew how much research I had done, and how much planning it took to get us this far. *She's angry and hurt. She's confused. Don't take her at her word, Maggie.*

"You're too late. You can't take it back. Mommy, it's too late. You can't take it back. You are too late. You can't take it back." She kept repeating this phrase to herself, like a little prayer that meant nothing. "Sero es, non potes recipere. Sero es, non potes recipere. Sero es, non potes recipere. Sero es, non potes recipere. Sero es, non potes recipere." She was muttering to herself like an incantation.

"We have to pray for her," my mother whispered, her voice shaking with fear. "That's all we can do when a child is possessed by the devil."

"She isn't possessed by the devil, Mother. There's a medical explanation for what is going on with her."

"Si diabolus sum, tunc videbo te in inferno." Isabel grinned at my mother, threatening her with the fiery pits of hell. Color was coming back to my daughter's face. The attack was almost over. "Diabolus sum. The devil is waiting for you. You have angered the good Lord and the devil is waiting for you!"

It was enough to make my mother break down in tears.

I was sitting between a woman and a girl, each unraveling in a different way. I felt for my mother; it wasn't her fault that she had been abused every day of her marriage. I'd seen photos of her before she married my father. My mother was tiny; she was built like a pixie but was graceful all the same. Years with my father had made her skittish and frail. I wondered what kind of woman she would have been had she never set foot in this house.

How many more years would I last before I also went insane? My parents were clearly agoraphobic, probably from years of isolating themselves within this community and my father's influence creating an unsafe space for my mother and me. My daughter had temporal lobe seizures or PTSD—neither was much better than the other—and it was obviously caused by either her grandfather or her abusive biological father, Nate Moore. I was only barely keeping it together. Had I been a little farther out on that cliff of sanity, the hospital probably would have kept me for longer than a weekend.

"You'll never be sane, Mommy. You can't be sane in this house," Isabel said.

She was lying between my legs, looking up at me. Her attack was over. The child laying below me was a gentle and sweet eight-year-old. The whole spewing-Latin episode was done, just as quickly as it had started. Isabel had no idea what had gone on.

"Why do you say that, honey?" I asked her.

"It's impossible to be sane in a place as gloomy as this. You'll never have a moment's rest as long as you live here." Isabel pushed herself up and sat across from me. "If you don't leave, you'll become agoraphobic too, and I'll probably grow to be resentful and angry, and who knows what I'll do to you." She gave me a light kiss on the cheek and then ran back up the stairs.

I heard her tap-dancing in the parlor. My mother was still sobbing in the hallway behind me, whispering the Hail Mary and rocking back and forth. In the distance, I could hear my father yelling obscenities at the TV.

Did that just happen? I asked myself, *or am I still dreaming?* I waited there for a moment to see if maybe I'd wake up from this nightmare, but I had no such luck.

MY PLAN WAS FOILED for the day. I would never get out of the house without my father noticing. Not only that, but Isabel was too excitable to hide for a moment. I read about this online. Most people after a seizure experience a moment of euphoria and uncontrollable energy. Isabel tap-danced for the rest of the day in her clacky dress shoes. I lost count of how many painkillers I took for the headache I had.

I had to accept that maybe this wasn't *just* PTSD or a seizure disorder. PTSD didn't teach you a new language, especially not a dead one. As far as I knew, no one had ever spontaneously spoken perfect Latin during a seizure—only gibberish and aphasia. There was another explanation glaring at me, and I did my best to ignore it.

There is a logical, scientific explanation for everything, I kept saying to myself while trying to work out how to re-attempt my plan. There must have been a logical explanation a doctor could give me for all of it, including the spontaneous Latin.

Either that or I had to reconsider calling a priest.

26

"Hi, Lana. It's Maggie from across the street. I realize this is going to be a weird ask, but you did mention it before... um, when you were driving me home from the hospital—God, that sounds weird—I mean, not *God*, not if that offends you. Anyway, you mentioned something about a priest that you knew who would be open to performing an exorcism on Isabel at some time and I just wondered if you could maybe pass along his information? I know it's a long shot and I was really against it, and I'm not sure if you were being serious or if you were joking, but Isabel's behavior has gotten worse and more... erratic, so if you could give me his number, that would be pretty great. If you can't that's okay too. Thank you. Either way. Thanks either way. Bye."

I hung my head in my hands after I left that voicemail. I hadn't been so nervous since I first started dating Nate—I just didn't know what to say to Lana and Bill. I wanted them to help me, but I wanted them to understand it was urgent. I wanted them to take me seriously, but I wasn't sure how serious they were about the paranormal stuff. I was so desperate and scared that I would have done anything, and in this moment the most terrifying thing I could do was leave a rambling, crazy voicemail to my closest neighbors—the only people I could count on in an emergency. I felt like a fool, and I sounded like an idiot, and I wanted to disappear on the spot.

"Mommy, why are you upset?" Isabel asked, appearing at the door to my mother's office. "Why do you want to hide so bad?"

"I just feel a little embarrassed, sweetie. Sometimes when grownups have to do very simple things, like leave a voicemail for someone else, they feel a little overwhelmed with the anxiety that they said something embarrassing, so they need a moment to regain their composure before facing the world again."

Isabel nodded, satisfied with my answer, then she jogged away up to her room. She was reading *Crime and Punishment* again, the same dusty hardcover my father had given her from the library. I was starting to feel like one of the characters in the book, doomed to be punished for eternity for a crime I didn't understand.

My to-do list was growing longer and my parents were impatient. I'd spent so much time planning a failed escape that I neglected the duties I had for maintaining this house. The furniture, the papers, the peeling paint weren't going to fix themselves.

I was in my mother's office again trying to get her files in order, but I couldn't be in there for longer than an hour without growing exhausted. I had collapsed into a nap more times than I could count. It was all just so boring that the tediousness seeped out of the page and put me to sleep.

I balanced her office with my workshop, focusing on the furniture I found in the parlor connected to the crying room. It took half a day to get all the heavy chairs downstairs, but I didn't want to spend a second in there that I didn't have to. There was an aura of danger around the crying room. Call it my own PTSD if you need; that part of the wall throbbed with a threatening energy that chilled me to the bone. I didn't need to be in the parlor to fix its furniture. The room itself just needed the floors redone, the wallpaper removed and a fresh coat of paint. As far as I was concerned, it could be boarded up and filled with cement, and no one would miss it.

No one except my father. He'd have nothing to threaten me with.

My father's power had weakened somewhat during Isabel's last attack. Isabel speaking in tongues had spooked him, and he had taken to avoiding her. He still haunted me, constantly checking to make sure I was working to his satisfaction. If Isabel appeared behind him, or if she was sitting with me, he clammed up and backed away. Isabel was dangerous to him. She repelled my father thanks to her possible possession.

"That kid is crazy, and I don't like it," he once muttered through clenched teeth.

That kid was the only thing keeping me sane. Isabel's words inspired me—as backward as that may sound. But I couldn't get over what she said to me—that I was "too late" and "couldn't take it back." She must have meant my life and the decisions I had made. It was true; I had to live with my stupid teenage choices, like running away from home and getting involved with an abusive drug dealer boyfriend—but it had brought me Isabel, and I would never regret that.

"Mommy," I heard her, snapping me out of my dream. "Mommy, it's too late." Isabel was at the door again, her arms crossed against her chest. "It's just too late, and you can't take it back."

I sighed. "You're right, baby. I've left the voicemail. I can't take it back."

As it turned out, I had nothing to worry about. Lana called me back soon after with the number for her pastor friend.

"He is pretty superstitious and very in touch with the otherworldly. I'm sure he'll be able to guide you, even if it isn't for an exorcism," she said.

Lana sounded enthusiastic, kept saying this was "just the thing" to get us on track. I hoped she was right. Having someone visit the house was risky, but easier than driving off aimlessly, trying to avoid my father.

I called the priest, hoping he would come immediately.

"I'm sorry, Miss Conner, I'm more of a Unitarian minister. I'm happy Lana and Bill um... recommended my services. She is right, I do dabble in the world of Spiritualism, the study of spirits and the translucent veil between the dead and the living—however, on a daily basis I'm more of a general practitioner of Christianity." He chuckled at his own joke over the line.

I tried to laugh, but I was crumbling to pieces inside.

"Is it because I'm Catholic?" I asked. "Because honestly, I haven't been to church in ages. I hardly remember the last time I confessed my sins. Catholicism was really just carried over from our Irish ancestors. My parents just put me in

Catholic school for the education." I was trying and failing to mask the desperation in my voice.

The pastor released a sympathetic sigh. "No. I'm happy to welcome all those who believe in the power of the Lord under the roof of my temple. Besides, even if I was Catholic, I still don't think I could do it. Catholics don't really practice exorcisms anymore; that's more of an overseas thing. They do it in Europe, maybe sometimes in South America. I think horror movies from the seventies ruined the practice for us over here." He chuckled again.

He was a lovely man, but I didn't have the time or patience for these little jokes. Not with the strange and stressful weeks I had been living through.

"The problem is, I am sure there is some spirit trying to communicate through my daughter. The house is old and our rooms are on the third floor. It's probably some angry old maid or a widow who threw herself from the roof—I'd like to know what it is. I want my daughter to have a normal life," I said, trying not to sound like I was begging.

"Why wouldn't your daughter have a normal life? Is there something else I can counsel you in, my dear?"

Oh, what the hell. This is a protected conversation, isn't it? He can't just rat me out to CPS.

"My daughter has been having these strange seizures—I'm sure Lana told you all about it."

"No, she hasn't. Even if she had, I would like to hear it from your mouth." I could hear him settling into his seat.

I walked around my mother's desk and shut the door. If I was going to tell this story I would need a little privacy. "It's these seizures. They started a few weeks ago—maybe three weeks ago? I don't know, sometimes time escapes me in this house. They start off innocently enough. I thought they were asthma attacks. I've been working through a remodel—refurbishment, really—of my house, so I thought maybe there was more dust in the air, or the fumes from the varnishes I was working with had hung in the atmosphere of the home."

"That sounds quite logical, so tell me why you've turned to the paranormal."

"It's escalated. Isabel has these breathing attacks that end with her choking and convulsing on the ground, and suddenly they are over. Just as quickly as they began, the attacks stop and Isabel is fine. She usually doesn't remember what happened during the attack. I think it's some kind of seizure—that's the medical explanation for it, but it doesn't mean there isn't someone or something controlling her from the beyond, does it? The last time she lost control, she started spewing curses in Latin to me, my mother, and my father. Her face was blue, but she growled obscenities at us in a dead language. That seems a little supernatural, don't you agree?"

"Yes, I would have to. It's not unheard of that a spirit touches the soul of another who is struggling. These phantasms we call 'ghosts' are really looking for someone who can listen to them and help them heal. I think that's why they go to those who are also experiencing mental difficulties—they know what the 'ghost' is going through."

Hogwash, but very comforting hogwash.

Sometimes I wondered what my father was doing in my head. He was the one who would call this hogwash; I didn't know what to believe anymore. Why not believe in spirits and ghosts, and the fine line between the living and the dead?

"I can come and do a blessing," the pastor continued, "to

cleanse the house of whatever plagues it. Hopefully, the blessing can help your child with whatever she is... experiencing."

He sounded uncomfortable. I'd heard him clear his throat when I mentioned the Latin, like any desire to have contact with my daughter was leaving his body. There was something in the way he was describing the way ghosts sometimes came to people who were struggling too, like he was afraid it was contagious or something. I wasn't sure what a blessing could do on this house, especially when it came from someone who wanted nothing to do with it, but it was better than nothing. Until I could leave and find a specialist for Isabel, this would do. Maybe he'd even be able to undo the curse that kept this house wrapped in misery.

"Sure, um, okay. Yes," I stammered.

"Okay? You don't seem entirely convinced."

I wasn't used to inviting strangers into my home. Even before my parents became agoraphobic, I remember I always used to avoid play dates at my house, or sleepovers with my friends. It was better to go somewhere else. Mary and the paramedics were the last people who came into my home, and neither of those experiences ended well.

"It feels strange inviting you here after you said there may be a struggling spirit roaming the halls. I almost want to spare you the trouble or the haunted feeling you'll have when you come visit my house."

"It won't be the first, and it certainly won't be the last. I can sense from your voice you may need my help. Lana and Bill—especially Bill; he was very insistent— said that you could use a kind ear in your life. The least I can do is bless your home and listen, so why don't we start there?" His voice was softer now. The dad jokes faded away and revealed a very serious man who knew it was his calling to help others when they were lost.

Even if he doesn't bless the house, maybe he can see what's going on and will be able to help Isabel. I might be a lost cause, but Isabel isn't, no matter what she says about it being "too late."

"Yes," I said, more confidently this time. "Come and bless the house. We could use your help and guidance, Father."

"Oh, you don't need to call me father. I'm Pastor Jacobs." I could hear him smiling on the other end of the line as I hung up the phone.

I asked Pastor Jacobs to come over that same day. I didn't want to wait. If this didn't work, I still had the bag I packed in the car. My parents didn't know about it. I could wait until they were asleep and sneak out in the middle of the night.

He arrived a little over an hour after our call. I was in the middle of preparing lunch.

"Smells wonderful," he said, his smile lighting up his face. Pastor Jacobs was a short, square man with little round glasses. It gave him the effect of an old monk from Renaissance Italy. All he was missing were the plain brown robes. He carried a little briefcase with him, like he was going to a business meeting rather than a blessing.

Well, I guess for him it is a business meeting.

"We were about to sit down," I said. "Do you want to join us?"

His smile faltered for a moment, and he glanced back at Lana and Bill's home. "I actually just ate. I had some lunch with the Cabots; I hope you aren't offended."

"Not at all. They're friends of yours, right? It makes sense you'd go over. Let me just set the table and I can, um... do whatever you need me to do, I guess." I smiled and led him in. The TV was blaring from the living room, so loud I knew it would drown out the priest. I poked my head into the living room to gently tell my parents to turn it down—

"What was that?" Pastor Jacobs called. He was standing awkwardly in the middle of the hall, staring into the library.

"Oh, nothing! Don't worry about it."

"You really think he's going to bless *this* house? This place is cursed, Maggie, we all know it," my father called out.

I flinched, but Pastor Jacobs didn't hear. He was wandering into the library, in awe of how many books were in there. I heard him make a comment about the collection, but I was distracted by my parents.

"Lunch is in the kitchen if you want it. Or if you want to have it in here, I can bring out a tray?" I offered. Behind my back, I crossed my fingers hoping they'd opt for the latter.

"Obviously, we'll have it in here. I don't want to eat with some religious zealot roaming the halls," my father answered.

I tried to hide my excitement as I backed out of the room. I rushed, putting my parents' dinner on two trays, speeding back to the living room. When I settled them, I went to the library to find Pastor Jacobs. He had various instruments, including a tuning fork and an incense ball, laid out on the table.

"Your meal smells wonderful."

"Thank you. My parents are eating in the living room. You can meet them, if you like, but they don't like visitors. They're a little bit agoraphobic, I think," I said, smiling weakly.

Isabel, of course, chose that moment to run into the

room to play with her dollhouse. She stopped in her tracks when she saw Pastor Jacobs loading incense cones into his ball. "Is that a priest?" she asked, with all the attitude of a teenager.

I cleared my throat in answer, just as Pastor Jacobs looked up.

"Hi," Isabel continued. "Don't mind me. I'm just here to play Mommy the Contractor."

I smiled at her and then the priest. He looked toward Isabel, smiled, and let out a little hum in response. I thought it was a strange greeting, but then he pulled out a tuning fork and struck it against the table.

I saw Isabel flinch, and I cleared my throat again, cuing her to be a little kinder to our guest.

"It's quite dry in here, but I think it is a good place to start. Do you want some water for your throat? That tickle will only get worse once the smoke starts."

I felt like I was in Catholic school again. Priests and pastors and nuns, they all had a miraculous ability to cut you down with a single passive-aggressive comment.

I followed Pastor Jacobs around the house as he banged his tuning fork and swung his incense ball. He said a short incantation in Latin as we entered each room. "Benedic spatium hoc nunc tibi et nobis."

Bless this space for now, for you, and for us both. It had a nice ring to it, like he was welcoming everyone to occupy the same space and coexist peacefully. I opened my mouth to say so, but Pastor Jacobs quieted me with an open palm.

"Mommy," Isabel whispered, suddenly by my side, "are we allowed to talk to each other?"

"No, honey, I think this is supposed to be a quiet time," I hissed through my teeth at Isabel.

The pastor didn't say anything. I assumed he was ignoring us while he focused on blessing the house.

Isabel slowly marched behind us, her mouth open as she stared at Pastor Jacobs. She had never seen this sort of thing before. I remember when I was a kid, the few times my mother took me to Catholic church, I was mesmerized by the little ball of frankincense. The tendrils of smoke that were so opaque as they left the ball but completely dissolved into the air above were mesmerizing and I would often rush my mother in the mornings so we could get a seat on the aisle, closer to the procession. Isabel had the same expression I had when I was her age.

Luckily for us both, every time Isabel wandered off and then joined our little parade, Pastor Jacobs didn't notice, or wasn't bothered. I didn't take any notice of it, until we passed the living room. My father, in order to drown out the chanting, had turned the television to an obscene volume. It practically shook the walls in the little room. Pastor Jacobs calmly smiled at me, persuading me that he actually *was* an Italian Renaissance monk in a former life. We were in and out of there quickly and as we walked away, I noticed Pastor Jacobs had to hold his tuning fork a little closer to his ear.

Fantastic! My parents have deafened a priest.

We slowly walked up the stairs, narrowly avoiding Isabel. She was over it. The stranger was repetitive and she was protesting by getting in our way whenever she could. She froze when she saw Pastor Jacobs turn toward the parlor, where the crying room was. His tuning fork would probably go flat when he was in there. He'd have to spend hours to properly cleanse that space. Isabel refused to go into the room, so I had to follow the pastor into the one room that desperately needed a blessing.

I was right; we spent more time in there than in any other room in the house. I almost screamed when I first heard it. A heavy fist pounding on the wall, from the direction of the crying room. After I got over my fright, I ran out into the hall, expecting to find a giggling Isabel with her fist against the wall. No one was out there. Isabel was standing at the top of the stairs.

"Is something the matter?" Pastor Jacobs said.

It was the first time he acknowledged his surroundings, and I was embarrassed to have been the one to break his focus.

"I thought— I heard something on the wall. An animal or a tree branch, probably, but it scared the life out of me," I said, trying to laugh it off. "I'm so sorry for ruining your focus."

"That's okay, it wasn't completely broken," he said, closing his eyes and banging the tuning fork against the windowsill.

The banging responded to the tuning fork with a wallop of its own. This time I couldn't ignore it—the sound of someone trying to get out of the crying room. My muscles contracted and I felt cold all of a sudden. A small, irrational part of my brain was sure it was a spirit reacting to the pastor's blessing. But it was too concrete of a sound to be some angry ancestor.

The pastor didn't seem to notice it. He did two turns around the room, as I predicted he would. As he walked around the room a second time, the thumping got louder and faster. Each step the pastor took, the thump doubled in speed and sound. By the time we left the room, I was almost on my knees with my hands over my ears.

Pastor Jacobs didn't notice until he was almost at the

stairs. "Miss Conner," he said, dropping his tools and rushing over to me, "are you all right? Do you need an ambulance?"

"No, I don't. It was that knocking or banging that was making me crazy."

"The fork? Yes, it is an aggravating sound, but—"

"No, not the tuning fork. Didn't you hear that? It was coming from the wall. It couldn't have been an animal—right? It was too loud."

Pastor Jacobs looked down at his hands, at his tools, at the wall—everything to avoid looking me in the eyes. "I don't know if I heard any of that."

"You were so focused you were probably in the 'zone,' as they say, communicating with a spirit beyond this mortal plain." I smiled, hoping to avoid another embarrassing moment.

It was too late. Pastor Jacobs looked skeptical that I took this seriously.

I pulled him back into the room where the thumping had turned into a rhythmic bang. "Don't you hear that? *Bam-bam-bam*—you could set a metronome by it."

Pastor Jacobs looked uncomfortable. He didn't say anything but coughed slightly and pointed at his tools. I cleared the way for him. He moved onto the other wing of the second floor, but when I went to follow him he stopped me.

"I think I need to do the rest of the house alone. Why don't you wait for me downstairs, in the library perhaps?" he said.

Isabel came out of the parlor and into my arms. "Mommy, we should let him do his work. It's important, right?" she said, pulling me down the stairs.

I felt rejected and embarrassed, but I dutifully followed Isabel into the library and waited for Pastor Jacobs to finish his blessing.

BAM—BAM—BAM!

I could still hear it from upstairs. My body seized each time. It always came in threes, was silent for a few minutes, and started up again. I could tell by Pastor Jacobs' footsteps that he was still in the parlor. He hadn't gone upstairs just yet.

"Mommy, do you want to play with the dollhouse?" Isabel asked, trying to draw my attention away from the pastor and the banging upstairs.

"Sure, honey," I replied distractedly, still staring up at the ceiling.

The pastor's work had obviously woken something in the house. Would he be able to get rid of it, or did I just invite the ghost to torment us on this mortal plain? I didn't know. I couldn't know until he came back downstairs and debriefed us.

BAM—BAM—BAM!

The noises got louder, and I stopped hearing his footsteps. All I could hear was the ghost that was locked into the walls of this house.

PASTOR JACOBS TOOK his time blessing our home. It was hours before we saw him again. He found me in the kitchen fixing Isabel's dinner.

"Smells delicious."

"I can prepare you a little to-go container, as a thank you," I said.

The pastor shook his head kindly and beckoned me to follow him. He had packed his things in the library, in the same place he started.

"Well, what do you think? Did you get rid of all the demons?" I asked, trying to sound jovial.

He chuckled to himself as he locked his briefcase. "This house is very old. You can feel its history everywhere you go. I have given it a blessing, and I hope you can feel that too." He took my hand and smiled at me. "I hope Lana and Bill bring you by the church. We're Unitarian, so we accept all denominations, so long as you are willing to be guided by light. I think, perhaps, it would be good for you to come and visit us. It could relieve your soul of what ails it, and bring peace to your own life."

Not knowing what to say, I just smiled and led him to the door. I wasn't looking for a religious conversion. I just wanted whatever was haunting my daughter to be banished back to the fiery pits of wherever it came from. I was starting to think this was some sort of savior grift.

Sure, I'll come bless your house, but it'll only work if you come down to the church and start donating tithes.

The banging upstairs hadn't stopped, and the pastor didn't acknowledge it once. I wanted to ask, but he scurried out the door before I could.

I went back to the kitchen and Isabel's dinner, doing my best to ignore my feelings that something was going to burst out of the wall and drag me down with it.

"Of course he ignores the *actual* problem in here. You can't invite those religious nut jobs in here. They just want to take your money and run off before you realize they didn't fix anything," my father growled as he sat down at the dinner table.

"Maybe he's hard of hearing, or he didn't want us to think—"

"He didn't want us to think! Period! What did you think he was going to do here, huh? He walked around the house with his little ball of incense, making the whole place smell like a hippie commune, and nosed about in our things. He came in here to give Mary Albertson a new crop of gossip and poke around in the medicine cabinet."

"You don't know that. I doubt he knows Mary. I found him through Lana and Bill Cabot—they're new in town. Besides, Mary's a quack. She's probably going off to California soon to live with her daughter even though her daughter doesn't like her," I said, more harshly than I intended. I was angry at the pastor. I expected more; at least more detail about what he felt in this house. I wanted to defend Pastor Jacobs to my father, but there was a part of me that felt he had a point. He hadn't fixed anything—he made the haunting worse, and then ignored what he had done.

"He probably made some kind of error in his blessing and felt too embarrassed to admit it. I'll hear from him in a couple days, just you wait," I said.

My father laughed into his drink. "You were always weak like that. No wonder you believed in this religious bullshit— y'know, he saw you as a mark the second he set foot in that door. He's not going to come back and *apologize*. Hah!" He stood up and swung his body out the door, stumbling back to the living room.

"I'm not weak!" I called out. "I'm doing my best to help this family!"

My father just laughed his way down the hall.

You're not weak, I thought. *You've had some back luck, but you're not weak.*

I had a hard time believing that, when every plan I concocted seemed to crumble. Pastor Jacobs did nothing but stir up a troublesome spirit. He provided no answer for what might be ailing Isabel. I should have ignored it. I should have driven her to the hospital while I had the chance. My father couldn't chase me on foot. He'd never get far.

"Mommy, is my dinner ready?" Isabel asked. "I'm pretty hungry. It's been a long day."

"Of course, honey. Sit down and I'll serve you."

Isabel was on her best behavior that night. She ate her dinner, dutifully bathed, and got into bed without me having to ask twice. It was like she knew that this day hadn't gone as I planned and was sparing me the eight-year-old tantrums.

"Honey, we're gonna wake up early again tomorrow, okay?" I said. "We're gonna take a little trip. For real this time, I promise."

Isabel nodded and yawned. "I'll be up bright and early tomorrow, Mommy, and I promise not to have an asthma attack."

I gave her a kiss on the forehead before leaving her room. I couldn't wait again. Waiting around for the right time wasn't helping at all. At this point, there was nothing to do but act.

27

I waited a few hours, wide awake and staring at the ceiling. I had no cash. I needed to get some, and I knew my father kept a stack of cash in his nightstand. I used to steal some from his little stash when I was a teenager, replacing hundred dollar bills with dollar bills so he wouldn't notice the stack getting smaller. It was the perfect plan, until one day he replaced his wad of cash with a wad of dollar bills and laughed at me for falling for his trick.

I waited until past midnight, and then I crept out of bed and down the stairs to my parents' bedroom. They were fast asleep, snoring soundly, and I crawled over to my father's side of the bed. There it was, right where he always left it. A wad of hundred-dollar bills. This time I took the whole thing, and scurried back up to my room. I needed to get at least a couple hours of sleep before we left.

"Isabel," I whispered, "wake up." I stood over my daughter, gently shaking her shoulder. She looked so peaceful it felt criminal to wake her.

I had waited until my parents were awake before, thinking I could plan around my father. That plan had disastrous consequences, so I changed gears and decided we had to leave before anyone was awake. I wasn't going to work around my father's "schedule" this time. I wasn't going to give him an opportunity to lay a hand on Isabel. We were leaving before dawn. I packed some extra things in another backpack—clothes and medication—because this time I didn't plan on returning right away. If it took a few days to find a doctor, I would be prepared. I was more determined than last time to not give up until I got my way. I wanted a doctor to see my daughter and tell me exactly what was wrong with her.

Even if it was just some ancient soul inhabiting her little body.

"Mommy? What time is it?" Isabel asked, slowly pushing herself up in bed.

"Early, very early. Do you want to go watch the sun rise?" I asked, trying to distract her from what she probably knew was *really* going on.

"I don't like this idea, Mommy," Isabel said, suddenly awake and very serious. "I don't think this is going to work."

"I know you're probably scared. Grandpa has made it very clear he doesn't like it when anyone leaves the house, but that's just what has to happen—"

"I'm trying to keep your expectations tied to reality, Mommy. It's not going to work. He can follow us everywhere," Isabel whispered and looked past me out the door.

What she said made me more determined. Even if my

father hadn't lain a hand on her, she was still so afraid of him that he could control her life without doing anything. He'd instilled so much fear in the mind of my eight-year-old daughter that she couldn't fathom fighting him.

"Well, honey, we don't know if it isn't going to work until we try, isn't that true?"

"I guess," she said, "but aren't you scared he's going to put you in the crying room? There's something in there, you know," she said, slowly getting out of bed. "You heard it when Pastor Jacobs was here, and I just don't want—" Isabel interrupted herself with a choked out sob.

I wrapped her in my arms, petting her hair and pressing her into my chest. "Shh, shh, honey, it's okay. I know you're scared. Trying anything can be really scary, but I don't want you to grow up afraid. I don't want you to be thinking about the crying room or having panic attacks or anything. I want you to be a kid again, so we need to try and run away for a few days, and then we'll come back, okay?"

"Aren't you afraid of what will happen?" Isabel asked, wiping away her tears.

"Of course I am, but that doesn't mean we shouldn't try," I said, smiling at her.

I kissed her forehead and Isabel gathered her things—a toy bunny that lay on her bed, and a small backpack of clothes.

We crept down the stairs slowly. My parents were deep sleepers but I wanted to be careful. I knew they wouldn't be up for another few hours at least, so we went slowly.

"Like spies," I whispered. "We have to get to the payload."

Isabel just rolled her eyes, but she played along.

We got to the car and I opened the garage door, painstakingly rolling the car out onto the driveway.

"Look, Issie, the sunrise. I don't think you've ever been awake to see the sunrise, not since you were a newborn," I said, smiling at the first few rays hitting my face.

Isabel squinted and hid in the car, peeking out the window.

"It's pretty, I guess," she said, "but it's still way too early to enjoy pretty things," she said as she sank back into the backseat.

My plan was to drive to the city. It wasn't as affluent as my town was, though. A lot of residents in my town, many who lived in the large Victorian mansions, worked in the city, despite the distance. The city had a well-regarded children's hospital, so I felt it would be a good place to start off.

Nate often drove there when he was dealing drugs, and he'd take me along, so I was pretty familiar with it. The drive was only two hours, and there were plenty of stops along the way. I wanted to stop by this cute little ice cream truck that I remembered going to as a kid. It was one of those places just off the highway that also sold fresh fruit and eggs, a real road trip staple that I hoped Isabel would be awake for.

It took two tries to start the car, but she was purring smoothly. We drove away so quickly, but in the rearview mirror, I noticed my father open the bedroom window and see us leave.

Isabel slept for the beginning of the ride. Once we got far enough out of town, I pulled off the highway into a gas station parking lot so I could get a little extra sleep myself.

The anticipation of leaving kept my adrenaline pumping all morning, but I was starting to feel the crash coming. I didn't sleep for long, but I had a horrible dream while I did.

I dreamt that I was walking out of the gas station to an empty car. Isabel wasn't in the backseat, but her bag and her toy were there. Her toy looked strange, like it had been accumulating dust for years. Suddenly I realized the whole car was covered in a pile of dust, like it had been forgotten about. I ran back into the gas station to ask how long I had been in there.

"I don't know, ma'am, I don't remember when you came in here," the attendant said.

I went back outside again and the car looked worse than it had before. It had rusted over and the bright red paint was faded and chipped. It looked like some forgotten beater at the impound. I walked closer to the car and could smell something putrid coming from the backseat. It was as if something died or food had been left out for weeks in there. As I got closer, the smell got stronger and stronger; it brought tears to my eyes and I had to hold my breath. When I touched the handle of the backseat I—

"Mommy, wake up! I'm so bored. I finished my book but I didn't pack some coloring stuff so I was wondering if you could buy me some so I could make a drawing, but you were asleep so I couldn't ask you to buy me anything. I was going to go in the store but I got scared that Grandpa would see me so I stayed in here but then you started shaking all over and you got really sweaty and you kept muttering something to yourself so I decided to wake you up because I think you're not having a nice dream. Are you okay? Mommy, wake up. Are you okay?"

I blinked and looked around. The dream felt so real that

I momentarily forgot where I was. I sniffed the air, shoved Isabel aside to make sure there wasn't some dead animal hidden in the backseat. It smelled fine. It smelled like car freshener and the cleaning products I'd used.

It was only a dream, Maggie, it was all just a dream.

"So, Mommy, is this where we get sundaes?" Isabel asked, her nose pressed up against the window.

"No, honey, that place is a little farther down the highway. Besides, I think it's still a little early for a sundae."

"Mo-om, you *promised* to get me a sundae. It's already almost lunchtime because you slept for soooo long, and it'll be even later once we get there because we still have to drive there. That's what you said when we stopped, that it wasn't open and you still had to drive there," Isabel said, her puppy-dog eyes staring up at me.

I couldn't resist them. She knew I couldn't resist them. "Okay," I caved, "but you have to sit down and put on your seatbelt or you're getting nothing at all," I said, settling back into the driver's seat. We had a long way to go. Might as well butter Isabel up while I could.

THE WEIRDEST THING happened when we were driving. There weren't very many cars on the road, but I kept seeing the same car. A red car, similar to the one I was driving, that was tailing me.

I shook my head a few times, blaming it on the paranoia I had that my father was following me, but the hallucination persisted. My double was chasing me down the highway.

WE PULLED up to the farmer's stand. It was just as I remembered—a little stall with some fruit and eggs, and a cashbox for people to pay. Beside it was a little trailer that served freshly churned ice cream and giant soft-serve cones. Isabel's nose was pressed to the glass.

"Do you want to come with me and pick whatever flavor you want?"

She was smiling, but she shook her head. "I want you to surprise me. I want to try your favorite flavor. I'm gonna close my eyes and try to guess what it is."

"Sounds fun to me. I'll get us one sundae with two spoons, but you have to sit with the door open, okay? I don't want you suffocating in here or anything."

Isabel nodded and opened the door, swinging her legs out and beckoning me to go. There were a couple of other families waiting for their own sundaes. I pointed at the kids but Isabel just waved me away.

"Johnny. John—Johnathan! What flavor do you want?"

"I want poo flavor," screamed a four-year-old boy to his very tired-looking mother.

She hung her head and looked at the ice cream man. "He wants rocky road. He means to say rocky road—"

"It looks like poo. Because it has stuff in it and it's brown." The little boy giggled at the funniest joke he had ever made in his life.

I couldn't help but giggle, as did the ice cream man. I hardly remembered what Isabel was like at that age. This summer's stress had worn me down so much.

"Do you have boys?" the mother asked. She had dark circles around her eyes and was searching for a friend in mine.

"No, sorry, I have a girl," I said, nodding toward the car.

The mom nodded and looked back at her son, who already had ice cream dribbling down his front. "Lucky you," she said. "Girls are cleaner."

"Maybe, but at that age, they're just as obsessed with poo."

The mother and I laughed and she picked up her son and took him to their car. This woman, whose name I didn't even know, was the first friend I had made in years. Another mother, someone just as exhausted by life as I was, who would do anything for their kid—including taking them to a lonely ice cream stand so he could ask for poo ice cream. *This time, what I'm doing for Isabel will work.*

"What can I get you, Miss?" the ice cream man asked.

"Vanilla sundae with whipped cream, cherry syrup, and a maraschino cherry on top. Oh and an extra scoop of rocky road on the side of it, please." Sundaes were my favorite dessert. I never really got it with rocky road, but the kid had inspired me. His joy and carefree nature was contagious.

I brought it back to the car with two spoons, walking quickly so the ice cream wouldn't melt. "You ready, Issie?" I asked.

She nodded and closed her eyes.

I handed her a big spoonful with ice cream and all the fixings on it. I kept the cherry off for fear of setting off a breathing attack.

Isabel's eyes widened with joy and a smile spread across her little face. "Mommy, this is the best thing I've ever tasted," she said, taking the spoon from my hand and messily digging into the sundae.

"Right? It's my favorite. I've never had it with rocky road before." I followed Isabel's lead and devoured the sundae.

"You know, he makes all the ice cream himself. Even the rocky road and the cherry syrup."

"I love it so, so much. Mommy, can we have a second one?" she said between mouthfuls.

"I don't think so. Too much of a good thing can make you feel sick."

The last thing I need is to clean an eight-year-old's puke from the backseat, I thought. That explained my odd gas station nightmare—a premonition of what would happen when Isabel gobbled down a sundae and couldn't hold it in.

"Slow down, honey. I don't want you to get sick," I said. "We still have a bit of this drive to go."

Isabel continued shoveling ice cream into her mouth. "It doesn't matter anyway; none of this is going to last," she said.

"What did you say?"

Isabel looked up at me and put down her spoon. "It won't last. This happy feeling we both have, the carefree nature of our roadside stop. It won't last for much longer. I'd like to savor it as much as I can." Isabel started slowly spooning the sundae into her mouth, savoring each bite like a little food critic.

I lost my appetite. Once she was finished I threw away the bowl of melted ice cream and got back in the car.

"Mom?" Isabel said from the backseat. "I hope you understand that I do love you, and I don't blame you for doing your best. I just want you to know that even though this freedom isn't going to last, I have enjoyed every moment of it with you."

"Thanks, Isabel," I said as I pulled out of the roadside stop. Was this another symptom of her mental disorder? That all-or-nothing, negative world view? I remembered that for both PTSD and temporal lobe seizures, one of the key symptoms was sudden, drastic mood changes. I chalked it up to that. Isabel was so overwhelmed with happiness that her brain short-circuited for a moment, pulling her back past reality and into the pits of despair.

The rest of our drive was silent.

28

The plan was harder than I thought. We arrived in town in the early afternoon, since we slept for quite a bit in the car, and I had to wait a few hours before I could check into any of the hotels because it was only just after noon. I wanted to use a fake name and avoid using any credit cards so that it would be harder to trace me, but no one I spoke to seemed to understand why I wanted to do that. There must not be very many runaway daughters or abused mothers checking into the Holiday Inn around here. Everyone preferred to live with their secret until that very same secret killed them.

I kept seeing the same car that was following me all morning. It was in the parking lot of the hotel, it was waiting behind me at stop signs and streetlights, it even drove by a coffee shop I stopped in. It could have been a coincidence, but my father's car wasn't a common model, and it made me feel more paranoid every time I saw it. Both my parents would have woken up by now. My father would have waited at the kitchen table until he realized I wasn't going to make him breakfast. He would have made some stupid comment about the pastor and then come upstairs to search for me, before finding my and Isabel's rooms were empty. Although I did think he'd even seen me drive away.

He might have taken it out on my mother, and I felt really guilty about that.

I got Isabel and me a couple of provisions before getting to work. She was entertained with a coloring book, while I went down the list and searched for a pediatrician in the area. There were more options here than in my rich, secluded town. There were children's mental health specialists and neurology specialists, there was an ENT doctor who only took adolescents on... A quick online search revealed that I had been looking in the wrong place. If I wanted someone to treat my child, I had to get out of a town that was made up of mostly retirees.

After making a few phone calls, I got up to stretch. The place I'd landed on was more of a designer motel than one of those high-rise places. It was only three floors high and surrounded a courtyard with a small tennis court and a pool. The parking lot was off to one side, and I could just see my beat-up red car in there. I liked the view because I could easily see who was pulling into the hotel.

Which was why I was so shocked when I saw my father sitting on one of the deck chairs by the pool. He wasn't doing much; he was lying back and drinking a beer. There were people around him splashing water in his direction, but they paid him no mind. He was staring in the direction of our room. I wasn't sure if he could see me, so I hid behind the curtain. It was definitely him. I was close enough to see his wrinkled face glowering at the beer in his hand. His clothes were unmistakable—clearly more expensive than anyone else's, well-pressed and starched like he was waiting for a date to go to the ballet or something. My father was tall and broad-shouldered and he dressed well, so from far away it was difficult to see his beer belly; he was an impressively imposing man, which made this casual scene more disturbing.

I closed the curtains and locked the door, and we didn't leave our room for the rest of the night.

I HAD a couple of appointments lined up for the next day. Over the phone I managed to find a way to sound urgent but not desperate, and I made some headway with a physician and a psychotherapist for Isabel. She was still mostly clueless as to what we were doing. According to her, this freedom and joy wouldn't last, and I began to feel guilty all over again. Her PTSD was so deeply ingrained that she couldn't believe we could start a new life.

Granted, she was right; I felt compelled to return to the house once Isabel's diagnosis was over. The money I stole from my father wouldn't take us very far, and I knew I could earn a little extra cash selling some of the antique furniture stored around the house. No one would miss it. There was plenty for my parents to use beyond what I planned to sell. Besides, all they did was sit and stare at the TV or at the books in the library. As long as there were two comfortable chairs, I doubted they'd notice if all the rest of the furniture slowly went missing.

"It's pointless, Mommy. None of this will go anywhere," Isabel said as I loaded up our car. "This won't last."

"I know you think that, honey, but I think you're wrong.

This is our first step—we're going to get you some medical help so that you can feel better, and then we'll start planning for the rest of our lives." I smiled, trying to remind Isabel of the joy she felt the day before.

She just sighed and stared out the car window like a forlorn teenager.

We had some time before the first appointment so I decided to take Isabel to the mall. At the risk of spoiling my daughter, I thought I'd get her a new dress to cheer her up a little bit. On the way there I thought I saw the same red car that was following us yesterday, driving in the opposite direction as we left the hotel. In the rear-view mirror I saw Isabel follow the car.

"That looks like our car," Isabel said.

I ignored her and refocused my attention on the road. I almost missed the turn into the mall parking lot thinking about the car. It was the same make and model as what I was driving—but who knew how many of these were produced? In different years, different shades of red... Just because it looked like our car, it didn't mean it was.

Not to mention the fact that you, Maggie Conner, are driving this car, which means your parents were left without it. How could your father be driving the same car you are? It's impossible, Maggie. Take a deep breath, and maybe tonight you should look for a therapist for yourself.

Isabel took her time choosing a dress. We went into various shops for girls, and she declared outright she didn't like any of them.

"They're all too frilly and girly. I feel like I'll ruin all of them," she pouted as we left another shop.

"You won't ruin them. You'll just have to be a little more careful, that's all. Maybe this dress is one you wear to dinner or when you want to look fancy, not when you're running around the house or doing an art project," I replied.

She took my hand and swung it around. "I guess that's true. I'm having a really nice day with you, Mommy," she said, and twirled off into the next store.

Just before I entered, I felt a shadow pass behind me. I looked to my left and there was a huge, burly man walking quickly through the crowd. From behind, he looked like my dad, but as he moved farther and farther away I wasn't so sure. It could have been another tall man, determined to get out of the mall before he lost his mind.

"Mommy! I found one I like!" Isabel called to me from inside the store, holding up a hot pink jumpsuit with a pointed lace collar. "It's perfect!"

"Sweetheart, this is wonderful, and it looks like you'll be able to play around in it too," I said, fingering the doily collar. I felt incredibly tired all of a sudden, like an anvil had been dropped onto my shoulders. What if that man was my father? What could he possibly be doing here? Not only that, but there was no way he could have driven himself; we didn't have another car. It was possible he took a cab, but then how would he know which hotel we were at, or that we'd be going to the mall?

I paid for the jumpsuit and took Isabel to the food court. We shared a burger, fries and a milkshake, adding to our decadent vacation. As I was sitting there, I saw him. My father was sitting a few tables away, eating his own burger and fries. He saw me glaring at him and cheered me with his burger, smiling like the devil. My insides twisted together in knots.

"Isabel! Look at the time! We are going to be late to your appointment. We have got to get out of here!" I sprang up and started cleaning up.

Isabel looked up at me while slurping her milkshake. "I told you," she whispered. "It can't last." She slid off her seat and followed me out of the food court.

I glanced behind me to make sure my father wasn't following us, but he was already gone, lost in the crowd.

The first doctor's appointment was an absolute wash. He acted as though Isabel wasn't even there, addressing all his questions to me and none to the patient in question. I knew all the answers, but it still felt strange that a doctor wouldn't even try to get to know his patient, even if she was an eight-year-old who was more interested in playing with the toys in his office than sitting still.

The doctor eventually descended into a lecture about the history and manifestation of trauma in family settings—his specialty. He loved discussing his research and I stayed in his office for a half hour longer because I couldn't get him to stop talking. After describing the environment at home, I was afraid he'd call CPS and wash his hands clean of us, but I was wrong. It seemed he wanted me to understand what could happen in these cases where a patient experiences unending traumatic events, as he called it.

He sent me home with a questionnaire to fill out, in order to give him a better view of my mental state so we could come up with a treatment plan. He didn't make it entirely clear *whose* treatment plan he was talking about. I was trying to weigh it out when I saw *him* again.

My father, walking across the parking lot and getting into his car. *My* car—well, the car I had been using the past two days.

I didn't know what to do except hide. I ducked into a coffee shop with Isabel, ordered a bottomless coffee and beelined to the very back of the shop where he wouldn't be able to see me. My mind was racing trying to come up with a plan—we were in an area where you had to have a car if you wanted to get around easily. Sure, there was a bus system, but it was wildly unreliable and I wasn't sure if it could even get us back to the motel.

"Mommy, can I have a cookie?" Isabel asked, completely oblivious to my dilemma.

"Sure, honey, here," I said, handing her a twenty. The wad of cash was dwindling faster than I expected. If my father took the car, it wouldn't last us longer than a week. I hadn't expected this to happen. I never thought my father would leave the comfort of our home, or even our neighborhood.

Isabel came back faster than I expected her to, with no cookie in hand.

"What's wrong? You didn't like the cookies they had?" I asked her.

She just shook her head, her serious face settling into a frown. "It's almost over," she said. "I lost my appetite."

We waited in the cafe for an hour. I kept my eye on the window waiting to see if the car drove by, but it never did. I had two cups of coffee and bought a slice of cake, and every time I did I checked on the car. My father was waiting in the driver's seat, his hands on the wheel, eyes staring forward. I thought I could wait him out, that he might get bored and leave, but it didn't look like that was a possibility.

"Come on," I said. "We have to get going." I still wasn't sure what to do. I could either get in the car and get driven back to my house, or run in the opposite direction, hop in a cab and deal with public transit. I took a deep breath before leaving the cafe, ready to accept the consequences of whatever decision I ended up making—but my father was gone.

I crept over to the car, looking into the backseat and the bushes behind the parking lot, but he was nowhere to be found. I opened the car door and could smell the aura of my father's beer-and-whiskey diet, so I knew he had been there. It had been him waiting for us in the car.

"Maybe he got tired of waiting?" Isabel breathed.

But I knew better. My father played the long game. If he wasn't here, it meant he was waiting for me someplace else.

I WASN'T sure I wanted to go back to the hotel just yet. We had another appointment scheduled, but I decided to cancel it because I was so afraid of another run-in with my father. He hadn't done anything yet, hadn't approached us directly, but I didn't want to tempt fate.

I drove around in circles for a while before coming across the Unitarian church that Pastor Jacobs led. It had all these flags outside, with a large banner that said:

We welcome all. Let us give you sanctuary.

It was the sign I needed, and I pulled into the church.

It was empty inside. I supposed not much went on in

between services. The building wasn't huge and it seemed very new, but the inside was cavernous.

"Hello?" I called out, my voice bouncing off the high beams. "Pastor Jacobs?"

I heard a flurry of footsteps, and Pastor Jacobs came out from behind the altar, wearing a bib.

"Miss Conner! What a surprise. I-I was just having a little snack," he said, walking down the aisle toward me. "How have you been?" Pastor Jacobs shook my hand vigorously before looking to Isabel. "Hello, Isabel."

Isabel immediately hid behind me and didn't say a word.

"She's shy," I said. "Kids go through a phase like that at her age."

I smiled and he awkwardly smiled back. I wasn't sure what to do or say, and neither did he.

"Did you need some guidance?" he finally asked.

I shook my head. "I just needed a place to sit down for a moment or two. Is that okay?"

"Of course. I'll be in my office if you want to talk. Which you don't have to, but if you want to talk about what might be going on, I'm here." He smiled and backed off.

Pastor Jacobs was a nice man. It wasn't his fault that my daughter and home needed an exorcism, not a blessing. I could see why Lana and Bill had recommended him.

"Make sure you say goodbye before you go!" he called back.

I waved at him. I didn't know what to say to his kindness. I just sat down. Isabel went for a walk between the pews, picking up the programs and reading them. I just stared up at the altar, begging this day to be over.

"Mommy, we have to go back now," Isabel said, appearing in the pew in front of me. "We can't stay in this church forever, and also I have to pee. And I'm tired. And hungry. And I want to color. And—"

"I get it, you little maniac," I said, tickling Isabel. "I'll drive us back to the hotel. We can order room service if you want."

"Yay!" she said, running past me and out the door.

I started walking to the altar so I could say goodbye to Pastor Jacobs, but something stopped me in my tracks. There were loud footsteps coming from that same back room. They were slower and heavier than Pastor Jacobs' and something about them sent a chill up my spine. A second later, as I took another step toward the altar, I saw the figure of my father pass through the doorway. He was so tall he had to duck underneath the door frame as he slowly advanced like the monster in a horror movie.

I didn't wait to see what he would do. I turned on my heel and ran out the door.

My mind was racing as I drove back to the hotel. Was I dreaming or hallucinating? Was my father stalking me or was he hunting me down? How could he know where I was or what I was doing? *He must have put a tracking device in your car. That's what he was doing in the driver's seat for so long.* I wanted desperately to check but I was driving and I could feel my heart rate rising. A stunt like that would get us into an accident, and my father already knew where our hotel was. The only person who stood to lose anything was me.

When we got to the hotel I hurried us up to the room, terrified that my father was lurking around every corner. Isabel complained—she wanted to go in the pool, she wanted to throw balls in the tennis court—but in that moment I didn't care. I had to get her up to our room before my father did something dangerous.

"Mo-om! You left my new jumpsuit in the car!" Isabel cried. "I wanna wear it. You have to go get it!"

"Isabel, it's safe in the car. You can wear it tomorrow."

"No! I want to wear it tonight. We were gonna do a fashion show. It's not fair. You haven't let me do *anything*. You said I can't swim in the pool, you made us run away at the food court... It's not fair, Mom. Please, please, *please* will you get my jumpsuit?" Isabel cried, dropped to her knees and threw a classic tantrum.

I didn't want to deal with this. I couldn't right now. I wanted to go to sleep and hope that today was a horrible dream, but I knew I wouldn't be able to if—

"Okay," I said. "I'll go get it."

Isabel celebrated as I left the room. I felt off-balance and terrified. The hallway was tilting like I had been drinking and I had to hold onto the walls to steady myself. My legs propelled me forward to my inevitable fate.

My father was leaning against the car, holding the bag with Isabel's brand new jumpsuit. "Looking for this?" he asked.

My dad had a smug smile on his face. He caught me in a moment where I had no choice but to confront him.

"Would you care to explain why you stole my car, and my money? You also left, even though I *explicitly* told you that you could not leave with Isabel and you could not take her out of my home." He grabbed my arm. "I don't think you understand that I do this for your own good. It's for your own safety that you need to—"

"Dad, I get it, but you don't have to lie and say this is for my own safety—"

My father cut me off by slamming my head into the car.

I couldn't even scream because my nose started bleeding. I felt so angry that this was happening, that my plan had failed yet again. My father's determination to kidnap my daughter and me knew no bounds. If I didn't understand that before, I certainly did now. It was just as Isabel said—this freedom wouldn't last.

I couldn't let go without a fight. My father picked me up by the arm, but I swung my fist into his chest. I swung as hard as I could, but my fist collapsed when it made contact. He was a sturdy man. He worked construction before he got into real estate, and kept his muscles by using my mother as a punching bag. My limbs felt weak and my father just laughed at me as I struggled to hurt him.

"You can't hurt me. I'm bigger than you, I'm stronger than you, and you'll never escape me. I control you, and your little embarrassment too. You're not going to embarrass me by running away and telling everyone how I ruined your life, you hear?"

All the strength drained out of me. I sank down to the ground, defeated. My arms and legs felt like jello and my head was throbbing with pain. What could I do? I couldn't escape him. He knew how to find me even when I wasn't near home. He was like a solid brick wall. I couldn't beat him if I tried.

My father followed me to my room and watched as I packed it up. Isabel was, thankfully, quiet. I had paid for the room in advance so I just had to tell the front desk I was leaving.

"Leaving so soon?" the concierge asked. "Well, I hope

you enjoyed your stay with us and you'll remember us next time you're in town!"

I looked at her like she had three heads. My nose was red, I could feel bruises starting to form around my eyes, but this girl saw none of that.

I walked back to the car. My father was sitting in the passenger seat. Isabel was in the back.

"You drove her here, you can drive her back," he growled. "Besides, I'm exhausted. I'm not interested in having to drive back home. You seem to thrive in the night. Your nocturnal self can drive in the dark."

No one said a word on the drive.

No one said a word when we got home.

My father and Isabel went straight to bed, leaving me to unpack the car. I did it slowly, covering the vehicle with a tarp. I didn't know how he did it, and I didn't want to know anymore. Now that I'd seen what would happen if I just ran away, without someone else protecting me, I had no hope of getting very far.

All I could do was avoid him, until I had a plan to escape once and for all.

29

I felt like I was underwater all over again, except this time I knew I wasn't being sedated. I went through the motions of my day, but often found myself frozen in time, staring at a chair or out the window, unaware of what to do next. When I walked through the house, I was silent. The voice in my head, my moral and critical center, had nothing to add. I smiled while playing with Isabel, but she could tell I was never in the mood.

"Mommy, do you want to play witches? Maybe we can brew a potion that will help you feel better," she said.

I didn't answer. I didn't know how to answer anymore because I didn't know how to be positive. I could no longer hide what kind of man her grandfather was—not that I ever had—and I couldn't dream of a day when I would be able to escape.

Isabel kept disappearing. She would be in her room, sometimes in the library, but I kept losing track of her throughout the house.

My mother kept checking on me and my progress. "You know the parlor isn't finished yet, don't you? Half the dining set has to be stained and re-tufted. Not to mention the half-painted walls up there. The house is an absolute mess, Maggie. What are you going to do about it?" she kept asking, but I never had an answer for her.

I understood why she was so often on her phone, or staring at the TV, or watching the dollhouse. My mother was also stuck, unable to move forward in life. Vacuumed into the misery that surrounded my oblivious, controlling father.

My father watched me like a hawk. He kept tabs on me throughout the day, and I had to report to him what my plans were. If I was in my workshop, the door had to be open so he could poke his head in the door and make sure I was still there. I couldn't leave, even if I wanted to. I didn't have the energy to work around my father's gaze.

I wasn't sleeping either. I didn't sleep a wink the night we came home, nor did I sleep the next night. When I looked in the mirror, I saw dark circles under my eyes, so dark they practically blended in with the bruising around my nose. I didn't think it was broken. I checked when I got home. It was tender to the touch but not painful or anything. It would heal just fine, and no one would even notice since I never went out anymore.

I was truly a prisoner in my own home.

What if he hurts her again? What are you going to do? the little voice at the back of my mind kept asking.

My father had never hurt Isabel before, yet I was

convinced he was going to do something "again." I didn't understand it. The few times I was able to close my eyes for a nap, I woke up screaming, thinking my father was hurting Isabel again. She was fine. He'd never touched her. He grabbed her arm once, but my brain was turning it around and making me feel he had done something worse.

"Isabel, has your grandfather ever hurt you?" I asked her, hoping to explain this strange train of thought.

Isabel said nothing; she only shrugged her shoulders.

What if he hurts her again? What are you going to do? the little voice whispered continually to me whenever I lost track of Isabel.

My father was just annoyed and ashamed of her. He preferred to think she didn't exist, but he'd never physically hurt her. Then again, what did I know? I was starting to lose track of Isabel during the day. She would be by my side one moment and would vanish in the next. In those moments, Isabel might have been hurt by my father—but she'd tell me if that happened, wouldn't she?

I THOUGHT Isabel had started avoiding me because of my father. That was the only reason I could think of for her sudden disappearances. She would be handing me a fresh brush in one moment, and the next she was gone, replaced by the specter of my father.

"Where's Isabel?" I kept asking, but my father didn't know or care.

"Why do you need her? She's eight. She can't use a power sander, can she?" was the most he would say.

I'd find Isabel later, reading in her bed. Sometimes I

wouldn't see her until it was bedtime, but she never seemed to remember where she went.

"Issie, you disappeared today when we were painting. Where'd you go?"

"I dunno." She shrugged. "I'm here now; isn't that what's important?"

"I guess, but I worry about you. I don't want you to get hurt."

"It's too late for that," she whispered.

It cut me down to my heart to hear her say that. My disappointment must have rubbed off on her, or perhaps she was coming to realize that we were confined to this old house and there was nothing I could do to free us. It hurt me and added to the depression I was experiencing.

I turned out the light and went to my room, glancing back at Isabel's sleeping body. There was nothing I could do anymore. I didn't know how to change this situation we were stuck in. I lay in bed, staring up at the ceiling, waiting for the morning to come.

"Mommy, what happens when people die?" Isabel asked me as I was finishing up with my mother's office.

"What do you mean?" I asked her, trying to figure out where this line of questioning was going.

"Where do they go? What do they do? Do they get sad when people forget about them?" she asked, her voice serious and steady. She could have been asking me for homework help with that same tone.

"It depends. Some people believe in a place called heaven, which is like... the most perfect place ever."

"A utopia?"

"Yes, heaven is a utopia. Some people think that's where you go, or you might end up in hell, which is the absolute opposite in every way. Some people think you come back in a new body—that's called reincarnation. You might come back as a human, or as an insect or an animal. It all depends on how you act in your current life. Some people think your body might die and be buried, but your soul or spirit will hang around for a while, especially if you have unfinished business."

"That's what ghosts are. That's why we got the blessing done on the house—right?" she asked.

I nodded and beckoned her over for a hug. "Why are you thinking about that, my sweet? Is there something scaring you?"

"No, I was just curious. Do you think a lot of people will come to my funeral?"

I was taken aback by that last question. It was normal and healthy for kids to have a fascination with death. Isabel was at the age where kids started to get curious and needed to find answers to what lay beyond what we saw. Still, with the state of our family, it scared me.

"Of course, honey, why wouldn't they? But why are you asking? Are you scared of something?"

"No, I was just curious," she said before running out of the room.

I truly didn't know what to make of that interaction. She didn't seem sad—at least, not until she started asking about her funeral—but it was possible she could be depressed. I would never be able to get a proper diagnosis of PTSD, but I was sure it caused her to think about her own mortality. What kid wouldn't in a house like this one?

I left my mother's office to find Isabel and make sure she was really okay, but I couldn't find her again. It was as though she had disappeared into thin air. I didn't see her until an hour later, when I went upstairs to change out of a dusty shirt. She was lying in her bed, drawing in a sketchpad.

"Hey, kiddo, you feeling okay? I wanted to check on you but I couldn't find you," I said, leaning against her doorframe.

"I'm fine. I'm drawing what I think the afterlife looks like, but so far all I can think of is a dark room. It's not very imaginative."

"That might be the afterlife for some people."

"I hope I have a better imagination than they do," she said, passing me and heading to the little bathroom we shared.

Her mood was swinging to the angsty side of the pendulum today. Isabel had a way of making sure she couldn't be found if she didn't want to, so I guessed I could chalk her latest disappearance up to that. Someone who didn't want to be found while she pondered the deep questions of the world.

THAT DAY WAS long and oddly grueling. I barely saw Isabel, except in glimpses as I worked in my mother's office. My mother wanted me to clean up in there, and I was happy to have another project to keep me as far as I could be from the crying room.

My father pulled up a chair and started reading just outside the door, like a bouncer or a prison guard. He sat wearing his favorite smoking jacket, slippers, and pajama set, reading *Crime and Punishment* all day as I continued working. He was there to make sure I wasn't distracted by silly things, like being a mother to my child.

I kept closing my eyes and ducking behind my mother's desk. I would squeeze my eyes shut and tell myself this was nothing but a bad dream, and that I was going to wake up on an inflatable pool raft in the hotel we were staying at.

"What do you think you're doing down there?" my father called from the hallway. "Think you're going to find an escape hatch?" He roared with laughter at his own joke, slapping his knee and almost choking on his cigar.

"Nope, just a lot of dust bunnies," I said, straining to smile at my father.

It took me ages, but finally I finished. We had dinner together as a family, almost completely in silence except for Isabel occasionally asking about songs to play at a funeral. She disappeared as soon as she was done, leaving me to clean up alone. I didn't mind. It meant I could go at my own pace, which had slowed considerably since I came home.

I dragged myself up the stairs to my bedroom and collapsed on the bed in sadness and exhaustion. I looked out my door, expecting to see Isabel's light still on, but I saw nothing. There was just an empty room, just as gloomy and dark as my own. There was a fine layer of dust covering the sparse furniture—a small crib bed, a dresser, and an old rocking chair. I squeezed my eyes shut and opened them again, but there it was. A strange room that had replaced Isabel's.

"Isabel?" I called out. "Are you there?"

No one answered.

I pushed myself off the bed and went into the room. It

was completely empty except for the three pieces of furniture. No one had been in there in years, decades maybe. The room smelled stale, and the light didn't work, so everything looked grey. It wasn't Isabel's room.

Am I hallucinating? I'd heard that happened with insomniacs. Eventually they needed sleep so badly that their minds started to dream when they were still awake. I touched the crib—it was real, and it felt like it was about to fall to pieces. It meant my daughter was missing—my daughter and her whole life were erased.

My hands started shaking and I could feel a scream catch in the back of my throat. Where was Isabel? What happened to her room?

I ran out of there and went to the attic, hoping this was some kind of strange and stupid prank. Isabel had been talking about her funeral all day; what if she had done something to hurt herself?

"Isabel!" I screamed. "Isabel, are you up here?" I wound my way through the junk in the attic, searching for my child. She was so little she could fit inside most of the furniture up here. It would be a perfect hiding spot for her. Was her bedroom furniture up here? Her books and toys and everything else that was once in the bright pink room? Where was the jumpsuit I bought her? She hadn't even worn that yet.

I ran back downstairs, opening every door and crying out her name.

My parents both screamed at me when I got to their room.

"Do you really think that little brat cozied up to us and we're keeping it from you? I've told you, keep an eye on her or I'll deal with it myself!" my father yelled, before slamming his face back into the pillow.

I stumbled down to my workshop hoping to find her, but had no such luck. I started crying, sobbing by myself down there. Without Isabel I doubted I would survive. I'd turn into a zombie like my mother, alive because my heart was beating and my lungs were breathing, but completely disconnected from the world of the living.

"Mommy?" I heard a whisper from the top of the stairs. "Are you okay? You're not in bed."

I whipped around and saw Isabel standing sheepishly, waiting for me in the kitchen. I felt a wave of nausea wash over me but I was relieved.

"Where were you?" I asked, more harshly than I intended.

"I was reading and then I forgot where I was. When I went upstairs, you weren't there."

"What have you done with your room, Isabel? Everything is gone."

Isabel's face screwed up and she started to cry. I realized I was gripping her arm hard, harder than I ever had. I didn't want her going anywhere. I wanted to tell her she could never leave my sight—no more disappearing acts, no more pranks. Instead, I wrapped her in my arms and carried her upstairs. She could sleep in my bed for the night.

Isabel's room was back to normal the next day, but she still didn't explain what had happened. She kept disappearing, but she'd always reappear in her room a few hours later. I grew accustomed to turning around and finding that Isabel suddenly wasn't there. My father was always there, always watching, and she avoided him at all costs. I rarely saw my mother, who now spent most of her days in bed, eyes staring aimlessly at the ceiling.

Meanwhile, I kept moving. Continued fixing up the house, organizing my parents' things, cooking and cleaning. All of it was done in a haze, like I was underwater, only this time I wasn't sure that I was sedated.

30

The Cabots noticed I hadn't been going out lately. Lana came to my door to bring me cookies and offer support. "Sometimes we see you in the window upstairs, and you look a little... distracted. I was wondering if you might need some help around the house?"

I didn't know what to say in return. She meant well but how could she help?

"I'm just fine. It's a lot of work, remodeling this old place. I think you've caught me when I'm tired." I smiled weakly, hoping to get her off my case. "Babysitting and construction work don't really go hand in hand."

"Bill worked construction once. A long time ago, before we met. He did it a few summers. I'm sure he'd be happy to lend a hand with whatever you need."

"Right now I'm more focused on furniture. You know, re-staining, reupholstering. It's not heavy-duty stuff. It's actually quite fun. I really enjoy it."

"That's wonderful. I feel like young people nowadays don't know how to fix things anymore. They just buy a new one from Ikea and call it a day. How did you learn to do all of that?"

I thought about my answer for a minute. I probably looked like an android that short-circuited, but if I was being honest, I couldn't remember how I'd picked up that skill. I knew what I had to do and did it, but I couldn't remember when I was taught.

"I get a lot of advice from the guys at the hardware store. Tony especially; he's great, never tries to sell you on something more expensive just for the sake of it." I started closing the door, feeling my father's presence behind me. "I actually have to get back to it now—don't want Isabel getting into the turpentine or anything. Thanks, Lana!" I closed the door on her, which felt rude, but she wouldn't leave otherwise.

I desperately wanted to reach out. I wanted to run into Lana's arms and tell her everything—how my father was my prison guard and I didn't know how to help my daughter. That I suspected my daughter was suffering from PTSD and she would sometimes disappear for hours on end and not remember what she was doing. The only help I needed was to escape this situation, but deep down I knew that even if Lana flew me halfway across the country, I would never be able to shake off what happened in this house. Bill was lovely, but having him sand down the hardwood floors to help me refurbish them or repair and re-paint the crown moldings wasn't what I needed. I needed so much more, and so did Isabel.

It wasn't lost on anyone in town that I had now joined my parents as shut-ins. In an instant we became the scary house on the hill, the ones children would avoid and tell stories about— starring the wicked old lady who lived in there. The stories would involve the full moon, and every once in a while a kid would be dared to jump the fence into the backyard or run up and ring our doorbell. Maybe Lana would chase them away, out of sympathy for me. I could get used to it—play up their suspicions by building fires at strange times of the year. Play really loud music on every full moon—or better yet, just a recording of me laughing maniacally. I could at least have a little fun in my zombie state. Instead, I got awkward pauses whenever I asked for my groceries to be delivered.

"Are you sure you don't want to come by? We have a couple of um... in-store deals today," the cashier would sometimes say to lure me out of the house.

I was too exhausted to do it. Going to the store would involve at least one argument with my father, phone calls to make sure of where I was, and I wouldn't be allowed to take the car *or* my wagon, on the off-chance that I was planning something.

"No, thank you. I'm so busy today; it's just easier to have my groceries delivered." I always said the same line, and she always sighed when I did.

Sorry to disappoint. The crazy woman in the big old house isn't going to be your source of gossip today. Try again next time.

I DID TRY to get some sunshine, at least for the vitamin D. I sat on the porch with a book in my lap. I usually didn't read. I'd just stare out at the street and bask in the warm rays of the late summer sun. I waved at Lana or Bill, but I didn't really see anyone else. That's why it was so surprising when I saw Mary rushing down the street one day. I'd just had a few bags of groceries delivered, and decided to stay outside for a little while. Mary must have seen the groceries getting picked and bagged, and decided to follow them to their destination.

Her disease had gotten worse since the last time I saw her. It hadn't been very long, but you could tell. Her curly grey hair was frizzier than usual and she was more erratic as she came rushing down the street.

"Maggie!" she called out. "Maggie Conner!" Mary stopped right in front of my house. Her large dress had a gaudy colorful pattern and it made her look even more frantic. "Maggie Conner, you have to wake up! Wake up right this instant! This has gone on long enough. You have to wake up!"

At that moment Lana came running out of her house and rushed across the street.

I hesitated to help Mary, because she was clearly going through an episode and I was afraid she might attack me.

"Mary, is everything all right? I'm not asleep, Mary. I promise I am awake, okay?" I called out to her.

Lana took Mary by the hand and whispered something in her ear. They had a strange little argument, but I couldn't hear what they were saying. Something about hallucinations and being confused. Lana was right. Mary was confused. I felt bad for her but how many other episodes like this one had occurred? Her daughter needed to come back from California to take care of her mom. I didn't care if they got along or not.

Eventually, Lana led Mary away, in the direction Mary had come from.

Later, when she came back, I waved her down. "Lana! I was watching you from the window. Is Mary okay?" I asked.

Lana hesitated answering at first. She bit her lip and looked at me with tearful eyes.

"It's okay," I said. "Mary is the town gossip. We all know her—though she probably knows us better. Is it dementia, like her mother?"

Lana shook her head.

I could see that she was too upset to say anything further and I retreated back inside.

"I didn't know they were close," my mother said when I joined her in the library. "Funny."

THE NEXT DAY, Mary came by again. I had called the hardware store to put in an order, which they quickly delivered to me. No comments about why I was getting deliveries—I guessed because most people needed to buy so much they couldn't fit it in their car. Minutes after the delivery boy left, Mary came rushing down the street again, huffing and puffing, her hair wilder than ever.

"Maggie Conner. No one wants to tell you this, but I will. I realize it won't make me very popular, but I think it's unfair that you don't understand—your family is dead," she yelled at me from the sidewalk again.

"Mary, are you okay? Are you feeling safe?"

"No—nope—absolutely not. I will not be talked down to that way. I am sixty-four, not dead! Your family is in the past. You are alone here, do you understand? You are *alone*."

"I don't understand. Why are you so upset about me living alone?" I asked as I started walking down the porch steps.

"You are alone! You are alone, you are alone, you are alone! You need to wake up, Maggie Conner."

"Mary," I said, trying a calm but forceful tone. "I live with my parents and daughter." I held out my hand, mimicking Lana's behavior from the day before. I wasn't sure if that was the right thing to do with a dementia patient—did you allow them to believe their own delusions, or was it better to pull them back to reality?

"Maggie, that is all in the past. You have to move forward. It's unhealthy for you to live like this."

"Live how, Mary? How am I supposed to live?"

"Like a normal person! You have to come to terms with the fact that you are *alone*. You are a single woman. You don't have your father controlling you anymore. You need to get help, real psychological help, and stop acting like your life is over. You're still young."

Something about what she said set me off. How dare she judge me and my living situation? She had been in this town for years; she knew very well what my father was like, and *now* she cared? *Now,* after years of casually observing us and spreading gossip all over town about my family, I was supposed to believe that Mary Albertson was *concerned*?

"Mary, I understand this isn't you, it's your condition talking, but you can't come to my house and start insulting me like this. You know very well how dangerous my father can be—don't try to deny it. You're the nosiest person in this town; you probably know what's going on in my house better than I do. I'm doing my best for me and my child, and I may not make the right decisions all the time, but I am trying." Tears started streaming down my face as I continued, "You, meanwhile, are a judgmental, cantankerous woman whose undiagnosed dementia is turning you into an even bigger menace than you once were—if that is even possible."

"You. Don't. Have. A. Child, okay? You are not a mother. You are just a crazy young girl who got into trouble and now—"

"What? Mary, I may have got into trouble in my day, but you're no better. You were so sour that your own daughter moved to the other side of the country to get away from you. I hope I am never like you, you crazy old bat!" I cracked. I pushed Mary into a parked car.

She was shocked. It threw her off balance and her blue eyes went as wide as saucers. "You are just like your father. Out of control, mentally unwell, and unfit to be a parent. How dare you bring me into this, as if my problems compare to yours. Well, I won't do it anymore, Maggie. I won't play along. Mark my words, you are in for a rude awakening." She shook her finger at me before stalking down the street, muttering to herself.

I watched her turn the corner and then deflated, collapsing to the street. I felt confused and exhausted. It was wrong of me to shove an older woman who was going through mental distress. What kind of person was I becoming?

"Maggie?" I heard Bill's voice pierce through my sobs. "Maggie, are you all right?"

I couldn't answer him. I was just crying and crying, wailing at my inability to control myself. Mary was right. I was turning into my father. The other night I grabbed Isabel's arm with the same steely grip. I was starting to feel like she couldn't leave my sight. I needed to control her and I kept saying it was for her own good. I wasn't fit to be a mother. No fit mother would keep her daughter in a living situation like mine.

"I'm going to run and get Lana," Bill said. "Will you be okay waiting? Please wait. I'll only be a minute, okay?"

I ignored him and just kept crying on the street. If only Mary could see me now, she'd have me committed and send Isabel off to some horrible orphanage or something.

"Maggie, what's wrong, dear?" Lana's soft voice came through, her hand gently touching my shoulder. "Please can you tell me what's wrong?"

"Can you take Isabel?" I sputtered, my whole body shuddering with tears.

"What was that?" Lana whispered.

"Can you take her? That way she'll be right across the street and I can still see her, but she'll be able to grow up in a loving home. You had kids so I know this isn't ideal but—"

"We can't take her, dear," Bill cut in.

Lana gave him a look and he pressed his lips together.

"What Bill *means* to say is that I don't think we'd be the best home for her right now. Because of our CBD business, we have a lot of products around the house and it makes it unsafe for children." Lana started to quietly cry. "I don't think we can help your little girl. I wish we could, I really do, but we can't."

"Please," I wailed, "please take her. I don't know what to do. I'm a horrible mother. I can't make any decisions. It's like Mary said. I'm just a troubled girl."

"My dear, please listen to me. Mary is a judgy busybody. You are doing the best you can. I don't know what is going on that we don't know, but I know that you are a very resilient young woman, and you'll get through this soon."

"If you could just take her," I said, leaning into Lana's

shoulder. She was so comforting, the perfect mother or grandmother. She knew what she was doing, she knew how to help people. I could barely even take care of myself.

"I wish we could do that for you, but we can't. I think you need to work through this," Lana whispered. She started to get up.

Bill took my arm and lifted me to my feet. He was holding a little business card with a phone number scrawled on it. "Take this. It's my phone number. I don't think you have it, though I think you have Lana's. Call us when you feel up for a visit, or if you ever need to chat with another grown-up. It's hard for moms when they feel alone. You can even call if you see Mary coming and we'll run interference," Bill said with a wink.

It was the tiny act of humor I needed in that moment.

He patted me on the back and helped me up the steps to the house, and then the couple jogged back across the street.

I went inside and closed the door, wishing I could forget it all.

31

quelch.

I remembered that sound. I started having dreams weeks ago with that sound.

Squelch.

The sound was hard and soft at the same time, it was wet and gushy, it was followed by the feeling of hot, sticky blood dripping down my arm, and the sound of someone crying out in agony. My heart was beating as I watched the blood drip down and cover my arm, more and more of it cascading from that invisible wound. The blood rushed out covering my arms, my legs, my torso, my shoulder, it kept rushing out until I was covered in blood from head to toe.

I tried to scream, but no sound came out, and when I opened my mouth I swallowed blood. I felt myself choking on the blood, and I was grabbing at my neck unable to breathe. I tried to scream. I tried to call for help, but blood sputtered from my mouth and made me choke faster. I couldn't breathe. My limbs felt cold. I could feel my body seizing up uncontrollably.

"Helllp," I managed to breathe out, but the sound was drowned by the blood. I was dying; I had to be dying—that could be the only explanation. I didn't know where I was. It was all dark, and I was going to die here, all alone.

I GASPED for air as I sat up straight in bed.
It was a nightmare, Maggie. Nothing but a nightmare.
I touched my limbs and my throat, but there was nothing there. My throat felt dry. I drank some water, swallowed it normally. Everything was fine. It was all just a strange dream.

Since coming home I had on and off insomnia. I couldn't sleep, and my waking hours were starting to bleed into dreams. My brain was playing tricks on me, and I had to find a way to get myself to sleep. That night I took a sleeping pill, and the next, and the next.

I didn't know which was worse: not sleeping at all, or sleeping but having terrifying and vivid nightmares. My dreams were all terrifying, and I woke up in a panic every time. In the first one, I was reliving the day I ran away, but it was remixed with the day I drove off with Isabel. Nate kept appearing in her bed asking me where Isabel was, but I couldn't find her. I searched all over the house, in the basement, even in the parlor. When I was in the parlor I heard a knocking coming from the crying room and I started to cry as I realized who it was. I clawed at the wall with my bare hands, tearing it apart to find my daughter, but the wall never came away. I dug through the drywall, insulation, through the wood, but it was never-ending, and I couldn't find Isabel.

"She's gone," Nate said behind me. "Stop digging."

But I couldn't stop. I kept searching for Isabel in the walls of this house. Finally, I dug my way out and found myself on the roof. I watched as another version of myself—the younger, sixteen-year-old version—hopped out of a window and climbed down. She ran across the yard to Nate's waiting car. I tried to scream out to her, to stop her, but I was frozen on the roof of the house. The younger version of me left bloody footprints on the green lawn.

BECAUSE MY NIGHTMARES were so vivid, I was still exhausted in the mornings. I needed rest, but rest was out of the picture. My waking hours felt catatonic and anxious at the same time. All I could do was wait for it to be over, and work as hard as I could. I got slower and less productive, causing my father to yell at me more often. My mother joined in, criticizing my work ethic, telling me I'd never get this remodel done and I was doomed to live in a crumbling home for eternity.

"Maybe you won't even be in this home. If you can't renovate the house, you'll have to find some other way to pay rent, or we'll have you out on the streets." My father laughed.

My mother, who was never a cruel woman, joined in.

Their laughter made me feel physically ill, and I couldn't escape it. I would often hallucinate the sound of my father laughing while I was working on the house.

The crying room started knocking again, after I had the nightmare where Isabel was inside. This time it didn't stop. The banging was constant throughout the day and night, but it didn't seem to bother my parents or my daughter. They didn't even notice it, and I felt like I was being driven crazy by the sound. I wanted to open the door and find out what it was, but I couldn't find the lock. It was buried under wallpaper which my mother wanted to keep as an accent wall. I wasn't even sure the knocking was real, but I was compelled to find out. I tried to find it, slice open the wallpaper, or hammer the door down, but as soon as I got close, my limbs went weak. It was like the crying room had a force field around it. I could hardly lift the sledgehammer, and would never be able to scratch through the wallpaper.

"Don't do it," Isabel said, standing in the hallway looking in. "It's not a good idea and I think it will give you nightmares."

She was right. There was no good reason to relive those memories.

I ordered earplugs from the pharmacy, to be delivered with the next refill of my prescriptions.

I WAS STAINING *the floor again. I thought I had finished this part of the hallway, but my father needed it redone. It was uneven. I dipped my brush into the can and started painting, but soon I realized I was painting the floor with blood. I couldn't stop myself. I was out of control. It smelled metallic. The blood was sticky. It was still warm. It was fresh blood. I don't know how I knew but I did.*

Down the hallway I could hear someone moaning. "Maggie," it said, "Maggie, no."

I ignored them; they didn't need my sympathy. I was growing angrier with every stroke. The blood was dripping off my brush and onto my leg. One drop grew until it was covering my body. I was getting closer to the person moaning—was it a man or a woman? I couldn't tell. I just kept painting the floor with blood. The blood got on my hands and in my hair—what did it matter; no one ever saw me nowadays. The floor was dyed a deep maroon color and it smelled like soil and iron mixed together.

I kept painting as my heart started to race. What if they found me? What if the person moaning found me and killed me? My heart was beating faster, my breath was getting faster, my arms were getting faster too. They were angry, I could tell. They were going to attack me but I was ready for them this time. They weren't going to get me this time. I was painting the floor with their own blood—

I woke up sweating.

Isabel was shaking my shoulder. "Mom, are you okay? You were screaming."

"What was I saying?"

"I couldn't tell—you were kind of mumbling—but it was really loud and you sounded like you were in pain. Are you in pain?"

"No, honey," I said, turning away to grab my glass of water. "I just had a bad dr—"

I turned back but Isabel was gone. Did I dream that too? I got up and padded over to her room to check on her. Isabel was sound asleep clutching one of her toys.

It must have been a dream, I thought. Strange; it had felt so real.

THE NEXT MORNING I was making breakfast when Isabel disappeared again. She was right beside me, drying the dishes, but as soon as I turned away, she was gone. Every time I lost track of her, she reappeared in her room a little while later. I was starting to see this pattern, so when I finished doing the dishes I went upstairs to meet her.

She was sitting at her desk drawing.

"Isabel, that wasn't very nice. You ran off in the middle of doing chores. It's rude to just disappear like that."

"Sorry, Mommy, I didn't realize I was doing it. Sometimes it just happens."

"Seems to me that when you're doing something you *enjoy*, it doesn't 'just happen.' Why is that?" I asked her, putting on as stern a voice as I could. I wasn't angry, I was worried. If Isabel was having her seizures again, I didn't want her to hide them from me. I was also afraid of what my father might do; he'd become more aggressive since we came home from our 'little journey,' as he called it.

Isabel shrugged at me. "I guess it's harder at those times because you're watching me."

"I don't want to do that. I don't want to turn into your prison guard, but these disappearances make me worried. Even if you are just going up to your room, I want you to tell me, okay? Please."

"Okay, Mommy."

She did not listen at all. An hour later, while I was having Isabel help me fix the banister in the main stairway, she disappeared again. This time while I was reaching back to hand her a hammer. I had felt a little off all morning because of the dream from last night. After I woke up I could never get back to sleep, and my hands were shaking from exhaustion. Isabel disappearing was just what my fragile mind *didn't* need.

"Isabel. What did I just ask you?" I said, storming into

her room. "If I am asking for your help it's because I need it. I'm sick of this bizarre disappearing act."

"Mom, I've been in here all day. I don't know what you're talking about."

Was that right? I could have sworn she was helping me with the banister. "That's not true, Isabel. What have I told you about lying?"

"Mommy, I promise, I don't remember helping you. We were washing dishes, then I left, then I came here, and that's it. Are you sure I was helping you? Maybe it was Grandma?" Isabel offered.

She looked so innocent and genuinely confused, I had a hard time believing this was a malicious prank. Still, every time she disappeared I panicked. Every time I ran up the stairs, I was worried she wouldn't be there. I couldn't have that happen, not today, and especially not after my confrontation with Mary.

"Honey, I want you to come downstairs with me. You can bring your book if you want to."

Isabel dutifully picked up her large copy of *Crime and Punishment* and followed me.

I sat her down on the top step of the main staircase, right where I could see her. If I was working on the banister, I could work it out so that she was always in my field of vision. I'd keep a little mirror with me as well, just to make sure I could have my eye on her at all times.

"This is what Grandpa does with you. Did I do something that made you upset, Mommy?" she asked.

"No, but I don't like this habit of yours. Disappearing without a trace isn't a very funny prank, especially when Mommy hasn't slept in days. So, I'm going to make sure you are right where I can see you."

Isabel's shoulders tensed up when I said it. My voice sounded more aggressive than I meant it. I probably sounded angrier than I was, but I was terrified of losing her. It was making me lose my sanity.

Isabel sat on the steps all day. She didn't move, except once when she asked to go to the bathroom. I stood in the bathroom with her because I didn't want her to disappear when I closed the door.

"Mommy, you're scaring me," she said, too nervous to do her business anymore. "This is scary."

"I have to keep you in my sight, Isabel. If I don't, I might lose you, and that's not okay," I snapped.

Isabel jumped and went about her business. I heard her sniffle as she washed up, and she was crying while I escorted her back to her chair. Isabel buried her head in her book, lifting it up to cover her face. I could hear her crying all day. It irritated me.

Doesn't she understand that this is for her own good? What if she bothered my father and he hit her? Or what if she ran outside and had a seizure, and I wasn't there to help her? Isabel was fragile and I had to protect her, and if that meant she was a little upset with me, I'd just have to live with that.

BY THE END of the day I had changed my tune. Isabel refused to speak to me, and she'd been crying nonstop for hours now. She wasn't dramatic about it, but her face was puffy and red and she was sniffling. When I put her to bed she refused to let me touch her, or kiss her forehead as I usually did.

"I'm really sorry, Isabel," I said, standing in her doorway. "I got really scared and I let that take over today. I feel like since we came back from the hotel everything has gotten worse. I can't sleep, I keep dreaming of someone dying, and I am so worried that—" I cut myself off as I started to cry. I couldn't manage it—losing Isabel. I thought if she was gone, I would fall down and die.

32

"Maggie, I need you." My mother appeared in my doorway, her hands in bandages again.

I was lying in bed staring at the ceiling. I spent another night awake, hoping to bore myself to sleep with no luck.

"Maggie, get out of bed, please. I need your help."

The night before, I cried until I had no tears left. It scared me how easily I turned into my father when I was afraid. There was a reason abuse cycled through a family this way. The moment I was challenged and stressed I acted exactly as he did—I tried to control every part of my child's life, beyond the point where it was reasonable. My head felt foggy. I could have had a hangover and I wouldn't know the difference.

"I'm coming, Mom. Just let me wash my face."

"It's important. I'll meet you downstairs," she said, and walked away.

I didn't know what that was supposed to mean—was I to follow her, or could I have a moment on my own? I decided to ignore her and wash my face. Whatever it was, it could wait. I needed an ice-cold shower to get me ready for the day.

My mother was waiting for me by the front door. There was a manilla envelope on the floor at her feet that she wouldn't pick up. "I can't," she said. "My hands are wrapped."

I thought this was over. She seemed fine yesterday and the day before that. I don't understand why her hands are wrapped up again. My mother's hands were bandaged around the palms and down her forearms. It was probably another burn, one that she treated herself in the middle of the night. My mother was never the type to bother anyone with those kinds of problems. She was used to it and didn't like to explain. Any time she could avoid lying to a doctor, or looking them in the eye as they ignored the real problem, she would.

"What happened this time?" I asked as I picked up the envelope.

She didn't reply, just turned and walked away, expecting me to follow, which I did, dutifully. *Never complain, never explain—a motto fit for royals and royal disasters.*

My mother went up to her office, which wasn't locked anymore. I kept it open nowadays, hoping to air out the room. It had an oddly stale smell, like the room had been locked up for years. The decaying pages released a musty scent and I was hoping to get rid of it.

"You cleaned," she observed, scanning the room before sitting at the large desk.

"Yeah, the room looks bigger now that the papers aren't cluttering everything. I made sure to keep them together. I didn't quite understand all the papers, but I think I did a pretty decent job. You'll be able to find everything—"

"Maggie, open the envelope. It's important. The lawyer sent more pages that we have to sign and you need to pay attention this time. I don't want any mistakes. This is important. Do you understand me?" She swerved to look at me and jerked her head to get me to sit down.

I looked through the pages as my mother stared at the top of my head. "Mom, did you ever think about leaving?" I asked as I rifled through the pages. Once again, they were impossible to understand. She was right; I had to really pay attention.

"I can't say. I suppose I did think about it," she said, her eyes wandering to the window.

"Did you ever try?" I asked her.

My mother didn't answer. She pushed herself out of the chair and exited the room.

I guess that was my answer. My mother was a dutiful wife. She wasn't raised to leave her husband and child, no matter the circumstances. Maybe if she had been born in a different generation…

I didn't want to think about that. It made me sad because ultimately, wasn't I in the same position as her? Bound to this house and to the Conner name and all the baggage it carried?

How many women had married into this family and found chaos waiting for them at the altar?

THESE PAGES WERE JUST as confusing as the last set of documents. They were steeped in legalese, and I felt like I was drowning in page flags telling me where to sign, print, or initial my name. This time I was determined to make my way through and actually understand it. That meant I had to ignore my father's questions about housework, and I had to let myself forget about what Isabel could be doing—she was avoiding me anyway, so the papers came at the perfect time.

It took me hours, and what I found chilled me to the bone.

These are probate papers. These pages were from my family's lawyer, officially signing my parents' estate over to me. But that was impossible, because why would my parents' estate go to me while they were still alive?

"THE LORD IS *my light and my salvation; whom shall I fear? The Lord is the stronghold of my life; of whom shall I be afraid?"*

"Amen."

There were more people at her funeral than I expected. Half the society ladies in town showed up, each clutching a handkerchief and quietly crying.

Where were their tears when my mother was hiding bruises behind sunglasses? They hid behind their society husbands then. Hid behind money and fear, and finally when they realized they did more harm than good they felt guilty, so this was all they could do. Show up at her funeral and cry, and ignore their part in her suicide.

"Helena Conner's daughter has chosen to read a poem as a eulogy."

I read some poem by Alfred, Lord Tennyson. The man spent years writing eulogy poems so it seemed appropriate. The society ladies cried at the appropriate moments and smiled nostalgically at others.

The day went off without a hitch. The only problem was that my mother was dead. The only person I had left in my life was gone.

The lawyers approached me at the wake. A team of old men hired by my father, who didn't have a sympathetic bone in their body.

"We would like to get the matter of the will and estate settled as quickly as possible. Our team is able to handle all the finances, but it would be good if you came into our office so we can run everything by you."

"Did you have to do this at my mother's wake?" I said. "Could you not have called, rather than ambush me on the day I buried my mother?" I was raising my voice but didn't realize it.

The entire party turned to watch the drama unfold. One of the old men—I couldn't keep track of their names—patted me on the shoulder. A calculated gesture he'd learned from some body language expert, no doubt.

"We apologize. It was difficult to get a hold of your mother in the first place, so we didn't want to take any chances. Estates and wills get more complicated the more time passes. It may be uncouth, so we did what we—"

"I'll set up a meeting. Please leave now."

The team of lawyers left. The party went back to normal. I called them a few days later. In a week I was sitting in a large conference room with a team of old men in suits who were running through the assets that made up my family's estate.

"Have you been managing it for them? What did my parents do?" I was completely flabbergasted at how comprehensive the document was and how expansive my parents' estate was.

"We managed the finances. When your father would add new

pieces of real estate we would do the day-to-day management of the same. Your parents paid us on retainer. If you wish, we can maintain this system going forward." There was one spokesman for the others.

I didn't understand their power structure. How did they decide who got to speak? Did they draw straws before going into the conference, or was there a complicated rehearsal process beforehand?

"That sounds fine to me. What do I need to do?" I asked.

"We'll send some papers soon. They will be quite clear. No one here has any interest in meddling in the system your father created. It is quite complicated but it is a well-oiled machine. You just have to sign some papers and we'll take care of the rest. You'll also receive a package of documents detailing the Conner estate's assets, and once per quarter you'll receive a dividends report that explains your revenues and the state of your financial positions."

"Sure." I shrugged, unable to process what was happening. My father was rich, my mother was rich—that meant I'll be rich for a long time. I was too tired and too traumatized to think about it now. All I wanted was to go home, fall asleep in my bed, and never wake up again.

"Do you have the keys to the house? The one we actually lived in?"

"Of course," the lead lawyer said. "There should be keys...?"

Another more junior lawyer jumped up and handed me an envelope with the keys to my childhood home. It would just be one giant Victorian mansion, and me.

I WOKE up at my desk, my head spinning. Once I signed these papers my mother's estate and her assets would be mine, because she was dead. There was a funeral. Mary Albertson was there. There was a wake, we had buried her, and there was a meeting with the lawyers detailing my inheritance.

My mother was dead.

These papers proved it.

I looked up, and my mother was sitting across from me, her hands bandaged. "Have you finished yet?" she asked.

I opened my mouth, but I could not scream.

33

"Maggie? I asked you a question. Are you going to answer, or are you going to sit there with your mouth open?" My mother was sitting across from me, in her office, in my childhood home.

My mother also had a funeral several weeks ago, where a team of lawyers passed her estate onto me. I had the papers in front of me, clearly stating that her entire estate was being passed to my hands. All I had to do was sign below and her fortune was all mine.

It didn't make sense.

"Um, sorry, what was the question?" I asked, training my eyes on her hoping to find some clue to what she was. Was this the ghost of my mother, or was it my own hallucination?

"Have you finished yet?" she asked. She was annoyed. Her arms were crossed and she was drumming her bandaged fingers on her arm. Or was she? Was I seeing all this right?

"Yes, I've finished. But I have a couple of questions about the paperwork, and I was wondering—"

"I didn't ask if you had questions, I asked if you were finished."

"I think so."

"Well, go mail it."

"Mom, did you read what these were?" I asked. "Do you know what it says in here?"

My mother sighed and rolled her eyes. She took the pages from me and quickly flipped through them. "It says something about an inheritance. What more do you need to know?"

I was shocked to find she didn't react to the contents of the documents at all. Did she actually read the pages in my hand?

"Mom, do you see whose inheritance it is?" I asked, truly concerned that she wasn't paying attention.

"Why do I have to? It came from the lawyers, it has to do with inheritance, someone died and is leaving me money—what else do you need to know?"

My mother was completely oblivious to the actual contents of the documents, I was sure of it. The same way that I couldn't understand what I was signing when we got the first pages from the lawyer.

She's from a different time. No one taught her the nitty-gritty of reading contracts and knowing your status in life. She was taught to follow her husband's lead, do what her husband asked of her, and do the same for the other male authority figures in her life.

My mother stood up abruptly. "If you're done in here, please make arrangements to mail the papers and get back to work. You have wallpaper to replace all over the third floor. You don't have a very consistent method for working in here, do you? If I were you, I'd have worked on a plan for how you were going to renovate this house before attacking the place. At this rate, nothing will be done, and your construction will be haunting us for years to come," she said, and walked out of the room.

My mother was dead, but my mother was also roaming around the house giving me orders. My mother might be a ghost, which wouldn't be very different from how she acted when she was alive. She might have been a ghost for weeks, and I hadn't noticed. How could I? My mother rarely ever paid attention to me or anyone else around her. It explained why Mary barely batted an eye when she could hear my mother being beaten by my father. I had to know why she was still here, what kind of unfinished business she had with this house that she had to haunt the place for weeks. It was terrifying thinking that my mother couldn't let go of life, when she could have so much peace in death. What did she come back here for, to be beaten and berated by my father?

Could this be the reason behind Isabel's attacks? Bill did suspect that something paranormal was behind Isabel's sudden breathing problems. That was why they recommended Pastor Jacobs to me. Did he refuse to do an exorcism because of my mother? That didn't make sense. She wasn't a demon. It would have been a simple matter of asking the ghoul to leave my daughter alone, right?

I wasn't sure I had what it took to confront my mother's ghost. Not yet, at least. I had to find more evidence before I could say it. If only she'd slip up and walk through a wall while I was looking—that would make it easier to prove she truly was no longer with us.

"Maggie, have you sent off those papers?" my mother asked later that night, at dinnertime. We were eating a roast I spent the afternoon making—a tangible dinner where I could see just how much my mother ate. As usual, she took a few bites and abandoned her plate.

"I scheduled a pickup tomorrow. A courier is coming from the lawyer's office." That was a lie. I scheduled a pickup with the post office, but I wondered if the threat of being spotted by a courier would draw my mother's secret out.

"Good. I'm going to bed. I've had enough dinner," she said, slowly standing up.

"You've barely touched your plate," my father barked. "Sit down and finish."

I shuddered. My father took the words right out of my mouth. I wanted my mother to finish, and I wanted her to stay here while I cleaned up. I needed to confront her. I needed to know the truth. If she was a ghost, why was she trying to possess Isabel? Was there something she couldn't do in her current form?

While cooking dinner, all I could think about was my mother's behavior these last few weeks. The hours and hours she spent in front of the TV or staring at that dollhouse. How often she seemed to be staring into space, the way she seemed to appear out of thin air everywhere she went. As much as I didn't want to say it, I was starting to believe it. The hallucination I'd had about her funeral—it felt too real. It felt more like a memory than some delusional dream, and while I didn't trust myself much lately, I really believed in it.

My mom took two more bites, then got up and left the room.

When I looked at her bowl, the food seemed to be

completely untouched, even though I saw her bring the fork to her lips.

"She's a ghost, isn't she? That proves it."

I jumped at the sound of my father's gravelly voice. He was staring at me like an animal devouring its meal, looking for the next.

"You're gonna confront her and she's going to deny it. You shouldn't do it. Don't disrupt the balance of the system, Maggie. If you do that, you don't know how she'll react. She might turn into a poltergeist and it'll be all your fault. You'll regret this when you have to clean up after her."

He'd read my mind. I was terrified at confronting my mother and having it blow back on me. It was entirely possible that I couldn't banish her from my home and would turn her into an aggressive version of herself. If she was able to survive Pastor Jacobs' blessing, she was obviously a powerful spirit. I felt terrified and unsure of what *could* happen if I confronted my mother. What would it do, anyway? We had lived a somewhat comfortable life together as daughter and specter. What was the harm in letting it continue?

"That's a bad idea, Maggie," my father said. "Your mother has to move on. She can't linger in this house forever. If she doesn't go, this house will be haunted long after you're gone, and you'll never be able to grieve your mother's death."

My father stared me down, reading my mind and answering questions I didn't have a chance to voice. It was creepy, but maybe he was thinking the same thing. *Or this was another mind trick he's learned to keep you under his control?*

Behind me, my father laughed.

I ignored the feeling that he was listening to my thoughts, and chased my mother.

I MANAGED to corner her in my parents' bedroom. She was sitting on the bed, staring out the window.

"Mom?" I asked. "I need to talk to you about those papers."

"Go ahead. I'm not doing anything," she said.

She didn't turn around, so I talked to the back of her head. "The lawyers sent over probate papers—"

"I know that, Maggie. It's for an inheritance I'm receiving."

"No, Mom, it's for an inheritance *I'm* receiving. Your inheritance—I'm receiving the proceeds from the will that *you* wrote. Don't you realize that?"

"Maggie, don't be ridiculous. I'm sitting right in front of you. How could you be inheriting my estate?"

"That's what I was wondering. But then I remembered we had a funeral for you several weeks ago. There was a funeral mass, we buried you, we had a wake and everything."

My mother was silent.

I braced myself for what could be coming. The woman was small, but I had no idea what she was capable of.

She slowly turned around to face me, her face showing no emotion at all. "Is that what you think?" she asked, so quietly I had to strain to hear her. "That I'm dead? Is that what you've been waiting for, then? For me to die so you can leave us here?"

"No, I—"

"Do you think I'm stupid, Maggie? Do you honestly think I am that stupid, because I think you are. I think you must be sick in the head to believe that I am *dead*. Clearly this was a mistake, and we have to *call* the lawyer's office to make sure the pages are corrected with the proper names in the right places. How *dare* you accuse me of that? Do you honestly not see that someone is playing a cruel prank on this family, acting as though I have *died?*" Her voice got louder with each word.

I immediately started backing away, terrified of what was coming. My mother seemed to get taller as she got louder. Her face was screwed up with anger. I had offended her. I had woken up the ghost who was in denial about their reality. She wasn't ready to go back, not at all. She wasn't ready to accept reality—

"Mom, please," I begged, "I only want to help you."

"Help me? By murdering me, or by stealing my money! Was that your plan? To persuade me that I had died so you could steal my money from under my nose? I bet you already have a death certificate forged and ready to go. You were going to leave me destitute, and for what? A dollhouse and a few old pieces of jewelry? Or was there something else in your little plan? Were you going to leave us with nothing? Tell me, Maggie, are you *stupid* for believing in a practical joke, or are you *evil* for planning on stealing all my money?"

"Stop it!" I screamed. "Please! I'm sorry, Mother, I am sorry. I didn't mean—" I cut myself off as I tried to catch my breath. Tears were streaming down my face, I couldn't control my own breath, and my mind was spinning out of control. Had I imagined that? Did I really see that funeral or was my mother right—was this some kind of sick joke?

I backed out of the room, just as my father appeared and slammed the door shut. I had no idea how he got up here so quickly. I hadn't even heard him coming up the stairs.

"I told you not to disturb your mother!" he yelled.

Behind him, my mother was pounding on the door, screaming at him to open up, calling me an idiot and a liar. I'd never seen this side of her before, and I felt frozen in place.

"You see what you did?" my father roared. "I told you to leave her alone, let her believe she was real, and now thanks to you we have a friggin' banshee living in this house! How do you think that's going to make us look, huh?" He slapped me upside the head and entered his room.

I heard my parents struggle, until finally he quieted her down. The door locked.

I caught my breath and dragged myself upstairs. I sat down on my bed to recharge and think about what happened. I was sure of the funeral, even after my mother's diatribe. Her defensiveness confirmed for me what I had seen. My mother was dead. Everything that was once hers was now mine, just as soon as the lawyers processed the paperwork. But what if—

"What if your mother destroys the papers?" I whipped around to see my father standing behind me.

"What are you doing in here? I thought you were downstairs, helping Mom calm down. I didn't even see you—"

"Maggie, this is my house. I don't need your permission to walk around my own home, do I?"

"N-no. I guess you don't."

"I locked your mother in our bedroom. The papers are fine; she won't destroy them. Even if she does, the lawyers will send another set. They are good lawyers. They don't want to trick you."

I wanted to get out of here. I didn't feel safe with my father in my room—

"Don't you worry about me. I'm not up here to hurt you

or your 'precious daughter.' I just wanted to warn you that behavior like this won't be tolerated. I am your father. You will listen to me and do as I say; do you understand that?" my father hissed his threats.

I edged away from him, nodding in agreement. I just wanted him out of here. The sooner I agreed the sooner I would get my wish.

He smirked and stalked out of the door.

I listened carefully to make sure I heard his footsteps go down the stairs.

I don't know how he did that. He must have used one of the house's secret passageways. But that didn't explain how he knew what I was thinking. Was I talking out loud and didn't realize? I was afraid, disoriented, and confused. I felt so confused! Why did my father care about my mother's mental state all of a sudden, after years and years of torturing her? If I accepted this money, what did it mean for him? Logically, if my mother was dead, her estate should revert to my father, so why was I getting it instead?

There must be some explanation. If this was some kind of cruel joke, I needed to find proof of it and tell the lawyers. I could only imagine how that phone call would go.

"Hello! My father sent a phony will that said my mother was dead and I would be the one to receive her estate. Do you mind making sure it doesn't see the light of day, and go back to his old will? Nope, that will be all. Haha, yes, we really are pranksters here at the Conner house!"

My father had the answers. He knew this house inside out. He hired the lawyers and controlled what they did. He was the one who tortured my mother physically and mentally. If this was a prank, it was coming from my father. His predictions of my behavior made sense if he was the one to set this argument in motion. If he was the one pulling the marionette strings, it explained why he knew what I would say before I said it.

I couldn't do anything now. I had to wait until everyone was asleep before I could act.

I WAITED until midnight and crept downstairs. I had to break into my father's office, on the first floor near the library. I used a bobby pin to pry the lock open, hoping I was quiet enough that everyone kept sleeping while I was working. It was dark, and my father's office was a mess. I could hardly see a foot in front of me, even after I turned the old lamp on. The whole room was covered in dust. He hadn't been in here in years. Something felt off. This room felt forgotten, more so than any other place in this house. I hadn't been inside while renovating, and now I saw my father hadn't either. I turned on his ancient computer to continue my search—was the inheritance my father's prank, or was my mother really dead?

There was no death certificate on his desk, nor was it saved on his computer. When I looked through the folders it slowly dawned on me that the most recent folder was time-stamped with a date from eight years ago. *That's impossible. My father made a fortune, but I don't believe he hasn't worked in eight years.*

That was the moment everything clicked. I couldn't think of a single moment in the past eight years where my father was present. In fact, I couldn't remember the last eight years of my life. I tried to remember Isabel's birthdays and where my father might have been, tried to remember my own birthdays, holidays, anything that could ground my father in reality, but the fact was he was missing from my memory. I could feel my father's presence—his suffocating aura permeated every thought in my mind—yet I didn't *see* him in my mind's eye. What had he been doing? Had he been a shut-in for longer than I remembered?

The computer's screensaver blinked to life, pulling me out of my mental spiral. I suddenly realized there were huge gaps in my own memory and I had no way of filling them. Why was I inheriting my mother's estate? That was the only question I wanted answered when I came in here, but this dusty office—a room that couldn't have been touched in ages—propelled me to keep going. My mother was just the start; there were other answers here.

My father might have had something to do with her death. That's probably why he didn't want me investigating. If he killed her—

I opened a browser. The computer was slow; the internet down here barely worked, but it chugged along. I had all night to find the truth. My father had probably killed my mother and I allowed myself to forget. My traumatic past wouldn't let me face the real truth, and now my father was taunting me with a prank. Rather than inherit my mother's estate, he passed it along to me, to play games with my mind and manipulate me further.

I typed my father's name into the search bar, but nothing came up. There were too many Joseph Conners in the world. I searched for "Joseph Conner—New York State," but that didn't narrow it down as much as I needed. There were old profiles dated ten years prior about my dad as a real estate mogul. There was a picture of me with my father, but my mother wasn't mentioned in the article at all. When had he killed her? How long had he been keeping this secret?

That's why she possessed Isabel. She needs someone to understand what happened to her. She needs someone to find the body.

I heard a distant thud coming from upstairs. The thud turned into a bang, a rhythmic bang coming from the crying room. Shivers ran up and down my spine as I thought *my father locked me in a room with my dead mother and I didn't even know it.*

I typed in my father's name and our home address. That narrowed it down to a single Joseph Conner. There wasn't another one in this town. I scrolled down past profiles of my grandfather, my father's namesake, and then I found it. An old news article that made me stop in my tracks. I read the headline over and over and over again, willing it to make sense.

Joseph Conner, Local Real Estate Mogul, Declared Dead in Absentia after Exhausting Eight-Year Search.

"So, you've finally found my secret."

I looked up, and my father was smiling, leaning against the doorway of his office.

34

"You're dead," I said, still staring at the headline.

He is remembered by his wife, Helena Conner, and his daughter, Margaret "Maggie" Conner. Joseph Conner disappeared eight years ago, and despite numerous searches by police, his body has never been found. His wife has been notified and police are attempting to locate his daughter. A memorial service has been planned thanks to the legal team in charge of his estate, as per specifications set out in Joseph Conner's will.

"That I am. That's been my little secret." He smiled. "I'm surprised you didn't figure it out yet, with all the people you've had coming in and out of this house. I tried to stop you, but you just wouldn't listen. You were always a stubborn girl, never listened to me or your mother no matter what we did."

"Your methods of enforcing rules were cruel. I did what I could to survive."

"And look at where you are now! You're living, and I'm dead, and yet you're still here. For all your rebellion, you have nothing to show for it. A crazy daughter and a reputation as the town wacko; the lady on the hill who talks to her imaginary parents all day long."

"Shut up! This is your fault! You've been haunting me and my daughter, and for what? This is all some kind of sick game to you, but this is my life!"

I ran at him with all my might. He was dead—what could he do?

My father grabbed me by the throat and pushed me up against the wall.

"You can't hurt me," I croaked. "You're dead."

He just smiled and tightened his grip around my throat.

C'mon, Maggie, you saw that headline. Your father is dead. There's been no trace of him. He ran off. He probably killed your mother, isn't that right? He came out of hiding and killed her, or even if he didn't, that doesn't matter now. What matters is that you save Isabel and go. Live your life. You can't die here. You can't die at all; he's all in your head. Maggie, he is all in your head. You are doing this to yourself. C'mon, Maggie, snap out of it!

I squeezed my eyes shut and tried to drown out the sound of my father's laughter. He was dead. I knew that. No ghost or spirit was this strong. I must be doing this to myself. I had to snap out of it and fight back. I couldn't just let the thought of him kill me. Isabel needed me.

When I opened my eyes, I quickly glanced down and saw my own arm at my throat, my legs braced against the doorframe. It was only a flash of reality, but that was all I needed. My father's face came back into view, but now I knew it wasn't real. I peeled his fingers off my throat, willing myself to believe I was stronger. It worked. My father stumbled backwards and I ran away from him. I bolted up the stairs with only one person on my mind.

"Isabel!" I screamed.

My parents' bedroom door opened and I willed my legs to move faster. *This house is too big; I won't make it in time.* My father's laughter was ringing in my ears. I had to ignore it, I had to get Isabel and get out. I would run to the Cabots' house. They could put us up for the night and maybe help form some kind of exorcism plan. Pastor Jacobs couldn't do it, but someone could. Someone had to help me. I had to get rid of my parents' ghosts even if it meant burning the house to the ground.

"Isabel, wake up!" I screamed as I made it to the third floor and whirled around the corner to her room. "Isabel!"

I was too late.

My daughter was lying on her bed, fighting against a pillow that was pressed down on her face. It was being held there by nothing, but her little arms and legs struggled against it. I could hear a muffled cry, someone squealing and gasping for air under the pillow. It didn't sound like Isabel. It sounded like a baby crying.

35

I ran into Isabel's room as the sound of a baby's cries echoed off her walls. I didn't understand how the pillow was suffocating her. It could have been my parents, but I didn't understand why.

"Why are you doing this!" I screamed. "Why can't you leave us alone? Why won't you just let us live!"

Isabel's hands were starting to go limp. Her grasps at the pillow were getting weaker and weaker.

I tried to pry it off her face, but something kept it vacuumed over her. I tore at the pillow, my nails digging into the fabric, scooping out feathers and throwing them onto the floor. I could feel the force of whoever was choking her forcing the fabric into her tiny mouth, gagging her as she tried to breathe.

"Isabel, please, just stay with me—please!" I screamed as tears streamed down my face. Somewhere downstairs I heard it again—the same banging as before, faster and more desperate this time. Whoever was in there was suffocating.

Their lungs were running out of oxygen faster than they could drag a breath.

Her hands fell limp to her sides as I finally tore the pillow in two. I brushed the feathers away from her face, scooped a couple out of her mouth.

She was lying still but she wasn't breathing. Her body was convulsing. It looked as though she was about to throw up.

Please, not like this. I can't lose you like this. I gently picked her up by the shoulders and rolled her to the side of the bed. I did the Heimlich maneuver as best as I could, slamming the heel of my hand into her back, just as you were supposed to. *That's the Heimlich for a baby, Maggie. It's different for children, isn't it? Is it?* I couldn't keep my head straight. I could barely see because I was crying so badly, and my ears were ringing due to the noise coming from downstairs. It was shaking the walls of the house down to the foundation. I felt that at any moment, the whole house would fall down around my feet.

"C'mon, Isabel, they aren't real. They can't hurt you! I promise, honey, I promise they can't hurt you."

I slammed the heel of my hand against her back one last time, and Isabel sputtered to life. She choked out a few last feathers and vomited. Then she started coughing and wheezing, doubled over the side of the bed, her whole body shaking as it tried to suck up as much oxygen as it could.

I rubbed her back trying to make her feel better while looking over my shoulder. We had to get out of here. I wasn't sure we'd have very much time. Even in death, my father was determined to cause me as much pain as possible. I wouldn't put it past him to take Isabel away from me somehow.

"Isabel, we have to go. We don't have any time."

"We're all out of time, Mommy," she rasped, her voice gravelly from asphyxiation. Isabel was staring up at me, holding her neck with both hands, like someone was choking her. I heard her breathing become labored. She started coughing and wheezing again, her skin was instantly paler and her lips were turning blue. It all happened so quickly that I didn't even have time to react.

Snap out of it, Maggie! I picked Isabel up by the armpits and carried her, the way I had when she was a baby or a toddler, one hand supporting her head. I bounced a little, trying to get her to breathe again. "It's okay, honey. You'll be okay, I promise."

The banging from the crying room got louder as I said it. My head was spinning and Isabel's body felt heavier than ever. I turned and saw my father standing across the hall in my bedroom. He was smiling, leaning casually against my dresser, wearing his favorite smoking jacket.

"You're too late. That kid is lost," he said. "You hear that knocking? That means it's time. It's the witching hour, the time all the spirits come out to play, oooooh." He laughed as he wiggled his fingers and mocked me.

I turned and ran down the hall as fast as I could. Isabel's legs were limp and slipping out of my grasp.

"C'mon, honey, wrap your legs around my waist. We have to get going, okay?" Her body felt limp and she was moaning in my ear.

"Mommy, I can't. I can't do it, Mommy, I'm too tired." She was crying. I could feel her tears on my neck. My daughter's voice got weaker and her crying slowed down. She sounded like a little baby.

I remembered what it was like, at sixteen, not a clue in

the world, trying to take care of a colicky baby while my father screamed at me to keep her quiet.

"There's nothing I can do!" I would scream. "She's in pain, but you won't let me take her to a doctor."

"You're not taking that kid anywhere," he said. "I won't have you parading that shameful mistake all over town, embarrassing me and the good Conner name."

I needed a doctor. My goal was to get Isabel to a doctor who would be able to take care of her. They could put her on a ventilator, pump her with steroids, anything that got her lungs working again.

"You won't get out of here." My mother was waiting for us on the second floor.

Behind her, I saw the furniture and the lights shaking in the parlor. The door to the crying room was ready to burst open. Whatever was in there wanted out. I didn't want to hang around to see what it was.

"Had enough secrets for the day?" My father laughed from behind me. He was sitting on the stairs, watching as Isabel slid from my grasp. "I think you'd be interested in what's behind that door. You've been curious, I know. Don't forget I can read every single thought in that silly little mind of yours. Part of you is wondering who that could be. That's the last secret of this house, right? Who boarded up the crying room? When did they do it?" my father hissed.

I stumbled backward, bumping into my mother.

"Don't make fun, Joseph. You've been cruel enough. She knows there's no turning back now. It's far too late to keep the crying room quiet."

I ran down the hall and down the stairs. Isabel could barely hold her head up. Her feet were dragging on the ground. I kept hoisting her up onto my hip, but then one of her arms would fall, and then her head, and soon I felt her body slipping out of my grasp.

"Maggie, come join us in the living room, please. Let's work this out like civilized adults. You've had a good life with us. We've provided for you, haven't we? Why don't you just put Isabel down and stay right here. It's better for all of us if you do."

"Better?" I spat. "Better if I stay? How can you say that? Do you know what it was like, living in this house? You were a zombie, Mother. You were weak and you let him belittle you and manipulate you and abuse me at every turn! I read the article. I know you ran away. I know everything now—"

"You don't know everything," my father said, appearing behind my mother. "There is a lot you still don't know. Your mother is right; it's better if you stay and we can work things out."

"Please, Maggie. I promise, no more lies. Just don't leave," my mother pleaded.

I was done. She was dead and gone, and she wasn't my problem anymore. I didn't need to sympathize with her as a relic of a bygone age. I didn't need to understand her, I didn't need to get angry with her. I wanted to take Isabel away and start a new life, and leave my parents' ghosts to rot in this old house.

"Let her go, Helena. It's the only way she'll learn. Look at her, look at the disgust and pity in her eyes. She hates you. She thinks you are a pathetic woman who couldn't think for herself, couldn't act for herself. She doesn't know anything. Let her learn the hard way what life is really about." He stepped back and sat down in one of the high-back chairs, disappearing from view.

My mother's teary eyes implored me to follow her, but it was too little too late.

I turned and started walking away.

"You're too late, Maggie!" my mother called after me. "If you stay then maybe—"

But I didn't hear her. I opened the door and dragged Isabel outside. The heavy wooden door muted my mother's cries.

I took a deep breath of the warm night air. I could see the stars in the sky and I could smell the dewy grass. It was late.

"Hopefully the Cabots won't hate us for barging in in the middle of the night."

Isabel didn't answer me.

Isabel was gone.

36

"What have you done?" I roared as I re-entered my house. "What have you done with her?"

No one answered.

"I know you're here. Don't start hiding out on me! Don't you dare start picking and choosing when you want to appear *now*."

My father walked out of the library and leaned against the door frame. "I've told you before, she can't leave."

"That's bullshit. I left with her a few days ago. We made it all the way to a different town. What did you do to her?"

My father just sighed and rolled his eyes. "Maggie, don't make me out to be a cruel man. I'm not trying to separate you from your daughter, I'm just trying to make you understand that as long as you leave this house, she won't be with you for long. I will make *sure* that she won't be with you."

I was done with this. "Isabel!" I screamed. "Isabel, where are you?" I checked in the living room, the hallway closets, even my father's office, but I realized he had more tricks in this house than I knew about. Dead or alive, my father knew this house like the back of his hand, and he knew what was hidden behind its walls better than anyone.

"You're not going to find her," he called out.

His voice filled my body with rage. In a blind panic I stormed to the kitchen, grabbing the first knife I saw out of the butcher's block. I came back slowly, hunting my father.

He was laughing in the doorway of the library. "What are you going to do, stab me?"

"You can get hurt. I've seen it. I've seen you burn your mouth on hot foods. Besides, I control you, don't I? You're just a part of my imagination. I can hurt you if I want to." My voice was low and guttural. I sounded like my father at his angriest. I was ready to fight for my daughter, until I died or my father went back to hell where he belonged.

"I don't think this is going to have the ending you are imagining."

"I want Isabel. Wherever you have her, whatever secret little closet you've put her in, I want you to show me. I won't let you do this to her. I won't. I won't let you drive her crazy like you've done me."

My mother appeared behind me, pleading with me, "Maggie, please, just let this go. Stay here and leave it be." She sounded caring and sweet, everything I *wanted* my mother to be, when in reality she was oblivious and cold.

"Shut up, Mother. That little innocent act won't work on me. I know you're part of this too. I know you've been working with him for weeks now—how else do you explain it? That's why I feel so afraid, why I feel so suffocated by fixing this house. You're creating work for me to lose myself and become just like you—weak and clueless."

I was shocking myself; I'd never spoken to my mother like this. I knew deep down that she deserved my compassion, but the part of my brain that could process that was turned off. My mother started coughing and wheezing, holding her throat.

"That's how I used to feel too," my father said. "I knew what I did was wrong, but I didn't care. I couldn't care. I put my needs before yours and your mother's, and you know what? I'd do it all again just the same way." He was reading my mind again. I didn't know how to turn it off. "I would also go into these rages where I would threaten my family, remember?"

"You aren't family. You never protected me. You cursed me and tortured me—that's not what family does," I raged, my voice going hoarse from screaming. "Give me back Isabel. Whatever you did with her, wherever you took her, go find her and bring her back to me."

"You don't want to know that."

"I don't want to know what?"

"What we did to Isabel. You're better off not knowing," my father said.

"Why don't you go back to remodeling the house? There's still a lot to do. As long as you keep working on it, you can keep seeing Isabel," my mother piped in behind me, her voice quieter than usual. She was trying to talk but something was caught in her throat. She was acting the way Isabel did right before one of her strange panic attacks.

"So you're holding her hostage? Why? You can haunt this house no matter what state it's in. Why do I need to be *fixing it up* for you? All you do anyway is sit in the living room watching TV or sit in the library staring off into space. Even in death you are barely living, so tell me, why should I keep renovating this house for you?"

"Because," my father's steady voice cut through my

screams, "you can be with Isabel. But only if you stay. If you'd prefer to leave, that's fine, but it means she stays."

"You think I'm going to let two vindictive, abusive ghosts raise my daughter?" I screeched.

The knocking started again, louder this time.

"What is in there?" I fell to the ground with my hands over my ears. The pounding was louder than ever. I could feel it down in my bones. The chill from whatever was behind there was permeating my flesh. Behind me, my mother started coughing and choking in earnest. She fell to the floor, clawing at her neck, the same way Isabel would fall to the floor. It was horrifying watching it, but I knew she wasn't mocking Isabel. My mother continued to paw at her neck, stretching out her collar to give herself more air.

"Maggie, look at what you're doing to your mother. She's dying to have you here. Her only request is that you fix up the house and *stop* asking about Isabel. Is that so hard? She's perfectly safe, your daughter. Once you agree that you won't leave the house and that you'll continue working on it, we can bring her out." As my father continued talking, a dark spot appeared on his smoking jacket. It looked like black ink at first, but it didn't spread as quickly as ink would. No, this spot slowly expanded, like a drop of molasses that was getting bigger and bigger.

"Maggie, just agree. Things can go back to normal if you just behave." My mother could hardly speak, her eyes were bulging and her face was turning blue. She kept clawing at her blouse, breaking the top few buttons on her shirt.

"Your mother is right. Listen to her. Just behave, stay in the house, stop trying to get rid of us, and you'll be just fine," my father said. The spot on his robe was starting to drip on the floor. It was blood, not ink or molasses or anything like it—the drop was my father's blood.

Am I dreaming? I asked myself.

"You aren't dreaming," he answered. "That is my blood." He smiled and laughed at my confusion and disgust.

I didn't understand; too much was going on and it was too loud. That incessant banging was driving me insane.

BAM-BAM-BAM-BAM-BAM-BAM-BAM-BAM-BAM!

"Stop that!" I screamed at the top of my lungs. "Get it to stop!"

"We can't," my father said. "That is out of our control."

I looked back at my mother. She was lying on the floor. The first few buttons of her blouse were open. She had a bright red mark around her neck—it had grown red from her scratching at it, and was scabbing over in parts. I couldn't see where it went. It looked like a necklace borne from abuse. I reached out to touch it, but my father grabbed my hand.

"Haven't you ever seen a rope burn before?" he said, throwing me back to the ground.

My mother's lifeless body was lying at my feet. Her hands and lips were greyish-blue, and her eyes were staring off into the distance, unfocused on anything at all. She had a bright red scar around her neck, a flesh-colored ribbon of rope burn. All the air drained out of my body as I looked at her.

"She could never handle it—any of it—life, her guilt over you..." My father shrugged. "What did you think was going to happen?"

I had nothing to say. The rage had seeped out of my body and been replaced with apathy. I didn't care anymore, not about either of them. Nothing in this house was as it seemed, nothing at all.

I'm not afraid of you anymore.

My father roared with laughter.

I got up and, without saying a word, turned and started walking up the stairs.

"Where do you think you are going?" he asked me. "What do you think you're doing?"

"I'm going to find out what's in the crying room, and then I'm going to find Isabel, and then I'm going to do everything in my power to banish you from this house forever."

"You're going to regret doing that," my father said. He was smirking in his strange, mocking way.

"I'm sick of hearing whatever is back there, clamoring to get out. I know you're afraid of it, and whatever scares you will relieve me. Whatever is back there that is scaring you is the only thing that will truly kill you, and that's all I care about now. I'm not afraid anymore. You can't actually hurt me. All you can do is laugh and spew these empty threats and ultimatums. Well, I don't care anymore. I don't care about you at all, and I'm not afraid of you anymore. You are a sick, sad old man and you're just hanging around here hoping to avoid the pits of hell where you belong. Mom, I can have sympathy for. She was pathetic, but you left her no choice. She tried to relieve herself. I'm only sad I didn't get here before she did; I might have been able to save her. Oh well, it was bound to happen, right? You always said my mother had no backbone. Well, look where that got her. I might be a little late, but I'm going to grow a backbone against you, and the first step is opening up that room and letting whatever is inside chase you down to hell."

I turned away from my father before he could say anything, and slowly walked up the stairs.

THE KNOCKING WAS DEAFENING, and it got louder and more physical as I got closer. I could feel the house vibrating beneath my feet with each step I took. I walked slowly, bracing myself for what lay behind that door. My head was spinning. The truth was knocking at the door of my consciousness. I wasn't sure if I truly would survive this.

I used the knife to pry up the wallpaper where I knew the lock was. It took longer than I expected. My hands and the walls were shaking from the knocking, and my heart was beating too quickly for me to concentrate and peel up the walls properly. I scratched at the peeling wallpaper until my fingers started to bleed. No one was around me. The only sound was the incessant knocking coming from behind the door. Finally, I found it—the light switch that acted as a hidden lock to activate the wall. I flicked the switch and scrambled to find the door hidden behind a layer of wallpaper—

"Mommy, no! Please, please, don't do it! Don't open that door, Mommy, please! No!"

I whipped around to find Isabel behind me, bawling her eyes out and pulling on my nightshirt, pulling me away from the door.

37

"Isabel, you don't understand—"

"No, Mommy, *you* don't understand. Please, don't open it up. Please, please, please don't open that door."

Isabel wasn't hysterical or creepy. She was plainly standing in front of me, begging me not to open the door. I didn't know what to do. This threw me off. What did she know about the crying room?

"Did Grandpa tell you what was inside there?" I asked her.

Isabel didn't respond. She pressed her lips together and looked right at the door.

The door was shaking now its hinges were revealed. The wallpaper had peeled to reveal the corner of an old door with rotting, splintering wood. I wondered why the wood was rotting up here; there was no moisture coming from the bathroom upstairs or the roof.

"I'd follow the little brat's advice," my father said. He was standing in the doorway wearing his smoking jacket. The blood soaked the bottom part of his jacket and was trailing him on the floor.

"I won't. I have to open that door. It's the only way this will end," I said, tears stinging my eyes.

"Mommy, please, don't open it. We can end this in other ways. I promise I won't let Grandpa hurt you anymore. I'll do whatever I can, but if you open that door I'll have to go away again, and I won't be able to come back." Isabel started crying. She wasn't bawling; this wasn't a tantrum. She was truly saddened by the thought, but I still couldn't comprehend why. "I'm scared, Mommy. I'm scared of the dark and I think if you open that door I'll go back into the dark."

"What do you mean, baby? I won't let you go into the dark, okay? I'll be here to protect you." Tears were streaming down my face. The answer was right in front of me, but I couldn't bear it. "I know I haven't been the best mommy lately, but I tried. I tried really, really hard to be the best mommy I could be, and I will only do what's the best for you, okay? I think if I open this door, you'll finally start to feel better."

Isabel was crying and staring at the door.

The knocking wasn't as loud anymore, but it was faster. Whatever was behind it was pounding on the door. It knew I was close. It knew the torture it had felt for years was almost over, and it was impatient to get out.

"You'll never do it." My father laughed. "You can't! You don't have the backbone to do it. You're just like your mother—weak. Especially when it comes to your sad little girl—a weakling who thinks she can bargain with me. Please... You won't open that door. Go to sleep. Let this night be over. In the morning we can get back to normal."

"You won't be able to take it," my mother said.

I spun around in complete shock. She had recovered completely, just as Isabel always did. Around her neck was a bright red ribbon matching Isabel's.

"I don't think your mind can handle what is behind that door. You think it's a release but really, it'll just suck you into your life before all this. A life of sadness and disappointment. Maggie, I think you'll go insane. Grief is a driver of our worst mental selves. If you open this door, you'll lose your father—but you'll also lose your daughter. You'll never be able to see her again."

"She's right, Mommy. Don't you love me? Don't you want me here?" Isabel cried.

I did want her here. I wanted to see her grow up. I wanted to tear my hair out when she was an irritating adolescent. I wanted to drop her off at her college dorm. I wanted to meet all her boyfriends and disapprove of each and every one, because no one could be good enough for my little girl. And she would still be my little girl, even when we were both old ladies muttering to each other in an old folks' home. That was supposed to be the only good thing about having kids when you were young—that you'd grow old together. You'd have a companion in your life forever. I didn't want to lose that because I wasn't sure I'd ever get it back.

"If you open that door, the Conner family will cease to exist. You'll probably change your name and disappear from this place. You'll forget about Isabel in a couple of years. Soon she'll be nothing but a footnote in your story."

My father was taunting me. He knew how much I loved my daughter. I couldn't bear to be away from her.

"If you leave now, just go upstairs and get a good night's rest, when you wake up in the morning everything will be back to normal."

"What does that mean, 'normal'? Isabel having seizures at random times, before suddenly feeling fine? All of you disappearing at will, leaving me disoriented? If we go back to what you think is normal, I'll lose my mind." I was crying, holding Isabel's hand, trying to communicate to her that I loved her. "Isabel, I love you more than anything, but I can't do that."

"Sure you can, Mommy. I'll be good, I promise! I won't get sick, ever, and I'll do everything you ask. I'll do chores and I'll help you around the house and everything." Isabel folded herself into my arms and I held her close.

I could smell her floral shampoo in her hair. Her body was warm and I could feel her little heart beating through her chest. She was real, she had to be. She couldn't be like my parents. I couldn't believe that—

"Maggie, I can tell you, as soon as you abandon your child, your life will never be the same," my mother said. "You won't be able to cope with the guilt. I can promise you that."

I ignored her, breathing with my child wrapped up in my arms. Isabel's tears were soaking my shirt. Her sniffling almost drowned out the knocking coming from the crying room. I didn't know what to do. I wanted a moment alone with my daughter, so I could understand what was happening. I had a headache, my stomach was churning, and I felt devastated. I didn't know why. Isabel was still here, she was still with me. I couldn't lose her. My mother was right; I wouldn't be able to cope with the guilt, and my life wouldn't ever be the same. I spent so much time this summer trying to find a way out of here. Searching for resources to help Isabel, searching for a way to bring peace to this house. The only thing that could bring us peace was the truth, to step out of this horrifying fantasy and learn why so many strange things went on in here.

The problem was that truth would break my reality. The truth would tear me away from the only thing in the world that kept me sane. I would never have this feeling again, of holding my daughter in my arms. I didn't know if I would remember this summer of playing witches in the attic and reading oddly mature books to my daughter before bed. *Crime and Punishment* would never be the same.

"Maggie, you have to make a choice. If you're going to leave, then leave."

I gave Isabel a kiss on the forehead. "I love you, Issie. You are the perfect daughter, but I need to know the truth. I need to know what's behind that door, or else nothing will ever change. It won't be normal. I'll just be waiting for the next time this house is overwhelmed by its demons. If I don't open that door, we'll just circle back to the beginning and we'll never move forward."

"Mommy, I'm scared."

"I know you are, and I'm scared too. The dark isn't so bad; it's just a place where you get to be as curious as you want, and that curiosity can build a whole new world just for yourself."

"Really?" Isabel sniffled. "I can do whatever I want?"

"Sure you can." I was trembling as I reassured my daughter. "Just like the dollhouse. It's what I've been doing all summer, isn't it? Making up my family out of the dark?"

Isabel nodded. She knew what my parents were.

I didn't want to think about what she was. I was trying so hard. I was using every cell in my body to avoid thinking about who was knocking on the door. They still hadn't tired, they were still ramming their little fists against the rotting wood.

"Can I make you out of the dark?" Isabel asked. "Is that okay? You were the best mommy I could have asked for. Anybody would be lucky to have you as a mom, no matter what you think."

Her voice was starting to sound more mature. She sounded more and more like me as she spoke. The spell was breaking. I knew what decision I had to make. I stood up and my father was behind me, blocking my way to the door.

"Please, Maggie, don't do this," my father begged. "You don't *want* to do this. What we had going was just fine. I promise we'll stop bothering you. I promise I'll change. We can all change. You know how to control me now, so you can change everything. Please, Maggie, please, I'm begging you, have mercy. Help me, Maggie, please help me—"

"Get away from me," I said, and I walked past him.

My father can't hurt me if he's just part of my imagination.

I scratched away the last bits of wallpaper blocking the door.

I wormed my fingers into the crack between the rotting door and the rest of the wall.

I closed my eyes and threw the door open, and once I did everything stopped. The knocking stopped, my daughter's tears ceased, my heartbeat stopped for a moment. I was completely alone for the first time in recent memory. Once I opened my eyes there was no going back.

I took a deep breath and opened my eyes.

Lying there in the crying room, slumped on the floor, leaning against the wall close to the door was a dead body wearing my father's bloody smoking jacket.

38

I stared at my father's withered corpse and all my memories came rushing back.

"NATE, can you pass me the kettle?"

"What for?" he snapped, slamming his fist down on the table. "You interrupted my count, so it must be important. What the hell do you need the kettle for?"

I froze, muttering to myself. I wanted to hide and scream and run away. My hormones were raging but I knew if I started to cry, Nate would probably slap me.

"I wanted to make some tea," I mumbled. "My stomach is a little upset because of the baby. I have some heartburn."

"You interrupted me for that? Do you know how fucking important this is? These guys aren't some cutesy dinner party guests. I owe them money. Do you know what they can do to us if we don't pay them money, huh, Maggie? Of course you don't. Poor little rich girl doesn't understand the basic concept of consequences, does she?"

Nate got up and grabbed the kettle, slamming it down on the table. The boiling water spilled over and onto my hand.

I gritted my teeth and tried not to react. He was stressed out; I didn't want to provoke him. How was I to know Nate was an angrier version of my father, with a shorter fuse to boot? Didn't he tell me tonight was an important night? I ought to have taken that as a cue to stay in my room and not come out.

"There's hot water in the bathroom tap, isn't there? Can't you make your tea with that, or are you just trying to annoy me?" he said, before sitting back down and starting his count over again.

I didn't say anything. It was better to stay quiet in times like this. I took the kettle and waddled to the little side table where I kept tea. It was hard to maneuver around our cramped apartment. Between the bags of drugs, piles of money, and furniture, it was not a pregnancy-friendly place. I was in my last trimester and somehow my belly kept getting larger. I couldn't go a day without irritating Nate. I waddled back and tried to reach the kettle onto the counter. My belly knocked the table, and I spilled a little boiling water onto one of the piles of bills.

"What the hell!" Nate screamed, backing up. He tried to grab some of the bills that fell, but they were too hot and he recoiled from them. "Augh—you idiot. What are you trying to do, kill me? Huh? Is that what you want? You want these guys to come in an get rid of me?" Nate roared, shoving his chair back and rounding the table toward me.

"I swear it was an accident, Nate. It's hard getting around the table with my belly—"

"Oh, don't use your pregnancy as an excuse. That's pathetic. What, are you gonna use that kid as an excuse too when it's born?

You won't be able to work because of the baby, you can't fuck me because of the baby—is that it?"

I stammered, opened my mouth only to close it again. I didn't know how to respond. I'd never seen Nate get so angry so quickly before. He was ready to kill me; I could feel it.

Nate smacked me across the head and grabbed my neck. "Apologize, you idiot. Apologize to me." His hand tightened around my throat. With the other he held my scalding tea, ready to throw it on me.

I knew our knife block was behind me. This time, if I let him, Nate would kill me, and kill my baby too. I couldn't let that happen. I couldn't let this baby not have a chance at life.

I kicked him as hard as I could. I couldn't see past my belly so I just closed my eyes and hoped my aim was true—it was. Nate released me, doubling over in pain, spilling the scalding hot tea all over his hand and arm. He was groaning on the floor as I grabbed the knife nearest me out of the block. I brought my hands down and stabbed him in the back as hard as I could. The knife squelched beneath my hands, and I screamed in shock. Nate's hand moved, so I pulled the knife out and stabbed him again—a strange, knee-jerk reaction I had to the thought of him waking up. I twisted the knife, and warmth spread across my body. If I did this one more time, he'd be dead. I could feel the life draining out of Nate's body. If I did this again, he'd never wake up. If he didn't wake up, I could blame it on the dealers who came by. No one would need to know it was me. Nate moaned again. I stabbed him again. It scared me how much power I had. I got up and backed away into the kitchen. Would my fingerprints on the knife matter? No. If anyone asks, it's normal for you to hold the knife in your own home. Why wouldn't my fingerprints be on it?

I wiped the handle anyway. Didn't hurt to be careful.

There was blood all over the floor, dripping down my arms

where it had splattered. I ran into the bathroom and washed my hands. I changed my shirt, hiding the dirty one under the mattress —no one would think to look there.

Then I passed out.

MY HEAD WAS SPINNING. I had never remembered what happened that night. The police said it was a drug deal gone wrong. They didn't bother with a more detailed investigation. They were already investigating Nate for dealing in cocaine and ketamine. The police were only disappointed they wouldn't have someone to turn in the bigger guns in the operation. They sent me back home, at eight months pregnant, to live with my father, who at first had acted happy to see me but then showed his real, hateful self.

"You couldn't send her somewhere else? There isn't a convent around that'll keep this embarrassment until she pops?" he said. Before they could say anything, my father pulled me inside and slammed the door. I remembered he had been drinking. I could smell it on his breath.

"I guess your boyfriend wasn't the knight in shining armor you thought, huh?" was all he said, before stumbling back to the living room and giving me the silent treatment.

I WOKE UP ONE MORNING, and I knew things were different. The house was quieter than it usually was. My parents weren't arguing. My room was above theirs; I could usually hear it. I crept downstairs after washing my face and changing for school. I peeked in their room—the bed wasn't made. That was unusual; my mom always made the bed first thing in the morning.

Downstairs in the kitchen my father was making breakfast. He was usually at work by now. He was always the first one in the office to "set an example" for everyone else. He was trying to make pancakes but he wasn't very good at them.

"Daddy, do you want some help?" I asked him. Mom had shown me how to make pancakes before, and I was almost tall enough to flip them.

"Does it look like I need help? They're pancakes; it's not rocket science. If your imbecile of a mother can make them why can I?" he yelled.

I didn't know what to do. My dad always yelled at my mom, but he never yelled at me. I looked around for my mother. She usually came between us if my dad was angry.

"You looking for your mom?" he said. He laughed as I nodded. "Yeah, so was I."

I didn't see Mom again, and I knew better than to ask where she was.

SHE WAS RIGHT. The ghost of my mother was right. Opening this door brought back a flood of memories that I had been happy to forget. The grey cloud that descended over the house that day had never moved on. My mother left when I was ten. She left me behind. She did what I did—stole money from my father's nightstand after he passed out from drinking, packed the car and left in the middle of the night without a single trace. She never explained why she didn't take me with her. I guessed she thought my father would be less likely to chase her if he had his daughter. I was ten years old when my life started to change, just a little older than Isabel.

MY FATHER DIDN'T LIKE babies. They were loud, dirty, and unpredictable. I wouldn't let him near Isabel, so he was angry that he couldn't control her.

"She's a brat, and she's an embarrassment. You should have given her up."

"I'm not going to give up my baby—"

He shoved my head against the wall. "You don't tell me what to do. I tell you what to do. I'm your father. You have to respect me and my word. You can't give her up now, anyway. That would be even more shameful. People would think I didn't have a handle on what goes on in this house. Do you know how that would reflect on my business? These idiots would start taking me for everything I'm worth." He stormed off, muttering to himself.

I could never tell when my father started drinking. Most days he'd always seemed drunk.

Isabel was a sweet baby. She was always smiling and giggling. Her cheeks were the brightest pink, like two little apples. She had the chubbiest little arms and legs. She almost always slept through the night, and when she didn't, I could usually calm her down pretty quickly. She had a small mop of light brown, almost blonde hair, and bright blue eyes. I hoped she'd always have them, but I knew blue eyes were a newborn thing. She was smart too. She rolled over and started crawling early. I was sure she was going to be a little genius. I read her books that were way beyond her level, just so she could get used to the words.

My father didn't let me take her to a doctor. "It's impossible to find a pediatrician these days. You can take care of her at home. I'm not going to be driving you everywhere for your little overgrown toy."

For the most part that was fine. I had the internet; there were forums and articles and books online where other mothers and professionals gave you all sorts of advice. I could keep this up for a little while, at least. Soon I could get a job, save up some money, and get out of this house. I'd do what my mom did—get out in the middle of the night and never look back.

Sometimes I wondered where she was. For the most part I didn't care. She wouldn't be much help right now anyway. She wasn't a warm parent. She did what she was asked. She taught me how to take care of myself and how to keep a clean house. Apart from that, my mother was busy keeping my father away from me.

I wanted to make sure I did everything I could so that history didn't repeat itself. Isabel was going to have a very different childhood to mine.

ISABEL HAD COLIC AS A NEWBORN. According to everything I read online it was supposed to go away on its own, but four months in and she was still crying on and on and on. I changed from breastfeeding to formula, I changed formula multiple times, I did massages on her tummy to help with excess gas, but she still cried for hours and hours at a time. I didn't know what to do. I was always cuddling her and crying myself. I was exhausted. It was hard to sleep. I would have strange dreams about Isabel where she would suddenly disappear or she'd start choking on her own tears. I woke up sweating and crying, clammy and hot at the same time, rushing to get up and check on her.

My father noticed, of course. He often complained about Isabel crying.

"She's a baby. Babies cry. It's normal."

"This isn't normal. You need to take that thing to a doctor or something."

"You won't let me take her to a doctor. You said there aren't any pediatricians around—"

"Don't talk back to me, you little brat. Just make sure she shuts up at night so we can actually sleep. Even your mother would know to do that."

"I'll try."

But nothing helped. I called around to pediatricians in the area, but they were so dismissive about taking Isabel on as a patient. I suspected my father bribed them. He hated when I left the house with her. The shame he felt about my pregnancy ran deep. He thought people were whispering about him, even claimed some of them were telling lies about the paternity of the baby. It wasn't true; everyone knew about Nate. They often stopped to comfort me about it on the street, always saying something along the lines of "I'm sure he would have cleaned up his act once he saw this little angel." I never knew what to say. I usually just smiled and walked off.

I was slowly becoming like my mother. I rarely talked to other people in town, and spent almost all of my time at home. I was afraid of my father, and would get between him and Isabel any time I could. He wanted to get rid of her, but he didn't realize she was the only reason I was sticking around. If it was just me, I could run away. Maybe I'd change my name and become some anonymous teenager in the city, or I'd try to find my mother. I couldn't do that with a baby in tow. No, with Isabel around I needed some kind of a plan.

One night, I fell asleep early. I was exhausted, having stayed up the whole night before. Isabel cried for a solid eight hours, and I had to stay awake with her the whole time. The next day I had to clean the house from top to bottom because Isabel spit up on the stairs and my father felt the suitable punishment would be for me to clean everything. From the stairs, banisters, and floors, it had to be spotless so that I would understand the consequences of not controlling my baby. I kept her in her crib all day, running upstairs to feed and change her before running back down to finish cleaning.

As soon as dinner was over, I fed Isabel and collapsed into my own bed. I kept both our doors open so I could see her sleeping and make sure she was okay. I fell asleep watching Isabel's mobile go round and round and round.

Hours later I woke up to a strange sound. It sounded like Isabel was crying, but she was far away. Had my father taken her downstairs? Where was the crying coming from? For a moment I panicked, thinking my father might have put her downstairs in the crying room. He was always threatening to do that, but I refused. I'd go in there instead, and take care of Isabel when I came out. But if I was asleep, then I couldn't stop him, so maybe—

"You little twerp, it's one o'clock in the morning. Don't you understand we have work to do?" I heard my father's whispered grumbling. He was slurring his words a little bit.

I wanted to stay in bed, I wanted this to be a horrible nightmare and I would open my eyes and his voice would disappear.

Instead, I looked over and saw my father bent over Isabel's crib. He was holding a pillow, and she was crying and wheezing. I saw him bring the pillow down again.

The rest happened in slow motion. I got up and ran to the doorway.

My father looked at me smiling, pride beaming from his face. "I finally shut the little shit up," he said. "Now I can finally get some sleep." He pushed past me and strolled down the stairs.

I was trembling as I walked over to the crib. "No, no, no, no, please no, please, Isabel!" I picked her up gently and went to the rocking chair. I had learned CPR from a video online, and I tried to revive her, but her lips were already cold. "How is that possible? You were crying just a second ago!" I wailed, trying desperately to wake her.

Isabel was dead. Her face was pale. Her lips were blue. Her beautiful blue eyes were cold. There was a red ring around her neck, where my father had grabbed her.

He'd killed her with his own bare hands.

I gave her a kiss on the forehead and gently placed her back in her crib. I decided then that my father had to learn what consequences really meant. I was punished for Isabel spitting up on the carpet by having to clean the house. How could I punish my father for murdering Isabel?

I went downstairs to the kitchen and pulled out a knife from the butcher's block. While reliving this memory, it felt like so much of my life hinged on these wooden blocks. I never had one in my house again, not after this. I walked up to my father's bedroom, the room he used to share with my mother, and I stabbed him in the stomach.

He woke up, screaming in pain. "What the hell do you think you're doing?" he asked, sitting up in bed and holding his stomach. "You realize you're going to have to clean this up, don't you?"

I was standing over him holding a bloody knife. I brought it down again, just under his shoulder this time. I twisted it as I brought it back up over my head.

"Is that the best you can do? I can still stand. Just watch—"

Before he could continue, I stabbed him in the heart. My father just laughed. This was harder than Nate. It was like my father's anger kept him alive for longer. He slowly started to get out of bed, and I backed away. I ran out into the hall and stopped to stand my ground. He plodded behind me like a zombie, stopping at the door. He had to lean against the doorframe for support, but he was still smiling.

"You're not going to finish me off that easily," he said, smirking at me.

I had no idea what I was doing. I sliced his chest and stabbed him in the stomach again. This time, blood bubbled up in his mouth, spilling out over his chin.

"You have to help me, Maggie," he spat. "You can't just leave me like this. Please, please save me. I'm your father. I'm your father; don't you have any compassion? Please, Maggie, have mercy. I'm begging you to please help me." My father slumped down to the ground, where I stabbed him in the back one last time. He kept talking for a while after. He just kept saying, "Please," over and over again. It took a couple of hours before his moaning stopped.

Once I was sure he was dead, I moved him to the crying room, tossing the knife in after him. I'd made a mess. I remember thinking I had to clean up before my father woke up.

I spent the rest of the night cleaning. I tore up the carpet in the hall and washed the blood from the floors by hand. I changed the sheets on my father's bed and burned the bloody fabrics in the fireplace. I wanted to forget that this night ever happened.

And I had.

The next morning I woke up and saw Isabel in her crib. She looked so peaceful I thought for a moment that she was just asleep. Of course, I was wrong. The rest was a blur. I called the police. They sent out a search for my father. I was sent to live with my mother, who couldn't believe my father was gone. I never spoke to her about Isabel.

I moved out as soon as I could.

I became a carpenter.

Then, my mother died.

I moved back home.

And now, here I was. Staring at the rotting corpse of my father.

I felt overwhelmed with emotion. I was going to be sick, but I also felt elated. I was free. I was truly finally free from the curse of Joseph Conner. I could do anything I wanted. I had his fortune. I didn't have my mother or my daughter, the only women in my life who knew what it was like to live under the scythe of Joseph Conner. I had killed two men, and watched as one of them killed the two women in my life.

I was starting to hyperventilate as I realized I would never see Isabel again. I didn't even remember where her little body was buried—that had been taken away from me too. I whirled around hoping for a moment to catch one last glimpse of Isabel's ghost, but it was gone. Everything was gone. My mother, whom I had hated so much, was gone. My father, who had tortured me, was gone.

And the only good thing that ever happened to me was gone as well.

Suddenly I felt suffocated in my own home. I was hyperventilating and my heart was racing. I was starting to feel dizzy. I had to get out of there. I slammed the door to the crying room and ran downstairs. The sun was coming up as I stumbled out onto the walk. I didn't know where to go or where to run, and I was quickly overwhelmed with emotion. I fell to the ground, but a pair of strong arms caught me. I heard a little dog bark, and someone asked what was wrong.

"My daughter is dead," I sobbed. "My baby girl is dead."

39

I came to in a strange bed. There were doilies all over the room, and the bedspread was a very dated floral pattern from, I think, the 90s. I had been in this house before, when I was a kid. This was Amelia Albertson's room. There were still posters on her wall from bands she liked. The wallpaper was also floral. I vaguely remembered Amelia talking about how much she hated her room but her mom wouldn't let her change the decor.

"This was my room, and then it was Amelia's room. I had her a little later, so I never really changed it. I love flowers." Mary appeared at the door, smiling gently and holding a cup of tea.

I felt simultaneously embarrassed and grateful that she'd found me, crumpled on the ground outside my house.

"I brought you some tea. Green tea with jasmine—only a little bit of caffeine but still very calming. I hope that's okay," she said, hesitating to enter the room.

"Tea would be wonderful, thank you." I smiled weakly and patted the bed. "You can come in if you want." I was still feeling a little lightheaded, but the deep sleep I'd just had was helping me to pull through. It was the first time in weeks I'd had a dreamless, relaxing sleep.

"I need to apologize to you," I said. "I kept thinking you were suffering from dementia, and I blew you off. Now I realize you were trying to help bring me back to reality."

"That's all right. I should be the one apologizing. It was quite harsh to do that. Lana Cabot gave me a telling off for doing so. She felt you needed to take your time, that there was something traumatic in your grief causing you to act that way. She convinced most of the town to play along once we all realized you appeared to think your parents were still alive. I'm not part of a very soft generation; I'm sure you realize that." She looked down at her hands.

I took them in my own as a gesture of goodwill.

"I understand. Never complain, never explain, just like the Queen says. That's how my mother acted too," I said, patting Mary's hand.

She immediately started sobbing into her hands and shaking her head. "Oh, your poor mother. I didn't realize... well... you see..." she trailed off and started biting her fingernails.

"Mary, please tell me. I still feel a little... confused. I need to know what happened with my mom," I asked.

Mary looked into my eyes for a long time before she took a deep breath and started telling me the story.

"Well, everyone in town knew about Joseph Conner. If you can imagine at all, his father was even worse, and the apple did *not* fall very far from the tree. Everyone knew what was going on in your house, but your father practically controlled this town. I remember once my father reported him to the police—he'd seen your father twisting your mother's arm and slapping her while she was taking you to the playground. The police looked him straight in the eye and threw the police report in the trash. 'Joseph Conner is what keeps this town going, through bribery and coercion,' I remember he said. And he was right. No one knew how to step in for your mother." She paused to clear her throat and sip some of her own tea.

"When your mother left—you must have been about nine or ten years old?"

"I was ten. She just disappeared in the middle of the night."

"Yes, I remember. Some people thought he might have—oh well, that's not the case. She always protected you. I don't think you understood what was happening, not really. When you would play with Amelia you were a little rougher than the other girls, but you were never malicious. After your mother left, it was clear your father turned on you in her absence. Amelia mentioned you stopped playing with her and you often had bruises at school. You became quite rebellious, I have to say. I was relieved when Amelia—"

"I mean, you can understand why, can't you?" I said, raising my voice.

Mary put her palm up to stop me. "I know it was wrong. We didn't know what to do. You didn't seem to have any relatives who could protect you, and your father was too influential in town for someone else to take you in. It was quite tragic. Then you ran away with that boy, Nate Moore—an even worse influence, if that was possible—and you came back pregnant. Your father shut you up after that. I remember I would sometimes catch glimpses of you with your baby girl in the window; you both were so beautiful. Like a princess in a castle."

"Guarded by an abusive dragon," I said, taking little sips of tea. Mary was right, it was gently waking me up. I was starting to remember my own history again.

"It's true. Soon after that I heard the news about your baby girl—you know, since your parents wouldn't share any information about you or your daughter, I didn't know her name was Isabel until recently. It's a lovely name." She smiled sadly.

If only she could have seen my Isabel—the feisty eight-year-old who read books beyond her age and maturity, and who invented the most clever games for us to play together.

"Did any of you know what happened?" I asked.

Mary raised an eyebrow and took a sip of her tea. "My dear, you are very well aware of my reputation in this town," she said, and we both giggled. "It's lucky I found you and not Lana. You'd be slathered in a CBD salve and changing meditative mantras while holding an amethyst crystal right now."

I laughed.

Mary's face took on a serious expression. "Apparently—and correct me if I'm wrong—you found your child in her crib the next morning, suffocated. The EMTs declared it a case of Sudden Infant Death Syndrome, but I always thought your father had something to do with it. The hospital would never dare implicate him, and the police would never investigate, but he disappeared after that day. No one ever saw him. You were still a teenager so the authorities tracked down your mother in Maine and sent you to live with her. I thought I'd never see any of the Conners again, but your mother resurfaced about seven or eight months ago. I don't remember the exact date. I saw her at the supermarket and honestly, I thought *I* was hallucinating. She barely said a word. She was so frail and looked like she was on the verge of crying." Mary got quiet again, staring into her tea.

I waited for her to finish.

"I'm afraid she—"

"I know," I said, stopping her.

My mother took her own life. I knew that now. I remembered it from the funeral. The technician couldn't cover the rope scars with makeup, so we bought a scarf and he strategically tied it so that no one could see.

"Several weeks ago, according to my sources," she winked, "you came back. I suppose you are now the sole heir to the Conner family fortune."

"Weeks? That's impossible. It felt like months." It was easy to lose track of time in that house. I rarely left it, and I lived on my own strange, insomniac schedule.

"Yes, it was really just a short time. It was terrible to watch—it was clear from how you behaved that you believed Isabel was still alive. Sometimes she would be with you. You'd call her, and most everyone in town played along. I just couldn't do it. I thought, you have had so much trauma in your life that it wasn't right for people to continue this charade. You are so young. You have your whole life ahead of you. If Tony at the hardware store is to be believed, you seem like a very skilled carpenter. I thought it was wrong to hold you back. Perhaps I was a little too harsh."

I shook my head. "It's okay, Mary, you meant well. Besides, I just assumed you had dementia so I felt just as sorry for you."

We both laughed. I had never realized how jovial Mary could be. She was my friend's mother, a disciplinarian, the town busybody, and now she was the mother figure I'd never had.

"It'll be pretty awkward next time I go to the grocery store, won't it?" I said, staring into my teacup.

"Don't you worry. Everyone in town means well. I think we all feel guilty for letting it go on the way it did." She paused, staring into her tea. "If you're really nervous about it, I can work some gossipy magic on your behalf."

I stayed with Mary for another day. She loaned me a few vintage dresses so I could get out of the pajamas she found me in. It was incredible how quickly everyone knew that I was "feeling my best." Based on the story she told me, and the reactions from a few older townspeople, everyone suspected my father of killing Isabel but no one thought I could have killed him, or Nate Moore.

Good. Let's keep it that way.

When I got home, the first thing I did was order some lumber and drywall from Tony. I went up to the parlor and opened the crying room. The room felt colder than the rest of the house somehow. I opened the door and this time the sight of my father's corpse didn't seem so scary. I carefully removed the smoking jacket and pulled the corpse out into the room, wrapping it in an old bedsheet. I used the new lumber to rebuild the parts of the wall that had started to rot, and I slowly and methodically sealed the crying room for good.

40

There was a rare moment of quiet in the Conner home. All you could hear was the occasional clink of cutlery against porcelain dishes. The nicest we had, as per my own request. I was sitting at the head of the table, eating scrambled eggs and drinking tea while scrolling through my phone.

I was alone. It was the first time I had been alone in what felt like years. I didn't know what it was like to hear nothing but the sound of slowly chewing my food.

The crying room wasn't finished. I had rebuilt the door and sealed the space, then realized I could easily have turned it into a powder room just off the parlor. I texted Tony at the hardware store to see what he thought of the idea.

> Hey, Tony, what do you think of making a bathroom off the parlor? Is that a silly idea?

> Hello, Mags. No, I don't think it's silly, but it's a little old-fashioned. No one needs a powder room and a parlor. However, a small ensuite could be a nice selling point to the house. Come by the shop and we can discuss. — Tony.

Tony was old and still signed off his texts as if they were emails. He was a former contractor, and had agreed to take me on as a sort of apprentice. I could earn money from my carpentry business, refurbishing old furniture, sprucing up cheap furniture, and building a few simple pieces for folks around town. While I did that, Tony would teach me the basics of construction and contracting, using my house as a training ground.

I met with the lawyers of my family's estate in person. First, I told them off for hounding me at my mother's funeral. It was amazing how apologetic people were when you were throwing money in their face.

I took a look at the probate papers again, this time with my *own* lawyers that I hired to consult on the pages. They noticed my family's estate lawyers had been padding their own pockets, charging higher than normal fees for pretty much everything to do with running my father's property business, so I took my business elsewhere. It was better, because I didn't want to deal with *anyone* who'd had a hand in perpetuating my father's abuse. They had known what was going on and turned the other way because my father was a high-paying client whose business was good.

With my new lawyers, I had all the properties registered to my name, and I suddenly found myself the CEO of a lucrative property and real estate management company. I had no interest in the company and didn't want a single legacy of my father's to exist. Anything with the Conner name didn't deserve to be remembered as a pillar of the community, not when its head was a manipulative abuser. I was in talks to sell the company's assets and close the business. My meeting with the new lawyers was later this week.

I wasn't sure what to do with my father's body. It was practically mummified from being in the crying room. His body could probably only be identified by medical records or something. Still, I wanted to be careful. I didn't want this crime to come back to haunt me, not again. Digging a large hole in the backyard would draw too much attention, and I worried that sealing him in the foundation would cause problems if anyone ever renovated the house.

Instead, I took a page from my father's book. I took an obscene amount of money out of his account and bribed the same funeral home that buried my mother to cremate my father.

"How long has this body... been like this?" the young attendant asked. It was the same man who helped me fix a scarf over my mother's rope scars.

"I'm not sure... a few years at least. I found him—it—while clearing out some rooms in the house. It's an old Victorian property and there were all these hidden passageways and closets that I'm trying to open up. It was in one of those."

His eyes went wide with excitement. "I've always wanted a house like that. You read about them in old ghost stories like stuff from Henry James. It's just so cool. Do you like ghost stories at all?"

"Honestly, I don't know if I believe in them." I smiled, and handed him an envelope of cash. "I know this is uncouth, but seeing as this house has been in my family for generations, I'd like to just leave it at this. I'm sure you know what went on at the Conner home. Frankly, I'd like it if someone started talking about a *different* family for once."

The attendant looked down at his shoes, unable to look me in the eyes. "Yes. I get it. This body can't have been there for long, though; it's not decomposed enough." After a pause, he looked right at me. "You know, my grandfather used to abuse my grandmother. She had horrible PTSD, as did my mom. They both took their own lives in the end, unable to deal with the specter of my grandfather haunting their psyche. That's why I got into this business. I think no matter how your life went, there's always hope for the beyond."

He took the envelope of cash. "I'd do this for free, but the machine is actually quite expensive, so..."

"Don't worry about it," I said, waving away his apology. "We can consider it a very generous donation to the people who made my mother's resting place a peaceful one." I winked.

He wrote me a receipt. I handed the receipt to my lawyers, and my father's body was a wonderful write-off on my income tax.

Finally he did something right.

I WENT HOME that night and sat in the library for a long time, staring at the old dollhouse. It needed about as many repairs as the house. In my delusional state I'd thought it was magically fixing itself. Sadly, that was not the case.

Since I had stayed at her house, Mary made it a habit to stop by my house with some tea. I had been asking her more about my mother, what she was like before she married my father.

"She was always really good with her hands. It's funny that you're a carpenter, because I think your mother wanted to be a sculptor. She would never admit it—her mother was too conservative to handle having an artist in the family—but she did a lot of ceramic pieces. Some of the porcelain bowls you have I believe are your mother's doing."

It felt good to have these meetings with Mary, although I did feel sad that I only learned about it after my mother passed away. All I remembered from the days when I was sent to live with her was a woman who was so depressed that she could hardly get out of bed in the morning. My mother lived off the proceeds of her trust fund, which thankfully was more than enough for small-town Maine. I never asked her about herself, because to me she was a weak woman who didn't even care to get to know me. I was disappointed to only have known the cold and distant Helena Conner, not the woman who predated my father.

Every night I went to bed crying. Isabel's room was still intact, as it was when she was a baby. A small crib bed, a dresser, a little desk in the corner. I could see it from my bed every night. Every night I cried, missing the baby I'd lost, the little girl I never got to know. Now I realized that the Isabel I'd invented was a reflection of myself at that age, I wondered what kind of kid she would have been. Would she have been as creative and passionate as the illusion of her was? I would never know, and that thought made me sadder than anything. More than once, I thought I would trade the truth to have that version of Isabel back in my life, even though I knew deep down that it was very unhealthy.

I was starting to see a therapist who helped me. It was the woman Dr. Bartesc recommended who specialized in trauma therapy. Dr. Esmeralda Bolton. She had me doing crazy somatic exercises to release tension in my body I never knew I had.

"I see it in a lot of patients who have suffered abuse. You spent half your life bracing yourself for what was coming next; now you have to learn to open up and receive the present moment."

I rolled my eyes at her, but her methods worked. I cried a lot, I was angry a lot of the time, but I was also more available to myself. Which was therapy speak for "I'm not hallucinating anymore."

My parents' fortune was going to be a complicated legacy beyond my father's real estate company. I wanted to move to the city, where I could expand my business and maybe meet a few new faces. People who had no idea who Joseph Conner was and why he was so powerful in a small, affluent community upstate. I wanted to meet someone who didn't know I spent three weeks one summer acting as if I had an eight-year-old running around, and I wanted to meet someone who liked me for who I was in the present moment.

I could take the money and run, drive up for estate and garage sales, and sell my wares to the people gentrifying cheap neighborhoods all over New York. Why not? It seemed as good a life as any. And if I didn't like it, I could just go someplace else. For so long I'd had no choice of what to do with my housing and money. The power to choose where I lived was freeing to me.

"Tony?" I called out into the empty hardware store. I had spent too much time that morning contemplating my new life. I came to the hardware store to forget about it a little bit. Tony was nowhere to be found, so I browsed the aisles looking for other supplies I knew I needed. I wasn't paying much attention, which was why I almost barreled into Charlie.

"Maggie! Hi, hello, how, um, how are you doing?" he asked, suddenly very sweaty in the air-conditioned hardware store.

"Charlie! I haven't seen you in a long time. How's your business going?" I smiled. He had the softest grey eyes I had ever seen.

"Great, actually. I, um…well, business is going well so I'm thinking of expanding. You know, so I can take on more clients and spread the work around a little bit." He breathed, laughing to himself, shifting his feet. Every time I looked up at him his face went beet red.

"That's fantastic! I'm also thinking of expanding my business. Maybe move to the city, but I'm not sure yet. It feels good to be a little more settled in town."

Charlie blinked at me, clearly unnerved about how to approach what had happened to me.

"It's okay," I said. "I had a little mental breakdown, but I'm on the mend now. Feels pretty good." I smiled. There was something about his demeanor that made me feel relaxed.

"I get it. I had something like that happen after the family dog died. I'd had him since I was a kid. He was so old, but for a long time he was the only consistent thing in my life. I, um… my family was also kind of, um… turbulent."

We didn't say anything after that. Charlie suddenly became very interested in the side of some drywall anchors, and I followed suit.

"Hey, um... I have a question for you. It might be—I mean you don't have to, um—" His face was getting redder and redder. I was almost concerned for the boy. "Before you leave... maybe... we can have dinner... and talk about stuff... anything, really... it doesn't have to be traumatic..." He took a deep breath after that.

I had to as well. I held my breath while he rushed through his question.

"Sure," I said. "I mean it's a little— It would be nice to talk."

We both smiled, let out our pent-up air. Charlie nodded. I nodded. It was like a scene out of a high school drama.

"Maggie!" roared Tony. "We've gotta stop meeting like this. You're gonna make your boyfriend Mr. Barrows there very jealous." He laughed his loud belly laugh, a sound I was trying to disassociate with scorn.

This time I knew he was teasing. This time I knew I was surrounded by people I could trust.

THERE WAS one last thing I wanted to do, to wrap up this summer of trauma. I was honestly afraid to call Lana and Bill. They'd had a front-row seat to my mental breakdown, and it felt embarrassing to admit to them what I had been so adamant about before. I thought back to the day I begged Lana to take Isabel into her care, how sweet she had been with me when she said no. I wanted to explain to them the truth of what was going on, to provide some kind of context.

Anything to make sure they knew they didn't have to worry about me anymore.

"Hello. Cabot residence."

"Hi. Lana? It's Maggie. How are you?"

I called in the evening, after dinner, while drinking a calming tea Mary had brought over.

"Maggie!" Lana sounded relieved and excited, not as awkward or angry as I thought she might be. "Bill, it's Maggie on the phone!"

"Maggie! Hi! I'm so sorry for how I acted. By the way, it was completely—"

Lana cut him off. "Bill, she called *us*. Give the woman some space."

The two bickered playfully while I giggled to myself on the line. This was the kind of parental relationship I had always wanted.

"What did you call for, my dear? Is there something I can do?" Lana finally asked.

"I wanted to know if that invitation to chat was still open. I was hoping I could explain some things."

"Maggie, of course it is. Our door is always open to you." Lana's voice was smooth as silk.

We chatted on the phone for a little longer before I hung up. I stared at the dollhouse, thinking about what to do with it. In the little parlor room, I saw a tiny light switch, and the seam of a secret door.

I smiled, and tore the door off, revealing nothing behind it.

THANK YOU FOR READING

Did you enjoy reading *Vanished*? Please consider leaving a review on Amazon. Your review will help other readers to discover the novel.

ABOUT THE AUTHOR

Theo Baxter has followed in the footsteps of his brother, best-selling suspense author Cole Baxter. He enjoys the twists and turns that readers encounter in his stories.

ALSO BY THEO BAXTER

Titles by Theo Baxter:

The Widow's Secret
The Stepfather
Vanished

Printed in Great Britain
by Amazon